KALEIDOSCOPE EYES

KALEIDOSCOPE EYES

GRAHAM WATKINS

Carroll & Graf Publishers, Inc.
New York

Copyright © 1993 by Graham Watkins

First Carroll & Graf edition 1993

Carroll & Graf Publishers, Inc.
260 Fifth Avenue
New York, NY 10001

Library of Congress Cataloging-in-Publication Data

Watkins, Graham.
    Kaleidoscope eyes / Graham Watkins.
        p.   cm.
    ISBN 0-88184-929-4 : $21.00
    PS3573.A839K35   1993
    813'.54—dc20   92-38240
                                            CIP

Manufactured in the United States of America

For K, A, and R—those who toast the usual . . .

The author gratefully acknowledges the assistance of Dr. Andrew Krystal, of Duke University, and Dr. Linda Norton, of Dallas, Texas, in the preparation of this manuscript.

KALEIDOSCOPE EYES

Prologue

Tenochtitlán, 1518

THERE WERE FLOWERS everywhere.

So many their colors dazzled the eye; so many their combined aroma saturated the air, acted much like a drug. Even though there was no escaping the scent, Quetzalpetlatzin brought some of the plumerias she was holding up close to her nose, breathed in their characteristic perfume, and smiled.

Across the bustling marketplace, a young warrior saw her smile and, perhaps thinking himself the cause, smiled back broadly and started walking toward her. As any well-trained daughter of the Mexica nobility would, she averted her eyes; the marketplace was not the environment to make the acquaintance of men—unless, of course, she were one of the "pleasure girls"—which Quetzalpetlatzin was not.

Ignoring the warrior—although she didn't fail to notice his expression of disappointment—she moved away, examining an array of jewellike feathers offered in the next stall. She was not unaccustomed to the attentions of young men; at sixteen, she was considered one of the most beautiful of the still-unmarried noblewomen, and was thus sought after by many of the most desirable young men. That was her purpose in being in the great market of Tlatelolco today; she wanted to acquire a new statuette of the goddess Xochiquetzal, the goddess of love; to her Quetzalpetlatzin would make her petitions for a happy marriage, one filled with love and blessed with fine children.

Distracted by the plumes, she did not hear or sense anyone coming up behind her, did not know anyone was there until she felt a light touch on her shoulder. Sure it was the young warrior— and equally sure that, because of her striking beauty, he had taken her for one of the pleasure girls—she turned quickly, planning to set him straight with acid words.

But it was not the warrior. It was a young woman, a woman who held a swaddled infant in her arms. For a moment, Quetzalpetlatzin stared. This woman was astonishingly beautiful, and in many ways, like herself: they shared the same dark skin, the same large liquid eyes, the same spectacular manes of thick black hair. By the magnificent quality of her eagle-feather-and-doeskin headdress and her pristine bright-white *huipl,* Quetzalpetlatzin was certain that this woman, too, was a noble.

Hence she was quite polite—one never knew if one was talking to, possibly, one of the wives of Moctezuma. "Yes, my mother?" the girl asked, tempering her formal salutation on her impression that the woman was at least a bit—though surely not more than a couple of years—older than she.

"My daughter, I would request a favor," the woman said. Before Quetzalpetlatzin could reply, the woman handed her the swaddled child. "Keep my little one safe," she went on, "for a short while. I must go, quickly, across the market; there is a vendor of green chilies there I must converse with. I will return, in due time."

The girl peered down at the child; it was so thickly wrapped it could not be seen. "But, my mother—" she started to protest. She looked up; the woman was nowhere to be seen.

A bit exasperated—her family would be annoyed if she were to be late returning—but feeling she had no choice, she wandered over to a stone wall nearby and sat down. The child was quiet, required no real attention; she rocked it gently anyhow, to keep it that way until its mother returned. Thinking about what the woman had said, she smiled; there was a well-known story about a time the great god Tezcatlipoca had appeared, in person, in the marketplace in old Tollan. His guise had been that of a Huaxtec seller of green chilies, and he had appeared as the Huaxtecs often did, without the benefit of any garments whatsoever. In doing so, he'd excited passion in the loins of the daughter of Tollan's ruler—and the results had been, for that ruler, catastrophic.

Minutes stretched into hours; the sun dropped lower in the sky. Quetzalpetlatzin became increasingly impatient, increasingly annoyed, with the woman's failure to return. A shadow over the marketplace attracted her attention, and she looked up to see an eagle, impressively large, soar down and light on one of the buildings nearby; the bird fluffed its feathers and settled down as if to wait, and to the girl it seemed as if the bird were gazing right at her.

Or, perhaps, at the infant in her arms. A little belatedly, Quetzalpetlatzin realized that the baby had neither moved nor cried over the span of several hours—hardly normal. Concerned, she unwound the wrappings and peeked inside.

As she saw what was there, it seemed to her that everything inside her froze in place. There was no child at all. Instead, the bundle contained a knife—a black, elliptical obsidian knife, the type of knife the priests used when offering sacrifices.

The girl did not have to ask what it meant; no Aztec, no citizen of Tenochtitlán, would have had to ask. The lovely woman in the white dress had not been a woman at all; she had been, instead, a goddess—the goddess of the earth, the mother-goddess, sometimes known as Quilatzli or simply as Tonantzin—our mother—but revered here in Tenochtitlán as Cihuacoatl, the Snake Woman. Everyone knew that she did this on occasion, that she walked among them in human guise when her hunger became too great, that she left this sign in the hands of some woman in the market so that the priests would know of her hunger, of her need.

Quickly, Quetzalpetlatzin arose, turning her steps toward the temple complex in the center of the city. This omen, she knew, had to be delivered to the priests. The goddess could not be denied; to even think of such a thing was utterly inconceivable. For the well-being of all of the people, for the well-being of the earth itself, she could not be denied.

Soon, the girl thought as she hurried along, there would be a ceremony—a ceremony held on a day auspicious to the goddess. Men, war captives, would die what her people called the "flowery death"; they would die on the stone before her temple, at least four of them. And one other, as well—one who would die not upon the stone, but upon a dais formed from the four war captives' bodies.

This one would be a woman, she knew. This one would be expected to spend a day impersonating the goddess, acting as her *ixiptla*, dancing in the ceremonial area; this one would be expected to walk up the temple steps of her own free will, this one would be expected to sit or lie atop the bodies of the men, this one would be expected to make no protests, no cries, when the priests used this knife to cut open her breast and extract her heart.

She sighed. That she and the goddess had resembled each other physically had not been an accident. Those who gave their service to the gods and goddesses, whether their role was that of a priest or an offering, had a choice in the matter. Like a priest, she had been selected, she had been called, and yet she had to volunteer; the choice was hers.

A choice, she told herself, that she had already made. . . .

One

THE MAN WAS dead. Even though his hands clutched at the sleeves of those trying to help him, even though his eyes darted around frantically, even though he was begging for help in a barely audible voice, he was dead. Half his chest was flattened, collapsed; blood drained from the corner of his mouth and from both of his ears, and his pants around his hips were stained with red as well. Sam Leo stood and watched him, and he knew the man was dead. The man, he suspected, knew it, too.

Not wanting to approach him, not wanting to have to tell him how sure he was that there was no hope and knowing there was nothing he could do to help, Sam remained nevertheless, absorbing the drama of the scene. Late afternoon sunlight, midsummer-bright, gleamed on the dented grill of the truck that had struck the man, glinted just as brightly on the bent frames of the man's shattered glasses. The truck's driver, wide-eyed and as frightened as the dead man, stayed a discreet distance away, telling anyone who would listen how the man had walked out right in front of him, how he'd had no chance to stop his truck.

That much was true. Sam had witnessed the whole thing; the man, abstracted by something—perhaps some personal or business problem he would now never solve—had walked to the corner of Hillsborough Street, and, without so much as hesitating, proceeded into the crosswalk against the traffic light. The truck, which hadn't been speeding but hadn't been moving slowly either, had been a mere fifteen feet back. The shriek of brakes almost imperceptibly preceded the impact, which had sent the man's body hurtling a good forty feet down the roadway. The police and an ambulance had been summoned, but Sam doubted they'd arrive in time to do anything more than clean up the remaining mess.

The usual knot of spectators had gathered; Sam, still standing near the perimeter of the crowd, looked them over. Two were trying to help the dead man, arguing shrilly over what was best to do. One of these, a long-faced young woman with short and obviously artificaly blond hair, seemed to believe the man should be given CPR. The other, an equally young man with a square face and thick forearms, was justifiably ridiculing this notion. Both appeared to be students from nearby North Carolina State University, but the dead man didn't care who they were; he knew his life was slipping away and he wanted them to help him to somehow hold on to it. The long-faced woman was holding his hand and he in turn clutched hers, as if her grip could keep him alive.

For a few seconds, Sam focused on the interaction between the dying man and the student. Even though they almost certainly didn't know each other, his agony, his onrushing death, had created a closeness, a unique intimacy; a closeness that surely would not survive if the man, by some miracle, recovered. But for now, there was a visible openness between them; the dying man was, at this moment, undoubtedly closer to the long-faced woman than he'd ever been to any other person.

Turning his attention away from the two would-be rescuers, Sam noticed yet another young woman, possibly another student, standing near the dead man's head. In appearance she was striking; her skin and eyes were quite dark, her hair a wonderful waterfall of jet falling past her waist. She was crying bitterly, tears filling her eyes and even dripping to the pavement at her feet.

The dead man couldn't be helped, Sam told himself, but perhaps she could. He circled around the edge of the crowd until he was almost touching her shoulders, which were trembling with suppressed sobs.

"Is he a friend of yours?" he asked, leaning close to her.

She gave him the most fleeting of glances, her eyes not really seeing him at all. "No," she answered. "No, I don't know him." She took in a deep breath, composed herself a little; the flow of tears did not stop. "It's just—it's just such a waste, there's no point to it at all! He's really suffering, really fighting . . ." She had a trace, no more, of an accent that indicated Spanish as her native tongue. "And there's no need, he isn't going to live . . ."

He nodded even though she wasn't looking at him. "No, I'm pretty sure he isn't," he agreed. "But who knows? The paramedics are on their way, I'm sure. The doctors these days, well, sometimes they can just about perform miracles." Sam himself did not believe these last words but they seemed innocent enough—the sort of thing he might have said to the dying man, a minor consolation.

But the woman did not accept it. "Not for him. His life is gone, and even he knows it," she said flatly, echoing Sam's earlier thoughts. "He suffers so because he is trying so hard to hold on."

"Well, that's just human nature," Sam observed. "Nobody wants to die. We all try to hang on till the bitter end, no matter what."

She wiped her eyes, but succeeded only in spreading moisture across her face. "Yes. Most do," she acknowledged.

"No. We all do. Anybody lying there would do what he's doing. Fight for life, hold on. Hopeless or not."

"No, not quite," she murmured. "Not quite. There're—" She stopped speaking and turned her face toward him again, seeing him for the first time. She was really impressively pretty, he thought, wondering at the same time what she was seeing as she looked at his bearded and slightly rough-looking face, his tall and lanky form, his unstylishly long hair. She tipped her head slightly to the left, her eyes expressing a curiosity, at least—maybe just a curiosity about why he'd approached her. "You're a prof, aren't you?" she asked. "At State?"

He grinned, shook his head; he wasn't unaware that he presented that image, and it wasn't the first time someone had made that sort of mistake. "No," he told her. " 'Fraid not. Close, though. I work out at RTP; I—"

"RTP?"

She had to be a newcomer to central North Carolina, he told himself. Everyone who'd been here more than a week knew what those letters meant. "Research Triangle Park," he informed her. "The big research complex between Raleigh and Durham. I work at the Institute out there, I'm an epidemiologist, and—"

She shrugged; her manner said she wasn't terribly interested in his work. "You talk like a prof."

"So I've been told; maybe it goes with the territory. You're a student, right?"

"Uh-huh." Her gaze was steady, direct; for the moment, at least, she seemed to have forgotten about the dying man lying in the street. Sam felt flattered. "My name's Selinde."

He frowned for just a second; he'd never heard a name like Selinde, and he'd expected something more along the lines of Maria. But then, people with odd given names—especially women— did crop up more than occasionally these days. "Sam Leo," he told her.

"Sam Leo what?"

"No, no. Leo's the last name."

"Oh." She hesitated, as if about to say something else, but before she could a wail of sirens cut through the air, and both of them returned their attention to the accident victim. A woman was kneeling beside him, telling him that everything would now be all right, that the ambulance was here. He did not seem to be able to hear her; he was fighting for breath, squirming on the ground, his eyes darting around even more frantically than before. Before the siren's wail came to a halt, a loud rattling sound came from his throat; his legs pushed out hard and his neck bent backward. While his rescuers continued to argue over what to do, his body trembled violently for an instant, the trembling degenerating rapidly into grotesque and uncoordinated spasms. Then, as his pupils expanded to fill the irises of his eyes, his body became almost still. Only a few random flips of a wrist remained.

"He's dead, isn't he?" an older woman in the crowd asked. Her question did not seem to be directed toward anyone in particular.

"Yes, I think so," another woman answered. "Such a shame. Here's the ambulance right now—so close."

"Wouldn't have mattered if the ambulance had been sitting right here," Sam muttered in a voice so low that only the woman next to him could hear.

Though he wasn't really talking to her, she looked around at him again. "No," she said, almost casually. "We both knew that." She wiped the remaining tears from her cheeks. Her eyes appeared quite dry as she watched the ambulance screech to a halt. The paramedics jumped out and ran to the man, but they confirmed the older woman's diagnosis. Even so, following procedure, they hustled the corpse onto a stretcher and hoisted it into the back of the ambulance.

"Why are they rushing like that?" Selinde asked. "He's dead, it doesn't matter."

"Well, that's not for them to decide, really," Sam pointed out. "Guys like him are declared DOA, not DAS—dead at scene."

She gave him a quizzical look. "DOA?"

Again, he frowned briefly. "Dead on arrival," he explained. "Arrival at the hospital." He'd quite naturally assumed that anyone would know what DOA meant, and it again made him wonder if she was a native of some foreign country.

"Oh." She nodded, then shook her head. "You see what I meant, though," she went on. "All his suffering, all his struggle, was for nothing. What did it gain him to live on for—what? Ten minutes?"

"Not a thing," Sam agreed. "But I'd bet that you or I, in the same position, would do the same thing."

She smiled a little. "Perhaps you would."

"So would you."

"No, Mr. Leo. No, I would not. But then, I would not find myself in his position!"

"Sam," he told her. He allowed himself to smile now; the police had arrived, the truck was being moved to the roadside, all four lanes of traffic were moving again and the spectators were dispersing, allowing some of the tension of the incident to drain away. "You don't plan to step in front of any trucks, eh? Can't say I do either!"

She looked over at the truck, at the gesturing driver and the busily-writing policeman. "No. That would be a very bad way to die. Too sudden. Too unexpected."

Sam nodded. "Yeah. Too painful, too. Me, I plan to drift off in my sleep when I'm about a hundred and ten. How 'bout you?"

Her expression was one of confusion. "A hundred and ten?" she asked. "You want to live that long? To get that old?"

"Well, sure. I once heard somebody say that getting old is a privilege—not everybody gets to do it!"

Selinde put a hand on her hip. "I don't understand," she said. "You, well, by that time your body—it'll have fallen apart! You won't have any strength, you won't be able to see, you won't be able to hear—you probably won't be able to think clearly and it might be the worse for you if you can! What do you plan to do with all those years?"

He didn't quite know how to answer that question. "Well, hell," he said finally. "Nobody wants to die. You put it off as long as you can, no matter what—"

"That's foolishness," she said, bringing her hand down in a gesture of dismissal. "Foolishness. And if you believe that, then you are a foolish man, Sam Leo." With that she turned and started to walk away, headed generally back toward the campus.

For a moment Sam just stared after her, feeling a rising irritation. He'd gone out of his way to try to console her, and the ensuing conversation—mere chitchat as far as he'd been concerned—had ended with an insult. Finally he, too, turned away, began walking off in the opposite direction.

"Wait," she called from behind him.

He considered ignoring her, walking on. But in the end he did not; he stopped and turned, facing her, a challenging expression on his face. She was quite close by then. "Yeah?" he asked coldly.

She laughed; he could not help but notice that she laughed like a small child, her whole face transformed by it. "Oh, don't be like that," she chided. "You look so much better when you're trying to make a good impression! Like you were a few minutes ago!"

That stung, too. He didn't like to think of himself as quite that transparent. "Look, I was just trying to be helpful," he almost snarled. "I wasn't trying to—"

"No. I don't think you were, although I must say I wonder if you'd've been so concerned if I was sixty years old and weighed three hundred pounds! But I am sorry, Sam, if I've hurt your feelings. I didn't mean to, really. Look; I have to go now, there're some things I need to do today, and I think I can do them now. But if you want to talk some more, we can."

Silence hung between them for a few seconds. This wasn't something that was easy to say no to, to walk away from without leaving some thread of connection.

He'd let her do it, he decided, if she wanted to. "I don't know . . ." he allowed at last, temporizing.

She didn't reply immediately either. "Yes. Yes, it is . . ." she muttered, leaving him to wonder what she meant. Popping open the small purse she was carrying, she took out a scrap of paper and jotted down a phone number, handed it to him. "Call," she said, "if you decide to."

He looked down at it; all that was written on it was the number, seven digits. "Look, like I said, I don't know . . ." He held the piece of paper up in his left hand, making sure the wedding band on his ring finger was apparent to her. He was inclined to doubt that this was the nature of her interest, but he didn't want to mislead her if, by some chance, it was.

She didn't comment, and her eyes gave him no hint. "It's up to you. If you don't, have a good life. I'll send you a birthday card on your hundred-and-tenth." With that she turned and walked away briskly, leaving him to stand staring open-mouthed after her. He could not remember having met anyone quite like her before. And Sam Leo had always believed he'd met more than his share of odd people in his thirty-seven years.

Two

Tired and a bit irritated—the drive home through Raleigh traffic had been even worse than usual, and he was, as he often did, cursing the manners of virtually all North Carolina drivers—Sam resisted slamming the door as he entered his condo shortly after six that same evening. Cheryl was already home, he knew; he'd parked his six-year-old Dodge behind her Nissan. Music drifted from the stereo; one of the tapes Cheryl had asked him to put together from various CDs. At the moment, "Don't Fear the Reaper," by Blue Oyster Cult, was playing. It was a song he liked, though he'd never paid much attention to the lyrics. Cheryl loved it, often sang along with it under her breath.

He was just putting down his briefcase when a slender woman with short dark hair and large, startlingly green eyes set in a broad and full-lipped face leaned over the counter that separated the kitchen from the living room. In her hand was a spray mister; she held it like a weapon. "Ah, good," she said. "It's merely you."

"Merely me," he answered. "Not the mad rapist, lucky you. Is there coffee?"

"There is."

"You are a good woman, Cheryl."

"Oh, I know that."

The briefcase fell over, blocking the doorway; Sam ignored it, walked into the kitchen, poured himself a cup of coffee. While the carafe was removed, a stray drop fell onto the warmer pad, sizzled and bounced around. Sam watched it idly until it evaporated, then replaced the carafe and sat down at the table. Cheryl had turned back to what she was doing, misting the birdnest and staghorn ferns that decorated the sill. Sipping the coffee, Sam watched her work. She'd obviously been home for a while; she'd changed into her usual shorts and a pullover top that did not quite reach her waist. He found himself staring at the backs of her legs. Very fine legs, those, he told himself, very fine. Very familiar to him, but that didn't mean he didn't like looking at them.

The ferns moistened to her apparent satisfaction, she replaced the mister under the cabinet and came to sit at the table beside him. "So," she said. "Rough trip home?"

"As usual," he grunted. "Raleigh traffic gets worse every day. But that wasn't the worst of it, not today."

"Bad day at the Institute?"

"Uh-uh. I wasn't even there most of the day; I went over to State, to the library. Had to park down on Hillsborough, walk from there." He went on, telling her about the accident, about the man lying in the street dying while he watched. He did not mention Selinde.

As he told his story, the green eyes reflected concern. "My God, Sam!" she exclaimed when he'd finished. "That must have been horrible for you!"

"It was pretty bad," he admitted, looking down into his coffee cup.

"You didn't try to help him? At all?"

His eyes flicked up; her question could have been taken as an indictment, but he hadn't heard anything of that sort in her tone, nor did he see it in her eyes. "There really wasn't anything I could do," he told her, defending himself even though he was sure he was not being accused. "The condition he was in, there was no first aid that would've helped. Someone else had already called an ambulance, that was the only thing anybody could've done."

She reached out, touched his arm. "I can see how much it affected you."

"Yeah. Unless you're in a war or something you don't see people die like that every day. It shows, huh?"

Keeping her hand on his arm, she studied his face critically. "I think so," she answered finally. "Something does, anyway. You don't look quite the same as you did this morning."

He looked down again. Cheryl, as he well knew, was sensitive almost to the point of being psychic; she was a very difficult person to successfully lie to, as he'd discovered years ago, prior to their marriage. Rationally, he could not doubt that what she was seeing was the effect of witnessing the man's death.

But if it wasn't—if it was, somehow, Selinde and the odd conversation he'd had with her—he didn't want to talk about it, not at the moment. Not until he'd had time to sort out his reactions to the dark-skinned woman.

"I think I'd kinda like to get the whole thing out of my mind for a while," he told her. "What's new with you today?"

"Well, nothing anywhere near as dramatic," she answered. "But, I don't know, maybe more important in the long run. To us, I mean." She pushed back from the table a little, crossed her legs. "I left work early," she went on, "because—"

"You feeling okay?"

"—because Jenny called, and there's a problem—"

He rolled his eyes. "Oh, shit."

Cheryl looked a little pained. "Sam, she is a friend of ours, after all, one of our closest friends. She—"

"Is a friend who is constantly having problems and constantly embroiling us and everyone we know in them!"

"Well, maybe." Cheryl's face took on a hard set, the kind of look that said it wasn't going to be easy to argue with her. "But she is a friend. If she needs help and we can help, then we have to. Otherwise, what does friendship mean?"

"You're maybe just a little too idealistic," Sam grumbled. "But anyway, what's with Jenny now?"

Her features softening in rhythm to his concession, Cheryl shook her head. "I can't say for sure. But I will say that I'm really worried about her, Sam. She didn't come right out and say so, but I have the feeling she's thinking about suicide again."

"That's news? Cheryl, you and I can't help her with that. She needs to see a doctor, I've said that before—"

"She has, and it doesn't seem to help."

"Okay, okay. So what is it now?"

"Well, she thinks Rick is having another one of his affairs."

There was a lengthy silence. It wasn't that Sam didn't know why Cheryl wasn't going on; he knew quite well. This conversation could almost be a taped version of previous ones, and at this point he was expected to either confirm or deny Rick Mason's proposed infidelity. Since he and Rick were old friends, since they'd gone to college together, since they saw each other frequently enough—in the absence of their wives. Since they talked.

And, as almost always before, he did indeed know the answer to Cheryl's unasked question. That answer was yes; Rick was having another affair, his fifth or sixth since his marriage to the unstable and neurotic Jennifer, and the fifth or sixth Jennifer had somehow found out about. How, Sam didn't know. Maybe Rick was careless, though that seemed out of character; it seemed much more likely to him that Jennifer was constantly suspicious—which in her case was not unreasonable—and that she spent a good deal of her time checking up on him. It didn't really matter. Jennifer knew about it and now she was dropping hints that she was thinking about killing herself. Again. Sam couldn't take it seriously. This sort of behavior had characterized Jennifer since they'd known her, and not once had she ever made an attempt, serious or theatrical.

The problem, for him, was Cheryl. He had three choices; refuse to answer—that would lead to an argument. Lie—and she'd probably catch him in it like she usually did. Tell the truth—and she'd insist that he go see Rick, probably tonight, and rake him over the coals, make him understand what a vile bastard he was, what he was doing to the loving Jennifer and to their eight-year-old son Paul.

He didn't want to do that. It wasn't his business even if Rick did choose to confide in him, and besides, he felt tired and drained—he really didn't want to go out at all tonight.

But Cheryl was waiting—not too patiently—and he had to make a choice. He sighed, long and deep. "Yeah, well, she is right," he said. "He is."

Hardly surprised, Cheryl nodded. "Anybody we know?"

"No. New lab tech over at the hospital. Her name's Ann, she just moved to Raleigh."

"How long has this one been going on?"

"I dunno. I just heard about it last week. Can't've been too long."

"Long enough for Jenny to figure it out." She stared at the tabletop for a few seconds. "He isn't ever going to change, is he? He's just going to keep doing this, over and over, until he's so old no woman will even want to look at him." She closed her eyes for a moment and shook her head. "Right now there are plenty who do, that's for sure. Look at him, I mean. Uh, I mean, he's—"

Sam smiled internally. He wasn't unaware that Cheryl considered Rick to be a terribly attractive man—and she was quite right, many women agreed with her.

But she had never given him the slightest reason for jealousy. "He might not even quit then," he cut in, rescuing her from her fumbling. "Remember, he's a surgeon. There're a lot of woman out there who think all doctors—surgeons especially—are filthy rich."

"And worse yet—"

"Yeah. He is filthy rich."

Cheryl sniffed. "I think Jenny would be happier if he was digging ditches for minimum wage, if he'd stop doing this." She paused. "Sam, you should go talk to him. Make sure he understands what he's doing to his family."

Sam groaned inwardly; he rolled his eyes but didn't let Cheryl see it. "Honey, it isn't our business," he protested. "Besides, I've already talked to him. He's incorrigible, that's all."

"But why does he do this? Over and over? Jenny's more than pretty, she's bright, she's loving—"

Sam glanced up at her, then went back to studying his coffee. There were several reasons, that he knew well enough. Some of them he could talk to Cheryl about, some he could not. "Ah, I dunno," he answered. "He's never once, in all the times we've talked, had so much as one bad word to say about Jennifer—in fact, he's very—uhm—complimentary. He says it has to do with eyes."

"Eyes?"

"Uh-huh. He goes on and on about women's eyes; it's one of his favorite subjects. You know how some men call themselves 'tit men' or 'ass men' or 'leg men?' Well, Rick is an eye man. He claims they're always the first thing he notices about any woman, the first thing that attracts him. He has, by the way, had some very nice things to say about yours—things, I must say, I agree with. But he says he runs across dark-eyed women, or hazel-eyed women, and he just can't resist."

"What is the problem with Jenny's eyes? She's got those real pale, bright blue—"

"Yeah, nothing. He loves them, he says so. And he'll point out that he's never had an affair with a blue-eyed woman."

"That's one hell of a weird excuse!"

"Yeah, well, it takes all kinds. People have all sorts of funny kinks. I think our buddy Doctor Rick may have a clinical obsession here, actually—a fetish. Did you ever see Monica?"

"No—she was two or three of these back, wasn't she?"

"Uh-huh. I did, once. It would've amazed you, Cheryl. Monica was pretty enough in her way, but she was—shall we say, a little beyond the point where you could use the word *plump* to describe her. But she had these amazing gold-colored eyes. Really, I could see what he meant, in a way."

Cheryl grinned. "So you found Monica interesting too, huh?"

He snorted. "Not hardly! You know me, I've got a thing about fat. A reverse fetish, maybe. She could have the greatest eyes in the world—kaleidoscope eyes—and it still wouldn't do a thing for me."

She laughed briefly. "Yeah, I think you'd drop me like a hot potato if I started gaining weight!" She patted her belly. "Which reminds me, I do have to find more time to get down and work out."

"You do not have an ounce of fat on you!"

"Not true. Besides, I'm talking about out-of-shapeness more than fat." Pausing, she shook her head and smiled again. "Maybe you don't do what Rick does, but there's competition out there, Sam, I'm not unaware of that. You remember last week, when you picked me up over at the hospital?"

"Uh-huh. So?"

"Did you notice the new nurse? Small, dark?"

Sam had indeed noticed. Admiringly. "Well, I guess. Maybe."

"I thought so—I didn't miss all the eye contact you two were making. Well, the next day, she asked about you."

"She did?"

"Uh-huh. She didn't see us leave together; she just saw you standing there chatting with Pam. Anyway, she asked if I knew you, asked if you were married. I, of course, said yes—but I didn't say who you were married to. You know what she said?"

Sam felt truly flattered. "No, what?"

"She said, 'Of course—the good ones are always taken!' "

"Oh, come on, she didn't—"

"She did."

He grinned and cocked an eyebrow. "Uh—what'd you say this girl's name was?" he asked, deliberately stumbling over his words. "And, uhm—you don't happen to have her phone number handy, do you?"

Cheryl laughed again, but with a slight edge. "Her name," she said, "is Michelle. Her phone number is none of your business. You stay away from her, Sam Leo." They laughed together, but hers soon faded. "Really, Sam," she said after a few seconds, "to get back to Rick and Jennifer—I do think you should go talk to him, don't you?"

"Well, since you asked—" He stopped; her face had taken on the hard set again, and Sam made an instant decision that it was going to be easier, by far, to go see Rick than to argue with her. "All right," he agreed. "I'll go give him a call, see if he's free. If he is, we'll go down after dinner and grab a beer. Okay?"

She nodded. "Yeah, I think that'd be good. It'd be nice if they could get this straightened out before the vacation comes up."

"It's only two weeks away," Sam pointed out. "Jennifer is not going to be over it by then, even if Rick agrees to stop seeing Ann right now!"

Cheryl sighed. "No, I think she will. She really loves Rick, and—for better or for worse—she's really dependent on him. That's what's happened before, Sam. She forgives and forgets practically overnight." She stared off into space, her eyes a bit unfocused. "I don't understand that myself—don't quite know how she can do it. But she can, or at least, that's the way it looks. So no, I don't think she'll be dragging around with a long face. Not unless the problem is still unresolved."

"Well, that's good, anyway. I don't think the vacation would be a roaring success for us or for the Dixons if Jennifer and Rick were still having problems. Not the way Jenny is." He finished his coffee, stretched. "I'll go call now," he continued. "What are we doing for dinner?"

"It's your night."

He grimaced. "Okay. In that case, we're doing Lean Cuisine."

"Could I expect anything else from the Master of the Micro-wave?"

Three

THE THIN DETECTIVE leaned over the desk, resting both his palms on it. His bladelike face threatened a smile. "So you're saying we've got him? Is that what you're telling me?"

On the other side, a dark-eyed young woman with long, reddish-brown hair returned a cool and utterly professional gaze. "I'm neither an attorney nor a prosecutor, Dave. I don't know whether you've 'got him' or not. All I am saying is what's in that report. Mrs. Teal did not die of natural causes, she died of thalium poisoning."

"That's one I don't know."

"It's a heavy metal. Used to be used in some insecticides, rat poisons, things like that. Hard to come by now; it's fallen out of use. Too dangerous."

"I do got him, Stephanie," Dave Brennan said gleefully, the smile breaking out. "I do got him!"

Stephanie Dixon leaned back in her chair. "I wouldn't know. Just demonstrating that Janice Teal died of poisoning is a far cry from proving that her husband put it in her coffee."

His chin jutted forward a little, a quick and birdlike motion. "She get it in coffee? Can we prove that?"

"No, no. That was just an example. I don't know how it got into her system."

He looked a bit disappointed, but the smile didn't fade. "It don't matter," he said. "I got him anyway. He had motive—he hated the woman, everybody who knew them says so, and there was a fat policy with our perp as the beneficiary. And—here's the kicker—you wanna know what he does for a hobby?"

"What's that?"

"He collects old bottles, shit like that. I saw some of his collection already. Old iodine bottles, sealed, with the iodine still in. A nineteen-forties Coke bottle with the cap on, full of old Coke. You don't think it's possible he came up with one full of old rat poison?"

"It sounds possible. In any case, you probably have enough for a search warrant. You can go through his collection and see."

"Can you analyze empties? See if one of them had this—uh—"

"Thalium."

"Yeah, thalium—in it?"

She looked a little irritated. "Of course. If it hasn't been cleaned. And the cleaning has to have been very good, Dave. If it wasn't, and it was there to begin with, we'll find it."

"You're the best, Stephanie. The best."

Ignoring the compliment, she stood up, smoothed down her white lab coat. "Are you through now, Dave? It's almost seven, I'd like to be getting home."

"Yeah—yeah. I gotta go see about getting a warrant, anyway. You're sure about this, right?"

Her expression of irritation intensified. "Of course I'm sure," she said, her tone many degrees cooler. "You can count on my reports, Dave. You know that." She walked past him, slipped off her lab coat, hung it on a hook on the door.

"Yeah, I do," he said from behind her. "Thanks, Steph." He headed for the door, bumped her, murmured an apology, rushed out.

She glared at the open door as she picked up her purse. "I've told you, Dave," she said, though she knew he was long gone, "I don't like to be called Steph, I prefer Stephanie. Actually, from people like you, I prefer Dr. Dixon!"

Locking her office door behind her, she walked slowly down the hallway, wondering if there was any chance Art would be called on to defend Marvin Teal on what was now pretty certainly going to be a murder-one charge. If so, it wouldn't be the first time he'd had to work against evidence provided to the state by his wife. It wasn't a problem between them; so far, he'd never tried to discredit one of her reports, never attacked her testimony if she was called to the stand to testify in person—something that had only happened once. They had talked about it, and he'd said tactfully that since he considered her reports unassailable, he didn't bother with them. If he were to defend Marvin Teal, she was sure, his thrust would not be that Janice did not die of thalium poisoning, only that she must've gotten it from some source other than her husband. Perhaps, he might suggest, the woman found it in an old bottle and decided to use it to commit suicide.

Not likely, Stephanie told herself as she walked into the parking lot. But then she pushed the question of Marvin Teal's guilt or innocence out of her mind, refused to think about it anymore. It was not her affair; her role was merely to determine the cause of the woman's death, no more than that. This she had done; now she wouldn't speculate on the case anymore. Stephanie prided herself on possessing a very disciplined mind, and she dismissed the unfortunate Teals from her thoughts as she drove her small Ford through the streets of downtown Raleigh; instead, she focused herself entirely on some shopping she wanted to take care of before heading home that evening.

Turning north on Glenwood Avenue, she went up a couple of blocks before making a left on Johnson, here moving into an area of town she really wasn't too familiar with. She drove slowly, her eyes scanning the right side of the street. The bookstore was supposed to be there—if Becky hadn't gotten her directions mixed up, which was never out of the question.

No, this time she had not. There was the store—or actually, the house that had been converted into a store, the blue-and-white sign out front identifying it positively as a New Age/occult bookshop. She expertly parallel-parked the Ford, got out, and started to walk up to the entrance.

Almost guiltily, she glanced around, for a moment wondering if anyone from the office might be in the area, might see her. She felt absurdly anxious, as if she'd have to explain herself to a stern parent if she was caught going into such a place. But, straightening her shoulders, she firmly pushed her anxiety away and proceeded on to the door, telling herself it was ridiculous for her to feel this way. She herself might have no interest in "New Age" or matters of the occult, but she certainly had a right to go into this bookstore if she wished. Jennifer did have such an interest, and Jennifer had a birthday coming up, right after the planned vacation. Stephanie, never one to wait until the last minute to deal with such matters, was here to buy her a gift. No more, no less.

A bell on the door jingled as she entered; she found herself facing a short hallway, rooms full of books and records adjoining it on both the right and the left. In one, immediately to her left, a plump young woman with blond hair stood behind a glass-topped counter.

She smiled. "Hi! Can I help you?"

"I hope so," Stephanie said, returning the smile. "I stopped by to get a birthday gift for a friend of mine. Maybe you could make some suggestions?"

"I'm sure I can. What do you think he—"

"She."

"Oh. She would like? A book, some music, jewelry?"

"Any of the above, all of the above."

The girl grinned. "Be glad to sell you one each. Or ten each."

"That might be overkill. I was thinking maybe a book—"

"What's she interested in?"

"Things Celtic. Druids, stuff like that. Old myths."

"Ah. Right back this way." Leaving the counter, the girl led Stephanie into the room immediately behind the one she'd previously occupied, pointed out a four-foot-wide, floor-to-ceiling shelf two-thirds filled with texts on Celtic studies.

Stephanie pulled one at random. It dealt with the adventures of some Georgia group that was trying to live in the woods and follow what they saw as Druidic ways. She put that one back. "I don't think she wants anything too wild," she told the girl.

"Well, this is a standard," the girl said, pulling out a book by Stuart Piggott entitled simply *The Druids.*

"Looks good, I haven't seen this one on her coffee table. You have it in hardback?"

"Sorry. Trade paper, that's it. We could maybe order—"

"No, this'll be fine. But maybe something else, too—"

The girl continued to be helpful; a short while later, after a visit to the room across the hall, she headed back to the front counter with the Piggot book, a larger book—hardback—on Celtic art, and a CD by a group called Ossian—whom she'd never heard of, but who the salesgirl raved about. She laid them down, started digging in her purse for her MasterCard while the salesgirl began ringing them up.

She'd just gotten it out when she noticed the little glass-fronted display case on the wall behind and to the left of the counter. Bright objects sparkled within. She moved closer, looked.

"What're these?" she asked.

The girl glanced up. "Oh, wands, stone eggs, crystals—stuff like that. And kaleidoscopes. Open it and look if you want."

She did, picking up and examining an eight-inch silver wand encrusted with crystals and decorated with pewter filigree. It was attractive; it also carried a price tag of three hundred dollars. She put it back, touched one of the carved and smoothed stone eggs. She had no idea what they might be for. Passing over them, she went on to the kaleidoscopes, a number of which lay on an upper shelf. She picked one up, turned it to the window, looked.

This was different from any kaleidoscope she'd ever seen, but then, all she was familiar with were the cheap dime-store models with a cardboard tube, a few chips of colored plastic in the end, and two mirrors. This one had a five-inch painted and inlaid brass tube, filled with natural crystal chips, the image multiplication achieved with prisms.

"Nice," she said, taking it away from her eye. Again, the price tag; a hundred and fifty. Not that nice. She put it back.

But there was another, longer and narrower, down at the end, that commanded her attention. In a way, the tube—it seemed to be of cast and beaten copper—was much more artistically designed than the other, though much less ostentatious. The surface of the tube was encircled by engravings; they were vague, it was hard to see what they might be intended to represent. To Stephanie, it looked like an illustration of a stylized nude woman holding —or perhaps wrapped by—an equally stylized snake. She picked it up, put it to her eye, swung around to the window.

And gasped.

This one was much more different from the first than the first had been different from dime-store kaleidoscopes. The colors of the tumbling pieces almost sang with vibrant color; that blue, Stephanie thought, that's the most intense and attractive blue I've ever seen! And that red, that's incredible . . .

Beyond that, the patterns created by the multiplying prisms did not seem, somehow, to be random. Almost like colorful Rorschachs, they suggested images they did not really form; that one gave the impression of some tranquil place in the country, and when she turned it the next gave her an unexpected erotic jolt.

"That's a nice one, isn't it?" the counter girl said with a grin. "About the nicest one we've ever had in here."

"It really is," Stephanie agreed, taking it down from her eye and rolling it over in her hand, looking for the price tag. There wasn't one. "How much is it?"

The counter girl's brow furrowed. "Well, I don't think the owner really and truly wants to sell it. Now, she didn't say it wasn't for sale—she didn't say that. But see, we didn't get it from the same place we get the others. A woman came in and sold that one to us; I don't know what we paid for it, we just got it yesterday. I think maybe it's an antique one, it's so nice, it—"

"How much?" Stephanie repeated, cutting her off.

The girl looked embarrassed. "Well, she said if anyone asked, I should say the price was fifteen hundred dol—"

"I'll take it. Put it on the card."

The girl stared at her. Stephanie was sure that if it were possible she'd be staring at herself. She had not intended to say that, but now that she had, she couldn't seem to take the words back.

The girl shrugged, then grinned broadly; nice commission, no doubt. She ran Stephanie's card through the machine, waited for the confirmation. It came; the transaction was complete. With books, CD, and very expensive kaleidoscope, Stephanie left the store.

For a few minutes she just sat in her car, staring at the hood. Why had she done that? Art wouldn't raise hell—he wasn't the type. Instead, he'd get uncontrollable giggles and she'd be forced to control her impulse to hit him.

She wouldn't keep it, she decided. She'd give it to Jennifer; she'd love it, she'd go crazy over it.

She'd by God better, Stephanie told herself as she pulled away from the curb.

Four

USING HIS NAPKIN, Rick Mason wiped a bit of beer foam from his carefully trimmed mustache. "You don't have to explain," he said. He looked almost forlorn. "I know full well what's happened. Jennifer's caught me again, she's talked to Cheryl and Stephanie, and Cheryl's insisted that you point out the errors of my ways. I know, I know. Lord, we've been through it all before, haven't we, Sam?"

"Well, I don't know about Stephanie, but as for the rest of it, you've got the picture," Sam answered. He slouched in his chair, stared into the darkness of a half-full mug of Dos Equis. "What I don't understand is why you aren't more careful. Damn it, you get your ass caught every time! It never is more than about a week after you tell me about your latest lady love that I start hearing about it from Cheryl!"

Rick wiped a hand down over his face. "I don't know, man," he muttered. "But hell, you haven't seen Ann. She has the most fantastic—"

"Yeah, yeah, you told me. The most fantastic eyes. What was it? Oh, yeah: 'mahogany flecked with brass.' Rick, they all have fantastic eyes. The point is that Jennifer always finds out—always. You've got to do something about that, man. Do something about that or stop doing this shit."

"Stop? Come on! You've never cheated on Cheryl? Not even once?"

"Not even once. You would've heard about it if I had. But—"

"Never been tempted?"

He started to say no, but even as his tongue moved into position to frame the word the image of Selinde sprang into his mind and rendered him momentarily mute. Rick would go apeshit over those endless dark eyes, he told himself.

The other man grinned. "I rest my case," he said quietly.

"Being tempted and creating a situation that fucks over my family are two different things," Sam argued. "You know me, Rick. I'm by no means a prude, and you could hardly call me a traditional sort of guy. I'm not going to sit here and tell you that what you're doing is wrong, that some god is going to strike you with lightning. If it affected you and you alone, then I'd say it's your business; hell, it is your business, anyway. It's just that your family and ours, and the Dixons, well, we're all so close—"

"And Jennifer tends to wash all the laundry in public," Rick agreed. "Yeah, I know. I know. It does sort of make it your business too. I know." He sighed, swigged his beer. "You know, ol' Art Dixon had one affair—one I knew about, several years back—"

"It wasn't the same," Sam interjected. "Stephanie didn't know about it then and, as far as I know, she doesn't know about it now. In the second place, Art's affair was with an old girlfriend, one of his lovers before he and Stephanie got married. What he told me was, he just hadn't gotten her out of his system."

"There're all kinds of excuses."

"I'm not making an excuse for Art. All I'm saying is this: you knew about his affair and I knew about it. But Stephanie didn't, and neither did Cheryl or Jennifer. It didn't cause any problems at all for anyone except Art. But now, Cheryl's all upset because she believes Jenny's thinking about suicide—"

Rick made a rude snorting noise. "That's ridiculous! She gets all upset and she wants to talk it to death with anyone who'll listen, but God damn, she's not crazy!"

"Well, I wouldn't know. I didn't talk to Jenny."

"I think I can set your mind at ease about that. The chances of Jennifer doing something that crazy are somewhere between nil and zero. Things just aren't like that between us, Sam. I know she doesn't like it, but she gets over it—"

"That she does. Real quick. But I'd say you take advantage of that, Rick, and—"

"Oh, I know that's what everyone thinks. I'm not sure I can disagree. But I tell you, old man, I wouldn't be doing this if I thought for one minute that it was going to cause Jennifer to do something like that! Shit, you know me better than that, don't you?"

Sam took a long draw from his Dos Equis and watched his friend's eyes. He'd known Rick Mason for a long time; longer than he'd known Cheryl, longer than Rick had known Jennifer, far longer than either of them had known Art or Stephanie Dixon. They'd met and become friends in high school; unlikely friends, according to those who knew both of them. Rick was a rising entrepreneur, a man everyone knew was headed for a lucrative career. Sam, on the other hand, was a rather eccentric "semi-nerd"—an unflattering term he'd once heard used in reference to himself. Headed for something creative, perhaps even fame, but not fortunes.

Even so, their college careers had run in parallel; they'd both gone into pre-med in college, and both had continued on through med school at Vanderbilt. Afterward both had migrated eastward along I-40 to Raleigh, to internships and residencies there.

After that, their paths had diverged; Rick became a surgeon, a good one, and went into private practice; it did, indeed, quickly turn lucrative for him. Sam strayed into research, for which he was well-recognized but for which he was not being rewarded with riches. The predictions of their classmates had come true.

Throughout, in spite of their differences, their friendship had remained intact; Sam often felt their relationship was more that of brothers than college chums. Whatever of the rites of passage they had not experienced together they had later shared, and that had generally included such detail as Rick's habit of involving himself with other women. Sam was a little more reserved, but not much. Overall they knew each other better by far than their parents and their true siblings knew them.

Their wives, too, were the best of friends, independently of them and prior to the marriages; Sam and Cheryl had met at a party hosted by Rick and Jennifer. This tight web had expanded some years back to include Dr. Stephanie Dixon, after her residency a junior partner in Rick's practice but now working for the State Medical Examiner's Office, and her attorney husband Art.

And they were now included as well in the tradition of the shared vacation, something Sam and Rick had begun years ago and still continued. For this Rick had footed most of the bill; he had purchased the remote beachfront property north of Kitty Hawk on North Carolina's Outer Banks, the large vacation home where the six of them had, for the past five years, spent ten days or two weeks in August.

The vacation that was supposed to start in two weeks, that Sam felt was threatened by Rick's untimely affair and Jennifer's equally untimely discovery of it.

"No," Rick was saying. "No, you don't have to worry about Jennifer doing anything foolish, she won't." He sighed. "She doesn't do that sort of thing anymore," he added under his breath, making another reference—there'd been such in their conversations before—about something "foolish" that Jennifer used to do. On this point, Rick had never yielded to Sam's pressure for information, and Sam had no idea what was meant by it. This time, he didn't even ask. "But I guess, now that she knows, I'll have to stop seeing Ann," Rick went on. "She is not going to be happy about this, damn it."

"Unless I miss my guess, neither are you."

"No, I'm not. Ann is—well—Ann is—"

A long moment of silence interrupted the conversation. Sam closed his eyes before speaking. "Don't tell me. Don't tell me you've found another one to play your little games, Rick."

Rick rolled his lips in so that they disappeared under his mustache. "Well—yeah. She, uh, uhm, well—"

Sam shook his head. "I do not know how you do it. I just do not. She wasn't into it before, am I right? You introduced her."

"Uhhh—yeah, I suppose—"

"How do you do it, Rick? How do you bring such things up? I mean, I wouldn't have a notion about how to approach it!" He leaned closer to Rick, lowered his voice. "Directly? Do you just come right out and ask them if they would mind very much if you tied them up? If they enjoy a little pain with their sex?"

Rick grinned. "Looking for some pointers, Sam?"

"No chance! That stuff's not for me, old buddy! We've been over this ground before!" He shook his head, sipped his beer. "No, I'm just baffled, that's all. I can't imagine how you get around to it, that's all." He looked back up at his friend. "Nor can I quite see what you get out of it."

Rick gazed off into the distance, across the bar. "Well, as to how I get into it—I start a conversation about fantasies, that's all. You'd be surprised, Sam. You'd be surprised. I start talking about fantasies with a girl and nine times out of ten I'm not even the one that brings it up."

Sam laughed. "You've told me that before, Rick. I find it hard to believe that there're that many people running around out there who sit around and fantasize about this stuff. I can imagine what Cheryl would say if I suggested it to her. I'd only do that if I had some heavy-duty self-destructive urges. No, I think you pick them out somehow. Some sort of radar or something." He smiled and again shook his head. Since college, Rick had been fascinated with what he invariably used a technical term to describe—algolagnia, sexual pleasure associated with giving or receiving pain.

The first time he'd found a young woman willing to play such games with him, he'd been almost obsessed with it for a while. Sam was not judgmental about this—he was aware that for most people a mild form of sadomasochism is common enough, expressing itself in love-bites and fingernail scratches—and Rick's games, from what Sam knew of them, were not much more serious than that. It was his attitude that was different, his active interest, his evident need.

"The thing is," Sam continued at last, "that we've talked about this, oh, I guess about a hundred thousand times now, and I still don't get it. I don't get what you get out of it. I make love with Cheryl and I want to be gentle with her, I want to make her feel good."

"Well, that's the way I am with Jennifer, too."

"So you've said. But not with Ann."

Rick sighed. "No. It's different with Ann. Although what we do makes her feel good, too."

He couldn't help his next question. He might insist that Rick's games held no appeal for him, but that did not mean that hearing about them wasn't titillating. "So what do you do?"

"Well, we bought these handcuffs—my idea but she went down and bought them—and I cuff her wrists and ankles. Then, well, I talk a lot. You know, fantasies, what I'm going to do to her while she's helpless. And she gets so thoroughly turned on by it, she just gets wild, out of control. I say crazy things and she says do it, do it, but of course, I don't." He paused, sighed again, sipped his beer. "It's a real turn-on, Sam. Not because she's tied up. Because it turns her on and she gets so completely into things, and—well, because she lets me, because she puts herself at my mercy. Sex with Jennifer is good, it's real good, but it's never like that, of course Jennifer can't get out of control, and—" he ran down, gave Sam a sidelong look. "Does Cheryl ever get like that, Sam?"

"Completely out of control? Well, no. I guess I'd have to say no, not completely."

"You ever been with a woman who did? Who just went crazy, who just let her passion take over?"

Sam hesitated for a few seconds, reviewing. His experience with women, over the years, was neither vast nor nonexistent; he'd had a few lovers before he and Cheryl had gotten together and decided to make things permanent. "Out-of-control" focused his attention quickly on one in particular, a fellow pre-med student he'd known back in college, the daughter of an immigrant family from the Philippines. The physical part of that relationship, he reflected, had been very good; if that woman hadn't decided to do med school at Columbia they might well still be together—in spite of the fact that they had little else in common.

"Well, I do remember one that was pretty wild," he admitted. "But even that one, no, I wouldn't say so."

Rick gave him a knowing smile. "Talking about Elena, right?"

Sam colored a little. "Closest thing I can remember."

"You used to rant and rave about her. You remember how crushed you were when she broke it off?"

"Yeah, well. Love conquers everything except distance. With me at Vandy and her in New York, there was no way it was going to work out."

"Told you then you shoulda gone on up to Columbia."

"Yeah, but I couldn't stand the city. You were right, though, in a way. But look: if I'd taken your advice I never would've met Cheryl. Look at it that way; it worked out for the best in the end."

"That wasn't what you were saying back then."

"No, but I was drunk a lot then, too. That really wasn't an easy one to handle. I can tell you now, Rick, I was always sort of jealous of you back then. Whenever a thing you had going folded up you just shrugged it off, and two days later you'd have some other knockout hanging on your arm."

"A matter of perspective," Rick said carelessly, waving his arm. "You did all right too. And anyway, most of those knockouts you're talking about were hanging on my arm because they imagined I was going to get rich."

"You did get rich."

"Well, sorta, I guess. That doesn't change anything. Fact was, they weren't interested in ol' Rick, they were interested in bucks, in easy living with a doctor husband who isn't around much. High-priced hookers, that's it. I'd rather go down to the local massage parlor, the girls there are honest. And they don't charge nearly as much. You remember what happened to Jeff Bancroft, don't you?"

Sam grimaced. "Yeah. Got married in med school and right after he set up his practice in plastic surgery his wife dumped him, sued him for a share of his future earnings. Got it, too."

"She sure did. That lady is living in high style today, old buddy. And Jeff works his butt off for nothing."

"Not exactly nothing; as I understand it Jeff turns nearly a mil a year. He has to give Shelly thirty percent, but that still leaves a lot more than I make. Anyway, I agree; it doesn't make what happened to him right. But I'm not sure I see your point."

"Oh. Well, you said you were jealous back then. I'm just saying you didn't have anything to be jealous about. It took me a long time to meet someone like Jennifer."

"Who you proceed to treat like shit."

Rick looked pained. "Oh, come on! I don't think that's quite fair!"

"No, I think it is. You go off doing whatever you want, chasing after every pair of eyes that attracts you, and what does she get out of—"

"Now look. I'm not going to say that I started this affair with Ann for Jenny's benefit; I'm not that altruistic, and I know you, you'd call me down if I tried to hand you any bullshit like that. But the fact is—well, hell, you know what I'm talking about, a man's relationship—his sexual relationship—with his wife gets stale after a while. There's no adventure, no excitement, no discovery. But when—"

"Jennifer," Sam pointed out, "is not having any adventure or excitement. And all she's discovering is that you—"

"No, you're wrong. Like I say, this isn't the reason I do these things, but sex between me and Jennifer is never better than when we make up after one of my—ah—transgressions. It follows a sort of a pattern now; I find out she's found out, I go and confess. She cries, she raises hell, threatens to get a divorce. I act meek, I let her call me names; sometimes she even slaps me, I don't protest. Then there's a period of about four or five days when she doesn't want anything to do with me, no kisses, no hugs, nothing. Sleeps on her side of the bed and wriggles away if I touch her."

"But finally she comes around," Sam put in, twisting his mouth cynically.

"Yeah, but she more than comes around. There's a kind of a trigger point, and she—well, she's never articulated it but as I see it, she sets out to show me she's a better lover than whoever. And, besides that, I might've learned a new wrinkle or two from whoever, that comes into it, and we're—I don't know, restored, renewed. It gets back—well, it almost gets back—to where it was when we first met."

Sam stared at his friend in wonder. "Rick, as rationalizations go, that one is a classic. You positively amaze me."

"No, it's true," he protested. "It really—"

"So why don't you go out and buy Jenny a couple of pairs of handcuffs? See if she wants to put that wrinkle in?"

Rick bit his lip. "I can't do that. I just can't."

Again, Sam sighed. "More ground we've been over," he observed. "You want to tell me why not? You're the one always saying your little games are harmless, just play. Jenny's always been eager to please you, she's been that way from day one. Why not try—?"

Rick's hand waved in a gesture of dismissal. "That's not for Jennifer," he said firmly, his tone that of a man pronouncing an obvious truth. "It just isn't. This isn't something I can talk about, Sam; close as we are, some things are private. Take my word for it, this stuff isn't for Jennifer. She knows nothing whatever about this, and it's going to stay that way." Continuing to wave his hand, he sipped his beer again. "But it doesn't matter. I'll stop seeing Ann, and everything'll be straight between me and Jennifer again. You'll see."

Sam didn't show it by facial expression, but he could not deny, to himself, that he found Rick's matter-of-fact confidence a little irritating. "I think you take her for granted. I think one day she'll surprise you and leave your sorry ass."

"That'd be a black day for me, for sure," Rick admitted. "I don't know what I'd do without her, Sam."

"Then maybe you'd better take a long hard look at what you're doing. Before that black day shows up, when you least expect it."

"Maybe you're right. Look, let's have another beer, then let me get on home. I've got some confessing to do." He sighed yet again, emptied his glass. "Tomorrow isn't going to be fun, either. Ann isn't going to be delighted."

"You set it up. You have to tear it down."

"Yeah, right." He raised his hand, motioned for the waitress. "So let's drop it now, all right? I'll take care of it; like you said, I started it. Tell me about what's doing with you, I ain't seen you in nigh on to two weeks."

Sam leaned forward, resting his elbows on the table. "Well, today was not a good day for me either. I had to go over to the library at N.C. State, and so there I was, walking down Hillsborough Street, when this man—"

The waitress arrived at that point, interrupting him. "Two more, gentlemen?" she asked, her voice low and pleasant. Sam looked up at her; he hadn't seen her before, she was not the same girl who'd waited their table previously. She was reasonably pretty, and she wore glasses that both magnified and enhanced her eyes—which were bright, alert, and the color of freshly turned earth.

Rick burst into an exaggerated smile. "Yeah, two more of the same!" he said enthusiastically. "And look, don't you have some nachos on the menu? I think we might like to have a basket of those, too! And—"

He babbled on for a while, the waitress nodding at each new request. Rick even requested a clean ashtray, though neither of them smoked and the ashtray contained only damp napkins he'd used to dry his mustache. Finally, after giving Rick a smile that could only be termed seductive, she left; the surgeon watched her go until she'd disappeared through the swinging doors leading to the kitchen.

"Anyway," Sam said, resuming his story, "there was this man, standing at the corner, and he—"

"Did you see her eyes, Sam?" Rick asked, his tone rhapsodic. "Oh, man, did you ever see eyes like those in all your life?"

Sam could only groan. For Rick, "incorrigible" was clearly an understatement.

It was after midnight when Sam finally got home. Cheryl was already in bed; he entered quietly, undressed, and crawled in beside her. Drowsily, she raised her head, told him good-night, kissed him. Then she rolled over, facing away, and he interlocked his nude body with hers, his chest against her back, their legs folded together, his penis nestled between her buttocks. Coming around her side, his hand found her smallish but firm and softly rounded breast; she allowed him to hold it for a moment before moving his hand gently down to her stomach. No, he told himself, she was not rousable tonight. He contented himself with reaching down to stroke her smooth thighs. To this she did not object.

Closing his eyes, he thought about Rick's friend Ann and tried to imagine Cheryl handcuffed, cold steel encircling her slender wrists and ankles, she struggling halfheartedly against them, then yielding readily to his whim. It doesn't do a thing for me, he told himself, it does not interest me at all. There're so many problems; how can she spread her legs if her ankles are cuffed? And her hands—Cheryl's hands were very active during lovemaking, and he could not find in himself any desire to reduce or eliminate that activity. No, he decided. Perhaps, if Cheryl were enthusiastic about such things, he could play along. But it was not interesting to him, and he was quite certain it wouldn't be to Cheryl, either.

Passionate and uninhibited as a lover she might be, but in such areas she stuck pretty close to traditional ways. Adventurous or kinky she was not.

After a while he rolled over on his back, started drifting off into sleep. In the hazy transition world between waking and sleep where the images in a person's mind are neither directed fantasies nor true dreams, he saw the dark girl, Selinde, again.

She was standing on a ledge on some mountainside somewhere, dressed in a long white gown so sheer she might as well have been nude, and she was holding a bundle of some sort in her arms, something wrapped in cloth. She was smiling richly at him, and he felt a deep and powerful hunger for her. He wanted to go to her, but there was no way for him to even think about climbing the slope leading up to where she was, it was far too steep, far too dangerous.

She said nothing, but it seemed to him she wanted him to come to her; he studied the slope again, decided he just wasn't capable of negotiating it. Up above, she shook her head in disappointment, and, after laying the bundle down on a convenient rock, turned away from him.

The emotional force of her disappointment and rejection slammed into him like a runaway locomotive. Throwing aside all caution, he lunged at the slope. Words were ringing in his head, whether his or hers he couldn't tell. There's only one chance, he kept hearing. Only one. No hesitations or inhibitions, no doubts or vacillations, no equivocations or reservations of any sort were permitted.

Once he'd committed himself to the slope, it wasn't nearly so hard as he'd expected; he bounded on up like a mountain goat. But it was already too late. Before he could even get close to her her form became hazy, dissolving into a welter of bright white sparks that shot out over the mountain like miniature comets.

He stopped, tears of frustration stinging his eyes, and looked around. Above him, the entire hillside was covered with roses, all of them in bloom, a riot of scarlet. Among them, just for an instant, he glimpsed a large white snake, crawling away from him.

Finally, he looked back down at the bundle she'd left. Reaching down, he pulled up a corner of the cloth; but before he could see what it contained, he fell deeper into sleep; other dreams, more normal ones, crowded the vision out. He was no longer aware that he was dreaming, but, paradoxically, he was aware that he would not remember these dreams the next morning.

Five

"You look funky this morning," Cheryl said bluntly. "Something about your eyes. They look really funky."

Sam looked up from his morning paper and peered at her across his coffee. He'd only been up for fifteen or twenty minutes, and he wasn't really able to focus on much of anything yet. "You look kind of funky too," he said jokingly. "Sort of blurry."

"No, I'm serious." She leaned across the table toward him, looking him over closely. "I can't see anything," she announced. "I don't know what it is, I can't put my finger on it. Something about your eyes."

He shrugged, looked back at the paper, tried to focus. "Things look normal from this side," he told her. "I don't think there's a problem."

"I hope not. How did things go with Rick last night?"

"You could've waited up," he chided. "I come back and find you cutting the z's."

"Sorry, I was beat. I have to work all day, too, you know—"

"Yeah, yeah. I know. Your job is always harder than mine. How hard can punching a computer terminal be? That's pretty much what you do now, isn't it? How long has it been since you cleaned a bedpan, anyway?"

"A while," she admitted. "But just because I'm working on that nursing efficiency project right now doesn't mean that punching a computer is all I do! Besides, what do you do during your average day?"

"Punch a computer terminal. All right, all right. In answer to your question, I think things went very well. Rick has agreed to stop seeing Ann, to patch things up with Jenny. But I have to tell you, if he doesn't do the same thing all over again a couple of months from now I'll be surprised."

"You're probably right, I know. But I—"

"Rick thinks the notion that Jenny might commit suicide over one of his affairs is ridiculous."

Cheryl took a bite of a cinnamon roll—along with coffee, the totality of her typical breakfast. "Well, I don't think it's exactly ridiculous, Sam. Remember, I've known Jenny longer than Rick has. Maybe not better, but longer. She invests a lot of herself in a man; she really invested a lot of herself in Rick." She paused, chewed, swallowed. "Besides, they have a child. It's not something we can really identify with. I know she worries a lot about the effect Rick's antics might have on Paul. If he were to ever find out, I mean."

He waved a hand, slightly irritably. "Well, it's over, I think, at least as far as we're concerned. Rick and Jenny will have to patch up their marriage as best they can, by themselves. I've done all I'm going to do."

Cheryl reached out and patted his hand affectionately. "And that's a lot, sweetheart. I really appreciate your doing that last night."

"You could've shown it by being awake when I got home," he grumbled.

Her patting turned into a squeeze. "I'll make it up to you to-night," she said with a seductive smile.

"Sounds good to me," he told her with an answering grin. He gulped the rest of his coffee. "But I have to get going. AIDS and Peruvian cholera epidemics await."

"Such fun."

"Tell me about it."

As the day wore on, though, Sam found it very difficult to concen-trate, very difficult to work. He sat in front of a computer screen whose hi-res super VGA showed a detailed map of Peru; he could scan that nation and its neighbors by pressing the cursor keys. Red blotches spread here and there on the green-and-yellow land sur-face like acne, illustrating the spread of the cholera epidemic. Ridiculous, he told himself, in this day and age. Such an easy disease to prevent; all you had to do was to boil the water before you drank it and avoid fresh vegetables and such that might come into contact with contaminated water. Simple.

Of course, vast numbers of Peruvian peasants didn't know that. The government might be trying to tell them, but they had other problems as well; Sendero Luminoso guerrillas, the leaf trade in coca—an epidemic in its own right, an epidemic of quick and easy dollars.

Problems with easy fixes, Sam told the screen silently. Legalize cocaine and undercut the illicit trade, put it out of business. Put some reasonable land reforms into effect and undercut the guerrillas, dry up their support, watch them and the drug dealers blow away in the wind overnight. As easy as boiling water.

Far harder, in his view, was what he was to do about the little scrap of paper that was currently resting on his keyboard, lodged between the TYUIO and the GHJKL. The scrap of paper with nothing on it except a phone number: Selinde's phone number.

A stray breeze from the hardworking air conditioner caught the paper and moved it back and forth a little, as if inviting him to pick it up and do something with it. He did pick it up; holding it so the VGA map formed an out-of-focus border, he examined each number minutely, as if that would offer a clue to his dilemma. Interesting, the way she'd written a 6, with the top curled down like a numeral formed by a printer. Even more interesting the way her 9 curled up in exactly the same way.

Realizing which two digits he'd chosen to examine, he curled his lip, accused himself mentally of being juvenile, and put the paper back down on the keyboard. As soon as it was back down the breeze caught it again, waving it back and forth rhythmically.

"I am not obsessed with you," he said aloud, though in a low voice. "You hear that? I'm just curious, that's all."

"I've noticed," came a voice from behind him, "that epidemics don't usually care. And if you mean the computer, well, they expect obsession. They demand it. Along with an occasional sacrifice, like maybe a goat. Or a virgin."

Trying to look casual about it, Sam plucked the paper off the keyboard and stuffed it into his shirt pocket. Only then did he turn to face his coworker—and perennial irritant—Ken Colburn. Colburn was the analyst and programmer for the numerous computers used in the research, a man everyone had to deal with. And a man no one really wanted to deal with.

Ken leaned over a little, peering into Sam's pocket, almost spilling a Styrofoam cup half full of cold coffee on him. "What's that?" he demanded. "Your mistress's phone number? Great! That means that fox of a wife of yours'll be home alone at night, all lonely, just waiting . . ."

"Damn," Sam growled. "You leave your office door hanging open and you never know what's going to crawl in." Colburn merely kept grinning, and Sam felt an irrational urge to at least try to explain the phone number. "The number," he went on, "is for an, uhm, ah, auto repair place, I have to get the car checked—"

Ken laughed, but the washed-out blue eyes behind the Coke-bottle glasses were, as always, mirthless. "Oh, sure," he jeered. "And that's why you were sitting there staring at it like a lost puppy. Sure. I have love affairs with my mechanics, too."

"Ken, you've never had a love affair in your life. Not with anything human, I'm sure."

Ken blinked, and the smile faded from his wide, pockmarked face. "That's right," he admitted. "You are right. Doesn't it get tiresome, Sammy boy? Being right all the time? You know, you're the rightest person I know. Rightest person I've ever known. How come you didn't become a preacher, huh?"

"C'mon, Ken. Don't start laying any trips on me. I've got work to do. Isn't there a computer somewhere around here that's feeling sick, that's just crying out for your none-too-gentle touch? A program with a bug that needs ironing out?"

"Nah. Got all of 'em up and running fine. Maytag repairman, that's me. Just hang out and wait for something to go blooey. You better be nice to me, Sam. If you aren't, I'll go fuck with the network and lock all your files. Then you'll have to come begging for the password."

Sam closed his eyes for a moment. Ken was not, he knew, kidding. The man was obnoxious and antisocial, but his intelligence exceeded the genius level, and his bent had carried him into computers and their languages. He could indeed lock Sam's research files so that he couldn't access them, or even wipe them out, and do it in such a way that the administrative authorities wouldn't be able to prove a thing. Ken was the sort of person who created software viruses and loosed them on an unsuspecting world, just for the hell of it. Just for the kick of creating chaos.

"All right," he said finally, opening his eyes. "You came over here for a reason. What is it?"

"I wanna borrow some of your expertise, Sam."

Sam's eyes narrowed. Generally speaking, his expertise was in tracking epidemics so they could be stopped. Ken's might well be the reverse. Many of the rules that applied to nucleic-acid viruses also applied to boot-sector and file-allocation viruses, and Sam had long suspected Ken of some major-league hacking in his considerable spare time.

But then, he didn't have much of a choice. Not unless he wanted trouble—possibly major trouble. "Okay," he agreed finally. "What do you need?"

Ken leaned over, pointed to his screen. "Clear that out," he ordered, "and call up—"

"Wait a minute, wait a minute! I haven't saved anything, and I don't want to lose two hours' worth of—"

"I put you on an autosave before I came down here. You're fine. Just whang an 'alt-F8' there."

"You sure?"

"Sure! Just do it!"

A little reluctantly, he did. The screen blanked, returned to the system prompt.

"Okay. Now: CD to 'k-backslash-pvt' and hit enter." He did that too. Some unconventional batch filename flashed up for an instant —too quick for Sam to read it—before the screen turned green and prompted for a password. "Good. Now look out." Ken reached down, and his stubby fingers danced on the keyboard for a moment; it looked to Sam as if he'd typed twenty or more characters.

But the green dissolved to black and a menu scrolled down. Many of the entries, each of which was coded by a number-letter pair, were themselves in some sort of code. Instead of words, the entries showed little square smiley-faces and graphics characters.

"Here we are," Ken said. "Now call up M8."

"Just M8 and enter?"

"Uh-huh."

He did; the screen flashed, then went to a map of the United States, Hawaii and Alaska in the corners. There were scroll bars in pale green, top and right.

Sam looked at it for a moment without enthusiasm. It was much like the map of Peru he'd just been studying; it was generally rendered in cool colors, but there were red spots here and there. As he focused on them, he realized they ran in an irregular line, from the Mexican border in Arizona up toward Phoenix, then turning eastward and continuing right across the country—ending perhaps fifty or so miles west of Raleigh. Closer inspection indicated it wasn't really a line; it was a broken series of tiny red and orange dots. But all those dots would've fallen within a hundred miles of a line drawn from Flagstaff to Phoenix and from Phoenix to Greensboro. "What's this?" Sam asked.

"You tell me. What's it look like to you?"

"Hell, I dunno. All I can see is some little blobs in what appears to be a probable line. There's not enough detail to—"

"Look here." From the side of the computer he slid the mouse down across the desk, clicked the right button; a little white arrow appeared. As Ken moved the mouse the pointer slid onward, coming to rest somewhere near Oklahoma City. Here he clicked again, and an outline rectangle appeared. After moving the mouse to adjust its size, he clicked once more. The image changed, zooming in on the rectangle so that it filled the screen completely. Sam was now looking at an area that covered only about a quarter of the state.

"See, here's how you work it," Ken told him, and spent the next few minutes explaining how to create the square, how to zoom-in and zoom-out. Sam tried it himself and discovered that he could repeatedly zoom-in on Oklahoma City, expanding the apparent image until he was looking at a detailed map of just a few streets; houses and even garages showed up as little brown or black squares.

"Christ, this is good!" Sam exclaimed. "Mine won't do this, not even the one I've got of the U.S.! It isn't anywhere near this detailed! Where'd this program come from?"

"I wrote it," Ken said offhandedly. "And spent a few months scanning in topo maps. Pain in the ass, royal."

"You gonna put it on the net?"

"Shit, no!"

Sam looked at him in consternation. "Well, why not? This'd be invaluable, especially in studies like AIDS epidemiology. Right now we can't track the spread inside a city, and we—"

"Fuck. Who cares? I put a lotta work into this, Sammy boy. I plan to market it and make me a mint. When I do, the Institute can buy a copy like everybody else."

"But—but—it might help us get a better handle on—"

"I don't give a shit. I don't shoot drugs and, as you said, I don't fuck anybody. I'm not at risk."

"You truly are an asshole, Ken. Class-A."

"Thank you, I appreciate the compliment. But back to business, Sam; I didn't come down here just to spoil your perfect day, nor to show you my new software. Like I said, I need your expertise."

Sam sighed. "All right, all right. Let's do it, let's get you out of my face."

"Good. Glad you see it my way. Zoom back up to the full map; control-F10'll get you there immediately." Once they were looking at the whole country, Ken started pointing out some spots. "You can't see it from here, but there're two colors, reds and oranges. Reds are certains, oranges probables. Put the pointer on one of the clusters."

Sam did, clicked the mouse; a detail of western Tennessee sprang up. Around Memphis was a group of red and orange dots, and there were a few more proceeding eastward. Each dot was coded by a number, too small to read; Ken showed him how to bring the number up to visibility by putting the pointer on a dot and touching a function key. Then the numbers revealed themselves to be dates and times.

"Epidemic?" Ken asked succinctly.

Sam studied it for a few moments, moving the pointer around to several of the red dots in turn. "Can't say for sure, but it doesn't look like it," he said finally. "More like a carrier; like a Typhoid Mary. Early points spread a little but then die out, and the chain moves on, new centers cropping up. I'd have to do some distribution analyses to be—"

Ken was grinning—a grin that Sam could only see as triumphant, as self-satisfied. "They're done," he said. "You can call them up in a window, use alt-A."

He did that too, examined the figures. "Uhm. Now it looks even more like a carrier," he said. "Almost classic for that. What is this? What's the source data?"

Ken's grin had expanded, but still, he looked pensive for a moment. "Well, it's a game," he admitted finally. "I got right much money riding on it, Sammy boy."

Sam sighed again. "So it's meaningless. Not real."

"Oh, no. It's real enough. The source data is from newspapers and such; each point represents a murder. The game was to see who could best predict when and where the next one would go down. We figured, at first, that we were tracking a serial killer."

"We?"

"Me and this guy from California. Like I said, we've been betting money on the predictions."

Sam looked back at the screen and nodded. "Yeah. A serial killer does sort of make sense, I guess. You working with the cops on this?"

"Shit! That's a damn stupid question! The cops don't even know there are a bunch of related killings!"

He looked back up at the programmer. "You gonna call them? Tell them? I could ask Art or Stephanie who—"

Ken laughed coldly. "Hell, Sammy, if they solved it it'd end the game! We've made sixteen predictions, some pretty much on the money. Town and date; best I've done so far. I'd like to—"

"You have got to be kidding me! Sixteen murders you might've prevented, and you just go on with your game?"

Ken grinned; to Sam he looked like he was about to vomit. "It ain't my business," he said. "I ain't about to get myself involved. Neither are you, because if you talk to anybody all this stuff'll mysteriously vanish from the net. All I want you to do is help me figure it out."

"I thought you already had. You said a serial killer—"

Ken shook his head. "No, that's what we thought at first, like I said. My buddy in California still thinks that, as far as I know. Me, I don't think so, not anymore. As I see it, there're problems with that scenario."

"What problems?"

Ken reached for a nearby chair, rolled it over, sat down. Taking the mouse in hand again, he wheeled the pointer to one of the Memphis dots. A click, and some data sprang up; geographical coordinates and a date from the previous January. "Take this one, for example," he said. "It was a good one, it fell right in our window of predictability. But the Memphis police made an arrest."

"So?"

"There're more after that, Sam. They either arrested the wrong dude or this wasn't one—one of the serial killer's hits, I mean. I think that's impossible."

"I don't think I'm following you."

"Hit F6, pull down the case screen."

Sam did; the map vanished, replaced by a plain text screen. There were several references; evidently the information had been compiled from various news sources. Paging down as required, he read the information. It told of the death of one Leah Cooksley of Memphis, a woman of twenty-two, a waitress. She had been killed with a knife; evidently a rather small one, since she'd been stabbed some twenty-eight times before she expired. Her body had been found nude; there was semen in her vagina and, in spite of her numerous injuries, there was no evidence of defensive wounds, no evidence that she'd so much as argued with her killer. The Memphis police had charged her husband—who'd also been stabbed— with the crime, and he'd committed suicide in jail. Without making a statement.

For a few seconds Ken and his questions went right out of Sam's mind. The brief piece commanded all his attention. He could not deny it; the victim's apparent acceptance of her own death—particularly since she'd been killed with a knife—was, for him, erotic. Even as he'd told Rick, just the other night, that he had no idea what Rick got out of his sadomasochistic games, he wasn't unaware of the link that existed between sex and violence. He'd read about the erotic appeal of a bullfight, he knew that the Roman writer Ovid had commented on the same phenomenon associated with the gladiatorial contests, knew that the antiwar demonstrators of the late sixties were sometimes shocked by the aphrodisiac power of a police riot. Personally, Sam did not consider this in any sense a problem, since for him, any erotica inherent in such situations quickly faded in the face of a terrified and struggling victim; a certain acceptance, at the very least, was required. Which meant, he told himself wryly, that his personality would make the avocation of serial killer virtually impossible. Just as it made the avocation of rapist impossible; Sam hated to be forced to do anything, hated to see others forced, and could hardly bring himself to force his desires on anyone—even though his self-assured manner and his quickness in an argument often allowed him to do just that.

Many times he'd told himself that this sex-violence link was normal, just a part of human nature; even so, he found that it vaguely embarrassed him when it popped up unannounced. He blinked and glanced up at Ken as if afraid that the programmer could somehow see his thoughts.

There was no indication that he could. "So?" Sam asked. "Sounds like a domestic thing. So you blew it. So what?"

"Can't be," Ken said intensely. "First of all, the M.O. is there; multiple stabs, no defensives, recent sex. That's what got us interested in the first place; why no defensives? How does this guy get his victim to sit quietly and let herself be killed? Now you consider this: I called this one from the stats, city exact and date within two days. What do you think the odds are of there being a coincidence like that? A husband offs his wife that way, that week, that city? I'd say it's out of the question."

"I have no idea what the stats are," Sam told him. "But it looks like it happened. If it was your rapist that killed the woman and attacked the husband, why wouldn't he say so?"

"Good question. But it can't be a coincidence, Sam. I can show you half a dozen more like this; it's been going on a long time.

Can't tell how long; we've only researched it back to about 1965. It goes back that far, at least."

"With how many deaths?"

"A hundred and twenty-nine certains. Close to four hundred we consider suspicious or probables."

"Christ! There's never been a serial killer with anything like those numbers!"

"Right you are, Sam. Now—"

Sam's patience was coming to an end. "Look," he said. "You want to know what I think? I think your program is screwed up somewhere, that it's skewing the data somehow. You're right, the odds of you guys making a prediction like this Memphis thing and having a husband kill his wife that night in that city in that way is pretty farfetched—" He paused, snapped his fingers. "I see," he said with a slow-developing grin. "I see. That's why you wanted me to look at it. You're thinking of something contagious, right? Something like a virus?"

Ken looked uncomfortable. "Well, I just noticed that it did look a whole lot like classic Typhoid Mary spreads—that's what you said, too, right off—"

Sam laughed out loud. "Of course, Ken! A virus! Or maybe a bacterium or, hell, who knows, a Rickettsia! Whatever, a contagious pathogen—something somebody is carrying, and when you catch it, it makes you want to stab your wife—and, sure, while we're indulging in these wild speculations, let's just propose that when women catch it, it makes them helpless to resist! A sex-murder virus!" He laughed again. "Ken, I think maybe your buddy has been playing some games with you! Games you aren't in on!"

Ken's expression was one of consternation. "No—no, look, Sam, wait a minute, all I want to know is—"

Sam waved a hand in a gesture of dismissal. "You have my opinion," he said firmly. "Now, can I get back to work here? Will you tell me how to get out of your program?"

Ken stared sullenly for a few moments. "Punch F10," he said. "Then answer yes." He stood up and walked toward the door as Sam pressed the keys. The system came back; he reloaded his working file on the Peruvian cholera epidemic.

To find that his work, two hours' worth, had not been saved. "Oh, shit!" he groaned.

Just outside the door, Ken laughed loudly.

Six

ART WAS GIGGLING. Just as Stephanie had predicted, he was giggling. In their home the dining room and kitchen were separated only by a subtle and spacious arch, and he sat at the already-set table, toying with the kaleidoscope, watching her stir spaghetti sauce. Her back was to him but she could still hear him giggling. For twenty-four hours she'd put off mentioning it to him, but that hadn't affected his reaction, nor her counterreaction.

"All right," she said without looking around. "All right. So I did something impulsive. So it's ridiculous, we can't afford it—"

"Oh, no," Art chuckled. "No, it isn't going to bust our budget, hon. It's not a problem. You want to go drop fifteen hundred on a kaleidoscope, no problem. You hear me complaining?"

"No, I hear you giggling like some kind of an ass!"

He got up, came to her, folded his arms around her waist. "C'mon, now, don't be mad," he begged. "You aren't impulsive very often, hon. You really don't, you just don't do things like this very often!" He didn't laugh out loud, but she could feel his body trembling as he tried to control himself. She had three or four new impulses; she could stamp on his foot, hurl hot tomato sauce in his face, elbow him in the stomach. Struggling with herself, she fought down the violent urges, pushed them aside. They didn't go very far; like wild animals around a campfire they lurked just outside her circle of consciousness, waiting for her to slip, waiting to enter.

Doggedly, she continued stirring the sauce. She did not slip, she would not slip. "We won't," she said evenly, "mention anything to Jennifer—or to Sam and Cheryl—that would give her any idea of what we paid for it. It wouldn't be appropriate. The next time an occasion came up, they'd feel obligated to return something of the same value."

"Well, what's wrong with that? Rick makes more than we do together!"

"It just isn't appropriate," she reiterated. "I bought that thing—as near as I can tell—just because it was so beautiful it took my breath away." She paused. "If you want to help, you can help me figure out exactly why I did that. You are right, that much I admit. It is ridiculous."

He let go of her and leaned against the oven side of the stove. As usual, Art was clad in a tight T-shirt and blue jeans; he still worked out regularly, and although his upper-body musculature was not that of a competition bodybuilder, he was proud of it. He liked to show it off, even to Stephanie.

And he looked good, that she had to admit—especially when his still-boyish face, his intense dark eyes, his quick and infectious grin, and the unruly shock of dark brown hair—the hair that he was constantly terrified might be thinning—were added to the athlete's body below. On the street or on the beach, other women sometimes stared at Art; the feelings that provoked in Stephanie were closer to pride than to jealousy.

Or at least, she told herself with a purely mental sigh, that was the way things used to be—before she'd learned how difficult it was to be married to a man like Art, before she'd learned how many problems his demands for closeness and intimacy caused her. These days, women still stared at him but Stephanie hardly noticed.

"Ridiculous," he said evenly, looking at her from beneath slightly lowered brows and commanding her attention again, "is your word, not mine. Mine was, as I recall, 'impulsive.' And I will say this, Stephanie dear; it is all right for you to be impulsive every now and then, even if it costs us fifteen hundred dollars. If that was a diamond bracelet of the same price, I wouldn't say a word and I wouldn't be laughing about it. You—"

"I don't do that," she said, her voice shifting to its cool tone. "I do not own any jewelry other than what I've been given as gifts. Mostly by you, Art."

"My point exactly. You never go out and buy yourself a bauble, a toy. You should, Stephanie. You deserve it; you work damn hard."

Her manner softened, and she began regretting the violent urges she'd experienced earlier. "I really don't think I can," she murmured. "You know what kind of background I came from; my family was poor as dirt. I have a hard time spending money on anything other than necessities, because I grew up not always having those. I don't know if you, or the Leos, or the Masons, can really understand that. All of you came from at least reasonably well-to-do families, and—"

"Not Sam. His family was blue-collar, he—"

"Even Sam. I've talked with Sam; there isn't a comparison. He didn't grow up doing without necessities. I did."

Art nodded. "So you've told me. Not in too much detail, I might add."

"I don't like talking about it. It has nothing to do with who I am now."

He sighed deeply; she gritted her teeth, hoping he would not try to push her into a discussion of her childhood—as he often had. "Everyone's childhood has a great deal to do with what they are as adults. You know that, Stephanie; everybody knows that. Why do you try to deny it?"

Tensing, she began stirring her sauce more violently. "My family," she said, her voice tight, "was, to use today's catchword, dysfunctional. Abusive. I'm not proud of what they were; I don't like to think I retained any of that." She started to go on, to tell him that her parents were dead, that she had no real family, that she'd left all that behind when she'd left the foster homes and entered Princeton on scholarship.

But he'd heard it all before. "Anyway," she finished, "you know I don't like talking about it. You know I don't appreciate being questioned about it." She was now stirring the sauce so vigorously that she splashed it up and out of the pan; a few droplets fell on her white shorts, a couple more on her thigh. It was hot, but she ignored those on her skin. She just stared down at the red stains on her clothes.

Art crossed the kitchen in three strides, ripped a paper towel off, came back, wiped the sauce from her leg. Then, after moistening another, he began to attempt a cleanup of her shorts.

"No, that won't help. They'll have to be washed, now." She pushed them down, stepped out of them. "Keep stirring this, would you? If it sticks it'll be ruined. I'll be right back." She turned away, headed for the laundry room.

"Your leg okay? This stuff is hot!"

"It's fine. I just have to deal with these shorts! And I have to do it now!"

She returned a few moments later, clad now only in her top and her underpants, and, taking the wooden spoon from Art, continued to stir the sauce as if nothing had happened. "Thanks," she said. "It's just about ready. We can eat in, oh, maybe five minutes."

"Look," he said, his tone conciliatory, "if you found my laughing offensive, I'm sorry. I really couldn't help it. It isn't the thing itself, Stephanie; it's just that, whenever you do something that seems irrational to you, you act like you've murdered somebody or something."

She was completely under control now. "No," she told him. "If I were to ever murder somebody, I'm sure I'd go much further off the deep end than this!"

Seven

FOR SAM, THE next day had been different from the previous one in only one respect, but for that he was grateful; it was already close to four o'clock, and as yet, Ken had not shown his face. Of course, he'd taken the precaution of keeping his office door closed, but he was sure that Ken, if he really wanted to see him, would barge in anyway. Or perhaps find some way to slither through his terminal; he wouldn't have been surprised to learn that the man had figured out a way to do that.

Again, however, the small slip of paper had spent a good part of the afternoon stuck in the keyboard, waving back and forth. Sam had spent a little more time talking to it today. He'd asked it nicely to leave him alone and it hadn't; he'd cursed it, but that had no effect on it either. It remained, moving constantly. Even, Sam would've sworn, when the air conditioner was not blowing. Persistently distracting him from Peruvian cholera epidemics and any other matters he was supposed to be concentrating on.

"All right, you," he told it. "Enough. Another hour or so and I'm out of here for today, and I've really got about three hours work to do." He plucked it out, started to fold it over, put it back in his wallet. It was already becoming brown-stained from its sojourn there.

With the paper half folded, he stopped himself. "Samuel," he said aloud, "why don't you just go ahead and call the woman? You know you're going to, sooner or later. Why all this agonizing? Just because you call doesn't mean you're going to do anything. Hell, she probably isn't even going to remember who you are."

He flipped the paper open again and picked up the telephone. For a moment he hesitated; his mouth felt suddenly very dry and his fingers actually shook a little. "She's just a student," he told himself firmly, "and you're not. Act your age, you stupid shit."

His self-reprimand succeeded in steadying his hand, and he punched out six of the seven digits written on the paper. He did hesitate again over the final 9, but he managed to key that one too. Tapping his fingernails on his desk as if he expected that she owed him an answer within the first couple of rings, he listened to the buzzes, counted them.

The fifth one passed; Sam felt a certain relief. She was not there —which really wasn't that surprising, considering that it was four in the afternoon. She was probably in class. Feeling absurdly victorious, Sam let it ring on a few more times.

Then, unexpectedly, there was a connection. "Yes?" a female voice asked.

Sam stared at the receiver for an instant. "Uh, uh, um, is this— uh—Selinde?"

"Yes, it is. I'm glad you called, Sam."

Again he stared at it. Clearly she remembered. But to recognize his voice? "Uh—yeah. I was about to give you up, I didn't—mm— think you were there."

"I'm sorry. I was in the shower. I'm standing here naked right now, dripping all over my carpet. I'm glad you kept at it."

He gave the receiver a third stare. This is not real, he told himself. She didn't just say that. She wouldn't've.

But, unless he was having auditory hallucinations, she had—and Sam was not able to clear his mind of the image her statement had conjured up. "Well, maybe I should call back—some other time—"

"No, don't worry about it. The carpet'll dry, and I will too. Sam, I wanted to apologize again for the way I spoke to you the other day. It really wasn't called for."

"Oh, it's all right. You've apologized for that already, and be- sides, it was a stressful situation. Watching that man die."

"Yes, I suppose. So. How have you been?"

"Oh, uh—fine—I guess . . . You?"

"Me too."

There was a silence, one that kept stretching on. Sam chewed his lip almost desperately, wondering what he should say to her. He began to realize that he had only four telephone personas; business, friend, family, lover. Selinde could only fit into the friend category, and he always had something of common interest to talk about with a friend. He and Selinde did not, at the moment, have anything in common—except a fatal traffic accident they both had witnessed.

"Are you still there, Sam?" she asked after the silence had grown long.

"Yeah—yeah—still here. Look, this is just a little awkward for me, but I—"

"Let me try to help," she cut in. "You called me because you wanted to continue the discussion we began out on Hillsborough Street. That, you are right now telling yourself, is the only reason. That's fine. We will both believe that as long as it's possible for us to believe that. Agreed? It only makes sense, then, for us to get together somewhere, sometime, to talk. Am I right?"

Again, Sam let a moment of silence ensue. He could not deny that she was right on all counts; he also could not deny that her implication of hidden motivations made him uncomfortable.

"You're right," he said finally, drawing out the words. "But I don't—"

"Yes, I thought so. Where shall we meet, then? And when?"

"I don't know, I—"

"May I suggest my apartment? You could come now. I could serve you dinner."

A series of excuses he could offer Cheryl raced through his mind, falling over themselves, becoming jumbled and confused. Honey, you wouldn't believe it. I had to work on the car lately broken down. The mechanic tells me the files weren't saved and besides that our computer network has burned out a wheel bearing. No. That wasn't going to work. He played through the possibility of telling Cheryl the truth: Look, honey, there's this fascinating and beautiful student I met the other day. I'm curious about her so I called her, and I'm going to her apartment for dinner. Don't know when I'll be home.

That one was only feasible if he decided that suicide was a viable option.

"No," he mumbled into the phone. "No, I can't. Not tonight."

"Too bad. When can you?"

He literally squirmed in his chair. "Well, I don't know, I—"

"You can call me back when you've decided."

And go through all that agony again? Leave the damn paper on the computer keyboard for two days again? No. Let's settle this now. Be reasonable, Sam. Tell her that you've reconsidered, that this was a bad idea. Tell her it was nice talking to her. Then hang up and throw the number away. You go see this woman and you're in trouble; you can smell that aroma, can't you? You can see those big red letters hanging in the sky, can't you?

"Well—I don't know," he repeated, thinking that that phrase probably constituted sixty percent of the words he'd said to this woman since he'd met her. He chewed his lower lip some more. "How about—maybe tomorrow?" She had plans. She had to have plans. Too short notice, a woman like her would have plans.

"Tomorrow's fine," she answered. "I have no plans. You want to come here?"

He felt lost, he felt doomed. But this, at least, he could avoid. "No, maybe it'd be best if we met in some restaurant or something like that," he told her.

"Okay. Which one?"

"What's convenient for you?"

"Anything. I live over by State. Not far from where the accident happened."

"You know where Two Brothers Pizza is?"

There was a brief silence on her end now; he thought he heard a muffled laugh. "Sure," she answered.

"Okay. Shall we say seven? Tomorrow night?"

"Seven's fine. At the Four Brothers."

"Two Brothers."

"Oh. Right."

"Good. I'll see you then. 'Bye."

" 'Bye." *Click.*

He took the phone away from his ear and looked hard at it before hanging it up. Maybe she didn't know where the place was. Maybe she wouldn't show. That'd be good; if she didn't show he could feel bad and get pissed, and while he was pissed he could probably throw away her number.

But he would be there, at seven, he knew that. And that meant he had to come up with a good, unassailable excuse as to why he wouldn't be home until late tomorrow.

He could do it, he was sure. Even though he had no practice or experience with this sort of thing, and even though Cheryl was almost impossible to lie to, he could do it.

Somehow.

Eight

"I JUST WANT you to know," Jennifer Mason was saying, "how much I appreciate what you did."

Sam leaned against the kitchen counter, his gaze moving between Cheryl—who was busy preparing dinner—and Jennifer, who was sitting in—or rather, on—one of their kitchen chairs, one slim leg tucked up under the other, her dangling foot keeping time with some unheard rhythm. As she spoke, his expression shifted between a smile and a scowl. He'd found Jennifer visiting—not a particularly unusual circumstance—when he'd arrived home that evening, and she'd almost immediately begun thanking him for having had his talk with Rick. Cheryl, evidently, had told her all about it.

He wished she hadn't. Intervening in their personal lives wasn't something Sam really wanted to do in the first place, and he wasn't comfortable accepting her gratitude.

"It's nothing," he said, waving off her thanks. "I just gave him my opinion, that's all."

Jennifer smiled. Her eyes were overlarge for her face and her eyelids always had a slightly swollen look, as did her lower lip; it made her look perpetually as if she were just about to fall asleep, or perhaps about to break into tears. That look was combined with a manner that made her seem much younger than her years and a slender body that looked almost fragile. Overall, it gave Jennifer an appeal that neither Sam nor any other man who knew her was unaware of; he knew quite well, from many conversations, how powerfully the combination had affected Rick.

"Well, it had its effect, and I'm grateful," she repeated. "I think maybe Rick has learned a lesson this time."

I very much doubt it, he said to himself; you should look out for a certain waitress. "I hope so." Knowing how she tended to thank him over and over, he searched quickly for some other topic of conversation, no matter how trivial. "Where's Paul this evening?" he asked.

"Right outside," she replied. "You didn't see him as you drove up?"

"Uh-uh."

"Oh. Well, Jeremy Peterson—you know, the boy who lives next door?—was outside tossing a ball around when we came in, Paul went over to see him." She paused, her brow folding slightly. "I worry about that, but you do have to let a boy play ball, don't you, Sam?"

"Well, yes, I'd say you do. It's a—"

"I just worry about his hands," she went on, rolling casually over Sam's answer to her evidently rhetorical question. "He's doing so well at his piano lessons, Sam, you just wouldn't believe it. The teacher says he's exceptional for an eight-year-old. You should hear him play Mozart, you'd really be amazed." She went on for a while, Sam by now only half listening. Paul was, he knew, a good musician—for an eight-year-old. He also knew that the boy wasn't yet ready for the concert stage, which Jennifer, with her tendency to hyperbole, seemed to be saying he was.

Then, with mercurial swiftness, she changed the subject and, suddenly ignoring him, looked past him toward Cheryl. "How's your new workout program going?" she asked.

Resting her hands on the stove, the dark-haired woman looked back at her and shook her head. "No better than the old one. Maybe I just don't go often enough, but there's never enough time . . ." She ran her hands down her thighs and sighed. "The cellulite is winning the war, I'm afraid."

Jennifer nodded. "Yeah, it's beating me too, and it seems like I live at the spa!" This new discussion went on for several minutes, both women bemoaning the state of their bodies—especially their thighs—and talking about their workouts, their aerobics classes. Both of them were wearing shorts; Sam moved his eyes from one pair of legs to the other. Cheryl's, he decided, could well have belonged to a professional dancer, they looked strong but smooth, athletic but sleek. Jennifer's, much slimmer, might have graced a fashion model.

"If either of you," Sam commented after a moment, "has even a trace of cellulite, it's totally invisible to the eye. These eyes, anyway."

"Oh, you're just being nice, Sam!" Jennifer scoffed. Like Cheryl, she ran her hands down over both her thighs, then leaned over to inspect them closely. "They're getting lumpy. I can sure see it." She sighed. "I guess it's just something that happens when you start getting older . . ."

Sam laughed. "Right. You two are crones, anyone can see that."

Jennifer looked sad. "It's not funny, Sam. A woman's prime is her twenties, and we've all left those behind. Maybe—"

"A woman's prime," Sam corrected, "is her thirties. That's well-established. And besides—"

Jennifer went on as if he hadn't spoken. "—that's why Rick keeps having these affairs—"

Not a subject I really want to get back into, Sam said mentally. "I don't think so," he grumbled. "I think it's just habit—a bad habit that's hard for him to break." With that he pushed off the cabinet and left the kitchen; flopping into a chair, he picked up the current issue of *Time,* opened it.

Cheryl, however, had returned to her cooking, and so taken herself out of the conversation; he looked up to see that Jennifer had idly followed him in. "Looking forward to this year's vacation, Sam?" she asked. There was no trace of her earlier melancholy in her voice or expression.

Sam put the magazine down and smiled. "Yeah, I am. Get me away from cholera epidemics for a while. I guess Paul is, too."

"Jennifer was just telling me, it doesn't look like he'll be joining us this year," Cheryl put in from the kitchen.

"Oh? Why not?"

"Well, his grandparents want him to come spend some time with them, so we're thinking about taking him up to Norfolk then, letting him stay."

"Your parents' home in Norfolk isn't that far. Maybe he could come down for a weekend. We'd all like to have him there for a while, at least."

"It isn't far as the crow flies. It's pretty far to drive; you have to go around the Sound or drive up the beach, you know—through the sand. But it's an idea, Sam. We'll talk about it."

"Have the caretakers checked out the house down there yet?"

She shook her head. "I think *caretakers* is too strong a word for Currituck Beach Associates, Sam. Their idea of looking after the place is to drive by once a week and see if it's still standing; if it is, they report that everything is fine. We got a letter from them the other day telling us, 'the land contour changed some after a recent storm.' Rick's been trying to find out what that means, but so far, no luck. We don't know what we're going to find. On the Outer Banks, 'contour change' could mean the house is right now about to fall into the sea, or it could mean the beach has moved ten miles away."

"Well, you build houses on a big sandbar and that's what happens," Sam observed. "It's kind of stretching the point to call the Outer Banks land at all."

"Uh-huh. Rick says that, too. But that old house has been there since the mid-nineteenth century; hopefully it'll stand there for a few more years."

"Hopefully. I'd miss it come August if it floated away."

Jennifer started to reply, but before she could the door popped open, almost violently. As Sam turned to look, a tall and slender but strong-looking boy with tousled dark blond hair burst in.

"Hi, Uncle Sam!" he cried. Then, after streaking past him: "Mom! Jeremy says they're getting up some teams down at the Y to play football this fall! Can you sign me up?"

Jennifer made a face. "Football? That's awfully dangerous, isn't it?"

"No! Dad played football in high school, didn't he?"

"He did indeed," Sam put in. "Quarterback. So did I; tight end." He laughed. "Of course, we were both second-stringers and we spent most of our time on the bench, but—"

While Paul, excited, danced around, Jennifer hung her head. "Paul, what about your piano lessons? Don't you want to—"

"I'll still practice! I promise!" He looked around at Sam, grinned engagingly. He was well aware that he could count on Sam's support in matters like this, but he was also bright enough to know where more effective support was to be found. "Aunt Cheryl?" he called. "Aunt Cheryl, will you talk to her?"

Smiling, Cheryl peeked out of the kitchen. "You can count on it," she said. "But you understand, I can't promise you it'll work out this time—"

"Oh, of course it will," Jennifer moaned. "I have to say, I just can't wait for you guys and the Dixons to have some children of your own, so I can pay you back for all this! Between you two, his 'Aunt' Stephanie and his 'Uncle' Art—not to mention his grand-parents—he always gets to do whatever he wants to do!" She shook her head. "I won't promise," she told the boy. "We'll talk it over with your father, okay?"

"Okay!" Knowing victory was in his pocket, Paul ran into the kitchen, gave Cheryl an affectionate hug, then rushed back out. "Uh—got any new games on your computer, Uncle Sam?"

Sam was compelled to rumple his hair a little more. "Well—I don't know. Have you seen the Camelot game, the one where you play the role of King Arthur?"

Paul gave him a disparaging grunt. "You know I have. We're stuck in the desert, we can't find water! Have you found a way out yet?"

"No, but I have a couple of ideas. We could—"

"No, you can't," Jennifer said firmly. She stood up. "If I let you two get in there on the computer, you'll be there for two hours, minimum. No. We have to go."

"Aw, Mom—"

"Don't 'aw, Mom' me. You heard me."

Sam could not resist make a face himself. "Aw, Jenny—"

"Not you, too!" Taking Paul's hand, she started for the door. "Cheryl!" she cried, "I'm being ganged up on, Cheryl! We're gone, I'm getting him out of here while I still can!"

"Okay, Jenny," Cheryl replied, laughing. "I'll be talking to you in the next couple of days."

" 'Kay. You all have a good evening." She moved on toward the door, towing Paul along. Sam did not immediately get up.

"Sam?" Cheryl said, a mild reproof in her voice. "Jenny and Paul are leaving."

He sighed—not quite loudly enough for Cheryl to hear it—and got up, walked them to the door, waited while they climbed into the BMW and drove off. Rick, Jennifer, and Paul were like family; he didn't feel he was necessarily required to walk them to the door. He returned to his seat, sat back down. Blankly he stared at the television screen, even though the set was not turned on. From the blue-grayness, Selinde's image seemed to gaze at him.

Cheryl came out of the kitchen, dispelling the vision. "What's wrong with you?" she demanded.

He glanced up. "Nothing," he replied. "Why?"

"You just don't seem to be yourself this afternoon, that's all. Did something else happen today? Ken, maybe?" She sat down in one of the living-room chairs facing him, crossed her legs, held up her hands, and pressed her fingertips together.

"No," Sam grunted. He picked up the remote control, punched

the TV on, switched it to ABC news. "No, I haven't seen Ken today."

"Then what is it?"

Scowling, he turned to look at her. "What is what?"

Her patient look was exaggerated. "What? Is? Wrong?"

He waved his hands around. "Nothing. I don't know. Maybe just the traffic on the way home. I-40 was jammed up as usual, and they were playing demolition derby on the Beltline again."

"The traffic's always bad, you complain about the traffic every day, day in, day out. You don't usually get an attitude about it, and you, my love, have an attitude."

"I don't have an attitude."

"Yes, you do."

"No, I don't."

She sighed. "Sam, I've known you for nine years, lived with you for eight." Her tone betrayed a rising irritation. "I know when you have an attitude."

He gave her a direct look. "I'm just tired," he said. "I'm just aggravated by the drive home. That's it. That's all. Okay?" He looked back at the TV, tried to listen to Peter Jennings's comments on the current state of what used to be the Soviet Union.

"I wish you'd look at me and not at the TV when we're talking," she persisted, her tone now close to severe.

Sam looked back at her, but his eyes kept darting periodically to the screen, and she did not fail to notice. Her left eyebrow was cocked and she'd shifted her mode of crossing her legs; now her left ankle rested on her right knee. Sam did not miss the body language; Cheryl felt he was brushing her off, and she was getting angry about it. There was an argument brewing, no doubt about it.

This one will be easy enough to defuse, he told himself; it isn't really over anything. Not that that mattered, some of their worst arguments had been over nothing. But this time, he was sure, all he had to do was accede to her demand that he admit that he had an "attitude," and that it was inappropriate for him to have one. It was easy, a small surrender, no cost to his ego. Not even as much trouble as going out to see Rick.

On the spur of the moment, he decided not to do that. He watched the TV for a few seconds, allowing her to simmer; then he turned his gaze back toward her. "If I have an attitude," he remarked, "you might want to think back to what you did a few minutes ago. When Jenny and Paul were leaving."

Her eyes narrowed a trifle. "What," she asked acidly, "did I do? Or should I say, what did you imagine that I did?"

"I didn't imagine a thing. I'm talking about your habit of correcting my behavior in public, as if I were a child. Maybe you don't realize it, but you used your parental voice in telling me I should accompany them to the door. I've told you before, I don't like that."

A flicker of chagrin colored her cheeks momentarily; she uncrossed her legs, the eyebrow dropped a few millimeters. As he read it she was ready to back down, though she wasn't quite ready to admit it yet. "I didn't, Sam! All I said was—"

"It had nothing to do with what you said. It was how you said it. I know, I know. All you said was, 'Sam, Jenny's ready to go' or something like that. But you said it as if you were speaking to a naughty seven-year-old. You used the same tone Jenny uses when she's correcting Paul."

She was silent for a few seconds. "Well, I don't think I did. But if you think I did, then I'm sorry. I didn't mean to."

There, he told himself. The legs are crossed at the ankles and the eyebrow is all the way down. I could drop it now and it's all over.

He didn't do that, either. "You know," he mused, looking back at the TV, "you never really offer a real apology. They're always couched in a bunch of qualifiers. 'If you heard me say' or 'if you think I did.' It puts part of it back on me. You won't say, 'Yes, well, I did that, Sam, and I'm sorry.' It has to be halfhearted."

The eyebrow was on the rise again. "Yes, well, I did that, Sam, and I'm sorry," she parroted stiffly.

"Now you're making fun of me."

"I am not! You told me what you wanted to hear and I said it!"

"Sure. But you don't mean it."

The leg went back up, too, and she folded her arms across her chest. "It seems to me that doesn't matter much. It seems to me you're in the mood for an argument!"

"I didn't start this."

"No, you never start them. Innocent as a newborn lamb, that's you. If you could observe some of the common social amenities without my reminding you, then this sort of thing—Will you stop watching that goddamn TV and look at me when I'm talking to you!"

He did look back. "You see?" he said calmly. "You see? The

naughty little boy is watching the TV when he shouldn't be. Mommy has to correct him."

"You know that irritates the shit out of me!"

"Your parental attitude irritates the shit out of me. And you know that, just as well. You are not my mother. I do not depend on you to—"

"I might as well be! You'd never have any clean clothes if I didn't wash them! If I didn't clean the house you'd be living in a pigsty, and I work just as many hours as you do!" She went on and on for quite a while, enumerating his faults and shortcomings, as she always did at some point during an argument. He listened, even though he had, in fact, heard them all before. Some of them were accurate enough to embarrass him; others, exaggerations.

"Maybe you just shouldn't do me any favors."

"Maybe I shouldn't! I think I'll just start leaving your clothes in a pile, see how long it takes for them to get washed!"

"Do that. That's fine."

"I will!" She jumped up, stalked into the kitchen. "There is a dinner cooked," she said icily. "You can eat it if you wish. A real dinner, not a microwave masterpiece!"

He rose from his chair, ambled in. "I will. Can't let it go to waste, can we? But tomorrow, maybe I'll just eat out."

"That's fine! That's just fine!" She put the dinner—a casserole, she'd worked on it quite a while, obviously—on the table. After setting a place for herself, and herself alone, she sat down, spooned food onto her plate.

Sam got his own plate and sat down to eat. There was guilt associated with all this; Cheryl was right, he knew, he'd taken a small thing and blown it up into one of their always passionate— and increasingly common—fights. It would be bad for him, he reflected, if it were to cause any long-range damage to their relationship.

But he didn't think it would. Their arguments, many of them much more venomous than this one, had not done so in the past. And for now, he was free to meet Selinde as planned. Without having to dream up some sort of excuse.

Nine

MORNING SUNLIGHT STREAMED through Stephanie's window as she sat alone at her breakfast table; it drew broad golden bands on the polished oak surface. Art was already gone, an early appointment down in Wilson having gotten him up and out of the house before six thirty. As always, Stephanie had risen with him, and now was left with some idle moments before she herself needed to go. A cup of coffee with exactly 2.5 teaspoons of cream—she always measured it—sat beside the morning edition of the *News and Observer,* which was open to the sports page—where Art had left it. On the other side sat a bowl of Life cereal with eight halved strawberries atop the little tan squares; beyond that was one cup of sweet acidophilus milk, also measured.

Beside the paper was the kaleidoscope, lying where it had been all night. It had no place in your home yet, she told herself, that's why it's still lying out. I'm not going to give it a place, either. I'm going to give it away. To Jennifer. No, to Paul; no, much too valuable for a young boy. Maybe Cheryl would like it better. She stared at it, her thoughts quieting for a moment. Maybe you can take it back, she argued mentally. Maybe they'll take it back. The girl at the store said she didn't think the owner really wanted to sell it, she'd probably be glad to get it back. Probably be delighted to tear up the credit card slip.

"It's just a damn kaleidoscope," she said aloud. "That's all it is. You bought it on an impulse, you threw away a sizable chunk of money, you had to put up with Art's giggling. Two costs. Why don't you just forget it, try to learn from the experience? There really isn't any point in compulsing about it. Read your paper, eat your breakfast, forget about it."

A cloud passed over the sun outside; the breakfast nook where Stephanie was seated darkened momentarily. When the light returned, a single narrow beam struck the kaleidoscope for an instant, hurling the etchings on the tube into sharp relief.

Insisting on discipline, she forced herself to take a sip of her coffee before she would allow herself to pick it up, even though the urge to do so was strong. She almost spat it out; it had grown cool. Surprised, she glanced around at the wall clock in the kitchen and discovered that she'd been sitting there for twenty minutes, just staring at the thing.

Irritated with herself, she put the cup down and picked up the kaleidoscope. Holding it with the eyepiece end downward and angling it so the again-abundant window light would catch it, she studied the carvings on its surface closely.

It was not easy to see what the designs were supposed to represent, there were too many swirls and flourishes surrounding them. As before, she thought she could see the form of a stylized nude woman, something along the lines of Winged Victory, and a giant snake whose head was resting on the woman's hand, looking into her face, and whose coils were wrapped around her lower body. Behind them was what appeared to be a tree, rising the length of the tube, its abundant branches spreading over them both.

Eve and the serpent in the Garden of Eden, she decided. She twisted her face. Not one of her favorite stories; how a woman was responsible for the Fall of Man from divine grace. That's us, she told herself. Wicked, sinful, lustful creatures. Men are such innocents, we bait them and lure them into their crude and violent ways, it's always our fault, they'd be such pussycats if it weren't for us. She turned the tube around, looking for a heroic or possibly a despairing Adam, or for a wrathful Yahweh gazing down from the skies.

She didn't find either one. The snake's coils and the tree's roots and branches almost encircled the tube, almost met on the other side. No Adam, no Yahweh. She was relieved, she didn't like either one of them. One was a pathetic wimp, impulsive but unwilling to take responsibility for his actions—like many of the men she'd dated before her marriage to Art. The other was overbearingly and violently paternalistic—far too much like her father.

Her well-honed mental discipline engaged itself without any conscious decision and those thoughts were expelled from her mind. She didn't want to talk to Art—or anybody else—about her childhood years, and she certainly didn't want to sit around during her spare time and think about them. Those years were over, done with, gone. She'd left them behind; no residue. As she'd told Art, nothing that had happened then had any effect on her life now, on the person she'd become. She continued to examine the tube, to study the images on it.

After a while she decided that perhaps it was not intended to represent Eve and the serpent, after all. The woman looked somehow too heroic and the snake too friendly. Maybe, she told herself, it wasn't really intended to represent anything at all, maybe it was just something the artist liked. Or maybe it was Eve and this particular artist didn't see things from quite the same perspective as the Genesis author. That was possible, too.

Or maybe something else entirely was intended; the designs were so vague they might really have been abstracts. She tipped the tube, held it horizontally, saw nothing different. Then she stood it on end again, this time with the eyepiece up.

What she saw now rather startled her. The carvings were the same, but what they suggested was quite totally different. She was sure she could see several human forms, some of them formerly part of the tree's branches; one looked like a man—or maybe more than one man—lying on his back, the other like a nude woman sitting astride him—or them—with her hands in the air, her pose suggesting that she might be having intercourse with the man or one of the men. Another figure—previously part of the snake—seemed to represent another man, a man holding the woman by one arm and holding in his other hand a long elliptical knife—either threatening the woman or, perhaps, actually piercing her chest with it. Nothing in the woman's posture suggested that she was being forced; her other arm was up, not reaching over to try to interfere.

Frowning, she flipped it over, saw the snake, tree, and woman reappear. Back, and the scene—a sacrifice, perhaps?—came back into view. She stared at it for quite a long while, finding it oddly compelling.

Finally, without really thinking about it, she turned it so that the eyepiece was aimed toward her face and lifted it to look through it, aiming it at the brightly lit window.

As before, the effect was visually stunning, fascinating. For a moment or two Stephanie thought she could see a hint of the sacrificial scene in the multitude of tumbling crystals, but she chalked that notion up to suggestion.

As she continued to turn the tube, though, she could not deny that the heavily saturated colors and symmetrical patterns were having the same effect on her as they'd had previously. In one frame, a trickle of scarlet ran down each side of each isosceles, the effect being transformed into blood-red spokes growing from the rim to the center of a multihued wheel. As the redness pooled at the center, several emerald crystals were dislodged sequentially, effecting a green spiral migrating back from the center to the rim. Red to green, chaos to order, she thought, unable to even consider tearing herself away until the greenness had been spread evenly around the wheel's margin. She turned the tube again and saw six pink roses leap into existence, saw a multitude of tiny blood-red streams pouring from them.

Eventually, with effort, she managed to take the tube away from her eye and put it back down on the table. Another glance at the kitchen clock told her she'd been sitting there for another thirty minutes, staring through the tube like some drug-addled relic of the sixties. With a vehement wave of her hand—one that threatened to knock over the cup of now utterly cold coffee—she mentally dismissed the kaleidoscope and pushed herself away from the table. As she started to walk toward the bedroom to dress, she discovered that her panties were soaking wet.

In disbelief, she stared down at herself; she was as wet as she might've been if she'd been heavily at foreplay for half an hour, if not wetter. That doesn't make sense, she told herself. How can those patterns be erotic? There's nothing there, nothing but the random fall of colored crystals.

But the evidence was undeniable. Even more irritated, she headed toward the bathroom; even before she got there she'd formulated an answer.

It was quite obvious, at least as she saw it now. There was nothing erotic about the patterns; it was what she was projecting onto them, that was all. As she'd noted before, like a Rorschach inkblot. The question was, why was she projecting things erotic onto them?

As she combed her hair and put on her makeup—she used only a touch, only a suggestion of facial colorings, mostly just to add a little emphasis to her eyes—she decided that the answer to that one was, unfortunately, pretty obvious.

Pausing, she rested her hands on the edge of the sink and stared blankly at the face in the mirror, not really wanting to think about the answer that immediately suggested itself. A pretty face, so she'd always been told; some had even said beautiful. She herself did not know—the face was too familiar to her, too commonplace, too everyday. There was nothing there that she could call ugly.

Her hair looked pleasant to her: shiny auburn, rolling smoothly and evenly over her shoulders and on down her back. Eyes were okay. On the large side and brown—"dark milk chocolate, sweet and rich," Rick had once said—but not striking green like Cheryl's or bright blue like Jennifer's. Her best feature, she'd always believed, was her lips—they were quite full, especially the lower. If there was a fault there, it was in the nose, which was hardly large but which she'd always felt was overlong. She stepped back, went on analyzing—bust was excellent, she'd managed to keep her body in reasonably good trim in spite of the limitations on her time—

She sighed, shook her head. She could not rid herself of the thoughts that had arisen, of her suspicion that she was seeing erotic patterns in the kaleidoscope because her sex life was, and had been for some years now, virtually nonexistent. She and Art had not made love for—she calculated mentally—four months? The eyes staring back from the mirror widened; she calculated again.

No, that was correct, four months. Worse, that last time had been hurried and mechanical, unsatisfying to her and, she was sure, to Art as well. Excuses were easy; Art was a busy lawyer with a heavy caseload, she was a busy doctor, a career woman headed for the top of her profession. Answers, solutions, were not so easy. There had been a time when her physical interaction with Art had been more than exciting, but that time had faded so distantly into the past that by now it was hard to remember.

With some effort, she shook off the sadness, the sense of loss, that such thoughts provoked. Her discipline engaged itself again. Your body is trying to tell you something, Stephanie, she said to the image in the mirror. You'd better pay attention, you'd better start searching for those solutions, you'd better start talking to your husband. And until you do—you are not to touch that damn kaleidoscope again. It has a disrupting influence on you, it isn't good for you.

Having decided on a course of action made her feel somewhat better, and she returned to her usual morning routine. After deeming herself acceptable to face the world, she gathered her things together and went out to the car, steering the Ford into the dense traffic of Raleigh's morning rush hour. She was over a mile from home when she realized she'd left the coffee, the cereal, and the milk sitting on the table. The coffee wasn't a problem for her, but she knew the milk would be spoiled before she could get home, that the strawberries would dry up and the cereal would become inedibly stale. Tears sprang to her eyes in a great rush, rendering her view of the traffic wavy and hazy; she grabbed a tissue from the dash and wiped them away. Damn nuisance, she told herself. Now I'll have to stop by and fix my eyes before I can go on in.

But first she had to get there, and the tears were not over. The often-hungry child inside Stephanie had reared her head, and this time she was not to be put down so easily.

Ten

STEPHANIE HAD ALMOST forgotten about the kaleidoscope, almost forgotten about her morning tears, almost forgotten about her problems with her husband. Gowned, with rubber gloves on her hands and a surgical mask over her mouth and nose, the auburn hair tied up under a cap, she stood beside a sterile white table looking down at the still form lying on it.

But her role today was not that of a surgeon; the gleaming instruments on the tray were not to be used to save a life. For this life, such efforts were much too long overdue. The woman on the table was quite dead, had been dead for a quite a while. She was here for autopsy, she was here so that Stephanie could determine the exact cause of her death, not so they could prevent it.

To the layman, the cause would've seemed quite obvious, since the corpse on the table was marked with several wounds, wounds that had evidently been inflicted with a knife. But for her—and for the courts—more precision was required.

She already knew a good deal about this particular person. Her name was—had been—Alice Near, twenty-two years old; she'd lived in a trailer park in nearby Morrisville. According to the police reports, she'd been employed, off and on, as a topless dancer in the clubs around Raleigh, and, according to speculations in those same reports, she'd occasionally worked as a hooker—although she'd never been arrested and charged as such.

Her body had been found in the trailer where she'd lived, amid a wash of blood—blood that they'd already determined had come from two different people, since there were two types, A positive and O negative. Only the O negative came from Alice; the police, not unreasonably, were assuming that the A pos came from her attacker. Since the body had been found unclothed, Stephanie had already run her "rape kit" on the corpse; she hadn't been surprised to find semen in the woman's vagina. A rape-murder seemed like a perfectly reasonable hypothesis already, but that scenario was complicated by the fact that the woman's husband, who'd worked as a veterinary assistant, was nowhere to be found. Since the trailer showed no signs of forced entry, Dave had already focused on him as the most likely perpetrator.

"It's too damn bad," Jack Bivens said from the opposite side of the table. "What a waste." He gazed down at the woman's trim figure, at her even-featured face. "She was one damn pretty girl."

"Pretty girls," Stephanie said, "get murdered too. It would be a waste if she was fat and ugly, wouldn't it?"

"I suppose. I just hate it when they look like that and they end up here."

"It probably wasn't her choice." She picked up a calibrated probe. "Okay, let's get to work, let's see what we have here." Leaning over the naked cadaver, she used the probe to test the depth and contour of the wounds. There were at least a dozen immediately visible. The woman's breasts had been repeatedly stabbed, as had her abdomen, both in front and down her sides; there were even some stab wounds in her thighs.

"Inflicted with a double-edged blade," Stephanie observed, speaking into a little voice-activated tape recorder she held in her hand. "Eight centimeters long minimum, approximately thirteen millimeters wide." She moved her probe to another wound. "The wounds are remarkably uniform," she continued. "There is no evidence of twisting or cutting." Her brow furrowed above the surgical mask. She picked up each of the victim's hands, examined them carefully.

"There aren't any," Jack offered. "I looked already."

"No, there are no defensive wounds," she agreed, speaking to the recorder rather than to Jack. "And there is no bruising of the wrists that would indicate that she might've been tied." Dropping the corpse's hand, she lifted the chin. "No neck bruising, no indication of strangulation." Turning the woman's head to one side, she ran her fingers through the hair, ruffling it. "No overt evidence of a blow to the head." She checked the woman's neck for stab wounds carefully; a puncture there, if it pierced the spine, might have converted the victim into an instant quadriplegic, helpless to resist her attacker.

But her neck was altogether unmarked, and none of her other wounds—virtually all of which were on the front and sides of her body—came anywhere close to her spine.

Shaking her head slightly—she had no answer to this yet—Stephanie continued to examine the wounds, methodically probing each and every one, determining the depth, the width, the angle of entry, and noting each on her body diagram sheet. "All the wounds," she told her recorder, "are remarkably uniform. Not one is over fifteen millimeters in width, although the depth varies from two centimeters to eight centimeters. All were inflicted antemortem." She paused, cleared her throat. "There are also numerous other small injuries apparent on the victim's legs and torso. Many of these are partially healed; it appears that most were inflicted days before death, at least. None were serious." She clicked off the tape recorder. "All right, people," she said, picking up a syringe and a small vial. "Let's get some fluids here, get them down to the lab. Then, after we get our photos, we'll get her open, see if we can find any clues inside."

Several hours later she sat alone in her office, red pen in hand, going over the transcript of her tape she'd already had printed out, and going over the lab reports simultaneously.

It wasn't, really, what she'd expected; at least, not insofar as any of the standard tests suggested. Alcohols had been done on the woman's blood, and on the vitreous humor from her eye; she had not been drunk, either at the time of her death or recently before. Nor did the blood and urinary screens suggest that she'd been drugged. Stephanie had even ordered an additional test: knowing that the woman's husband had worked in a veterinary office and knowing that barbiturates are ubiquitous in such environments— and that those drugs are easily capable of rendering a person unconscious and insensible to pain—she'd had them tested for as well.

But that test, too, had turned out negative.

The overall picture was actually fairly clear, but it left as many questions posed as it answered. Unless she'd taken some exotic drug, Alice Near had, most likely, been in full control of herself when she was killed. Her attacker—whom she'd been facing—had proceeded to repeatedly thrust a relatively small double-edged knife into her body. From all the available evidence, she'd done nothing whatever to try to stop him. She hadn't even squirmed around much.

Unusual, she told herself, but not unique. She recalled seeing a couple of reports on the same sort of thing. There'd been one, a few years back, that had received considerable notoriety nationally: a young woman had been bludgeoned, strangled, and stabbed, and the evidence indicated that she'd adopted the meditative lotus posture before the attack had started and had maintained it throughout the long and violent attack, even as she was dying; she was found with her thumbs and middle fingers still forming the classic circles. In that case, as in this one, the victim had offered no resistance at all.

Not for me, Stephanie thought, not for me. Anybody comes after me with a knife, he's going to have one hell of a fight on his hands. If he wins, there's going to be a shitload of defensive wounds found on this body when they do the autopsy.

But even as she told herself that, another image, unrequested, arose in her mind, an image of herself in Alice Near's position. If she believed that her death were inevitable—or perhaps necessary, for some reason—she was sure she'd be able to accept it without complaint, without struggle. If it were her choice, she realized, if it were her choice and if she were strong enough to master the pain, it could change, it might not be something horrible and terrifying, it might be . . .

"That's sick, Stephanie," she said aloud, blinking her eyes to dispel the images. "Sick." Maybe, she told herself, it was just the coincidence of having this sort of a case today, after seeing the apparently voluntary sacrificial scene on the surface of the kaleidoscope.

Putting the report down, she stared off into space blankly for a few seconds. That answer, she told herself, that Alice Near's death had been a sort of an assisted suicide, did not work. Firstly, because she was sure that fantasies such as the one she'd just had were hardly common; she'd imagined such things before, and she'd attributed them to her need—a need she did not apologize for, a need she did not regard as problematic—to be able to control, endure, or transform virtually any situation.

Secondly, it did not work because Alice Near's assailant had inflicted wounds—many of them—that were, from all appearances, not designed to be fatal. He—Stephanie was quite sure, in her own mind, that it had been a he—had done that intentionally, she was certain of it. There were no wounds near the woman's heart or throat and most of the stab wounds in her breasts had been directed at angles so they would not pass between her ribs and into her lungs.

She tapped the tip of her pen on her desk, trying to work out some other scenario that would fit the evidence. Maybe when she was attacked she'd been so frightened she'd fainted. That wouldn't leave any evidence for an autopsy.

But neither that theory nor a suicide hypothesis explained the blood that had been found in her trailer and on her body, the blood that was not Alice Near's type, the blood the police assumed had come from her attacker. Even Stephanie had to admit that he was the most likely source. Nor did either explain the small injuries, the previous, nonlethal ones. Maybe they weren't connected, she told herself. The only reason for supposing they were was there general appearance; several could have easily been inflicted by the same knife that had later been used to kill her.

She thought about it for a while longer, tapping her pen with rhythmic regularity. No other explanations suggested themselves to her.

It isn't your job, she told herself finally, throwing the pen down and packing up the report. You've done your job and it's all right here. Cause of death, loss of blood, cumulative. No defensive wounds. Evidence of recent sexual intercourse but no physical evidence of rape. Blood alcohol point-oh-two, no drugs. From here on, she said silently, it's all yours, Dave. You figure it out. We've got a bunch of tubes of blood from this woman in storage, we've got other fluids, we've filed away a piece of her liver, a piece of kidney, and the contents of her stomach. Anything you come up with, we can test for.

But maybe she'd run it past Art when she got home. Maybe he'd think of something she'd missed, something she could look for. It really was peculiar; it really begged for an explanation.

Eleven

THERE WAS NO question in Sam's mind that this day had been one of the longest of his entire life. By four, he'd begun to have little hope that the evening might be pleasant; so far, nothing else had been.

The first thing, of course, had been his own fault; Cheryl's icy demeanor this morning, the potshots she'd taken at him whenever an occasion presented itself. He hadn't responded in kind; he'd taken them, absorbed them, tried to dismiss them—even though a few of them stung. His behavior toward her had been cool but not hostile; he did not want to set up a situation where the fight would go on for days and days, always a real possibility. No, he'd gained his one night of freedom, he'd take it and then do everything he could to restore the status quo.

That hadn't ended the day's unpleasantness, though. Ken had shown up at his office door before lunch, demanding another conference on his fancied—in Sam's opinion—murder epidemic. As before, Ken had made it impossible to brush him off completely, but Sam had gotten rid of him by giving him what he wanted—a different statistical procedure to analyze the spread of the hypothetical epidemic, a possibly better way to predict the next occurrence—presuming that the model of a carrier-borne pathogen was viable. If it wasn't—as Sam had carefully explained—then the predictability should go down, not up.

After Ken had left, Sam had been somewhat bothered by the data he'd seen. An epidemic was of course nonsense, but it was possible, it seemed to him, that Ken and his hacker buddy were indeed tracking a serial killer's progress—with a few stray points thrown in. What was included and excluded, of course, made a great deal of difference when it came time to apply statistics to such problems, to try to make predictions based on previous occurrences. That, Sam was sure, was the weakness. Ken might be brilliant with computers, but he was not a trained researcher, and his data selection might be utterly faulty. If so, the well-known GIGO principal of computing would apply—Garbage In, Garbage Out. The appearance of a carrier-borne epidemic instead of the linear point-by-point tracing of a serial killer.

And if it was a serial killer, then, according to what Sam had seen in the data, he was now practicing his deadly pastime in North Carolina, not too far from Raleigh. After giving the matter some serious thought, he decided it would be best if local law-enforcement was made aware of these matters.

So, accordingly, he tried to call Stephanie; she had the proper connections. She was, he was told, busy with an autopsy; he left no message, called Art instead—only to find that he was in court. At that point he put the matter aside. He'd deal with it tomorrow, he promised himself; that'd be soon enough. Today, there were other matters to occupy his attention.

As five thirty rolled around, he had to force himself not to rush from the office. He continued to map the spread of the Peruvian cholera epidemic, telling himself doggedly that it would serve nothing to go out and engage in combat with the worst of Raleigh's afternoon traffic, only to arrive at the restaurant between six and six thirty—and sit there chewing his nails for a half hour or more.

As, he realized, he was chewing them now. Since about three, his adrenaline had really been flowing free; his mouth was dry and acrid, his stomach felt queasy, his bowels were grumbling and behaving in a manner that suggested that they might become somewhat unruly. To cap it off, he already had a slight tension headache. You're in great shape, Sam, he told himself silently. Great shape. You're going to make a wonderful impression. Pizza will probably push you right over the edge, you're going to spend half this meeting in the men's room with diarrhea. If you don't start barfing you'll be lucky.

It wasn't as if he didn't know the cause of the tension. What did the woman want? And worse, what in God's name was he going to say to her? He'd been awkward enough on the phone; in person, he was sure, it was going to be worse.

Or maybe not. At least he wouldn't be fantasizing about her standing wet and naked in her apartment. But that didn't help much; he still didn't really feel he had much to say to her. With a twinge of frustration, he realized that he was virtually without experience in this area; he had never met a woman anywhere, anytime, as a casual friend. A woman might be met on business or as a friend of some other woman—or man—but not as a simple friend or acquaintance in her own right. Sam only knew how to meet such women on one basis, and that was as a prospective lover.

Pushing his chair back from the desk where his computer workstation sat, he folded his arms across his chest, unconsciously mimicking Cheryl's body language, and looked down at his wrist. You are not a weak man, Sam Leo, he told himself as he watched the numerals on his digital watch shift from 5:33 to 5:34. You are not weak. You are going to go talk to this girl, or rather, let her talk to you. You are going to get her out of your system, quickly and permanently. You are not going to have an affair with her. One thing you aren't, you aren't a hypocrite; you've always taken a certain pride in that, haven't you? You can't criticize Rick for what he does and then go do the same thing yourself. Deciding he'd dealt with himself firmly, he pulled the chair back up and returned to his work. With all the distractions, he still had more than enough to do; he'd work until six thirty, he promised himself, then get up and go. That should put him at the restaurant within ten minutes of seven, one way or another. If he was late and she decided not to wait, well, that was fine. He'd eat, then go home and start patching things back together with Cheryl.

But, in the end, he left work around ten minutes after six, and he arrived at the restaurant twenty minutes early.

With a raspy voice—his mouth and throat were really terribly, annoyingly, dry—he told the hostess he wanted a table for two, that a friend of his would be arriving soon. She at first showed him one near the plate-glass windows in the front; he hesitated, then asked her for a more private booth, in the back of the restaurant. It wasn't likely that anybody he knew would wander in here or pass by on the street, but he didn't want to be conspicuous, didn't want to be noticed. With a smile that might have suggested something but might've meant nothing, the hostess picked up the two menus she was carrying and led him to the back, showing him to a corner booth. Flopping down on the brown vinyl-covered cushion, he asked her if she could send a waitress around with some water, soon. She nodded, left him; the waitress arrived with the requested water mere seconds later. Sam hardly even looked up at her; he just grabbed the glass, mumbled a thank-you, and gulped half of it down.

"Would you like something else while you're waiting, sir?" the unseen waitress asked.

He still didn't look up. "Yeah, beer, Dos Equis," he said. "No, no. Not a good idea, not before I eat. Ice tea, sweet. No, make that coffee. No, wait. Tea. That's it. Tea. I'll have the tea. Sweet." The girl giggled; he heard the scratching sound of ballpoint on pad, and she left the table. Sam held his head in his hands. "Shit," he muttered. "Shit."

As before, the time dragged. He emptied the water glass, drank all the tea; the waitress brought him a refill and he drank half that, too. This is stupid, he kept telling himself. There's no reason for you to be this nervous, no reason at all. She might not even show up.

But she did. At exactly seven, according to his watch.

When he saw her come in, he almost groaned aloud. Before, on the street, she'd been wearing demure yellow slacks and a rather loose-fitting blouse. Tonight, she was clad in brief white shorts and a thin white low-necked top that contrasted perfectly with her dark brown skin and black hair.

Every male head in the restaurant—and more than a few female heads—swiveled toward her, one by one or in groups. If Sam wasn't imagining things, a virtual hush fell over the place as she walked back toward the table. When she sat down, all those eyes that had been following her focused on him, asking a silent question. He felt like he was on stage, he could've easily imagined that the whole incident might've been in the headlines in tomorrow morning's paper.

"Hello, Sam," she said with an utterly engaging smile.

He couldn't even speak immediately. Her top made it obvious that she wasn't wearing a bra or was wearing one so light it didn't matter; he could see the dark shadows of her nipples quite plainly.

Her smile broadened a little. "Sam? Are you all right?"

"Uh, ah, yeah. How, uh, it's good to are you, uhm, Selinde?"

"I are good to fine see you too, Sam," she answered promptly.

He bit his lip. Get yourself under control, he raged at himself. She does not miss one damn thing, that should be obvious by now. He started to take another sip of his tea, bumped the glass as he reached for it, fumbled with it but caught it without spilling it, managed to stabilize it. After taking a deep breath he tried to take a sip but it ran into his mustache at the corners of his mouth; he felt twin lines of cool proceeding down toward his chin.

"Damn it," he muttered, putting the glass down and grabbing a napkin from the little silver holder sitting on the table.

"Sam," Selinde said quietly, "I am not going to eat you alive, you know." She added something he didn't quite hear; to him it sounded like "not at the moment" but he was sure he hadn't heard that right.

"I am sorry," he said as he wiped away the tea. "I'm rattled, I might as well admit it and get it out of the way. I don't usually do this."

"Drink tea?" she asked innocently.

He grimaced. "You know what I mean."

"Yes, I do. I couldn't miss that wedding band you're wearing, Sam, you were quite careful to show it to me. You aren't a man who goes out behind his wife's back. I understand."

"I hope so, because—"

"Why did you call me, Sam?"

Because, he said to himself, you are the most fascinating and spectacularly beautiful woman I've met since Cheryl—and when I first met her, my initial impulse was to fall on the floor, slobber on her feet, and whine like a puppy.

But he was more under control now. "You know, I'm not really sure I can answer that," he replied. "It just seemed to me we left things in sort of an unfinished state out on Hillsborough Street that day."

"Not as far as I can see."

He shrugged. "Difference in perspective, I suppose."

"Ah. Yes. Perspective. An important consideration."

He sipped his tea again; in suave fashion this time, he did not spill any. "You know, I don't even know your last name. Don't know where you're from, anything."

"Lorona. Selinde Lorona," she answered. "And I'm from Mexico."

He nodded; he'd figured her for Latin-American the first time he'd seen her. "Mexico? Selinde doesn't sound like any Mexican name I've ever heard."

"No, it's German, as a matter of fact."

He waited for her to explain how she came to have a German first name, but she did not. "So, Mexico. Are you just here to go to school, or—?"

She tipped her head and gave him a quizzical look. "School?" she asked.

"Well, yeah—didn't you tell me you were a student at State?"

"No."

"Oh. I must've been confused, then."

"Perhaps so. Perhaps you heard what you expected to hear. That can be a problem sometimes, Sam."

"Yeah, I suppose so. So what brings you to Raleigh, then?"

Her smile could only be described as mischievous. "I live here," she answered. "For now. What brings you to Raleigh, Sam?"

He was beginning to relax a little. "That," he told her, "is a long story. To capsule it quickly, a close friend of mine and I sat down one day while we were in med school and picked a place that both of us thought we could live in. That was Raleigh. Things worked out, so here we are."

"So you and your compadre came here to be together," she mused. "Unusual. Most Americans I've met go their own way regardless of such relationships. They're lucky if they can work it out so that they can live in the same city as their husbands or wives."

He nodded. "I guess we are unusual in that way, but we've been close for a long time. Compadres, you said. I know the word, of course, but—"

"In Mexico a compadre is a friend who is more than a friend. Like a relative, like a brother."

"That's it. A perfect word."

"Accept it, then, as a gift from me."

He grinned. "I will. A perfect word is worth a lot."

"And now you must give me a gift, as well."

He started to ask her, in half-joking fashion, what sort of a gift she'd like, but they were interrupted by the waitress, who'd returned to take their orders. This time, Sam looked up at her. Young, blond, blue-eyed. Not bad looking, hardly beautiful. And looking at Selinde with an expression of jealousy that bordered on hatred.

This girl does provoke emotional reactions, he told himself. "What would you like?" he asked her.

She shrugged. "I like all foods, all drinks. You choose."

"You sure?"

"Yes."

He looked back at the waitress. "Medium pizza," he said. "Pepperoni, onion, green pepper. Beer for me—Dos Equis." He glanced at Selinde and she nodded. "Make that two," he added.

The waitress, having gotten control of her expression, jotted it all down. She started to turn away.

"Excuse me, miss," Selinde said.

The waitress turned back. She smiled, but it was forced. "Yes?"

"Could you bring me some jalapeño peppers as well?"

The waitress looked at her like she was crazy. "You mean on your pizza?"

"No. On the side."

"You sure?"

"Yes."

"Well, okay." Shaking her head, the waitress jotted a note on her pad and wandered away.

Sam watched her go. "It isn't all that unusual a request," he observed. "A lot of people like jalapeño peppers, they're sort of standard now."

"Yes, I suppose they are. And I do like a few mild peppers sometimes."

He scowled, then laughed. "Right. Mild."

Again, she gave him the innocent look. "No, they are mild," she protested. "Hot ones, well, the hot ones just aren't available in the United States. So I carry my own."

"You carry your own pepper around with you?"

"Sure." She reached into her purse, brought out a small bottle, handed it to Sam. He examined it; it was full of crushed pieces of red pepper and yellow pepper seed. To him, it looked no different from the crushed cayenne that filled a shaker on their table. "These," she said, tapping the bottle with her forefinger, "are very good. You must try some, Sam."

He eyed the red fragments, and he started to tell her that he was no fan of hot peppers; as far as he was concerned, jalapeños were extreme, too much for him in most applications. But he didn't want her to think of him as wimpy. "Sure," he said offhandedly as he set the bottle down. "I'll try some."

The waitress returned, bringing two bottles of beer and the dish of jalapeño peppers, put them down on the table. "Pizza'll be up in just a couple of minutes," she said.

"Thank you," Selinde murmured. She picked up one of the peppers and slipped it between her lips, pulling the whole pepper off the cap and stem, which she discarded. Both Sam and the waitress stared as she chewed it casually, evidently savoring it. The first gone, she picked up a second, treated it the same way.

Sam's gaze went back to the bottle of red fragments. What, he asked himself, have I gotten myself into now?

"These are okay," Selinde said, munching a third. "But they're pickled, and they lose a lot when you pickle them. You want one?"

"No, I think I'll just wait, and—"

"I wish they had some fresh ones. You ever had fresh ones, Sam?"

"No."

"They're a lot better. A lot better." She polished off yet another, only then deigning to take a sip—a very small sip—of the dark beer in her glass.

Returning, the waitress put plates in front of them, then placed a pan containing the pizza between them. "That all for right now?" she asked.

"Yes, we're fine," Sam told her, watching Selinde extract a steaming red and yellow triangle from the pan. Picking up her little bottle, she sprinkled the red shards and seeds all over it before taking a bite.

"Here," she said as Sam pulled his own onto his plate. "Try some." Without waiting, she sprinkled his, too. Not as liberally as her own, but more heavily than he would have liked.

All right, bigmouth, he told himself, now just do it and take it like a man. You wanted to be macho, now you have to pay the price.

He took a bite of the pizza. Grinning at her, he chewed.

Then the pepper hit him. Looking back on it later, he was certain that the reason he hadn't been aware of it immediately was that every nerve in his mouth and tongue had gone into shock.

It literally felt as if someone had turned a blowtorch into his mouth; he was experiencing real pain. His lips felt numb and swollen, but at the same time they, too, felt the flames of the torch. He fought with his facial expression, trying to give her no hint of his agony, but he could not do it.

Eyes bulging, he grabbed for his beer and took a huge gulp, washing the remainder of the bite of pizza on down. It didn't help; it merely caused the fire to spread to all parts of his mouth and to run down his throat. Some of it settled in his stomach like a bunch of red-hot coals.

"They're too strong for you, aren't they?" Selinde asked solicitously.

He was managing—barely—not to claw at his mouth like a frog that had swallowed a bee. "They're—a little—strong—" he croaked.

"Here, try this," she suggested, handing him something.

He was in such pain he didn't even look, he just took it and popped it into his mouth, realizing only when it was there that it was one of her jalapeños. It was, as she'd said, much milder. But that didn't matter, it was like pouring salt into an open wound. He found himself literally squirming in his seat, trying to make the pain go away.

"You aren't approaching this correctly," Selinde said.

"What?" he groaned, reaching for the beer again. Unbelievably, the fiery sensation in his mouth was actually gaining in intensity, not receding.

"Beer won't help. Listen to me, Sam."

"What? What?"

"First, relax, as much as possible. The pain you're feeling is just a sensation, a sensation like any other. It does not have to be unpleasant. Stop trying to escape it; you can't, anyhow. It's going to run its course, and there's nothing you can do about it."

"I feel like I drank sulfuric acid. And it's still getting stronger, damn it!"

"Yes, these chilies do that. Sam, what you are feeling I, too, feel. With no less intensity."

"Why would you do that to yourself?"

She shrugged. "I like the flavor. And, as I'm trying to explain, the burning is just a sensation. You can get into it, you can learn to enjoy it."

"I doubt that!"

"Oh, I assure you, it's true. Close your eyes; concentrate on the pain. Feel where it is, where it's going. Picante has a pitch, it has a timbre. It can be smooth and mellow, it can roll over your tongue, wave after wave. It can be darting and violent, it can attack at many different points with a quick fury. It can envelope, warm and moist."

As she started to speak, he had closed his eyes, he had tried to follow her instructions. And, he had to admit, the effect was rather novel, rather interesting. The red pepper from her bottle was attacking his lips and tongue with millions of bright little triphammer blows; if he tried to compare it to a sound it would be like a keening, a high soprano. The jalapeño was lower, smoother, darker. As she said, rolling in waves. To a great extent, looking at it this way was helping him, not to control the pain, but to transcend it. In a weird way, to actually enjoy it.

He opened his eyes; the agonized expression on his face was gone. Selinde smiled at him. "Good," she said. "Good, it looks like you're getting it." She reached for the jar of crushed cayenne on the table, dusted a small amount into her palm, and picked out two seeds. One she placed between her own bright white incisors; the other she gave to Sam.

"Break it," she instructed. "Crush it between your teeth and press your tongue up against it."

His smile returning, he did as she said; watching each other, they crushed their seeds simultaneously, and as he saw her tongue push up to her teeth he did the same. A dull fire spread across the tip of his tongue and wormed its way up to the center of his lips. Midway between the other two, he decided. Alto, nasal. An English horn of peppers. Moving his gaze between her mouth and her eyes, he did not see her betray a trace of pain, but he knew she was feeling exactly the same thing he was. He had to repress an urge to reach out and hold her hands while their tongues were pressed against the crushed pepper seeds.

With a flick of her tongue, Selinde tossed the seed back into her mouth and swallowed it. She laughed. "Eat your pizza, Sam," she instructed. "I don't think you'll have any trouble with it now. And it's going to get cold."

Mechanically, he nodded and took another bite of the same slice—forgetting, until it was in his mouth, that it was covered with the violent red pepper. A million tiny hornets stung his tongue and lips again, but he did better this time. Again, he watched her do the same thing, knew what she was feeling. This time he couldn't resist. He reached out to her and found her hand lying on the table, waiting for him. Taking her hand, he clasped her fingers and held them while they chewed, savored, swallowed.

Rather abruptly—with the disappearance of the slice of pizza—the moment ended. She gently extracted her fingers from his and leaned back in the booth.

"That was amazing," he told her. "I have to confess, I've never really been much of a hot-pepper fan. That may change! I didn't know you had to have lessons in how to eat them!"

"Oh, you don't. Anyone can eat them." She picked up a jalapeño from the dish—the last one remaining—and held it by the stem so that the blossom end was pointing straight up. Bringing it to her mouth, she allowed it to rest against her lower lip for an instant before sucking it up and in. "It's the appreciation that requires the lessons!"

Watching her do that, it was all Sam could do not to reach across the table for her again. But the moment had passed; she had physically withdrawn a little, and a bit of his own self-control had been restored. She did not offer him more of her peppers as he took another slice of the pizza, though the bottle remained on the table, and he did not take them. As the circular pan began to grow empty, their conversation turned to more trivial things. Raleigh traffic, the heat and humidity of the North Carolina summer. This continued through another beer for each of them, and Sam began to feel just a little disappointed, began to feel as if he weren't getting anywhere.

That thought stopped him. Where, he asked himself, did he want to get? If he'd merely wanted to have a pleasant dinner with the woman, he'd already more than succeeded in accomplishing that.

He looked down at his almost empty beer mug, at the dark fluid remaining in it. I guess that's pretty obvious after all, he told himself. Asshole.

"Do you want another beer, Sam?" Selinde asked.

He raised his eyes. "No. I don't think so. You?"

"No. What shall we do now, then?"

He shrugged and averted his eyes. "I dunno. Leave, I suppose."

"Perhaps we should. Do you want to come to my apartment, Sam? It isn't far."

He was silent for a few seconds. Oh yes, he was saying mentally. Oh yes, I would like that, I really would. "I don't know if I think that's a very good idea . . ." he replied, dragging his words out.

"Perhaps not. Well. You have my number, still. You can call. As I have told you, Sam Leo, all these choices are yours." She stood up, opened her purse as if she was going to take money out.

"No," he told her. "My treat."

She smiled, and he felt like he was beginning to crack inside, felt like he might literally fall into pieces. "Why thank you, Sam." Leaning down, she kissed his cheek quickly. "Good-night," she said.

Then, before he could say another word, she quickly crossed the room and went out the door. Realizing she was gone, he jumped up, threw down a tip, and rushed to pay the check. But all that took a matter of minutes, and by the time he stepped out onto the sidewalk she was nowhere to be seen.

It didn't matter, he told himself. As she'd said, he still had her number.

Twelve

SAM WAS HALFWAY through his dinner with Selinde before Stephanie managed to tear herself away from Dave Brennan's incessant questions about this latest case. He was, she could tell, quite convinced—again—of the husband's guilt. Even though the man had not yet been found, even though there really wasn't any direct evidence against him yet. Dave, too, was puzzled by the case, and Stephanie couldn't help him there; no plausible explanations had occurred to her, either. She continued to review the evidence on her way home as well, but as she pulled the Ford into her drive she still had no new ideas.

Once she'd opened her front door, however, the strange case and its possible explanations went right out of her mind. Something was not right. Art should've been home for several hours; the TV should be on, the smell of the coffee he always drank in the early evening ought to be in the air. Neither sound nor smell was apparent.

"Art?" she called softly as she walked in toward the kitchen. She passed by the den, where the TV was; the screen was dark. "Art, are you here?"

Her anxiety jumped a level each time she called, each time she failed to hear an answer. Wasn't he here? If not, why not? If so, why didn't he answer her? She hurried her steps, but she peeked around doorways as she came to them. Looking into the dining room, she saw him sitting at the table. Still and silent, looking through the kaleidoscope at the reflected sunset light from the eastward-facing window.

She frowned and sighed. "Art," she snapped, "didn't you hear me? You scared me, I thought something had happened to you!"

"I answered you," he said, turning the tube in his hand. His voice was very low. "You didn't hear me, I suppose."

She put her things down. "No, I didn't, and if you answered in that voice you couldn't've expected me to!" At this point she glanced around the kitchen and dining room. The coffee, milk, and cereal she'd left that morning had been transferred to the kitchen counter, but not yet emptied. No fresh coffee had been made. The stove and surrounding area was still clear; there was no smell of food from the oven or elsewhere.

"You didn't start dinner?" she asked, confused.

At first he didn't answer her. But then, with obvious reluctance, he took the kaleidoscope away from his eye. "Dinner?" he echoed blankly. "What time is it, anyhow?" He was looking toward her, but she could've sworn he was looking right through her, staring at something distant, beyond her face.

"It's after seven thirty," she pointed out. "When did you get in?"

"I dunno—four thirty, five—"

"You've been here for three hours? What've you been doing?"

"Doing?"

"Yes, doing! What's the matter with you, Art?"

He blinked rapidly, several times. "I had no idea it was so late," he muttered. "No idea." He held up the kaleidoscope, showed it to her as if she'd never seen it before. "This thing," he told her, "is fascinating. Just fascinating. I picked it up when I came in, and . . ." His cheeks began reddening, he started stumbling over his words. "And, well, uh, I suppose that's what I've been doing." Putting it down on the table, he pushed his chair back, stood up. "Christ. I need some coffee. Damn, I've got a crick in my back, too!" He went into the kitchen, looked at the coffeemaker. Thick black sludge sat in the bottom of the carafe; he picked it up, dumped it into the sink, rinsed it out, refilled it.

Silently, Stephanie just watched him while he made the coffee. In one way, this was a relief; she was not the only one who could lose chunks of time looking through that thing.

But it made her wonder, too. Yes, the colors seen through the kaleidoscope were vivid. Yes, they were attractive. Yes, the patterns were interesting.

But that's all, or should've been all. Colors, patterns. Nothing more. Why was the thing so compelling?

"Maybe you can see, now," she commented, "why I bought it."

He poured water into the top of the coffeemaker and glanced around at her. "Yeah. It really gets to you, it's hard to put down. Funny. When I was a little kid I used to go out and lie in the backyard in the summer and look at shapes in the clouds. I could do that for hours, waste a whole afternoon doing that. It was sort of like that, I think. Sort of like that." He laughed, but it was a little strained. "At least I didn't waste a whole afternoon, huh? This time I won't get punished, huh?"

Stephanie stared; his eyes were distinctly, noticeably, misted. Art? She'd never seen Art misty-eyed, never. She'd suspected it a couple of times, when they'd watched some movie that she thought might have gotten to him, but he'd hidden it from her, never really let her see it. Maintained his macho. It wasn't something they hadn't talked about; he'd always said he believed there was nothing wrong with a man's tears, but he himself couldn't shed them—the message from his parents, that they were inappropriate and showed an unmanly weakness, was too deeply ingrained.

That didn't really bother Stephanie much. No one ever saw her cry, either. Although she was far from sure that she could have controlled her tears that morning, even if she hadn't been alone.

"Art, what are you talking about?" she demanded, her voice colder than she'd intended.

He turned away from her, faced the coffeepot, watched the brown stream of liquid flow into the carafe. "Are there any cigarettes in the house?" he asked.

She hesitated before answering. "Yes," she said finally. "There's an unopened pack of Marlboros in the—"

"I want one."

"No, you don't. We don't smoke anymore, Art. We have a deal on that. I haven't cheated, I haven't had a cigarette in six months. Have you?"

"No. But I want one."

"It isn't up to you. Our deal was that you can't smoke one unless I give you permission, I can't unless you give me permission. I'm not going to give you permission, Art."

"I'll give you permission, all right? You can have all you want, starting now."

She looked a little shocked. "Don't do that," she begged. "We've been very successful with this, we—"

"It's done. Now you do it for me."

"No."

"Then I want a drink."

She put her hands on her hips and stared at his back, amazed. It had been a long time since this had come up, but she hadn't forgotten that Art's drinking—his alcoholism, she told herself, call it what it is—had very nearly torpedoed their relationship in the first place. Art, though highly competitive with virtually all other men and a ferocious fighter in the courtroom, was always very gentle, very tender around women, especially Stephanie. Except when he was drunk. And, when Art drank, he always got drunk. He changed then; his personality darkened, violence could be seen clearly, lurking right under the surface, ready to erupt at the slightest provocation. It was not—and Stephanie had told him this, very clearly—something she could live with. Although she could not help remembering that he'd been drunk when she first met him, when she'd first realized how attractive he was to her . . .

She erased those memories, came back to the problem at hand. "Art, you don't drink anymore either!" she reminded him. "Damn it, that's a lot more serious than a cigarette! You know you have—"

"Yeah. A problem with it. I know." He sighed, very long and deep. "All this goddamn clean living is making me sick, you know that? I'm so fucking healthy I'll probably live past a hundred. Seventy more years without a drink or a cigarette. That's a pile of shit, Stephanie. A pile of shit."

"What in God's name is wrong with you?"

He still didn't turn around. "I was just remembering, that's all. About watching the clouds."

Stephanie's eyes narrowed. She might work as a pathologist, but that didn't mean she'd forgotten everything she'd ever known about psychiatry. "You remembered watching the clouds, and now you want a cigarette or a drink."

"They're not connected."

"I think they are. You want to tell me about watching the clouds?"

"I did already."

"Not really. You just said you used to waste a whole afternoon doing that, watching clouds and seeing shapes in them."

"Didn't you ever do that?"

No, she almost blurted. No, I was too busy trying to scrounge a crust of bread and trying to stay out of Daddy's way. "I guess so," she replied aloud. "It wasn't a big thing for me, I don't really recall. But it was to you, that much is obvious." She took a few steps toward him. "Is there a particular incident you remember?"

"Uh-huh."

"You want to tell me about it?"

"I don't know."

"Come on, Art. It's obvious to me that—"

"Yeah, yeah. 'Obvious to me.' You use that phrase all the time, did you know that? It's sort of insulting. It's sort of a subtle put-down. Obvious to you but not necessarily obvious to the inferior intelligence you're talking to."

Again, she was shocked; Art virtually never talked to her like this. "Let's not get into a fight," she said carefully. "If you don't want to talk about it, then that's fine. If you do, I'm listening. And I'd like to hear it, Art."

He sighed again. "I don't know what made me think of that time. It was a long time ago, Stephanie. I couldn't've been more than maybe eight or so."

"And you wasted an afternoon watching the clouds."

"Uh-huh. Wasted the whole day, really. I spent the morning reading my book."

She reviewed what he'd already said. "Let me guess. You were supposed to be doing something else, and you got punished for it."

His head dropped a little lower between his shoulders. "You guessed it. Mama had decided I was old enough to work around the house some, help out. It wasn't a big deal. Then, at that age, doing household things could be fun, sort of."

"What were you supposed to do?"

"I don't even remember. Clean up my room, maybe; do the dishes, maybe. Something. Some chore. I didn't do it."

"And you got punished for not doing it?"

"No. Well, not exactly. Mama came looking for me because I hadn't done what I was supposed to do. She found me in the backyard, behind the garage, lying in the grass and watching the clouds. She wasn't even that angry, not then."

"What happened?"

"She asked me why I hadn't—done whatever it was I was supposed to do. I remember, I said I'd been watching the clouds and I forgot. Like Clarence."

"Clarence?"

"*Clarence the Cloud-Watcher.*" He shifted his weight from one foot to the other. "That was my favorite book. I'd read it over and over, I could recite most of it. It was just a children's book, you know what I mean. Clarence was this little boy, like me, who liked to watch the clouds. He'd see a dog in the clouds and he'd play with it, throwing a stick. Or a train, and he'd get on board and ride to some strange cloud-land. Just a children's book."

"Sounds like it was important to you, if you can still remember it that well."

"It was. You remember me telling you about my Aunt Patricia? My dad's sister?"

"Uh-huh. The one you were so close to, the one that died in an auto accident?"

"Right. Well, she had a habit of bringing me a present whenever she came over. Mama didn't like it, she always said it spoiled me." He paused. "Jesus. Twenty-five years ago, I can remember it like it was this morning. Anyway, she brought me that book. Wrote in the front of it—wrote something. 'To my favorite nephew,' something. It made it a treasure for me. And especially since that book was her last present." Once again, he sighed. "The accident—the one she died in—it happened when she was leaving our house. That visit, she brought me that book. And she'd told me she'd come over just to bring it to me. Then she died. I felt responsible. If she hadn't brought the book she wouldn't've been killed."

Classic, Stephanie told herself. "Children often feel that way," she soothed. "They think they're responsible for accidents, for divorces—"

"Yeah, I know. But for me, it made the book—I don't know, it was like the book was her. Like I said, I treasured it. Besides that, I liked it. I daydreamed that I was Clarence, riding away on a cloud train to a cloud city where Aunt Patricia was still alive, where she'd meet me and hug me like she used to. Mama never hugged me. Never. She still won't. You know Mama, she doesn't like to be touched. By anybody."

Stephanie found herself wiping her own eyes, and she was glad Art was facing away from her. "You were telling me about the incident," she said when he stopped speaking. "The day your mother caught you cloud-watching—"

"Yeah. Well, like I said, Mama wasn't that mad, but she asked me what I thought I was doing, I was supposed to be doing— whatever it was. I said I was sorry, I forgot. I said I was watching the clouds. And I told her all about it, how you could see things up there. Like Clarence did, in the book, and I reminded her about the book. She said, What do you see, and I can remember she looked up, too. It was a close moment. Mama usually wasn't too interested in what I felt or thought."

Yeah, Stephanie told herself. We don't call her the Ice Lady for nothing, you know. "Go on."

"So, so, I told her. I pointed. There's a dog, I said. Over there,

there's a rhino, and an ocean liner right beside it. Just things. I mean, I don't know if I mentioned dogs or rhinos or ocean liners. Just things. But I do remember the last thing I mentioned. That I do remember."

"What was that?"

"I said—and I'm pretty sure I'm quoting myself—I said, 'That one looks like a naked lady with big titties, sitting down.' "

Stephanie couldn't restrain a little laugh. "You didn't! At eight?" His shoulders shook a little, and she thought he was laughing with her.

But his voice was flat, cold. "I did. There wasn't a thing sexual about it, I was too young, girls were gross to me then, I hated TV shows with what I called 'smoochy stuff.' It was just what I thought I saw in the cloud."

Don't know if I can agree with that, Stephanie thought. Maybe a little precursor of sexual urges, a subconscious argument to the "girls are gross" proposition. What you see in clouds—and in kaleidoscopes—are the things you project there.

But it was not a point worth arguing. "What happened then?"

"Well, Mama got real mad. She jerked me up off the ground and sent me back inside to do the chores I hadn't done. I remember feeling embarrassed. I hadn't meant to say that to her, I forgot who I was talking to. You could say things like that to Dad or to Aunt Patricia, but not to Mama."

"That's all? I thought you said you got punished."

"I did, but I don't think Mama thought about it like that. She brought it up when Dad came in from work, she was really upset about it. He had the same reaction you did, he laughed. She got madder and started yelling, and they got into a big fight."

"And you felt responsible for that, too."

"Uh-huh. But that wasn't the end of it, either."

"Did your father hit her?" Stephanie blurted. Then she bit her lip. Those words she hadn't meant to speak.

Art was involved with his own memories, he didn't question the possible implications of her words. "No. If Dad ever hit her, I never knew about it. They fought with words, with yelling and screaming and insults, not with their fists. But sometime during the fight, Mama went to my room and she got the book, *Clarence the Cloud-Watcher*. She brought it back into the living room, she was waving it in Dad's face, yelling about what a bad influence Aunt Patricia had been on me. I was crying, I was crying. Dad got furious, told her not to talk about his sister that way, that she'd been a wonderful woman, that the book was harmless. And then Mama—she—she—" He broke off, his voice hoarse and cracking.

Stephanie moved a little closer to him yet. His shoulders were still shaking. "What, Art? What did she do?"

He turned to her then; his mouth was twisted like that of the eight-year-old he was remembering, his eyes were red, and tears were streaming down his cheeks. "She tore up the book!" he almost howled. "She tore it up, she tore out every page and tore each one in half! Oh, God, I felt like she was tearing me in half! I ran in, begging, screaming, but she wouldn't stop, she wouldn't stop, she wouldn't listen, she just kept tearing out the pages and tearing them up and then she broke the cover and she threw it down and she stomped on it, she stomped it . . ." He stopped, put his hands over his face, and wept bitterly.

For a second or two Stephanie was stunned, paralyzed. She could not believe Art was doing this, that he was behaving this way, it was so utterly different from the Art she'd known. The children inside us, she told herself, seem to be erupting with a vengeance. Jennifer would, I'm sure, say it was something in the stars.

Then, breaking free, she went to him, folded him in her arms. He accepted her embrace, put his head on her shoulder, and continued to weep uncontrollably for several minutes.

Almost abruptly, he regained some of his control. "Christ," he said, lifting his head but not pulling away. "Christ. I can't believe that. That all came back so vividly, like it had just happened. Christ."

"The association," she told him, reaching up to stroke his hair in the back. "Sitting there with the kaleidoscope, seeing things in the patterns. Like seeing things in the clouds."

"Yeah, I guess."

"The coffee's done. You want some? I'll get it for you . . ."

"Yeah. Maybe." He wiped his eyes. "Damn it. I feel stupid."

"No reason for that." She released him, went to the cabinet, took out a cup, filled it, handed it to him. "Can I do anything else for you?"

His eyes were downcast. "Yeah. Stephanie, I don't ask for this sort of thing very often. But could you—uh—I mean, like you were a minute ago, could you—"

She smiled, very softly. "Hold you? Art, you could ask that of me every day if you wanted to!" She matched actions to words; he put the coffee down on the edge of the stove, bearhugged her body against his own.

She held him for quite a long time. It was far from unpleasant for her but it was different; it was not the way she was used to interacting with Art, and she found herself wondering if this was a precursor of a new phase in their relationship, a warmer and closer phase. That she would not object to.

Nor did she object when Art's hands began finding their way under her clothes, or when he began removing both his and hers piecemeal and guiding them back through the house, step by step, leaving a trail of garments in their wake. This, she told herself as they reached the bedroom door, was more normal—at least it was what used to be normal. Perhaps the problems she'd been thinking about this morning were solving themselves; perhaps the kaleidoscope had helped both of them.

If so, she thought as they rolled onto the bed, it would mean the kaleidoscope was well worth the money she'd paid for it. Worth every penny.

——— Thirteen ———

"I DIDN'T ENJOY eating dinner alone, Sam," Cheryl was saying. There was no rancor or accusation in her voice. "I didn't really eat dinner, as a matter of fact. I just had some yogurt and a glass of juice."

This, Sam told himself, was the best he could've hoped for. He wouldn't have been terribly surprised if he'd come home to find Cheryl either out or in a mood to proceed with the warfare. "Pizza for me," he muttered. "Not the world's greatest dinner either."

"I thought you liked pizza."

"I do. Sometimes."

She looked at him closely. "Your lips look red and maybe a little swollen. Did you burn your mouth?"

Do not get flustered, he told himself, lies are not required. "No. Well, in a way. I had some, uh, hot pepper on the pizza."

"Sam! You don't eat hot pepper!"

"I do now. I think I've discovered a taste for it."

"Really?"

"Uh-huh. You should try it, too."

"No, thanks. I have. I have no desire to cauterize the inside of my mouth, thank you."

"No, you have the wrong approach."

"Approach?"

"Yeah. It's hard to explain. I'll get some cayenne or jalapeños the next time I'm at the store, I'll have to show you."

"You're still mad at me."

He looked startled. "Why would you say that?"

"Well, you want to torture me with hot peppers. That's what you're saying."

He laughed; she joined him, and the remaining tension between them dissolved away. She came to him, put her arms around his neck, kissed him.

"I don't like it," she told him. "I don't like it when we fight. I don't like it when our bodies aren't touching when we sleep. I'm not right the next day."

"No, me neither."

She kissed him again. "You still hungry?"

"No." Pause. "Not for food."

She raised an eyebrow, smiled. "Back to normal, are we?"

"I am. What about you?"

Surprisingly, she let go of him, went back across the room, sat back down. "I think we need to talk," she told him.

He started to roll his eyes, but he knew full well that would reinstate the argument; started to sigh, but knew that would have the same effect. "I think we need to talk" was a key phrase for Cheryl; it had a meaning far beyond what the words themselves said. It meant, among other things, that she wasn't satisfied with the way things had turned out, that she expected something more from him. Not infrequently, if an almost-terminated argument entered this phase, the argument itself was reinstated—or, worse, entered a new arena, went off on some totally unrelated tangent.

Deciding not to expect the worse, he repressed the sigh, held back the eye-rolling, and sat down across from her. "What about?" he asked innocently, as if he believed the words had no meaning other than their superficial ones.

"About these arguments we have, Sam. We argue, we're distant from each other for a couple of days, and then we get back together—usually, in bed."

"So? It sure beats not getting back together at all!"

"Yes, it does. But sometimes it makes me think we don't have much of anything in common except sex. If we didn't have that, we wouldn't have much of a reason to stay together."

"But we do have that. I'm not sure I see the problem."

Her eyes flashed at him, and he was instantly aware he'd said the wrong thing. He tried to backpedal, tried to explain that he hadn't meant that that was all they had together, just that it was an important facet of their relationship, something they could count on.

She didn't give him the chance, she was off and running with it. "So that's all I am to you?" she snapped. "A good lay?"

"No. No, Cheryl, I think you took that wrong, I—"

The ankle was resting on the knee again, and the frost was back in her voice. "I think I took that just as you meant it, Sam. Oh, I know you didn't mean to say it. But I think you meant it, I—"

"Cheryl," he said quietly, "think about it for a few seconds. You know full well I don't feel that way about you."

For a moment her eyebrow stayed up and her ankle remained on her knee, looking as if it was about to move even higher on her thigh. Sam waited, knowing that the odds were that the argument was about to erupt once again but hoping that wouldn't be the case.

After several seconds of hesitation she relaxed visibly. "Maybe you're right," she admitted in a low voice. "Maybe I do know that."

He stood up; he did not want to lose the moment. Crossing to her quickly, he sat down on the arm of her chair and ran his fingers through her hair. "I'm glad you do," he told her.

Her anger seemed to be gone; she laid her hand on his thigh. But she was still staring rather blankly ahead. "So now, I suppose, we'll go to bed. We'll make love and everything will be fine. Until the next time."

"Maybe there won't even be a next time."

"No. No, Sam. There'll be a next time. I know there will be, and so do you."

"Not if we—"

"Whatever we do. And a next, and a next. And each time, it'll knock another little fragment off our relationship, until there isn't anything to hold it together anymore. Then it'll just crumble. It'll just crumble and we'll go our separate ways and that'll be the end of that."

He frowned down at the top of her head. "Cheryl, I don't think it has to be that way—"

She looked up at him. Her eyes were dry but sad. "I hope not. I'd rather we—rather we—"

He did not press her to continue; he pulled her up, hugged her. She did not resist him but she did not hug him back, either. "I know not," he said reassuringly. "We're just tired, I think. We need to get away from the grind for awhile, that's all."

"Well, we're going to. We're going on vacation." Almost tentatively, as if they didn't really know each other very well, she lifted her arms, put them around his neck.

"Look," he told her, "I don't want you to feel pressured about anything, and I don't think we really have to have sex to end an argument. If you'd rather not, if you'd rather just go to bed and sleep, then we can—"

"No," she answered. "No, Sam. That's not what I want to do." She broke free from his embrace again, walked into the bedroom; he followed her, watching her as she unbuttoned her shirt and slipped it off. Her bra followed quickly. He stepped up behind her, reached around her chest, cupped each of her breasts in a hand. She sighed softly, as if letting go of remaining tension.

After a few moments he let her go, and he removed his own clothing while watching her push her shorts down over her hips and step out of them. She sat down on the edge of the bed, and he sat down beside her, turning her head gently toward his and kissing her deeply while he fondled her breasts. He felt her fingertips graze over his own nipples—she was well aware that his were highly sensitive—and move downward toward his crotch.

Like professional dancers who knew the choreography perfectly, they moved through their steps with exact precision. He did not roll onto his back and she did not nudge his head downward when he began licking and sucking her nipples, each thereby giving the other the message that for tonight, intercourse was preferred over any variety of oral sex; all that remained undecided was position. When Cheryl started sinking backward toward the pillow, supporting her slight weight on his shoulders, he understood that at this time, male-superior and face-to-face was her preference. He moved back with her, laying first one leg between hers, then the other. After he'd scooted up a little, he felt the tip of his penis contact warm moist softness. He watched her face as he pushed gently; her nostrils were slightly flared, her lips just parted, her eyes were just dropping closed. It was far from an unpleasant view, but he wished she'd open her eyes. As Rick had often observed, she had wonderful eyes. It was a shame that she kept them closed during their lovemaking, almost always.

Afterward, they'd lain together for a while as they always did; then they'd gotten up and gone to the bathroom to clean up, another part of the familiar and well-established ritual. Once they'd returned to their bed, Cheryl had almost immediately started slipping off into sleep. The script, as Sam knew, called for him to snuggle with her and sleep as well.

He did not; instead, he rolled onto his back, staring blankly at the spackled ceiling above their bed, lost in his own thoughts.

Cheryl hadn't known it, he told himself, but she'd made love this evening with two quite different Sams simultaneously. One was, of course, the Sam she by now knew so very well; the other, the one who'd been a passive observer tonight, she probably wouldn't have recognized at all.

That second Sam had been awakened when he'd thought idly about Rick's remarks about Cheryl's eyes, about how lovely they were; from there Sam Two had gone on, thinking about his friend's former lover, about his statement that the girl "lost control" when they played their games. It wasn't, he told himself hurriedly, as if Cheryl wasn't passionate. She was by no means a woman to lie passive and unmoving during lovemaking.

But out of control? Never. Not even close. While they'd made love, she'd nibbled his ear; Sam Two had wondered what she would've done if she had been out of control, if she'd been swept away by her passion. Would she have bitten down? Would she have drawn a little blood, perhaps?

And how, he asked himself now, would you have reacted if she had done that? Would you have yelled, would you have jumped up, would you have demanded to know what the fuck she thought she was doing?

No, Sam Two informed him, continuing the dialogue. No, you wouldn't've. You've just learned a lesson, just today: pain is a sensation like any other, if the circumstances are right and you can approach it right, you can enjoy it. And while you're thinking about it, isn't that exactly what Rick has been saying all these years?

What about the other way around? Tonight, you bit her lower lip; you almost always do, her lips are so damn sensual when they get slightly swollen, and they always do when she gets aroused.

How would she have reacted if he'd bitten down hard, if he'd been the one to draw the blood?

That one, Sam One told his Other smugly, was easy to answer. There would've been screaming, accusations, maybe even a slap—there would've been problems. Still, lying calmly in his bed while Cheryl slept beside him, he allowed himself the latitude to pursue that fantasy, allowed himself to visualize a quite different reaction. The fantasy was so vivid he could almost taste the hot salty-sweet taste of her bright blood on his tongue, he could see her body go rigid, he could see her squirming violently on the bed as her passion raged beyond her ability to control it.

You've seen that, he realized in a sudden flash. When she has her orgasm, she reacts almost exactly like that. He considered that for a few seconds. A lot of women—concerning men, he had no way of knowing—react to orgasm and to sudden pain in precisely the same way physically: the eyes are closed, the head arched back, the face contorted, the body rigid and perhaps trembling; the breath is taken in sharply and held. Often there are moans—for some women there are shrieks.

He almost laughed at himself. You're a scientist, Sam, he reminded himself. Sudden terror can produce that same reaction too, and there are perfectly good reasons inherent in human physiology that explain it.

But explaining it, Sam Two noted, didn't mean it wasn't erotic.

Still staring at the ceiling, he curled his lip. You don't need all this, he told himself. Lovemaking with Cheryl was wonderful—just wonderful, even if it had become a bit—well, all right, maybe more than just a bit—stylized over the years. Physically and mentally, he insisted again, he felt completely satisfied.

So why, he demanded silently, were you seeing Cheryl with bloody lips when you came? And why are you seeing Selinde's image right now?

Fourteen

"I'M GLAD WE could do this," Jennifer said as she lounged in a booth in an Oriental restaurant in downtown Raleigh. "I know it's hard for you two to get away from your jobs. Especially at the same time." She put her purse up on her lap, began digging around in it.

"We have to eat lunch," Stephanie observed, poking at a white lump of wonton in her soup. "Even Dave Brennan admits that."

Jennifer extracted a small bottle from her purse, shook a pair of little tablets out in her hand. As usual, her manner was almost furtive; she tossed the pills in her mouth quickly, popped the bottle back into her purse, then took a quick swallow of water. Stephanie had no idea what the medication was; once, Jennifer had let it slip that it was something Rick had prescribed for her. "He's that detective, isn't he?" she asked hurriedly, perhaps to deflect a possible new question. "The one that always wants to talk over the cases with you?"

"Uh-huh. Thinks I should be a part of the prosecution team. I tell him that's not my job, but it goes in one ear and out the other."

"He's a man, isn't he?" Cheryl observed. Stephanie nodded. "Then what can you expect?"

Stephanie and Jennifer both laughed, but for Stephanie, the laughter was brief. She looked back down at her soup and poked the wonton again, as if she weren't quite sure it was thoroughly dead.

"What's with you?" Cheryl asked. "You aren't your usual cheery and vivacious self today."

"Leftovers from last night," she said. "Art was acting strange." She started to sigh, repressed it. A sigh now would invite questions from Cheryl or Jennifer, and those questions might lead her into areas she did not, at the moment, wish to discuss—her sex life.

Art's unusual behavior had not persisted as they'd begun lovemaking; very quickly they'd fallen back into their old—and to her, dull and uninspired—patterns. Before they were half finished she'd found herself wishing, again, that he would stop trying to play the stud, that he would get off of her and leave her alone. Naturally she hid this from him, but still, she found herself resenting him for —she wasn't sure what for. For luring her into lovemaking under false pretenses, perhaps. As she saw it, he'd promised openness, he'd promised something new and different, and all she'd gotten was the same old thing: Art the superstud, Art the hypermale, Art the energetic, Art the selfless, Art the overenthusiastic fulfiller of her every desire, spoken or unspoken.

In a nutshell, she thought cynically, Art the boring.

"Well, naturally," Cheryl was saying, drawing Stephanie back to the here and now. "He, too, is a man. They think they have a constitutional right to act strange. God knows, they do it often enough."

"So what was Art doing?" Jennifer asked.

Stephanie fixed her with a stare for a few seconds. "This does not go home to Rick," she said firmly. She turned her gaze on Cheryl. "Or to Sam."

"Secrets known to be secrets are kept," the dark-haired woman observed. "From the husbands, anyway. Such is the law of the sisterhood. Will you get on with it?"

Stephanie shrugged. "I don't know what brought it on. He got into something out of his childhood, for a while he was demanding a cigarette and a drink. He—"

"He didn't have a drink, did he?" Jennifer asked, her eyes growing a little wider. Neither she nor Cheryl had ever seen Art drunk, but they'd heard stories, tales about how frighteningly he changed, about the dramatic contrast between that Art and the kind and gentle Art they knew so well.

"No, he didn't. But you wouldn't believe what he did do."

"What? What?"

"He cried. Like a baby. Big tears."

Both of Stephanie's listeners looked stunned. "Art?" Cheryl asked. "Art cried? That, Stephanie, is hard to believe!"

"True. But he did."

Jennifer leaned over the table, her palms flat on its surface. "Well, what'd you do?" she demanded. "I don't know what I'd do if Rick did that. I'd think something was really wrong with him."

"Something is really wrong with Rick," Cheryl observed flatly.

"We've all known that for years. But then, he, too, is a man, so I guess it's normal. Anyway, you—"

"Sounds to me like there might've been a problem with Sam last night, too," Jennifer noted, glancing around at Cheryl.

"Yeah, but nothing that dramatic. I want to hear about this business with Art."

"Well, I came home late—after seven—to find him just sitting at the table, staring," she said. "No dinner started, no coffee made. You know how Art is about his coffee."

"Yeah, he's an addict. So's Sam," Cheryl put in.

"Right. "Anyway, I asked him what was wrong, and it took a while for me to get it out of him, but finally he told me. He'd been thinking about something that happened when he was about eight, something really traumatic." She went on, explaining about the book and about Art's Aunt Patricia. "But after we got into bed, he was fine," she concluded. "He was fine this morning, too."

"That is odd," Cheryl agreed.

"What do you think set this off?" Jennifer asked.

Stephanie sipped hot soup from her spoon. "I'm not sure. Just the association, I think. Pictures in the clouds and the images in the kalei—"

She stopped herself, felt her cheeks get hot. She hadn't intended to mention the kaleidoscope at all. But now she'd blown it, and for both Jennifer and Cheryl to have missed it would require a minor miracle.

"The what?" both of them asked, almost in chorus.

She sighed, took another sip of her soup. "Kaleidoscope," she answered, slightly under her breath.

"Kaleidoscope?" Jennifer echoed. "What kaleidoscope?"

"The kaleidoscope I bought the other day, at the Dancing Moon bookstore." There. It was out in the open, on the table.

There was a moment of silence while Jennifer and Cheryl turned face-to-face, staring at each other. "Did you hear what I heard?" Jennifer asked.

"I don't know," Cheryl answered. "I don't think so. I didn't hear her right, I'm sure. I thought she said she bought a—what was it? A kaleidoscope?—the other day, over at the Dancing Moon. But that isn't possible. I could've said that and you could've said that, but not our Stephanie. The mere fact that she would even show her face at the Dancing Moon is—"

"You forget," Jennifer observed with a smile. "I have a birthday coming up."

"I haven't forgotten, I—" She stopped, looked back at Stephanie. "Oh," she said. "Oh." Her head swiveled again. "But still, this begs an explanation, doesn't it? If she was there to buy you a birthday present, then why would she buy a kaleidoscope?"

"Maybe that's my present."

"I don't think so. Our Stephanie is not one to blurt out a secret like that. No, she must've bought the kaleidoscope for some other reason. Maybe she even bought it for herself, although the very idea boggles the mind. But there's one thing we can be sure of."

"Uh-huh. She wanted to talk about it, but couldn't say it straight out."

"Get out of my head, will you? That's what I was going to say!"

"Are you two quite finished?" Stephanie asked.

Jennifer's gaze came back around. "Not with you! You have yet to tell us about this kaleidoscope!"

"I bought it on impulse," Stephanie admitted.

Again, Cheryl and Jennifer went through their theatrics, facing each other and coming almost nose-to-nose, their eyes wide open in exaggerated expressions of pure wonder. "We must find out what day this was," Cheryl said. "What day this happened."

"Yes. And mark it down on our calendars," Jennifer agreed. "On this day, Dr. Stephanie Dixon did something on impulse. Never before in the history of the Western World has anything like this ever—"

"Come on, will you?" Stephanie complained. "Haven't you ever done something silly on impulse?"

"I do silly things on impulse," Jennifer replied, "all the time. Cheryl does them sometimes. We're not talking about Cheryl and Jennifer. We're talking about Stephanie."

"Maybe we ought to let her tell us about it," Cheryl put in.

Again, Stephanie sighed. "It's easy to explain and it isn't," she opened. "I picked it up and looked at it, and it sort of—I don't know, it sort of fascinated me. So I bought it, without thinking about it. As you two have already observed ad nauseum, that isn't exactly typical of me. But that's what happened."

"What does Art have to do with it?"

"Oh, well, that's what he was doing when I came home. Sitting at the table, looking though it. He'd been playing with it for hours, I think."

"I see," Cheryl said, nodding. "What you said about associations. Patterns in the kaleidoscope, patterns in the clouds. It set off a painful memory. But that still leaves a question unanswered, Stephanie."

"What's that?"

"Why would Art sit there staring into the thing for hours? I mean, we all know Art. He misses the evening news for no man—or woman. And I can't imagine him, with free time like that, not going down to his weight room to play with his toys."

"No, it is odd," Stephanie agreed. "But that kaleidoscope—it is, well, like I said, it's fascinating. I sat there myself, yesterday morning, staring into it. I forgot to eat my breakfast, I got so involved with it. This morning I wouldn't let myself touch it."

"Well," Cheryl breathed, "there's one thing I know for sure!"

"What?"

"I want to see this magic kaleidoscope! Anything that can cause Stephanie Dixon to act on impulse and forget things, I want to see! Don't you, Jenny?"

"Yes, I do," she agreed. Perhaps predictably, she had begun to look a little concerned. "I take it this isn't one of those run-of-the-mill cardboard things with chips of plastic. I take it this is something a little unusual."

"Yes, it's pretty fancy," Stephanie told her. She went on to describe, in general terms, the details of the kaleidoscope's construction. "The girl at the shop said she thought it might be an antique."

"Where'd the store get it? Did you ask?"

"As a matter of fact I didn't, but she mentioned that too, in conversation. Someone brought it in, sold it to them."

"So its history isn't really known."

"I guess not. Not to me, anyway."

"I see." Jennifer pushed her dark blond hair back away from her ears, a gesture that usually indicated nervousness. Looking down at her half-eaten eggroll, she now began poking at it as if it were alive, the same treatment Stephanie had previously given her wonton. Maybe we see too much of each other, she thought. We pick up each other's habits and mannerisms as if they were viruses.

"I know," Jennifer continued after a moment, "that both of you think I'm silly sometimes. But I think—maybe—you ought to be real careful with this thing, Stephanie. You never know . . ."

Stephanie sighed, but concealed most of her exasperation. This, from Jennifer, was hardly unexpected. "It isn't magic, Jenny," she said, firmly but not unkindly. It's just a kaleidoscope, that's all.

The patterns and colors are pretty, it's intriguing. Everything else is just what you project into it, your own thoughts, and—"

"You can't know that," Jennifer insisted. "Please, Stephanie, I really do think you should be careful with it!"

"Okay, okay. I'll be careful. Satisfied?"

She pouted. "You're just saying that to pacify me."

"Jenny," Stephanie said, her exasperation increasing, "I don't even know what being careful with it means! Honestly, I—" Realizing that Jennifer was staring at her, she stopped speaking. Jennifer was now using her patented helpless-little-girl expression, her bright eyes very wide, and her lower lip, while not actually tremulous, threatening. That look, as Stephanie well knew, was capable of converting an adult male like Art or Sam into a quivering heap of jelly. Rick had built up some immunity over the years, but even he was affected to a degree.

The effect of The Look, as Cheryl and Stephanie had—in Jennifer's absence—dubbed this expression, was not so profound on women. Still, to deny Jennifer what she wanted when she was using The Look felt much like kicking a cowering puppy. Some might get a thrill from it; for Stephanie and Cheryl, the result would be irrational guilt that would cling to them for days, like lint on their clothes.

"All right, Jenny," Stephanie muttered, surrendering to the inevitable. "What do you want me to do?"

Jennifer's face transformed immediately, The Look vanished; sunshine flowed over their lunch table once more. "Good. Now, what I want to suggest is that you don't look through it again, don't even touch it. Don't let Art mess with it, either. Take a cloth that's been soaked in some salt water and pick it up with that, put it away somewhere and lock it up, until we can all get together and check it out. Oh, and I want you to tell me, as near as you can remember, *exactly* when you bought it, what day, what time. I'll sit down at the computer tonight and cast a chart, and—"

She went on and on; Stephanie tuned her out, waited for her to finish. She had no intention of locking the thing away, even less of handling it with a saltwater-soaked cloth. In fact, she was deciding that she'd look through it again tonight. Just to prove that she, not it, was in control.

"Saturday," she said blankly after a few moments. "Saturday would be fine, I think. Art and I don't have any plans, at least none that I know of, and he usually lets me make them so—"

"I hadn't asked that question yet," Jennifer said reproachfully.

Again, Stephanie was a little flustered. "Well. You were going to."

Cheryl laughed; Jennifer twisted her mouth momentarily. "Yes, I was. And that's fine for me, too." She glanced around at Cheryl. "How about you?"

"I wouldn't miss it. I want to see this thing. Where?"

"My house. Rick's going to have to be at the hospital until probably midnight, and Paul is spending the night with his friend Brian." She smiled slyly. "And now that that's settled," she went on, gazing intently at Cheryl, "maybe we should start hearing the latest in the never-ending saga of Cheryl and her eccentric husband."

Cheryl gave her a direct look. "There's really no need to talk about it," she said. "Sam is not at all eccentric, considering."

"Considering what?"

"Considering that he's a man, of course!"

Fifteen

SAM HADN'T BEEN back in his office from lunch more than thirty minutes when Cheryl called. No, he answered in response to her initial question. I haven't planned anything for Saturday evening. Yes, it's fine with me if you go out for a while with Jenny and Stephanie, have I ever given you an argument about that? Sure. Love you too, honey, see you around six.

He hung up, he sat there staring at the now-silent telephone. Then he picked it up again, dialed a number he'd by now memorized.

"Hello."

"Selinde. It's—"

"Sam, I know. Good to hear from you again, so soon."

"You're busy Saturday night, aren't you? I mean, you have a date or something, I know it's—"

"No. I'm free. What did you have in mind?"

"I'm not really sure. This is sort of spur-of-the-moment."

"We're all impulsive at times, Sam."

"I suppose so."

"You want to come here? To my place?"

We sure as fucking hell can't go to mine, he told himself. "I don't know . . ."

"You say that a lot. You're welcome to, if you want to."

It wasn't as if he found Selinde intimidating, but he had the feeling he was some sort of rodent, looking up to see a swooping eagle, knowing there was no escape. "All right. Where is it?"

"Van Doren Place." She gave him the number. "The upstairs apartment. There's only one. Use the outside stair."

"Fine. I'll find it."

"Okay. I'll see you then."

"Don't you want to know when? What time?"

"It doesn't matter. I'll be here when you get here. I'll see you then, Sam. 'Bye now."

Click.

He held the phone for several long seconds; an outsider, seeing the expression on his face, might've thought it was a bomb, about to explode in his hand. But he didn't feel as if he could put it down. He had another call to make, an important one, one he'd put off too long already.

———— Sixteen ————

ON THE SECOND ring, Stephanie picked up her phone and answered it with her usual formality: "Pathology, Dr. Stephanie Dixon."

"Hi, Stephanie," came the perhaps a little shaky-sounding voice on the other end. "It's Sam, Sam Leo."

She was a little puzzled. Sam and Rick only rarely communicated with her outside their wives' presence. "Oh, hi, Sam," she replied. "What's up?"

"You still have your good solid ins with the folks at homicide, don't you?"

She grunted. "Uh-huh. Too solid, sometimes. Why? You contemplating a murder, you want to know how to get away with it?"

He laughed. "Hardly. Look, do you happen to know if the police are currently doing any investigations on a possible serial killer, here in the state?"

She frowned at the phone. "I know they're not," she answered. "Why do you ask?"

"You remember Ken Colburn, don't you? Works over here, the computer expert?"

She laughed. "I've never had the pleasure, of course, but sure, I remember your stories about him. The super-asshole, right?"

"You got it."

"You suspect him of being a serial killer, Sam? Somehow I just don't think he's the type."

"No, I'd have to agree. Not that I don't think the man's not a menace to society in his own way. But no, it's a little different from that. He and a buddy of his have been playing a sort of a computer game—I'm not clear on all the details—but anyway, the object is to predict when and where a serial killer will strike next."

She shuddered a little. "Sounds wonderful. Whatever happened to Super Mario, anyway?"

"You don't quite understand. This isn't a software scenario; they've been tracking a real live honest-to-God serial killer—or so they thought, and I'm not sure they weren't right. Trying to predict the date and place where he'll kill next."

Her manner now much more serious, Stephanie pulled a notepad over in front of her and slipped a pen from her lab-coat pocket. Sam Leo, she knew, was not one to go off the deep end; he wouldn't've made this call if he hadn't thought the matter was serious. And his skills as an observer were more than just respectable. "Tell me about this, Sam. You say some of these killings have taken place in North Carolina?"

"Uh-huh. I saw his charting map the other day. He's got points in Burlington, Greensboro, Winston-Salem, and Asheville. More back over in Tennessee, and west from there, all the way to Phoenix. The dates show a steady eastward movement."

"There're murders all the time, Sam. The stats are horrifying. But that doesn't mean that—"

"He told me," Sam cut in, "that they take them case-by-case, scanning in info from the news services and letting their computers look for murders with a specific M.O., just like the police might. But you know better than I do that the police aren't the most sophisticated people in the world when it comes to computers and stats. They rely on people like you to do science for them."

"True. Go on."

"Anyway, this M.O. is peculiar—I can't make sense of it, and the fact is, they can't either. Ken tells me this killer rapes women and then somehow gets them to lie quietly and let themselves be stabbed to death, or something like that. There're never any defensive wounds, and—"

For Stephanie, the image of the corpse of the young woman she'd recently autopsied sprang up in front of her face. "How many of these did you say there've been?" she almost barked.

"I don't know. I just got a glimpse. A lot. I only saw it because Ken is running into some trouble, he's got a few that fit his predictability window but the cops have busted husbands and boyfriends. It worries him, and he's come up with the notion—"

"Sam, I just autopsied one yesterday that fits that description perfectly. From Morrisville. And Dave Brennan is right now out trying to hunt down her husband."

"You're kidding! Wait, I did see something on the news—"

"Uh-huh. That's the one. I think maybe I ought to put a bug in Dave's ear, Sam. I'm sure he's not making any connection with any possible serial."

"Can we not use my name? I don't mind being the good citizen, but you have no idea how much trouble Ken can cause me around here if he finds out I was the one that spoiled his game."

"I don't think so, you've given me enough already to set Dave off like a bloodhound, I don't think he'll even have to talk to Ken. But if he does—you say he has all this on computer?"

"Uh-huh. On the net, here at the center."

"Well, he doesn't own it. I'm sure Dave could go in a little higher up, get access to the stuff."

"You probably aren't right about that. Ken has the stuff coded and locked and probably hidden from the system. The higher-ups wouldn't know it was there and wouldn't have a notion about how to access his data. He's a shithead but he's good at what he does."

"Okay. As I said, Dave probably won't need it anyway. If Ken's been taking all that stuff from newspapers and so on, the same data'll be available to the police. It's just a matter of knowing to look for it."

"That's the way I see it, too."

"But if he can't," she went on, trying to cover all options, "and he were to have to get a search warrant to force Ken to open his files—then I'm not sure there'd be a way to keep your name out of it, Sam. It wouldn't be up to me, it'd be up to Dave and the judge. Maybe Art could help on that end, but I can't promise."

"Damn. Ken'll send all my files to la-la land, you can bet on that. But if that's the way it has to be, I guess that's the way it has to be."

"I'll do my best to see that it doesn't come down that way."

"Thanks, Stephanie."

"No problem. I'm calling Dave, right now."

"Good enough. See you soon."

"Sure. 'Bye."

She didn't put the phone down at all; she simply pressed the release and dialed Dave's number at homicide. Amazingly, the detective was in; without mentioning Sam or the Center, she quickly and succinctly explained the situation.

"Where'd you get this info, Steph?" Dave demanded.

"Does it matter?"

"It might. Easiest way for us to go is look at these computer files. I could get Wally to issue a warrant—"

"My source," she said carefully, "does not wish to be identified, and has good reasons for desiring anonymity. I think I've given you enough for you to start an investigation, Dave."

"Well, maybe. But the easiest way is—"

"I'm not interested in the easiest way, Dave. I'm interested in the best way. And that's to keep my source's name out of this completely. And mine, since a connection might be made."

There was a substantial silence. "Steph, you know you oughta—"

"I'll remind you again. I don't work for you, I'm not a police-woman. You have your start; get to work."

Another silence ensued. "You know," he said angrily, "I could haul you into court and force you to—"

"Try it. Art'll have you for lunch. And it'd be a cold day in hell before you ever got me to stay late and advise you if you pull a stunt like that on me."

"Shit. Shit. All right, Steph. Your way."

"That's more like it. If you don't get anywhere, we'll talk about revealing sources. With Art present. My source didn't have to divulge this information, Dave; the source is not involved. The last thing I want to do is to create a problem for the source."

"Shit. You won't even give me a fucking pronoun."

"Damn straight."

"Okay, okay. Fine. I'm gone. I'll let you know what I come up with."

"If you wish. I have no legal or professional need to know."

"Right, right. No curiosity, either."

"I keep it under control."

"Sure. Okay, Steph. Talk atcha later."

"Okay." She hung up. "And don't call me Steph," she said to it after the receiver was down.

Seventeen

"I HAD A really strange dream last night," Cheryl was saying. Sitting at the table, she was still dressed in the short robe she wore almost every morning, a half-eaten cinnamon roll in front of her, her hands wrapped around her coffee cup. Turning herself in her chair as she spoke, she faced the window, stretched her legs out and crossed them at the ankles. "Really strange."

"Can you remember it?" Sam asked, looking up from his Saturday morning paper. Having hardly forgotten what he had planned for that evening, he almost jumped every time she spoke to him, wondering if he'd somehow given himself away.

There was no indication of it. Her face was blank. "Most of it, yeah." She glanced over at him. "You were in it. We were—I don't know, warriors of some sort, both of us, members of some ancient tribe. Maybe Celts; I remember reading somewhere that they used to go into battle stark naked, and that's how we fought, stark naked. We were the best fighters around; but at the same time I sort of knew that we weren't going to be for much longer, that we'd passed our prime, that it was pretty much all downhill from here. Anyway, in the dream I understood that we'd once been—on the same side, I guess you'd say, but now we weren't anymore. And there was a war, and we met each other on the battlefield."

An allegory for our arguments, Sam told himself, nothing more. "And what happened?" he prompted. He thought maybe he could guess, that perhaps the idea of fighting nude gave the clue; that after fighting for a while without a winner being determined, they fell into each other's arms.

"Well, we were fighting," she went on, "with swords. We fought for a long time, a very long time; we were both getting exhausted, but neither one of us could get through the other's defenses. And finally, well, in the dream, I sort of decided, this isn't right. We shouldn't be doing this."

Sam repressed a grin. Just as he'd thought. I wonder if she remembers the conclusion? "Is that all?" he asked her. "All you can recall?"

"No," she answered, her voice distant. "No. I was telling myself something like, there's only one right way for this to turn out. So I just dropped all my defenses. I let my shield fall to the ground and held my sword down at my side. So you could do whatever you wanted to do."

"And what did I do? Put my sword down and take you in my arms?" he finished for her, sure of it now.

She looked around at him, her eyes large, bright, quizzical. "No," she told him. "No, you didn't. You ran your sword right into me, ran it all the way through me, right here." She patted her stomach in the vicinity of her navel, and her face tightened a little. "I knew you'd do it," she went on. "In the dream, I knew, I had no doubts. It hurt me, Sam! I can't usually feel pain in a dream, but it hurt! But it was weird, too; it was hurting but it seemed like it was a good hurt, that there was a rightness to it. When you pulled the sword out I felt like I was turning inside out, like whatever was me was running out on the ground with the blood. I couldn't stand up anymore, and I fell. I was dying, I knew it, but that was all right with me; I was dying in battle, dying like I was supposed to die. I felt proud, I felt happy. You came and knelt down beside me."

Again she paused; Sam was so shaken by this sudden turn that he could not speak for a moment. Worse, he could hardly deny that he'd found the scene she'd just described to be erotically charged; he was seeing it vividly in his mind, and he could feel a tightness in his pants.

"Did I say anything?" he asked when he trusted himself to speak again.

"Not right away. You cradled my head, kissed me. You said you were sorry, but you'd had to do it. I told you it was okay, it was right; and I said the only thing that would make it better is if you were coming with me. You want to know what you did, Sam?"

Weakly, he nodded. "What did I do?"

"You put the hilt of your sword down on the ground, you put the point up in the pit of your stomach, and you sank right down on it." She rolled her lips, uncrossed her ankles, crossed them back the other way, fidgeted with her hands. "You sank right down on it, and then you were dying too, our blood was mixing on the ground. We held hands, we were dying together, our blood was mixing, sinking into the earth, mixed forever." She looked at him again, and her eyes were wet. "It was beautiful, Sam. I was happy. I was happy. When I woke up it wasn't like it was a nightmare at all, it was like one of those good dreams you want to go back to . . ."

Sam couldn't see it as a nightmare either; the tightness in his pants had, if anything, increased.

It isn't what it sounds like, he told himself. It's symbolic; piercing her with the sword is a symbol for intercourse, that's just Freudian. It's just what I thought it was, except more symbolic. He foundered for a moment on an explanation of why he'd then killed himself, but his ability to analyze symbols, honed during the psychiatry rotations he'd done as a resident, came back into play as if it had never fallen into disuse. That could symbolize his willingness to make a compromise to end the argument—the "war"—in the first place. It could also symbolize his orgasm. Yes, he told himself, that's correct. The mixing blood symbolizes ejaculation, his fluids mixing with hers. Simple.

But powerful. Very powerful. Sam remained silent, not quite able to dispel the images in his head.

"You think that's about the argument we had, don't you?" she asked finally.

"Sounds like it might be."

She shook her head. "It is and it isn't. I don't know. I can't quite figure it out. It feels like there's a lot to it."

"Sometimes dreams have more than one meaning," he agreed pedantically. In spite of his state of arousal he was still afraid of giving himself away, he was still being very careful about what he said.

"Yes," she agreed. "I know." She shook her head again, sighed.

"I've got things to do," she announced abruptly, rising from her chair. "I can't lounge around here all day."

Turning his head, he watched her go into the bedroom, slipping her robe off her shoulders as she went, giving him a quick glimpse of her bare back and rear. That might be an invitation, he told himself. It might be, and he certainly felt he was ready to respond to it.

But he did not, he sat still, he turned his back and he picked up his newspaper. It isn't safe, Sam. You say all manner of things when you're in bed with her, and today you have all manner of wrong things to say. Best to pass on it this time; you're probably too damn nervous to do it anyway.

She emerged a few moments later wearing her trademark shorts and an old shirt; if it had been an invitation she said nothing about it, gave no further sign of it. Instead she went straight to the kitchen sink, took out a can of Ajax, and began scrubbing it down.

After a few moments he put the paper aside. "You need any help with that?" he asked.

She glanced at him over her shoulder. "Oh, no, Sam. Not at all. Hey, you deserve to relax, you worked all week. Me, I'm all rested. All I did was work all week."

Things were normal, Sam said, smiling to himself. Reassuringly normal. He got up, gulped the remainder of his coffee, and set about helping her with the housework. While they worked, he told her about Ken and his "game," about the possibility of a serial killer, and about his call to Stephanie. This led to another argument—why hadn't he taken the time to tell her, didn't he think she was at all interested in such things?—but it was minor and short-lived. Otherwise, the day slipped by slowly but peacefully; there were no other altercations. Dinner that evening was a little hurried; afterward, Cheryl had to leave.

Standing in the doorway, Sam watched her go. He didn't know how long she'd be gone, but then again, it didn't really matter, he told himself anxiously. He was not expected to sit home and wait by the door for her return. If he wasn't there when she came back, she probably wouldn't even ask him where he'd been.

He struck the doorframe with his fist. Is that wishful thinking, he demanded mentally, or what? No, she wouldn't put him in front of an inquisition, that wasn't her nature. But yes, she would ask, very casually. And if he said, "just out" or something similar, she'd persist. Widely spaced and subtle questions, but she'd persist. He could say, truthfully, "I went to see a friend." The question would then be, "who?"

No, he told himself. If you aren't here when she gets back it's going to require a lie, sooner or later. And you know, Sam, how that goes.

But the alternative—going in and calling Selinde back, telling her he wasn't going to be able to make it—was equally unacceptable. He walked down the steps and headed toward his car, unable to shake the feeling that disaster was accompanying him, step by step.

The address Selinde had given him was, indeed, within easy walking distance of the restaurant where they'd met; he guided the car carefully through the narrow passages north of Hillsborough Street, among the confusion of fraternity houses and private residences, many of which were rented out to students at nearby N.C. State. He had no trouble finding the house; it was a two-story, of course, and a stone walk led to a stairway that rose steeply on the right side, terminating in a small, awning-covered porch. He parked his car, sat staring at the place for a few minutes, then made his way down the walk and up the stairs. Standing on the porch, he again hesitated, studying the door. Ordinary screen-wire door outside, wood frame with four panes of glass inside. Neat little curtains on each pane. A door, a commonplace door. He knocked on it, waited, watched.

The inner door opened, and Selinde stood there, dressed in the same white shorts and almost see-through white blouse she'd worn before. She smiled; he felt something crumbling inside himself.

"Hi, Sam," she said. Her voice was so musical it startled him each time she spoke. "Come on in." She pushed the screen door open; he stepped inside without speaking. "It's definitely humble," she went on, waving her hand around the interior, "but it is home." Still saying nothing, he paused to look around. From where he was standing, he could see the kitchen, its attached dinette, and the living room beyond.

The décor was definitely unusual. It seemed to him it reflected Selinde herself; dark, mysterious, tantalizing. Nothing in the kitchen even vaguely resembled a modern appliance, a Waring blender or microwave. Dry herbs hung from the walls, interspersed with strings of red peppers; on the counter sat a pottery juicer, there was a black cast-iron skillet and matching dutch oven on the stove. There was no coffeemaker, there wasn't even an electric pot, just an old and almost corroded-looking percolator of the type one might use over a campfire. There were electric lights, but he had to consider it possible that she didn't use them. Candles were scattered everywhere, most of them partially burnt.

In the living room, that most ubiquitous of American household necessities, the TV set, was missing. There was a stereo; at least there were speakers, he could not see an amplifier, player, or tape deck. The chairs and the sofa could be discerned only by their outlines, since they, like almost everything else, were covered by thick, luxurious-looking draperies. The living room contained four colors, and four colors only: bright white, jet black, blood red, and navy blue. No off-whites, no grays, not a green or orange or violet anywhere.

"Well, what do you think?" she asked.

"Interesting," he replied. "Unusual."

"But do you like it?" she persisted.

"It almost looks like some sort of shrine. I almost expect to find a body laid out in state in there, ready for viewing."

"Your body and my body are the only bodies here," she said casually. "But you can sit down at the table there for a while, until you get used to it. I know this doesn't look like most American apartments. But I like it."

He walked to the table. White tablecloth, looked like real silk. "I'm afraid to," he said. "Well, I'm not afraid to sit there. I'd be afraid to eat or drink anything, though. Afraid I'd spill something on it."

She cocked her head slightly, looked into his eyes for a long moment. Hers looked almost unnaturally bright. The lighting, he told himself. It's twilight outside and she doesn't have a single light on in here anywhere. "Sit down, Sam," she reiterated. "And don't worry about the tablecloth. That's all it is, a tablecloth." She paused, waited until he pulled out a chair and sat down. "Can I get you something to drink?" she asked, standing just behind him, out of his sight. "I have coffee, several juices, tea, beer, and tequila."

"Not the tequila," he answered quickly. "But anything else will be fine."

"Some tea, then," she suggested, crossing behind the low divider that separated the rooms and returning to the stove. "I have the water already heated."

"You do? I didn't see—"

She picked up a copper teakettle; steam poured from its spout. "I sure do," she said.

He shrugged. "I guess you do."

Opening the cabinet, she took out two stoneware cups; from a pottery urn she extracted some reddish leaves, dropped them in. Atop this she added the furiously steaming water. Then she came back to the table and put them down, one in front of him and one in front of the empty chair to his right. He looked down into the cup blankly, watching the water turn dark red.

"You're still worried about the tablecloth, aren't you?" she asked.

"Well, yes, like I said, I—"

Reaching over his shoulder, she dipped three of her fingers into his cup, as far up as the second joint. Pulling them back, she very deliberately allowed drops of the red liquid to fall onto the pristine white cloth in front of him. "Now," she said quietly. "You don't have to worry about it, Sam."

He frowned at her. "Christ! You didn't have to do that! That water was almost boiling!"

She sat down, showed him her fingers. They were not red. "A matter of attitude," she said with an enigmatic smile.

"You are weird," he said, shaking his head. "You are a weird woman. I thought I'd met some weird people in my day, but you take the cake. You are weird."

She laughed, sipped her tea; for him, it was still far too hot. "I don't think so," she countered. "But I wouldn't mind you telling me, Sam, about some of these weird people you've met in your past."

"Some other time," he said. "I want to talk about you."

"What about me?"

"Where you're from. What you do. Who you are."

"It takes quite a long time for someone to truly know who another is, Sam." She shrugged, toyed with her cup. "And I've told you where I'm from: Mexico. I—"

"That's a big place. Where? Some border town?"

"A place called Tepeyac. It isn't far from Mexico City."

"I've never heard of it."

"I'm sure."

"What brings you here? To Raleigh, I mean? I think I asked you that the other night, but you never really answered me—"

She ran a finger across the edge of her lip. "I'm sorry, I don't mean to be mysterious. I suppose you could say I'm on a tour, that I'm a tourist."

He glanced around the apartment. "But you're living here. Tourists stay in motels."

"A tourist comes to a place to learn about the place. You can't do that if you only stay two weeks, Sam. It takes time. I come to a place, I stay six months, I stay a year, maybe longer. Then I know the place and its people. Then I leave, then I go."

"You don't work, then? You're not in school?"

"No. I have—resources."

It didn't seem appropriate to pursue this. "So how long have you been here?"

"In Raleigh, you mean? About two months."

"You have any idea how long you plan to stay?"

"As long as it takes."

That confused him a little. He hesitated, took a tiny sip of the now deep-red tea; the flavor was very robust, and it caused his tongue to tingle a little. "As long as what takes?" he asked finally, unable to frame his question any more elegantly.

Again, the enigmatic—or possibly mischievous, possibly even mocking—smile. "To do what I came here to do. Learn about this place, learn about the people who live here."

"It seems to me you probably know a lot about them already. Most people would take you for American; second-generation maybe, but American. You speak the language very well, you know a lot of the idioms—when we first met you said I acted like a 'prof'—"

"Superficial things," she said with a wave of her hand. Then she looked away. "But, if you think I know enough already, perhaps I should just leave. Tomorrow, first thing. Or maybe I should start packing up right now. What do you think?"

Sam found himself almost desperately searching for something to say that would quash that idea, but he could not come up with anything. "Well, it's up to you, of course," he allowed finally. "So don't let me talk you into anything. I was just making conversation, that's all."

"Oh. I see." She looked back at him. "So what you said didn't mean anything, then."

"No."

"Your idea of making conversation is to say things that don't mean anything?"

She had him squirming, trying to find a way out. "Well, no—Jesus! It was just the first thing that came into my head, that's all!"

"No, Sam. That wasn't the first thing that came into your head. Why can't you be direct with me? Do I frighten you?"

You scare the shit out of me, he said silently. You scare me because I can't figure you out and I can't control my reactions to you. Outwardly, though, he smiled. "No, Selinde," he replied. "You don't frighten me."

"Machismo. Nothing scares Sam Leo."

He laughed. "Well, I wouldn't go that far!"

"What scares you, Sam?"

He shrugged. "I don't know. Lots of things. Nuclear war, the greenhouse effect, pollution, the destruction of the rain forests. Lots of things."

She nodded slowly, evenly. "The things men do. The things men do, the things men are capable of doing. Those scare you."

"I suppose that's accurate enough. The things men—or women—do mindlessly, the things that get out of control and threaten us all."

"Are you afraid of yourself, then?"

He frowned. "Well, no. I don't think I do things mindlessly, and I don't usually—I mean, well, I don't let myself get out of control."

"I see." She shook her head, paused to take a long slow sip from her teacup. "I have known many men like you, Sam. Many men, many women. Never out of control."

Peculiar coincidence, he thought. Just the other night I was talking to Rick about this, I got distracted thinking about it in bed with Cheryl. And now this conversation's come around to the same issue. "You say that like you think there was something wrong with it."

"No, no. There isn't anything wrong with being in control. It's not that. It's just that a lot of your control is, I think, an illusion. You just don't find yourself in situations that might test it, that's all."

He considered that for a moment. "There may be some truth in that."

She laughed. "Oh, there is! I assure you, there is!"

"Are you in complete control?"

"Me?"

"Yes, you!"

"We weren't talking about me."

He grinned. "Now we are!"

Smiling, she looked down into her almost-empty cup. "There is a difference," she said. "And it is, I don't try to be."

Christ, Sam told himself, a man sure could read a lot into a statement like that! "You don't try to be. You give vent to each and every impulse you have."

"I didn't say that. But I do follow my—ah—my instincts. As I did when I gave you my phone number."

"Well, that wasn't exactly wild and crazy—"

"No. But it's different for you, Sam. Here you sit, right now, trying to decide what you're going to do with me. Controlling yourself, so very carefully. Your instincts are clear; you know your desires. Yet you hesitate, you struggle. Why?"

He refused to meet her eyes. "There are—certain conflicts—"

"I understand that. But there would not be, Sam, if you knew yourself well enough."

"Maybe not."

"Certainly not."

His eyes flicked up. When he spoke again his tone was slightly accusatory. "If your instincts and desires are so clear, if you know them so well, then you could—"

"I have said that the choices are yours, Sam. So they are."

"You really are a strange woman, Selinde. Really."

"Perhaps."

He drank down the remainder of the tea. "What if my choice was to come over there and kiss you?" he demanded boldly. "What if my choice was to do more than that?"

She smiled. "The choices are all yours, Sam."

Eighteen

PUTTING HER ELBOW on the table, Stephanie rested her head against her fist. She and her two friends were seated around the Masons' formal cherry dining-room table, glasses of wine in front of them. Across from her, Jennifer was still staring fixedly at the kaleidoscope; it was lying on a piece of blue cloth that Stephanie had, in deference to her friend's sensibilities, wrapped it in before bringing it.

"Why don't you just pick it up, Jenny?" Cheryl asked.

Jennifer glanced at her watch. "It isn't time."

"Time?"

"Uh-huh." She proceeded to give them a long and convoluted explanation of the astrology charts she'd done on the kaleido-scope, of which Stephanie understood not one single word. She did, however, understand that according to Jennifer's calculation the safe time to handle it was merely four minutes away; she felt sure she could wait that long.

The four minutes passed; with an expression and a manner more appropriate to picking up a venomous snake, Jennifer reached out and first touched, then picked up, the kaleidoscope.

"Her head isn't turning all the way around, and there's no pro-jectile vomiting," Cheryl observed, looking over at Stephanie. "Must be safe."

"Don't kid around," Jennifer told her. "I just want to be sure, that's all."

"If the thing was accursed," the dark-haired woman asked, "how would you know?"

Jennifer looked embarrassed for a moment. "I don't know. I think I'd feel it, somehow."

"Why wouldn't I?" Stephanie asked.

"Well, you might. But you don't really believe in it, you're not looking for it."

That, Stephanie could not argue with. She merely nodded. "So," she said after a pause, "are you getting anything?"

Jennifer rolled the tube around and around in her hands for a few seconds before answering. "No," she said finally. "It feels sort of—nice. Like an old antique brass lamp or something. Feels nice to the touch, smooth and cool." She looked down at the tube, studied the engravings; Stephanie watched closely, waiting for her to turn it with the eyepiece up and wondering what she'd see if she did.

She did not turn it that way, however. She did see, did comment upon, the woman, the snake, the tree. Stephanie started to point out the other orientation, but she wasn't sure she wanted to try to deal with the conversation that might ensue.

"Could I see it, Jenny?" Cheryl asked.

"Sure." She handed it to Cheryl, who rolled it over in her hands a few times, just as the other woman had. Then, without comment, she raised it to her eye and looked at the light through it. Jennifer gasped theatrically and made a face, but the damage, if damage there was, was already done.

"It's very pretty," Cheryl said flatly after a moment. "Very

pretty, nice patterns, vivid color. I could play with it for a while."
She lowered it. "On the other hand, I can put it down without any
trouble at all. I can't quite see why you and Art are having a
problem with it."

Jennifer reached out and took it from Cheryl's hand. "I guess
it's my turn," she said as she lifted it, pointed it toward the light,
and looked.

Again, she gasped. "Oh, it really is beautiful!" she enthused. "It
really is! I've never—I've never—" She fell silent, turning it
around and around, breathing heavily, staring into it fixedly.

"I think it's claimed another victim," Cheryl commented, looking up at Stephanie. "The kaleidoscope from hell."

Minutes passed. "Jennifer?" Stephanie asked. "Are you all
right?" There was no answer. Stephanie touched her arm.
"Jenny?"

Even then she did not respond immediately. Stephanie shook
her shoulder, spoke more loudly.

Jennifer took it away from her eye, looked at Stephanie blankly.
"Huh?"

"I said, are you all right?"

She put the kaleidoscope down. "Oh, sure." She shook her
head. "Sure, I'm fine." She moved her hand as if she was going to
bring the kaleidoscope up to her face, seemed to fight with herself
for a moment, then put it down on the table again. "Maybe Cheryl
can't see why you were fascinated by it, but I sure can," she muttered. There was a brief silence. "Uh—look, Stephanie, when we
get together down at the beach house—uh, uhm, could you bring
it? I'd sort of like to—well—"

Stephanie shrugged. "Sure. I guess."

"And uh, uh, if you ever decide you want to sell it—"

The auburn-haired woman smiled. "I don't want to sell it,
Jenny. But it's in the family, if you know what I mean."

Jennifer picked it up again, held it up but did not move it toward her eye. Again she examined the engravings, and this time
she did turn the eyepiece upward.

"Look at this," she said, pointing. "When you turn it this way,
there's a whole different picture . . ."

"Yeah?" Cheryl asked. "Let me see." Leaning over, she, too,
examined the tube. With a mix of anticipation and nervousness,
Stephanie waited for them to comment on it.

Cheryl was the one to break the silence. "That's weird," she said at last. "Looks like a scene from some pagan sacrifice or something."

It wasn't your imagination, Stephanie told herself. It is there. Cheryl sees it too, and Jennifer is nodding agreement.

"That's a funny coincidence," Cheryl said slowly. "Just last night, I had this weird dream . . ."

"Dream?" Stephanie asked, seeing in her mind a fleeting vignette of the sacrifice with Cheryl playing the role of the woman.

"Uh-huh." She shook her head rapidly. "Oh, it's nothing. I can't remember most of it. It had nothing to do with that sort of thing anyway." Almost hurriedly, she picked up her wineglass and sat back in her chair to sip it. "That dream," she went on, "I'm sure, had to do with the fight I had with Sam a few days ago, and it might've had to do with—"

"You didn't tell us about that," Jennifer pointed out. "You ducked it at the restaurant."

Cheryl sighed. "Yes, well. The same sort of fights I always have with Sam, it really wasn't anything unusual. He just—doesn't think. Doesn't pay any attention. Lives in his own world." She looked off into the distance, her green eyes rather sad. "It wasn't always that way. I just miss . . ." She stopped, shook her head again, vigorously. "It isn't important. It's over, we're back to normal. For what that's worth."

"There was something else," Stephanie put in. "Something else it might've had to do with."

"Oh, right. At work, there was a guy who came in and gave us a talk about dealing with 'carvers.' You ever heard of them?"

"Yes," Stephanie answered.

"No," Jennifer told them.

Cheryl turned to face her. " 'Carvers,' " she opened, "are—well, let's say disturbed people—mostly teenage girls and young women, who cut themselves deliberately. Sometimes with knives or razors, sometimes with broken glass, even things like nail files and so on. Mostly they cut their arms and legs, sometimes the chest." Her voice took on a rather formal tone, as if she were lecturing student nurses. "Some of them are psychotic," she went on, "and some are suicidal. But most aren't either one, most are what we call 'borderline personalities.' They—"

"You'd better tell Jennifer what a borderline is," Stephanie put in.

"Oh, right. Borderlines are, well, they're people who—it's sort of difficult to explain. They're manipulative, they have problems in their personal relationships; they tend to be substance abusers; a lot of times their affect isn't right, they have severe emotional ups and downs. And sometimes, they like to hurt themselves. Not always, but often enough. Anyway, these 'carvers' I was talking about, the speaker was telling us about why they do it—what they say, anyhow."

"I've not heard this," Stephanie said, her interest aroused. "I mean, I knew about them, but—"

"Well, they say, mostly, it makes them feel good. Makes them feel alive, makes them sure they can feel something, a lot of times they don't think they have any feelings. Sometimes they say there's a tension that builds up, and when they cut themselves and bleed, there's a release. He was telling us that there's an idea that—"

Stephanie was listening to Cheryl; her interest, she was telling herself, was academic, professional. Yet in the back of her mind she was wondering, as she'd wondered before, if there was anything of her own personality in that description. She did not have the emotional ups and downs—she never allowed herself those—and she'd never been a substance abuser, except for nicotine, which she'd always told herself didn't count. In relationships she'd always had problems; she got along well with Art—most of the time—only because he almost always gave in to her in every respect, and sometimes even that wasn't enough. Certainly all her previous love affairs had been tumultuous, to say the least. And, she admitted, the term manipulative might well be applied to her. . . .

Her attitude toward pain, however, was another matter. She took pride in her ability to endure it without complaint, an ability her agonizing childhood had necessitated. But there was more to it than that, too, and she could not, even now, deny there was something a little familiar in Cheryl's comment about "making sure you can still feel something." As to whether there was more —she didn't like to think about it, and she normally didn't allow herself to. Trying to distract herself, she glanced around the room idly.

When her gaze fell on Jennifer, though, it brought her up short. The blond woman was repeatedly brushing her hair back behind her ears; her face was pale, almost ashen, but her eyes, in distinct contrast, were bright, feverish. To Stephanie, she looked like she was about to faint.

"Wait a minute, Cheryl," Stephanie said, cutting her off in mid-sentence. "Jenny, are you all right?" she asked then, echoing her earlier question.

This time Jennifer responded instantly. "Yeah, sure." Only then, it seemed, did she become aware that Stephanie and Cheryl were staring at her. She flushed. "What's the matter?" she demanded, her tone suddenly a little hostile. "I was just listening to what Cheryl was saying, that's all . . ."

"You looked like you were about to pass out."

"Well, I wasn't. I was just listening, that's all." Looking a little annoyed, she brushed her hair back hard.

"You did look a little strange, Jenny," Cheryl put in.

Jennifer turned on her. "What is this, get Jennifer night?"

"No," Stephanie said soothingly, resisting the momentary urge she had to shout at her friend. "No, we were just concerned, that's all."

"Well, you had no reason to be. I'm just fine. Let's just get back to what we were talking about, can we?"

"I was about through anyhow," Cheryl said. "It wasn't anything important . . ."

"No, you weren't through. You were telling us about these really really crazy people, these carvers, these borderlines . . ."

"They aren't 'really really crazy,' Jennifer," Cheryl protested. "There're a lot of people who have borderline tendencies who're otherwise pretty normal. They don't need to be locked up in asylums or anything like that."

"They don't?"

"No."

"Oh." Jennifer took a healthy swallow of her wine. "Well. We did get pretty far off the subject, didn't we?"

Cheryl seemed a little lost. "Which was?"

Jennifer's quick and charming smile reappeared as if it had never been absent. "The kaleidoscope, of course!" She began to prattle on for a while, mostly just ranting about the beauty of the patterns, comparing them to mandalas, suggesting that they might offer an effective tool for meditation. Stephanie watched her eyes while paying little attention to her words, wondering what exactly was happening here tonight.

Nineteen

THE KISS HAD lasted only a few seconds. Only a few seconds, but it hadn't even taken Sam that long to realize that he was, without question, not in control.

Selinde let her hand slide slowly down off his shoulder as she moved her lips away from his. Her eyes looked immense in the fading light of the early evening. Still facing him, she walked backward into the living room, never hesitant, never stumbling, as if she could see what was behind her. He followed her; there wasn't anything else he could've done. He'd made his choice, he'd risen from his chair and taken her hand, and she'd gotten up to meet him; when he'd moved his head toward hers she'd been ready, that was obvious, ready and waiting. The touch of her lips had sent an almost electric thrill through his whole body, an experience he hadn't had since his teenage years, an experience he hadn't even had the first time he'd kissed Cheryl—and that kiss, he'd always believed, had almost caused him to fall apart.

She knelt; from somewhere she produced a lighter or matches, he couldn't tell which, all he could see was fire, all he could see was that she was lighting candles, several of them. Warm yellows and reds spilled around the room, flowing into the crevices of the ubiquitous draperies. Sam felt a little disoriented; now that he was in that living room, he realized it was hard to tell where the furniture stopped and the floor began, the drapes made it all seem to run together, especially in the candlelight.

She sat down, showing him the location of what appeared to be a couch. He came to her, knelt down in front of her. For long seconds he merely stared at her achingly lovely face.

"Do what you will, Sam," she whispered. There was a ringing in his ears; her voice seemed to come from a great distance.

He wasn't sure of himself, wasn't sure he could do anything except stare at her. But he saw his hands come up, saw them reach for the buttons on her blouse. Looking down at them, she smiled richly. A button slipped from its hole; another, and another.

Then his trembling hands were pulling open the freed flaps. As he'd suspected, she was wearing no bra. Golden brown breasts began to come into view; perfect in shape, perfectly smooth, their color reddened a little by the candlelight. He pushed on, opened the flaps more, exposed the rest of them, exposed the darker nipples. Selinde sighed as he touched them gently, wonderingly.

"You hardly look real," he managed to mutter. "You're too perfect. Real women don't look this perfect."

"I'm real enough, Sam. Your senses aren't lying to you."

He lowered his head, allowed his tongue to glide over her skin, tracing a path to one of her nipples. She shrugged off the blouse with a single motion and her hands came around behind his head, clasping him to her chest. After teasing her nipple, after feeling it become rigid against his tongue, he moved his head on down, down across her stomach, pausing to insert his tongue briefly into her navel. He was a little surprised to find his hands already on her thighs, stroking them, finding them incredibly sensual, then moving inexorably on up toward the fastenings of her white shorts.

He snapped them free, pulled them open, pulled them down. There were no panties, either. He moved his head and lips down into the V formed by the opening, the V that deepened as he slipped them on down her legs.

His lips contacted pubic hair, and a heady musk swept into his nostrils. He pushed the shorts lower, moving his lips around her inner thighs, luxuriating in the feel and scent of her. Her vaginal lips were either unusually large or already swollen; he pressed his tongue between them, encountered warm moistness and an erect and prominent clitoris. She held his head tightly as he teased it lightly. After mere seconds her body shuddered, as if she was already having her first orgasm.

After she relaxed he worked his way back up her body until he reached her mouth again; he kissed her furiously, she nipped his lower lip and laughed. Finally releasing her, he pushed himself back to his feet and stared down at her as he began removing his own clothes. She looked back up at him, her nude body lying casually but gracefully among the folds of the cloth, her long black hair framing her head and shoulders, her dark skin looking very red to him now.

When he'd finished undressing, he knelt back down in front of her; she rolled slightly to one side and reached for something, he couldn't see what. Then she held it up, showed it to him. He looked puzzled; it was a jalapeño pepper, evidently a fresh one.

"Now?" he asked blankly. "Now, you have a craving for a pepper?"

"They brought us here," she told him. With a delicate nip she took a half-inch off the end off the fruit, held it between her teeth. Then, running her tongue around it, she pulled his head down to hers and kissed him again.

Fire spread through his mouth, far hotter than that from the pickled jalapeños at the restaurant, but he did not pull away from her. Using her tongue, she pushed the piece of pepper into his mouth, and he in turn pushed it back into hers. After several trips back and forth they treated it as they might've treated the worm from a bottle of Mescal, biting it in half, then chewing and swallowing the fragments remaining.

His mouth and lips continued to burn violently. Even though it was painful he didn't mind; it seemed he had already internalized her advice about the proper "approach" to hot pepper. He kissed her again, tasted jalapeño in her mouth, on her lips.

She pushed him back up; when his torso was vertical she leaned forward, cupping his almost painful erection in one hand. He watched her as she moved her head forward; she first let her tongue sweep softly around the glans of his penis, then pulled it in, between her lips. He felt another shock, as if his skin temperature had suddenly dropped forty degrees, countered by a quickly rising warmth in his penis, a warmth that was spreading throughout his lower body.

After just a couple of seconds, the warmth turned into heat, and the heat turned to fire. It took him a moment to realize that it was the pepper again, the pepper that was still in her mouth.

She obviously, however, knew what she was doing; she seemed to be able to wipe it away with her tongue, just before it became too painful. She was expert in other ways, as well. Several times in the course of the next five or ten minutes she drew him to within a fraction of a second of his orgasm, only to release him and let him drop back at the last possible moment.

At last, she released him and laid back among the folded drapes. "Don't wait too long," she advised with a knowing smile. "You'll suffer for it if you do!"

The heat around the glans of his penis was rising already; he knew what she meant. "But—won't it burn you too?" he protested.

"Yes. But together we can tame it, use it. Come into me, Sam."

He didn't need any further encouragement. Shifting himself into position, his thighs between hers, he slid the tip of his penis up and down between her vaginal lips for a moment, then pushed gently inside her.

She closed her eyes, just for an instant, then opened them again. Her mouth was slightly open; she looked more passionate then than any woman he'd ever seen. Winding his hands into her hair he began moving on her, and she shifted her hips sideways under him in a serpentine motion. The effects of the pepper had not vanished; his penis felt distinctly hot, but now that he was inside her, now that he was sharing it with her, it was far from unpleasant —even though it was a sensation that under other circumstances he knew he wouldn't have found anything remotely like pleasurable. Now, though, it seemed to be making a reality of the common "fire" metaphors of sexual arousal; he did indeed feel he was aflame with desire, and he sensed that she was too. In such a context, their shared pain—for pain it was, there was no question —simply drove him toward erotic heights he had not before, at any time, experienced.

Almost desperately, he kissed her again, grabbed at her breasts, her thighs. He was not, he knew, going to last long, and he wanted to take advantage of every instant, to make the most of this. This is unique, he told himself again, and even his thoughts seemed choked and strained. This is magnificent, this is incredible.

He was right; he didn't last long. Once his orgasm started to rise he thought it was never going to stop, he felt like he was literally turning inside out. She held him tightly against herself, her body rigid, evidently experiencing an orgasm at the same moment. He felt his semen spraying into her violently, felt like a teenager again, like a young boy with little sexual experience.

Afterward he shifted his weight off her body and put his head down on the—was that a pillow or just a pile of cloth?—beside hers. He made no effort to free himself. He couldn't've gotten up then if the place had started burning down.

She turned her head toward his; her wonderful eyes seemed to fill his entire field of vision. He felt almost drugged, his perceptions were not quite right. Deep down in her eyes he thought he saw bright colors, kaleidoscopic patterns, swirling, ever-changing. . . .

He blinked; the illusion was dispelled, he could see nothing in her eyes except reflections of the candle flames and a very hazy image of his own face.

"I don't know what I want to say to you, Selinde," he told her candidly. His voice was very rough, congested. "Right now I feel like I love you. But that's really—I mean, we don't—"

She stroked his cheek. "You don't have to say anything, Sam," she whispered. "Nothing at all."

"I don't want to get up. I don't want to leave."

"And yet you will."

He twisted his mouth a little. "Yeah. I will."

"You have not betrayed your love for your wife, Sam."

He felt like crying. "It seems to me I have."

Twenty

YOU HAVE TO get rid of this face, Sam told himself as he pulled up in his driveway. He hadn't been lucky; Cheryl's car was sitting right there, she was already home. If he'd been able to beat her home she might never have known that he'd gone out, and he wouldn't be expecting her to ask questions that required lies for answers.

But that hope was gone, and now he had to walk in there and face her. He would've sooner faced the fires of hell, but that wasn't one of his options.

Letting his car roll to a stop behind hers, he shut the engine off and sat staring at the front door. You have to do it, Sam, he told himself. You have to go in. Where've you been? Fuck, I don't know. Out of this world, that's where I've been. Getting out of the car, he ran scenario after scenario through his mind, considering and rejecting each one in turn. They all had a common problem; they were all lies, lies that would set off Cheryl's built-in radar in an instant. You might as well get yourself a huge placard, he told himself, one that says "I've been out with another woman." That's how obvious it's going to be.

He ground his teeth. No. No. You'll find a way. You have to. Yes, Selinde is fascinating. Yes, she's irresistible. But you can't lose Cheryl over this. You can't. You couldn't take that, so that can't happen. In truth, he had no idea whether she'd leave him over an affair or not, even though she'd repeatedly wondered aloud why Jennifer didn't leave Rick. For them, it had never been tested. He did know, however, that she would not be delighted. He did know that his life was going to be hell, at least for a while, one way or the other. If the truth came out. If.

Stiffly, listening to the sound of his own molars scraping against each other, he went up the walk and used his key to open the door.

"Sam?" Cheryl called from the kitchen. "Is that you?"

"No, it's the mad rapist," he answered. He walked on in, rather woodenly, feeling like he was painted all over with guilt, like he was absolutely broadcasting his indiscretion.

"So," he said, abnormally loudly, abnormally jovially. "How'd your evening with the ladies go?"

She was sitting at the table, looking like she was lost in thought. "Oh, fine," she answered. "Fine." She fell silent, just staring down at the wood of the tabletop.

He looked at her keenly. Something was wrong, something had happened. Seeing an opportunity to at least delay the inevitable, he decided to push a little. "What happened?" he asked. "You have an argument with Jennifer or Stephanie?"

She glanced up at him. "No," she told him. "Not really." Then, slowly and with more than an occasional hesitation, she told him about the kaleidoscope, about how Stephanie had said that she and Art had been fascinated by it, how Jennifer seemed to react the same—and how she had not. She also described, without comment, the engravings on the instrument's surface.

There was more to it than that. Sam knew that perfectly well, there simply was not enough there to account for her abstracted mood. He continued to nudge the conversation along. It didn't really go anywhere; he didn't really learn anything more. But it did succeed in occupying the time until they at last went to bed. As Sam drifted off to sleep, he realized that she had not yet even asked where he'd been; he counted himself, at that time, as a very lucky man indeed.

Twenty-One

ART HAD GONE to bed already, some two hours or more before. Stephanie could hear his soft snores from the bedroom; a reassuring sound rather than an annoying one.

For her, though, it looked as if this night were going to pass without benefit of any sleep whatsoever. Dressed in her robe, she sat at their dining-room table in near darkness. A little light spilled in from the bathroom nightlight that, operated by a photocell sensor, turned itself on each evening, off each morning; a little more was offered by the red glow of the cigarette she was smoking, her first in months.

Strange evening, she told herself as she dusted her ashes into a paper cup; they'd long since removed all the ashtrays from the house. Very strange evening. Strange behavior from Jennifer. Maybe it was the kaleidoscope. The strangeness hadn't started until Jennifer looked through the damn thing, had it?

She made a snorting noise, took a long drag on her cigarette, held the smoke in her lungs for a moment while she chided herself. That has nothing to do with it, Stephanie. That stuff is crap, you only put up with it because of Jennifer. Yes, Jennifer behaved as if she were fascinated by it too, but that isn't what set her off. What did, and that's pretty clear, was Cheryl's discussion of the characteristics of the borderline personality. She, too, must've seen something of herself in that, perhaps merely in the statement that borderlines have chaotic relationships. One of us should have explained, you don't have to be a borderline to have screwed-up relationships. All you have to be is a human being for that.

So where does that leave you, Stephanie? she asked herself. Why all the strange notions lately, why the fascination with that damn kaleidoscope?

Even as she questioned herself, though, she understood that it was not just lately that she'd had some ideas that most people would consider strange; she'd had them for a long time. A memory, an event that took place when she was perhaps nine, streaked through her mind like a runaway train. Her father, on one of his familiar rampages, had just beaten her mother unconscious, and he had then turned his attention to her. He'd knocked her down and kicked her in the chest a few times, but then he'd walked away, he'd left her alone. She could remember crying bitterly; not so much because she was hurt—though she was, he'd succeeded in cracking one of her ribs—but because, in the twisted way she'd begun to think, it meant he didn't love her anymore. He'd lavished thirty minutes on her mother, but had given her less than two. The pain was tolerable; his neglect was not.

Like Art's memory of Clarence the Cloud-Watcher, remembering made her eyes grow wet. She wiped them hurriedly, forced her now turbulent emotions back under control. Tapping her ashes into the paper cup, she again listened for Art's snores, as she'd done every few minutes since she'd first lit the cigarette.

But this time, she didn't hear it. She started to get up, to go check on him, but it wasn't necessary. He was standing in the doorway, stark naked, his arms folded across his chest, grinning.

"Caught you," he said.

Once again, she flushed. God damn you, Art, she said silently. How dare you sneak up on me? And how long have you been standing there spying on me? "You gave me permission," she reminded him, her tone close to icy. "Remember? That was a mistake. You shouldn't've done that."

"You said you weren't going to accept it."

"I lied."

"Oh. I see. Can I have one, too?"

"No."

"How about a drag? Just a drag, just one!"

"No." She got up, went into the kitchen, and extinguished the cigarette under the faucet. After tossing the now-soggy butt into the trash, she returned to the table.

"You want to talk about it?" he asked gently.

She sat back down and stared at the paper cup in front of her. "Talk about what?"

"About what's bothering you."

"Nothing's bothering me."

"Sure. It's after three o'clock in the morning and you're sitting up smoking cigarettes. No reason to assume anything's wrong."

"A cigarette. Just one."

"Is that what you'd say if I had a drink? Just one?"

She glanced at him. "You can't have just one, Art. That's the problem. So no, it—"

"You can't have just one cigarette either. Neither can I, any more than I can have one drink. Addiction is addiction, Stephanie."

"You make it sound like I was some sort of junkie."

"That's what you said when we decided to quit. You said we were junkies. I agreed. I still do."

"Well, I'm not going to smoke another one, so we can drop it. Okay?"

"That's fine with me. We can drop that and you can tell me what the problem is."

She sighed; she glared at him. Art didn't push her often, but when he did he was incredibly persistent. She'd have to give him something, anything, just to get him to leave her alone. She certainly wasn't going to drop all her walls and open up to him the way he'd opened up to her, that wasn't in her nature.

"Well, you know I took the kaleidoscope over to Jennifer's tonight," she opened. Deliberately hesitant, sprinkling her comments with *ah* and *uh,* she told him about Jennifer's reaction to it, about her interest in buying it and her own refusal. He listened silently throughout, nodding occasionally, but making no comments.

"Well, for what it's worth," he said when she'd finished, "I'm sort of glad you didn't sell it."

"Why? Jennifer would've given me what I paid for it. I'm sure of that."

He shrugged. "I like it. I agree with you, it's weird, but I like it. For me it's more than just pretty. It does something for me, it— well, it puts me in touch with myself. Or lets me get in touch, I don't know, something. All I know is, I start looking through it and I start thinking about things I haven't thought about in years." He paused, laughed. "Am I making sense?"

"More or less," she told him. "At least, I understand what you're saying. But Art, I've never heard you talk like this in my life!"

Still laughing, he shook his head. "I know. But I don't think it's a problem, do you?"

"No, I don't. And if I'd known that earlier, that would've been a good enough reason to keep it. But I didn't, Art. I just didn't want to sell it, and I don't know why not. That bothers me."

"As I told you before, you're allowed to be impulsive some—"

She slapped her hand down on the table, hard, and it made an almost gunshotlike report. Art jumped. "No, I'm not!" she hissed. "I'm not, I'm not allowed!"

His eyes went wide. "Jesus!" he said. "What in the hell was that all about?"

She'd gone too far, and she knew it. Now he was going to start demanding some answers, answers she did not want to give him. She trusted Art—more or less—and she loved him as much as she felt she could ever permit herself to love another human being. She still did, in spite of the fact that their sex life was currently in collapse. He was still the best friend she had.

But that didn't mean she could share everything with him. Not the things she'd put away in a locked box inside herself—a box that, when it cropped up in her dreams, always took the shape of a coffin.

"Stephanie?" he asked after she'd retreated into a stiff silence for a few seconds. "Could we talk about this some? Look, tomorrow's Sunday, we don't have to get up early. I'm perfectly willing to sit here all night if that's what it takes."

She took his hand and smiled at him; if the smile looked affectionate to him, that was nothing more than what she'd intended. "I know you are, Art. You're very patient with me, you always have been. Sometimes I think you deserve something better than what you get from me."

"I'm not complaining. But you've so secretive about yourself. Who knows, it might help if you'd share these things with me."

She nodded. "Maybe. Look, I'm sorry about the explosion. It's just that, well, in my family, you couldn't afford to be impulsive. Being impulsive could cost you a lot. I learned early on to think about things before I did them, to be ready to take whatever consequences there were." She shook her head and sighed, knowing that none of this was news to him. "Like I told you the other day, I just don't like to talk about it, that's all."

Falling silent, she watched his eyes; he wasn't going to leave it at that, she knew, he was going to continue to push, he was going to continue to pry. She felt a surge of rage, then an equal and opposing rush of self-loathing. He did not deserve that, she told herself firmly. He was only trying to help.

But she couldn't do it, she couldn't let him. The rage came back, overwhelmed the self-hatred, settled into place. You can control him, she told herself darkly. You've always been able to. All you have to do is distract him. For that, you've got a little trick that never fails.

Concentrating, she allowed a different persona to settle over her like a cloak. "Besides," she said, her voice becoming soft, "I'm not sure I can concentrate on it, not with you sitting there like that. You're a sexy man, Counselor."

Expectantly, she waited. Art's macho, as she well knew, would demand that he react, no matter how badly their last encounter had gone—if indeed it had been bad for him, she couldn't really be sure of that, since they hadn't discussed it. In any case, if he didn't respond now, it would be the first time.

He didn't disappoint her. "And you're a sexy woman, Doctor," he noted. "You look very sexy sitting there in that robe. Of course, you could look even sexier . . ."

She pulled the belt, opened the robe, pushed it back over her shoulders. She wasn't wearing anything else. "How about this?" she asked.

"Yeah." He scooted his chair closer to hers, pulled her to him. "You want to wander back toward our bedroom?"

"Not necessarily."

"And you say you're never impulsive."

That caused her a pang. She didn't like deceiving him, didn't like using her body purely as a diversion. But in a way, she told herself, she wasn't; his touch was, in fact, arousing her. From there the rationalization was easy; she was only doing what she wanted to do, she wasn't doing anything wrong. "I told you. Sometimes I lie."

He moved his knees apart a little. "C'mere," he said, tugging at her arm.

She got up, went to him, straddled his legs, sat on his lap; he buried his face between her breasts. After a moment he lifted his face, looked into her eyes. He started moving his hands up her body, beginning at her waist, continuing to her breasts, then on up to her neck. Stephanie's neck was quite long; Art often complimented her on it, often remarked on how attractive it was. As always his hands lingered there, his fingers barely touching her skin.

Damn it, she told him mentally. You don't have to be so fucking gentle, I'm not going to break! Do something; squeeze. Tighten up those fingers, squeeze. Squeeze hard: I can take it. Squeeze.

As she realized what she was thinking, her eyes flew wide open.

Art's head was down; he did not see it, but he felt her stiffen slightly. "Something wrong?" he asked.

"No," she replied smoothly. "You just caught a ticklish spot, that's all." My God, Stephanie, she asked herself. Now what? You've never had a notion like that in your life!

No, well, that isn't quite true . . .

She tried to dismiss the thought; it wouldn't go. For several seconds she was lost, adrift in a world whose inhabitants included her father, the woman on the kaleidoscope, and Alice Near. Vaguely, she became aware that Art was tickling around her neck, looking for a reaction. You have to behave normally, she told herself frantically, you have to get yourself under control. He'll notice, he isn't stupid!

"Oh, yeah?" he was asking. "I didn't know you had any of those!" His fingers continued to search her throat and neck. "Where is it, where?"

For a moment she didn't even know what he was talking about; then she remembered that she'd told him he'd tickled her. She raised her hands, touched spots just under her ears. "Somewhere around there . . ."

His fingertips followed hers, and, after an appropriate delay, she squirmed and leaned against him. He seemed delighted with this new discovery, his manner that of a small boy. She could feel him hardening between her legs.

No more wild ideas sprang to her mind; she began to relax, hoping against hope that somehow, tonight would be better. She was aware in a way that she wasn't helping; her body was responding to him but her thoughts were detached, coldly analytical. Art would not, she was sure, notice that; and, in a strange sort of way, her easy success in controlling him was itself at least somewhat exciting. Even if there was no improvement, she was sure she could get through this one without discomfort—as long as he didn't take too long.

You really are a bitch, she told herself as he entered her. You really are.

Twenty-Two

IT HAD BEEN a miracle. Sam had no doubts whatsoever about that, a miracle. Cheryl had clearly been focused on the odd way Stephanie and Jennifer were acting about the kaleidoscope; she'd spent a good deal of Saturday night and a part of Sunday discussing it with Sam, and just as long on the telephone with Jennifer. She was, evidently, almost completely preoccupied with it, as if it were a crisis of major proportions rather than a curiosity.

Sam wasn't complaining. It had prevented her from even thinking to ask where he'd gone Saturday, prevented her from noticing his stiff and tentative manner during the weekend. It had gotten him through to Monday, back to work, without further incident. It might not continue—she might well ask tonight, as soon as he walked into the house—but he was far better equipped to cope with it now, now that it was less fresh. Beyond that, the vacation at the Masons' beach house was looming in the near future, and preparations for it would occupy her attention, too. Even if it didn't—even if he had to face it tonight—he was eternally grateful, to whatever benevolent gods might have granted him such a boon, for the respite.

Not that it was helping him in terms of trying to concentrate on his work. There was considerably more data to be sorted on the Peruvian cholera epidemic; he felt obligated to have the material in some sort of usable form before he left for the vacation.

But he wasn't getting it done. He'd spent a good deal of that morning staring blankly at the map of Peru on the screen, unsuccessfully trying to force himself not to think about either Selinde or Cheryl. It wasn't until after he'd returned from lunch that he pulled his chair firmly up to the desk and started rattling the keys, creating the dataset that would permit a distributional analysis of the cholera victims.

Everything went fine until he tried to save the dataset matrix.

When he did, his screen blanked. Confused, he stared at it; he tried ESCAPE, tried RETURN, tried everything he could think of. Nothing worked. The system was clearly up, nothing had happened to the monitor, but he could get no response from it.

Then, quite slowly—as if being printed by an old teletype machine—letters began appearing on the screen, green on black. More bewildered than ever, he watched them appear.

"My dear Cheryl," he read, "I am so sorry to have to tell you this. I know it will come as a terrible shock to you, but as your friend I feel I must. Your husband, Samuel G. Leo, is having an affair. The woman's name is, I believe, Sally. She lives at—"

In a state of shock, Sam watched Selinde's address and phone number reel off. "I truly am sorry," the message continued, "but I felt you had a right to know. I will be in touch with you soon, Cheryl. Maybe I can help to console you in your grief. Regretfully, a friend."

For another two or three minutes, the letters remained; then the screen blanked again and the message repeated. After another pause, his original screen, his dataset on the cholera epidemic, reappeared. As if nothing had happened.

Pushing his chair back in a fury, Sam jumped to his feet. He was asking himself how, but he surely wasn't asking himself who. Ignoring the stares of people he passed in the hallway, he marched to the elevator, waited impatiently, then rode it up to the third floor. After another march down another hall he stopped at a door labeled COMPUTER SERVICES and slammed it open.

Ken was sitting facing the door, quite obviously expecting him. "Oh, hi, Sam," he said in an ordinary voice. "What brings you up here?"

"You goddamn, low-life son of a bitch," Sam growled. "What in the fuck do you think you're doing?"

"Now, now. Close the door, Sam. You don't want the whole center to know your business, do you?"

He was reluctant to accede to any request Ken might make, but no, he didn't want to broadcast this. He closed the door, then crossed the room and stood over the programmer. His arms hung stiffly at his sides, and his fists were opening and closing in a regular rhythm.

"You hit me," Ken warned, "and two things'll happen. First, that letter will go to your wife. Second, I'll charge you with assault. Think about it first, Sam."

"Oh, it'd almost be worth it!"

"I doubt it."

He fought for control. "All right," he snarled finally. "All right. So you haven't sent that letter to Cheryl? It's all bullshit, you know, I haven't—"

"Oh, come on, Sam. That's useless. But no, the letter hasn't gone out. Yet." He grinned hugely. "It's my game, Sam. Better get that straight, real quick."

The phone, Sam told himself. That's the only possibility. "What do you do, you scum? Sit around here all day listening in on the phones? God damn it, my line is supposed to be private—"

"Your line is linked in with the net. I can access it through the same circuit that operates your connection to the modems; it isn't hard. And no, I don't listen in, I don't have that kind of free time. Look." He swiveled his chair, tapped his keyboard with expert fingers. On the screen, both sides of his conversation with Selinde scrolled into view. The name "Sally" was bracketed, followed by a question mark.

"My voice-analysis software didn't recognize that," Ken said, pointing out the name. "Either you say it funny or it isn't Sally, it's something unusual. But it's close enough." He glanced up. "Okay, now look at this." He pressed some more keys, and Sam's call to Stephanie replaced the other transcripts. "You really are a jerk, Sam," Ken observed. "Shoulda made that call from home. You've pissed me off, Sammy boy. I told you that business was between you and me."

Sam was wilting a little, but he was determined not to let Ken see it. "You were born in the wrong time, Ken. You should've been born back in the Dark Ages. You could've been an evil wizard, you could've worn a peaked hat and a robe with moons and stars, and you could've cast your spells on the local virgins."

"You should quit giving me those compliments, Sam. You're going to swell my head. Besides, I like these times perfectly well. Even if there are no virgins around to cast spells on."

Sam began pacing. "Let's cut the crap, Ken. You want something from me, and you're going to blackmail me to get it; if you'd just wanted revenge you'd've already sent the letter. What is it?"

"Sit down, Sam. Have a cup of coffee, there's clean cups over there by the machine, and—"

"I don't want to sit down, I don't want coffee, I—"

Ken's smile vanished; his eyes were cold. "I told you to get some coffee and sit down, Sam. I'm calling the shots. You'll lick my shit out of the toilet if that's what I tell you to do. Otherwise, that little sex machine you're married to will, in fact, receive a letter. Got it?"

"Don't talk about Cheryl like that! You fucking worm, I'll—"

"You'll do nothing. I'll talk about her tits, I'll talk about her cunt, I'll talk about how it'd feel for me to stick my fat dick in her mouth and squirt my cream down her throat. I'll talk about porking her in the ass, if I want to. You won't do a thing."

Sam glared. He ground his teeth, clenched his fists, chewed the inside of his cheek. Finally, very stiffly, he went to the coffee machine. Most of the cups around it had brown scum with green mold growing on it in the bottom; he managed to find one that was at least approximately clean. After filling it, he came back and sat down. Of all the people who could've possibly learned of his indiscretion, there was no question that Ken was the worst.

Other than, of course, Cheryl herself.

"You're right," he said finally. "But I want to get to the bottom line, Ken. What you want from me."

Ken's grin came back. "Well, you mentioned blackmail, Sammy boy. You could pay me." He struck a theatrical pose. "One million dollars! One million or I turn canary!"

"I don't have that kind of money and I can't get it, either."

"Oh, I know. I cracked your bank's teller line, too, just to make sure you couldn't feed me any bullshit. Sixteen thou in savings, about four thou in checking at the beginning of the month. Little bullshit portfolio worth about twenty. You could raise fifty thou, maybe, and that's about it. It ain't enough. So I ain't gonna blackmail you—for money."

Sam shouldn't've been amazed, but he was. "Bastard," he muttered.

"Oh, come on! Nobody's finances are private now! You should hire me as an adviser, Sam. You throw away a lot of money."

"That's my business."

"Yeah. I don't give a shit, really. Point is, you don't have enough to buy me off. So we have to talk about other things."

"Like what?"

"Like the bimbo you're porking, Sam. What's she look like? As good as Cheryl?"

Sam wasn't going to give up anything he didn't have to. "She looks all right," he answered carefully.

"Good. I was afraid she might be some ugly brainy bitch. Women are better off without brains, Sam. Tits and cunts are all that really count."

"That's not my opinion."

"Who cares? You're a schmuck. Anyway: what I'm getting at is that maybe, if she looks good enough, your bimbo could buy your freedom."

Sam did not have to ask what he meant; it conjured up an utterly horrible vision. "You can forget that shit," he snarled. "There's no way I'd ask—ah, Sally—to do that! Besides, I thought you told me you never fucked anybody! You sure don't want to start now!"

For the moment, Ken's sickly grin was absent; his eyes looked sad, even pained. "That's maybe a little exaggeration," he admitted. "But it's been a long time, and I'm a normal man, I—"

"Let's not get ridiculous!"

That got to him, Sam noted with some satisfaction. Maybe just a little, but it got to him. "As I was saying," he went on coldly, "it's been a while. The last one was that grad student who was over here from Duke, Cindy Ellison, and that's been—"

Sam was staring blankly. He remembered Cindy Ellison quite well. Pretty, intelligent, ambitious, personable. It was as easy to see her having an affair with a rabid rhinoceros as with Ken. "Cindy? I don't believe it!"

Ken waved a hand. "Oh, sure." He laughed mirthlessly. "Oh, no, Sam. She didn't want to. No girl ever wanted to, not with me. She didn't have any choice. I coded her datasets, and she had to deal. If she wanted to get her Ph.D., that is. So she did. Not very well, though; she sucked me off and then she threw up on my floor, so I made her do it again."

Hardly able to look at him, Sam physically squirmed in his chair. This, he told himself, was even lower than he'd thought Ken would stoop. "You're lucky," he said, "that she didn't charge you with rape once you gave it back!"

"She thought of that too, she threatened me with it. But I jimmied her data before I gave it back to her, see. Nobody'd ever notice, not if they weren't looking, but it's rigged so that if certain stats are applied it'd look faked. She won't give me a problem, Sam. Not if she wants to keep that cushy appointment she got up at Dartmouth."

Still holding the cup of steaming coffee, Sam was silent for a few minutes, just staring. He was feeling an almost overpowering urge to hurl it into Ken's face. Fantasizing the other man's reaction, he almost smiled.

But, in the end, he did not throw it and he did not smile. "Ken, you are an evil man. You really are—I just don't think there's any other word for it. I'm not sure I believed in pure evil before I met you. Why are you telling me all this, anyway?"

Ken jabbed a stubby finger at him. "Just so you don't get the idea you can weasel out of this, to let you know I cover all the bases. You don't want your wife to find out about the bitch you have on the side, and frankly, I don't want to tell her. I'd get a few giggles out of watching your marriage go down the drain, but that's about all. And it isn't enough."

"What is enough?"

Ken leaned back again. "My game is enough. Winning is enough. You're going to help me do that."

Sam's eyes narrowed; this sounded too easy. "Well, naturally, if you want my expertise in examining the data you have—"

"I do. But that's not all."

I knew it, Sam said silently. "What else?"

"What else is your good friend Stephanie Dixon, over there in the Medical Examiner's Office. You said it yourself, on the phone; she has good ins with the cops. I want information, Sam. The keys the cops don't tell the papers, the stuff they hold back to check confessions and all that. They don't put that stuff on networks and services, I can't get at it. But she can, and if I can put it in it'll give me an extra dimension of predictability. You can get it from her, Sam. You follow me?"

Sam made a snorting sound. "You're crazy, Ken. I can't get that kind of stuff for you!"

"I think you can. It'd be easy for your buddy Stephanie to—"

"Ken, it's impossible! Stephanie isn't going to do that—I mean, she'd be risking her job, she might even be risking arrest herself, for obstruction of justice!"

"She's your friend. Tell her you're in trouble. Tell her you need it. I might even be convinced to try to dig up some dirt on her if you asked me nicely."

Sam was curious in spite of himself. "How would you do that?"

Ken shrugged. "I've got password-cracker programs written, Sam. You have no idea how much information there is wandering around out there now, on everybody. IRS, Social Security, credit bureaus—it's all over. All on networks. All password-protected. All accessible."

"You're incredible. How come you're not rich?"

"I do all right. But that isn't what we were talking about." He leaned forward, shook a finger at Sam. "I'm not unreasonable," he went on. "I'm going to give you a couple of days to give me an answer, I know all this is a shock. All you need to understand is this: you have three choices. A million clams, a turn at your bimbo's cunt—if she's pretty enough, if she's a dog you only have two—or the information I want. You got it?"

"Ken, you're being ridiculous, I can't—"

"If you can't, the letter goes to Cheryl. Bottom line, Sam."

Sitting and staring in silence, Sam thought he understood how Cindy must've felt. There was, he told himself, only one truly logical, truly reasonable, answer to all this.

And that was to buy a gun and blow Ken Colburn's head right off his shoulders.

It would be a heroic deed, he told himself wildly. The man is evil; he's admitted to rape, he came close to admitting theft, and he's a blackmailer. He's a menace to everyone, not just a nuisance. He deserves it. It'd be right. Justice.

"Sam?" Ken inquired. "You still here? Don't go catatonic on me, Sam."

"I'm not. Look, Ken, I don't know how much can be done this month. I'm leaving for vacation next—"

"I don't give a fuck. Postpone it if you have to."

"But so is Stephanie! She won't be seeing any of her cop buddies for at least two weeks!"

"She can postpone too."

Sam rose from his chair, put his cup down carefully. "Ken," he said, his voice low, "don't push me any harder. You're right, I don't want you to send that letter to Cheryl. But I'm trying to explain to you, you slimy asshole, what is possible and what is not. If I get the idea you're going to push so hard the letter is going to get sent no matter what I do, then I am—I promise you—going to take great pleasure in stuffing your head into one of those monitor screens. Believe me, Ken. The satisfaction of doing that is well worth the jail time."

Ken's eyes flashed fear, and he held up his hands defensively. "All right," he said hastily. "All right. For now, the letter doesn't go out. But I will expect to see you again, Sam, before—let's say, Thursday. You tell me then what you're going to do and when you're going to do it, and I'm not buying next year—who knows when the cops might blunder onto some answer about all this? Especially since you've put a bug in their ear about it!"

Sam nodded slowly. "All right," he said. "Before Thursday, I'll give you an answer. I'm leaving now; I can't breathe in here, the stench in the air is just too damn bad!"

Ken's triumphant grin returned. "Get used to it, Sam," he said. "One way or the other, you're going to be seeing a lot of me. Don't forget, you've already agreed to do the analyses on my data!"

Twenty-Three

"I SPENT THE whole damn weekend on it, Steph. I reviewed every one of the unsolveds we've had in N.C. for the past couple of years, and I even reviewed a bunch of those that've been listed as closed." Dave Brennan paced back and forth in front of her desk, his hands clasped behind his back, his head down. "I've got to admit that it looks like something's going on. But it don't look like no serial killer, not to me."

Her hands clasped and her chin supported by her fingertips, Stephanie listened. As usual, her attempts to convince Dave that this really wasn't her concern—yet—had fallen on deaf ears; she'd been contributing little to the discussion but she had been listening.

"I have a lot of confidence in that source, Dave," she said in a bland voice. "But that isn't a guarantee that there is a serial killer at all."

He stopped pacing and turned to look at her; he looked worried. "Maybe. Maybe not. What there is is a pattern of some sort. And there's something like an M.O., too, a common thread. It's hard to figure, it's real hard."

"I'm not following you."

He rubbed his hands together briskly. "You take the one we're working right now, Alice Near. What would you say characterized that one? What jumps out at you?"

"The lack of defensive wounds," she answered promptly. "The lack of any evidence of a struggle. We talked about that before."

"Uh-huh. Well, she isn't the only one."

"I know that, Dave. I've heard of other cases like that."

"Yeah, but that was a long time ago, and it wasn't here. We've had a bunch of these right here in N.C., over the past year or so."

Stephanie looked blank. "We have?"

"Uh-huh. I'm sure of it, Steph. With a knifing, it's pretty obvious; I'm pretty sure there've been a lot more. When somebody's been strangled or shot you don't expect defensive wounds, and—"

"It sounds to me," Stephanie cut in, "as if this is speculation and not fact, Dave."

"A cop's instinct," he countered. "You've heard of hunches, haven't you?"

"Mmm-hmm. Speculation."

His mouth twisted. "Maybe."

"Do you have any that aren't?"

"Look. I've got one from Asheville I was looking at. Unsolved. The victim was found naked, just like Alice Near. Raped. The report says she had a number of nonfatal injuries. No sign of a struggle. Killed in her own home and no sign of forced entry."

"How'd she die?"

"Gunshot wound. In the belly. Fired while the muzzle of the gun was pressed against her."

Stephanie touched her lip. "Okay. Let me run this by you. Her doorbell rings. She answers it, a guy says 'florist' or something. She opens the door, he points a gun at her, he says something like 'Do what I say and you won't get hurt.' She does. There's a rape, and our boy is sick in the head, he likes to cause pain, he inflicts these nonfatal injuries you mentioned. He keeps telling her that if she cooperates he won't shoot. She does, she lets him do what he wants, she thinks maybe that'll save her life. Maybe a lot of this time he's poking her with the gun. At the end, without warning, he pulls the trigger. Too late for her to struggle then. You're a cop, Dave; does that make any sense to you?"

"Yeah," he grumbled. "Yeah, I guess it does. It could've gone down that way."

"With Alice Near, it's strange because she had to know she was being killed; she was being stabbed, repeatedly. But she didn't fight. The one you described might be the same but it doesn't have to be. You see?"

"Yeah, yeah. You don't have to beat me over the head with it." He sighed. "You know, Steph, you might not believe in a cop's hunches but I do; I guess I have to. I went through all this stuff and I got these unsolveds that are doubtful, and, on the other hand, I got some that look just like the Near killing. But damn it, the books have been closed on those!"

Stephanie grinned and shook her head. "Dave, you of all people should know that real life isn't the movies. The cops don't always get the right guy! Have you considered that?"

He gave her a hard look. "We try to. Ninety-five percent of these things are open-and-shut, it's just all the damn rules the courts lay on us that—"

"I don't want to get into that again," she almost snapped. "You know we don't agree on that. I'm not saying you do it yourself, but I think most cops are just interested in closing books. And that means that one arrest is as good as another, whether you have the right man or not. The rules you're always complaining about help to control that!"

"I guess I can't expect anything different from a defense lawyer's wife," he sneered back.

"Art agrees with me, but he doesn't do my thinking for me. Now, you may want to stand here and argue this point, but I don't, I have things to do. Okay?"

He threw up his hands. "Okay, okay. It's dropped, all right? Shit, all I'm trying to do is follow this up with you, anyway. We have confessions in some of these; it's hard to doubt—"

"No, it isn't hard to doubt. You remember the girl who was killed down near Lexington a few years ago? Let me remind you that there was not one but two confessions to that one. No relationship between the guys that confessed. Both convincing. But everybody agreed, they both couldn't've done it! You remember Henry Lee Lucas? He confessed to dozens of killings, but—"

"Yeah, yeah, okay, you've made your point, Steph." He looked off into space for a moment. "That one in Lexington might give a clue to Near, though. One of those guys said the girl asked him to do it, that she wanted to commit suicide but couldn't do it herself. She was stabbed, too."

"Well, I don't know, I don't know all the details of Lexington. But if Alice Near chose that as a method of suicide, she sure chose a painful one. That went on for a while, Dave. She didn't go down quick."

"Neither did the girl in the Lexington case, she was stabbed a buncha times too. Lots of people watch too many movies, they think if you stick a knife in somebody they just fall over dead. You and I know it ain't like that, Steph. We see lots of cases where people have been stabbed dozens and dozens of times, and they just keep on screaming and fighting, they don't go down."

"You don't have to tell me that," Stephanie mused. "I've seen enough of them myself." She shook her head. "To commit suicide that way, though—so painful . . ."

Dave grinned. "You ever talked to a survivor of a knifing?"

"No. The knifing victims I see aren't the survivors."

"Yeah, well, I've interviewed a lot of them. What they say, usually, is that it doesn't hurt all that much, not when it's happening. A lot of 'em say it didn't hurt at all. That they didn't even know they got knifed, they just thought they got punched. Until they see the blood."

"I've heard that. Shock, probably."

"Maybe. I ain't no doctor and I ain't never been stabbed. All I know is what people tell me."

"No, I haven't either," Stephanie mused. She was silent for a moment, then she shrugged. "Well, so, what's the status of this? You're going to drop it, you don't think there is a serial killer?"

"Right now, I sorta doubt it. But no, I'm gonna burn some more midnight oil over it. It bugs me, Steph. You come up with this lead and I find a bunch of funny cases. It bugs me. I tell you what; I do think I'd like to talk to this source of yours."

"I don't think," she said carefully, "that the source can tell you anything you don't already know. The entire connection the source has with this affair is in assembling information that's been printed in the newspaper. You have access to more information than that."

"I still—"

"If you become convinced that there is a serial and you don't know where to start looking, I'll speak to the source, I'll see if the source can offer any assistance. Otherwise, there's no need in dragging the source into it. That's the way it's going to be, Dave."

He sighed; he knew he'd get nowhere arguing with her. "You know, you can be really tough to deal with sometimes, Steph."

She didn't allow herself to grin. "I know," she answered.

Twenty-Four

SAM'S LUCK HELD through Monday night; Cheryl remained abstracted by the matter of the kaleidoscope, and she spent a good deal of her evening on the phone, first with Jennifer, then with Stephanie. She did not ask about his whereabouts Saturday night, and she uncharacteristically failed to notice his tension. Normally this would've annoyed him. Naturally, on this occasion, it did not.

On Tuesday, he left work—ostensibly for lunch—at around eleven thirty. Hurrying home, he checked the mail, found nothing there that even might be a letter from Ken. Treachery from the man he expected, though probably not this soon. He'd wait, Sam was sure, he'd wait until he felt he'd gotten as much as he could get. Then he'd send the letter. Probably to Cheryl's work, or in some other way that would make it impossible for Sam to intercept it. Ken had to be given credit for intelligence, he could not be underestimated. But he certainly couldn't be trusted, either.

There was another matter to be taken care of too, he told himself as he left home again, having remembered to leave the mail in the box so he wouldn't provoke questions from Cheryl. Ken might not know Selinde's name, but he knew her address and her phone number. She had to be warned; she had to be told what was going on. He'd considered calling her, but in a moment of weakness he decided to drive by Selinde's apartment first, see if she was at home. Parking in front as before, he looked around guiltily before almost scurrying up the stairs and knocking on her door.

He sighed with relief when he saw her face through the panes of the inner door. She smiled, opened it. "Sam!" she greeted. "This is a nice surprise! Come in! But aren't you supposed to be working?"

"Lunch hour," he told her as he moved quickly inside. "I'll be late getting back, but that won't matter. I've got to talk to you."

She gestured toward the table. It was still covered by the silk cloth, but there were now no stains on it. He sat down, glanced around the apartment quickly, as if he expected Ken to be lurking there someplace. He saw nothing except what he'd seen before; she had the curtains drawn, and the interior of the place was almost as dimly lit as it had been at twilight. You're getting paranoid, Sam, he told himself. Ken is not the ancient wizard you compared him to, he isn't following you around invisibly.

He looked back at Selinde, who remained in the kitchen, watching him with evident concern. For an instant he closed his eyes. Today she was dressed in a floor-length white gown, so sheer he could see the outlines of her legs and body clearly through it, silhouetted against the sunlight from the door. In spite of the stress he began to react to her.

She came to the table, sat down. "Sam, what is it?" she asked, laying her hand on his arm. "You seem—distraught."

"That's a good word for it. That's a damn good word for it. Just let me tell you what's happened." Quickly he explained to her who Ken was, described him, outlined the situation. "So now he's blackmailing me," he concluded. "I don't expect you to do anything about that, but you need to know who he is. In case he calls or comes around here. I wouldn't put anything past him."

She squeezed his arm. "I'm sorry this has happened," she said softly. "You say he's blackmailing you. He wants money?"

Sam grunted. "Yeah. One million dollars. That, or some information I don't even know if I can get for him; I'd have to get from a friend, I don't know how I'd do that, and I'd feel I was betraying her if I did. Or—" He stopped, shrugged.

"Or what?"

He made a violent gesture with his free arm. "Or he wants you. If you look good enough to suit him, he says, and you do, believe me . . . Anyway, I've already told him that's ridiculous." He sighed. "But so's the million, so I'm sort of stuck. In the end, he's going to send that letter to my wife."

"I don't really see the problem, Sam," she said quietly.

He looked up at her and sighed again. "Look, Selinde, I have to tell you this—regardless of what's happening between you and me, I really do love my wife, and I don't want my marriage to break up!"

"I know that, Sam," she acknowledged. "But it seems to me you have several paths open to you."

"Like what?"

"You could tell your wife what you're doing. Bring her here, or invite me to your home, let us meet. You would take away his power over you."

He shuddered. "Believe me, Selinde, I don't think that's a good idea. Cheryl has a quick temper, I don't know what she might do."

She smiled. "Cheryl—that's your wife?"

He cursed himself, he hadn't planned to mention her name. "Yes," he admitted.

"Well, if you think that would not work, then I can see two other paths open to you. You said one of the choices he gave you involved me?"

He laughed bitterly. "Yeah. He says you can save me. If he, as he put it, 'gets a turn with you.'"

"You mean sexually."

"Uh-huh."

"I could do that for you, Sam. If you think it would end the problem."

He stared at her in amazement, he hadn't expected a response like that. "No," he said with a bitter little laugh. "No, once you met him you'd back out. Your average sewer rat has about as much appeal."

"That doesn't matter. I wouldn't be having sex with him for my enjoyment."

He began shaking his head, little swings at first that rapidly became more vigorous. "No. No. I don't want you to do that. No. Just forget about it."

"But—"

"No!"

Smiling again, she pursed her lips. "Very well. What about the money?"

"Out of the question. He asked a million. But he just pulled that number out of a hat, he doesn't really want money. He knows damn well I don't have a million."

She nodded. "I could get you that much, Sam. Once again, if you believed it would end the problem."

He was even more amazed than before. "You have a million?" he asked weakly.

She laughed. "Not here! But I could get it, yes."

"I can't. There's no way I could pay you back." ·

"I'm not asking that."

Now he was gaping at her stupidly; she seemed perfectly serious. "Are you telling me you'd pay this guy a million, right out the window, just to get me off the hook?"

"Yes. That's what I'm saying."

"You're out of your mind!"

"No, I'm not."

"Jesus! I can't believe this!" He shook his head again, covered her hand with his, gave it a squeeze. "But I can't accept that any more than I can accept your screwing him. Don't get me wrong, I do appreciate the offers. But even if we did it wouldn't end it. He'd end up betraying us."

"Then you have only one path left, Sam."

"Yeah. Get the information, somehow."

"No. You said this would involve betraying a friend, you cannot do that. In the end, you will not do that."

She was probably right, he told himself. "What, then?"

"It's simple, Sam. Kill him."

There was quite a long silence then, a silence Sam finally broke with a nervous laugh. "Don't think I wouldn't like to," he told her, grinning idiotically. "But of course, that's—"

Her expression became almost severe. "I am quite serious, Sam."

"You can't be," he said after another long pause.

"I am. What does it matter?"

"I can't kill anybody! Jesus Christ!"

"Do you want me to help you? Or do it for you?" There was nothing, not the slightest thing, in her manner that suggested to Sam that she was not, as she'd said, perfectly serious.

"You'd do that, too?" he demanded, his voice shaking.

"Of course."

He tried to laugh, didn't quite succeed. "You know, you once asked me if I was scared of you and I said no. That might be changing!"

She looked genuinely puzzled. "Why?"

"Well, God damn, Selinde! You're sitting there as calm as can be, telling me I should commit a murder! You're even offering to help me do it! Now I won't say I haven't thought about it, but—"

"You take it too seriously. You—"

"Well, what's more serious? We're talking about a man's life, Selinde!"

"Whether this man lives or dies makes little difference in the long run," she said flatly. "For any man, the—"

"What happened to the woman who was crying in the street because somebody she didn't know had been hit by a truck?"

"That was quite different. And I told you then, Sam, I was not weeping because the man was dying. I wept because of the waste. I wept because he was suffering needlessly. Not because he was dying; people die every day. It'd be a disaster if they didn't."

He scowled at her. "Why?"

She laughed. "Because, Sam, people are born every day! If people didn't die, there'd be far too many people! And besides—"

Sam rolled his eyes. "Well, sure, but that's in the abstract. Besides, a lot of those people you're talking about are dying of old age—"

"It wasn't abstract for that man in the street, Sam. And people don't die of old age; they fade away, there's a difference."

"There is not! They're just as dead!"

"Perhaps. But they've passed away slowly, over years, falling apart, one piece at a time. When they finally do die, there isn't much of them left. That man in the street died all at once, over the span of a few minutes—that's dying. And people must die, Sam. It's the way things are—life comes only from death. In more ways than one."

His gaze moved from one of her eyes to the other. "You're very religious, aren't you? Life after death, all that?"

"Yes, Sam. I am very religious, in my own way."

" 'In your own way'? What does that mean?"

"It means that, since I've told you I'm from Mexico, you'll naturally assume I'm a Catholic."

"And you're not? What is your religion, then? Protestant?"

"No and no. But this is not the time to talk about my religion. We were—"

"Are you a satanist or something?"

She erupted with laughter. "No, Sam! I'm not a satanist! Let's leave this subject for the moment, shall we?"

"If you insist. . . ."

"I do. You have a problem, you need to solve it."

"Not by committing a murder."

"It doesn't seem as if you intend to let me help you."

"It isn't a matter of that."

Her manner was now a bit formal. "It seems to me it is."

He sighed. "Now you're angry with me."

"No. This is, after all, your problem. If you wish to solve it yourself, then that, of course, is your right."

He shook his head. "I just wish I knew how to solve it," he muttered, as much to himself as to her. He glanced up. "Short of murder, that is."

She shrugged. "I'm not sure I can see any other way for you."

"I think what I'm going to have to do is face the facts. Cheryl is going to get that letter, sooner or later. I've got to start thinking in terms of damage control, not prevention."

"That, Sam, was my first suggestion!"

"I don't think getting you and Cheryl together is going to prevent damage, I think it's going to create a catastrophe!"

Her expression indicated helplessness. "As I've said, Sam. All the choices are yours. You are free to do as you wish."

"Yeah," he growled. "There just aren't any good ones, that's the problem!"

"You came here to warn me about this Ken. If he should contact me, what would you have me do?"

"Nothing. If he shows up at your door, don't let him in. If he calls, don't talk to him. Anything you say can and will, I'm real damn sure, be held against me!"

"I'll do as you ask."

"Good."

Watching her eyes, he fell silent again. You're finished here, he told himself, you've said everything you came here to say. She's been warned about Ken, you can only trust her not to make matters any worse. You need to go now, get back to work. You're behind, and if you don't get to it you aren't going to have that data ready before it's time to leave for the Outer Banks.

But he didn't want to go. Not yet.

As if reading his mind—or perhaps his gaze, which was wandering downward—Selinde's smile became seductive. "The choices are yours, Sam," she whispered.

Twenty-Five

ART WAS HOLDING up a hand for silence. Stephanie, a little irritated —perhaps even more than a little—at being interrupted, stopped speaking. She'd already given him most of the details about Sam and Ken and the possible serial killer, but she wanted to express her concern that Sam could somehow get tangled up in the Alice Near murder. "Art," she plowed on, "I'm trying to explain that—"

"The court," he said, cutting her off, "as of this morning, appointed me to represent Bill Near in Alice's death."

"Huh?"

"That's right, he turned himself in. He wasn't trying to escape; he's been in Wake Memorial Hospital since his wife's death."

Stephanie said nothing for a few seconds. "So I take it you've talked to him?" she asked conversationally.

"Yeah. This afternoon. For quite a while."

"You said he was in the hospital. Why?"

"Stab wounds. He'll make it, but he's in bad shape."

"Who stabbed him? Alice?"

"Uh-huh."

"You know I did the autopsy on her. I told you about that already. It didn't make sense, she didn't—"

"I know. And you might be interested to know that Bill confirms your reports exactly. He says Alice didn't struggle. He says she let him do—everything he did."

She found herself very eager to talk about this, very eager to hear the minutest details. But externally she showed no signs of it, and she managed to cram those desires down before speaking again. "But why?" she asked. "It still doesn't make sense!"

"Yeah." He shook his head. "It's craziness, Stephanie—Bill's way out in the ozone somewhere, and I guess maybe Alice was too. Assuming you can trust anything he says."

"Like what?"

"I don't know all the details, not yet. Today about all he could say was, 'It wasn't a murder. It wasn't a murder. I was only doing what she wanted me to do, what she asked me to do.' I asked him how it happened that he got stabbed too, within an inch of his own life, and he told me he'd let her do that, just like she'd let him do her. I don't know. I tried to explain the legal definition of murder to him, but I don't think it got through. It may be a while before I find out anything more. Naturally I'm going to go for insanity; he's up for a psychiatric evaluation, and I've gotten everything else postponed until we get back from vacation."

Realizing that he wasn't going to go into the detail she wanted to hear unless she directly asked him—and being unwilling to do that—she consciously latched on to the mention of the vacation to distract herself, jumping to it mentally like a trapeze artist leaps to the next swing. "Oh, I am looking forward to that!" she exclaimed, her mood shifting rapidly. "I've had enough of all this, for a while, anyway!" She leaned forward, crossed her arms on the table, smiled. "When we get there I'm going to turn into a beach bunny. I'm going to put on a swimsuit when I get up in the morning and I'm not taking it off until I go to bed at night!"

Art laughed. "The swimsuit I can believe. But you, a beach bunny? Never happen!"

"Just because it never happened before is no reason for you to assume it can't, Counselor," she said with a grin.

Art rolled his eyes theatrically. "Dr. Stephanie Dixon, a beach bunny! Lord, wonders will never cease! If that happens I won't have anything left to hold on to, nothing I can be sure of. I might even start believing my clients' crazy stories. Like Bill Near's."

The mention of the name almost caused her to lose her grip on her mental swing, but she managed to hold on. Her eyebrows bounced. "Let's not get ridiculous!"

"Yeah, I guess you're right. Even Bill says he's crazy. Oh, right, I didn't tell you that part of it yet."

"What part?"

"He says he was having a thing with another woman. Says she drove him crazy."

Stephanie laughed. "A woman drove him crazy, huh?"

"Yeah. He even made up a crazy name for her."

"What was it?"

"Selinde. Selinde Lorona."

Twenty-Six

"I NEED SOME answers from you, Sam. I'm trying to be patient, but I need some answers I can believe." Ken looked petulant, looked disappointed.

"I'm doing the best I can, Ken," Sam replied. He turned to Ken's computer terminal, tapped a few keys, watched the screen change. "Fact is, I've already laid some groundwork to try to get you some of the information you want."

"I don't have time for that," Ken whined. "I'm behind in the game, Sam! There was another fit, right here—in Morrisville, I mean—and he nailed it! He called it for Raleigh, and—"

"Well, that isn't right," Sam pointed out logically. "It wasn't Raleigh, it was Morrisville. Maybe you can disallow it."

The programmer glared. "That isn't the way the game works, Sam."

"I don't know how it works," he said offhandedly. Nor do I really care, he added silently.

But Ken was off and running. "It's complicated," he said. "We make our calls for a specific hour of a specific day and for an exact location, geographical coordinates, seconds of longitude and latitude. Once one of us has entered a call for a certain day, the other can't enter for that day—unless he's calling a second murder. Then, after it happens, we enter the data and the computer does the scoring; you get points if you get the right state—that's easy now—more for the right county, more yet for the right city. The time prediction works the same way—you get points for getting the right month, more for the week, more for the day, a lot more if you can nail down the hour—neither one of us has done that yet, but you see what I'm saying. The computer scales the points statistically—you can make up to around a thousand on one call if you get it exactly. But, if there isn't a fit within thirty-five days, then you lose points. Even if you do get a fit, the computer subtracts error points—it does that statistically too—it decides how well your prediction fits the data and then deducts points for how far off you are in miles and in hours—you can lose a lot if the fit's real bad." He sighed. "So you want your call to be right. I'd figured Wake, Durham, or Orange County for this last one—I was trying to work down to which one, but he put in the call first. County correct, one day off. He picked up 62.7139 points on me. I was ahead, but only by a little over forty." Ken shook his head. "Right in my own backyard, too. I don't want to miss the next one, Sam. I won't be pleased."

If the situation weren't so serious—from Sam's viewpoint—he might have laughed. Especially at the absurd precision: 62.7139 points. A typical programmer's game—overly complex and, as he saw it, hardly fun. "You say you have money riding on this?"

"Uh-huh. A hundred dollars a point. I had to transfer the bucks to his account. Now he's getting the interest and I'm short."

Sam stared for a moment. The precision was no longer absurd —not once it had been translated from 62.7139 to $6,271.39. "Well," he said soothingly, "I'm doing everything I can to help you. Let me get back to work here, let's see what we can come up with." He pressed a few more keys, then used the mouse to size the resultant display.

Stalling, he told himself. That's all you're doing, and at the expense of getting your own data ready before you leave. Not that it matters much; with all these distractions there was no way you were going to accomplish that anyhow.

After giving the matter much thought over the past couple of days, he'd decided to take Selinde's initial advice—partially. He still had no intention of getting the two women together, but he was figuring that his best course lay in telling Cheryl about his indiscretion himself, and doing it right at the end of the vacation. He himself would have some emotional distance from the situation at that point, and Cheryl should—assuming all went well during the vacation trip itself, and there was no reason to expect otherwise—be in a good mood. He would not mention Ken. If the letter came later, he would feign shock. His intention was for Cheryl to believe that his confession stemmed from pure guilt, not that he was, like Rick, forced into it by exposure or an immediate threat of it.

He'd gone over this plan repeatedly in his mind; he'd been composing, mentally, his confession speech and the subsequent groveling he'd be expected to do. There were, as he saw it, two problems. One, Ken had to be kept at bay until after they were safely away on the vacation. Two, he'd be obligated to promise Cheryl that he wouldn't be seeing Selinde again.

Neither of these, he was discovering, was easy. Ken was impatient, he was pushing hard. Selinde lurked constantly at the edge of his mind, calling to him, and her calls were almost impossible to resist. At the moment, he had no answer for her—or rather for that part of himself who was finding it hard to accept the idea of never seeing her again.

"I don't know what good all this is going to do," Ken grumbled, staring at the screen. It now showed an enlargement of central North Carolina; a red dot was visible near Burlington, and there was a new one over Morrisville. "I've already run some distributional stats on it, and I can't get better predictability than forty percent. That's nowhere near good enough to make a call."

"No, it isn't," Sam agreed. "You'll pardon me for saying this,

Ken, but you aren't much of a statistician. With computers you're a whiz, but you haven't used tests that'll take full advantage of what you have. I can; I'm trying to apply some parameters now that'll get rid of some possible outliers and reduce the variance. That may give us a better handle on things."

"Why didn't you do this before?"

Sam threw him a cold stare. "Because I wasn't interested. Because it takes time, and I was trying to work on my own stuff, on the cholera epidemic. You've got my interest now, Ken."

Ken giggled obnoxiously. "Yeah, I guess I do, don't I, Sammy boy?"

"The only problem is," Sam said as he turned his attention back to the screen, "is that these things take time, as I said. I don't know if I have that much time, not before I have to leave for—"

"Your vacation, yeah, I know. Like I said, you can postpone."

"No, I can't. Cheryl would know something's very wrong. I might as well tell you to fuck off and let you send your goddamn letter."

"Now, you don't want to do that, Sammy boy. You'll be happy to know that I see your point. So, I have a solution for you."

With a loud sigh, Sam took his hands away from the keyboard and swiveled his chair around. "Now look," he began, "I am not going to use some half-assed excuse to cancel my—"

"Not what I had in mind. There's a phone where you're going, isn't there?"

"Yeah. Why?"

"I can lend you my laptop. You can take it with you, and you can link up with the system here by phone. You can go right on working."

"I don't think the system here will accept—"

"That's my problem. The system here will accept whatever I tell it to accept. All I need is the phone number where you'll be."

Sam immediately became suspicious. "Right," he snarled, "so you can call Cheryl and—"

"I can call her now, Sam. At work. Tonight, at home. Tomorrow. Whenever I choose."

"You'll pardon me if I say I like the idea of being free from you, of not having to worry about you, for two weeks. I don't want to give you that phone number. No, let me rephrase that. I am not going to give you that phone number."

Ken puckered his lips, looked unhappy. "Well, all right. I suppose I can rig the system here to answer your call whenever you dial it up and tie you right in."

"Why didn't you just do that in the first place?"

"Security, Sam. I'll have to give you access through the password. Right now there's no phone net access to this stuff at all, it's blocked off. That's so my buddy in California can't snoop into my files, get an edge on me. He's been trying."

"And I suppose you've been trying to get into his, too."

"Why, sure. But I haven't had any luck."

Sam gave him a disgusted look, but then shrugged. Ken and his hacker buddy going after each other was a lot more harmless than breaking into the NASA and IRS systems or building computer viruses to release on an unsuspecting public.

"So what I'll do," Ken went on, "is lock the password in so you can't see it, don't know what it is. You're gonna have to guard that laptop with your life if I do that, though. Anything happens to it and your ass is grass. Not just at home but around here, too."

Sam grinned at him. "What'd you say your buddy's name is?"

Unexpectedly, Ken went into a rage. "I didn't say! I didn't say!" he shouted, jumping up from his chair. "And don't try to make me think I did! I'm in control here, God damn it!" As abruptly as the rage had come over him, it subsided. He smiled darkly, his eyes mere slits. "You talked to your bimbo yet, Sam? You asked her if she'd be willing to get you out of this mess?"

He really is psychotic, Sam told himself, he really is. "No, I did not. And besides, knowing you, I don't figure that'd be the end of it, anyway."

"Well, it doesn't matter. You know what I expect from you, and you know what the cost'll be if you let me down. And just to be sure you don't let me down, I've figured out a way to give you a little more incentive."

That sounded ominous. "What have you been doing, Ken?"

He giggled again. "I've been doing some work with your datasets, Sam. It's so easy to do. It really is. I had the software already written. Your data fitted the paradigm perfectly."

"You still haven't told me what you did, Ken."

"Well. You remember what I told you about Cindy? About what I did to her data so she wouldn't want to even think about bringing any sort of charges against me?"

"Yeah, I do. You rigged it so it would look like it was faked if—" His eyes went wide. "Ken, you didn't!"

"I did. It's just so damn easy! You remember that stuff about

Mendel, the father of genetics? How they figured out recently that the deviations from the expected in his data were too close to exactly what you'd expect the deviations to be? That's where I got the idea. Of course, it isn't the kind of thing anybody'd notice. Unless their attention was called to it."

Sam stood up, his fists doubling up again. "You bastard," he said quietly. "You goddamn bastard. But this time it won't work, Ken. All you've cost me is time, and you might've cut your own throat, too. That stuff isn't published yet, I can go back over it and compare what's there with the original source data. And when I find it doesn't match, I'll have proof the you've been messing with the datasets around here. That'll get your ass fired, Ken! That'll make it damn hard for you to find another—"

"Oh, I didn't do it to the current stuff, the cholera. Like you say, you can just fix that. No, I did it with some of your archives, the stuff you've already published in the journals."

Sam was struck dumb. No, he said over and over. No, he couldn't have. It isn't possible. "It won't fly," he said weakly. "There're data samples published too, the means and standard deviations won't match—"

Ken laughed. "You think I'm an idiot? Your papers are on file too. I made sure that none of the adjustments affected anything you published. It makes you look like a fraud, Sam. A real clever fraud, but a fraud."

Sam could only stare, unable to doubt that Ken could've done exactly what he was saying, even less able to doubt that he would. The utter ruination of his career as a researcher loomed before him, along with the collapse of his marriage.

"So. Do we understand each other, Sam?" Ken asked.

"Yes," he managed weakly. "You've made things perfectly clear, Ken."

"Good. You'd best get back to work, then."

"Yeah. Yeah. Let me do that, let me see how much I can get done here." Feeling a little sick, he turned back to his terminal, began working with Ken's dataset again.

But his thoughts were elsewhere. Maybe Selinde was right, he told himself, maybe she was. He did not think of himself as a stupid man; surely he could plan things well enough that there'd be little risk to himself, even taking into account what he'd already told Stephanie.

But he felt he had to consider it, had to think about it very seriously. Any man can be a murderer, he thought. All you have to do is push him hard enough. It's in our instincts, in our genes. We're all capable of it.

———— Twenty-Seven ————

"Now THIS DON'T mean I don't want to talk to your source," Dave Brennan was saying. " 'Cause there's still some unsolved murders, and it'd be good if we could get some leads on some of them. But I'm pretty damn sure now, there ain't no serial killer."

Stephanie looked doubtful. "You're sure?" she asked.

"About as sure as I can be. I guess your husband told you we've caught up with Alice Near's husband?"

She couldn't restrain a laugh. "He told me Bill Near turned himself in, yes. If that's what you mean."

Dave looked a bit embarrassed. "Yeah, well, same thing. We have him, anyhow. And he's been trying to confess."

"I doubt if Art has permitted that."

"No. But he is the perp. We know that now."

"You believe that now," she corrected. "And you've believed it all along, as a matter of fact. He hasn't been convicted yet, has he? But. Even if that's so, it shouldn't convince you that there is no serial killer. All it says is that Alice Near wasn't one of his victims."

"No, it doesn't, not by itself. I been burnin' more midnight oil on this, Steph. Your source said there's a serial killer hunting down women, who for some reason don't resist when he's killing them. Am I right?"

"Yes, as far as—"

He didn't let her finish. "So, at first, all I'm looking at is cases where women are victims. I kinda broadened that picture, Steph. I started looking at some other cases, too."

"What, cases where there's signs of a struggle?"

"Uh-uh. Cases where the victims are men. You know what I found?"

"Of course I don't."

"What I found is that there's a bunch of those, too. Cases that fit the M.O., but the victim is a guy! Now, what does that say?"

She frowned. "Maybe a serial killer who believes in equal rights?"

"No. It don't work. Serials aren't like that, they don't go after men and women alike. They kill women or they're fags or fag-haters and they kill men. That's—"

"Or they're women and kill men. Remember the female serial killer in Florida."

"Yeah, but so far, she's the only one. And she only killed men. No, this isn't right, it doesn't fit. A lot of these dead men were found just like Alice Near. Naked, in their bedroom or something. In a few we had direct evidence that they'd just gotten laid; dried semen. Just like the women." He began his characteristic pacing. "And in a few, a wife or girlfriend has turned up later on, dead— suicide. Those have been closed."

Stephanie was frowning deeply. "Now wait a minute," she said. "This doesn't sound right, Dave! These aren't average murders, there's something—"

He stopped his pacing and turned to face her. "Yeah. It still bugs me. There's something, all right." His expression became quite serious. "It ain't no serial killer, but all these murders where the victim don't even try to stop it—I don't like it." He lowered his voice, clearly for dramatic effect. "You wanna know what I think? I figure maybe this is cult activity. That's what I'm figuring."

Stephanie sighed. "Your favorite bogey rises to the fore again. The satanic cult."

"It happens, Steph. I'm convinced of it."

"I'm not. Or rather, not that it happens in any organized way, not that there's a worldwide network of satanists like you seem to think there is."

"It's gotta be. There's too much evidence—"

"There's no evidence at all. Hearsay, innuendo, and a lot of ranting by some people who're obviously mentally ill. Like those people that were on the Geraldo Rivera show that time."

He shrugged. "I don't expect you to believe it. But I do. And I got a feeling there's something here, that there's some connection between these murders."

"Like a cult. Like they're all members of a cult."

"The killers, yeah. So you can maybe see why I wouldn't mind sitting down and having a talk with your source."

"I don't know what that would accomplish, Dave," she told him firmly. "All the source did was call your attention to a pattern. You've got more of a pattern now than the source knew about. I think you're headed off on a wild goose chase with this satanic cult business, but that's your affair. Go with it if you want to."

"So you won't give me a name."

"No. If I thought it would do any good I would, but I don't."

"Taking a lot on yourself, Steph."

"Maybe so."

He leaned on her desk, glared at her. "Wish I could convince you about this, about these cults. You don't know some of the things that've happened. There's been a lot of reports from places like Florida and California. Sacrifices—babies mostly, but some adults. Some of 'em, Steph, were willing. I heard about one, happened out in California, they talked some girl into letting them sacrifice her, they used this special knife—" He stopped, shook his head. "You don't want to hear the rest. You wouldn't believe it, you just wouldn't."

Unexpectedly, Stephanie found herself caught up in the story Dave had started. Visualizing the scene, she was staring at him, bright-eyed, seeing herself as the voluntary sacrifice he was talking about, taking pride in the mental strength and discipline that was allowing her to lie still and smile while she felt the white-hot pain of a knife being driven into her breast. There was both a delectable sense of absolute abandon and at the same time a sense of tremendous power, in that this was of her own choosing and that she was strong enough to choose it, that it was being done only with her express permission; her fear of her onrushing death only added to the excitement, transforming the whole experience into something magnificently soft, delicate, erotic. It was all she could do not to lick her lips, she wanted Dave to go on, she wanted to hear all the details. She almost lost control, almost asked him to continue, but her automatic control circuits engaged, just in time.

"You're right," she said coolly, giving him no signal whatever about what she'd been thinking. "I probably wouldn't."

He sighed, scratched his head. "Yeah. I'm sure. Like I said before, Steph, you're tough. Well, look. Gotta go. I ain't gonna catch no perps around here, I don't guess."

"Guess not," she agreed as he walked to the door. He hesitated there, throwing her a hangdog, disappointed look; she didn't respond, and he went on out.

As soon as he'd gone, she put her head down on her desk. If she closed her eyes, she saw very clearly the scene engraved on the kaleidoscope, and it was hard for her to expel it. "Jesus Christ, Stephanie," she muttered, speaking aloud. "What is wrong with you?"

Twenty-Eight

"YOU SHOULD HAVE talked to me sooner," Rick was saying, a touch of severity in his voice. "You really should have."

Morosely, Sam stared up at the TV set in the bar, the same bar where they'd previously met. MTV had been tuned in; Madonna gyrated inanely on stage. "Why?" he asked. "You always get caught. That's exactly what I don't want to happen." He sighed, swung his head back toward his friend, picked up his beer, and drank quite a bit at one pull. "I'm not really asking for advice, Rick. I just need to talk, okay? I just need to talk to somebody I can trust."

Rick, having now heard much of the story of Sam's affair with Selinde—not all, he hadn't been told Selinde's name, he hadn't heard the details, and he hadn't heard about the ax Ken Colburn was holding over Sam's head—could not restrain a rather self-satisfied smile. "I must say again," he almost cooed, "that it's curious that you were sitting in this very bar not long ago giving me hell about being unfair to Jennifer, and now—"

"I'm not an addict like you are!" Sam snapped back. "This is my first time, all right? First time, last time!"

"Sure, sure. I told myself that too, my first time. At least, old buddy, I have a reason!"

Sam felt his neck grow hot. Yes, he told himself, Rick has a right to snicker. But there's a difference between snickering and the sanctimonious smugness you're getting now. "I don't see," he shot back, "that you have any more reasons than—"

"My games, as you call them, Sam. Shall we say, my prediliction for algolagnia. I can't share that with Jennifer, I have to find other playmates. You have no such—"

"You don't know everything, Rick. Maybe you think you do, but you don't."

That stopped him cold. His beer mug suspended in midair, he stared at Sam. "Don't tell me," he said softly, echoing Sam's own words on another occasion. "Oh, don't tell me. You, Sam? You?"

Embarrassed, unwilling to meet his friend's eyes, he looked back at the TV. "It isn't the same. It isn't—it isn't S&M, it isn't like your games. This woman—well, she's Mexican. She has some games of her own. Games involving, uh, hot peppers. Jalapeños."

At first, Rick looked like he was strangling. Moments later, the laughter erupted, but by then he'd controlled it a little, he didn't draw undue attention to them. "Sam, my boy," he said patronizingly, "I doubt very seriously if the games Ann and I played with handcuffs and belts were anywhere near as—algolagnic, if I can coin a word—as games with jalapeño peppers would be, not if the picture I'm getting is right! Jesus! I've eaten those things, I know how they feel going in and how they feel coming out! I just can't imagine!"

"Yeah, well," Sam agreed, still staring at the TV, "we're talking about a burning desire, that's for sure. I imagine you're getting the right picture, Rick."

Rick started shaking his head. "Sam Sam Sam," he muttered. "Sam Sam Sam. I never would have believed it if I hadn't heard it with my own two ears. Never. All these years you've criticized me and my games, and now—"

"I have never criticized you," Sam argued. "Never. Your games were always played between consenting adults. My philosophy is, when both parties consent, anything goes. I have criticized you for being inconsiderate of Jennifer, and I sure as fuck am down on myself right now for doing the same thing to Cheryl!"

"Well, she hasn't caught you yet so you have no reason to be," Rick said carelessly. "Unless she catches you it doesn't affect her. Am I right?"

"Well, not really, it—"

"No, I am. You think about it. Are you ignoring her? Planning to leave her? No? Then it doesn't affect her."

"Would you say that if Jennifer was having an affair?"

"Yes, I would!" he nodded vigorously. "If our relationship is going on the same as ever and she wasn't planning to run off, if I didn't know about it and it wasn't eating at me, then I'd say it wasn't affecting me. I'd say it was none of my business."

"You lie. You would not."

"Would too."

"Would not."

Rick laughed again. "This isn't getting anywhere. The point is, you have some problems with this. That's what we should be talking about."

Sam sighed. "Yeah. I swear to God, Rick, I just don't seem to be able to say I'm not going to see her again. And mean it, that is. And besides that, all this stuff—"

"The games, you mean. You like them and that bothers you."

Sam hesitated noticeably. "Uh-huh. But it isn't—"

Rick leaned forward, rested his chin on his knuckles, his elbow on the table. "It is my opinion," he pontificated, not letting Sam finish, "as an educated medical man, that these—tendencies, shall we say—are latent in just about everyone. Those of us who confront them, who deal with them, are simply more aware of ourselves than most. As I see it, your new playmate has broken you out of a shell, given you more freedom than you had before."

"I don't feel like I was in a shell," he grumbled. "But anyway, it just—it isn't the same, it just isn't. The—uh, the things she does with jalapeños—well, it just seems to me that it's a far cry from the whips and chains." He paused and glanced around the room, making sure that no one else was listening in on their conversation. "First of all, it's a mutual thing, it's something we're sharing, not something one of us is doing to the other, neither one of us is tied down. And the point is, well, the point is not to uh, just, well, cause pain." He was aware, by now, that he was pretty much babbling, but he couldn't seem to stop himself. "There's more to it than that, it's—the peppers are, you know, stimulating—"

Rick laughed again. "The point of any erotic game," he pointed out, "is stimulation!"

"But it isn't the same!"

"Sam," Rick cut in, "just stop. You have an image, I'm sure, of me playing my games all dressed up in black leather, the girl tied down with chains—"

"Handcuffs. You told me handcuffs."

"Okay, handcuffs. I'm sure you see her with a red rubber ball in her mouth, a spike collar around her neck and C-clamps on her nipples. Now, there're some people who get a kick out of all that paraphernalia, but I'm not one of them. I'm not sure I wouldn't just go ahead and do it if a girl I was with wanted it, but I haven't run into one yet who did." He shook his head vigorously. "You take Ann, for example. No leathers, nothing like that. Just the cuffs. I'd slap her with a belt sometimes, but mostly I'd just talk to her."

"You told me that. You never did tell me what you'd say."

"Oh, sort of—threats. Fantasies, nothing more. She liked that, and she'd challenge me, she'd say, well do it, I'm not afraid. I liked it too, because—especially after the first time—she knew I was going to make all those threats but she couldn't know, not really, not deep down, that I might not just decide to carry one out and really hurt her. It was all up to me, you see? My choice. She was cuffed, she was helpless, there was nothing she could do to stop it. That's erotic, Sam. There's a—I don't know, tenderness to it. She thinks enough of you to let you hurt her, thinks enough of you to put herself in your power completely."

Sam could not deny that this last struck a familiar chord with him. "It's so damn one-sided, though. What—this woman I was talking about—and I do is—"

"Mutual. Sam, would it surprise you if I told you I let Ann cuff me, too? Let her beat the shit out of me with a belt?"

Sam could only stare for a moment. It wasn't surprising; considering Rick's personality, it was downright stunning. "You aren't serious," he managed at last.

"Yes, I am. I discovered the pleasures of that years ago, Sam; reversing the roles. Not every woman wants to; when you find one that will—like Ann—it's really great. A whole new dimension."

"That's not exactly a typical attitude for someone who's into these things. Not according to the literature. Most people who're into this kind of thing are strictly active or strictly passive."

"Are you?"

Sam started to argue again that what he was doing bore no relationship to Rick's games, but he decided that was futile; it wasn't a proposition he could defend and he knew it. "Well, no, but I've never done anything like this before—"

"Doesn't matter. I'm not either."

Sam twisted his mouth, paused a moment before speaking. "You said this was a new freedom. I'm just not sure it's a freedom I really wanted."

Rick laughed. "That's a strange statement from you, Sam. You, the quintessential free man, the great advocate of personal freedom, the hater of all rules and restrictions, even reasonable ones!"

"Well, yes—I do believe that, but—"

Rick waved off his objections with a casual gesture. "All freedoms are good, Sam. You already know that, really. If I may suggest—why don't you take some of these ideas home to your wife? You might offer her a new freedom, too."

"As I recall, I suggested you do that with Jennifer. You pooh-poohed the idea. What makes Cheryl different?"

His manner immediately changed, to dead serious. "Jennifer," he said carefully, "has some things in her background that—prohibit it. I don't want to get into that, I'd be betraying confidences. As far as I know, Cheryl doesn't have any such."

"I wouldn't know unless you tell me—"

"I can't. The point is—"

"The point is that you, being the all-seeing god, make all the decisions for Jennifer. You don't even talk to her about it, you just cut her off. Deny her this grand freedom you're spouting. She has no say-so in it at all. Pretty damn paternalistic, old buddy."

Rick looked confused. "No, I'm protecting—"

"So said generation after generation of men when they were holding their wives down."

"Shit! You sound like Cheryl! You caught something from her, some feminist disease!"

"No. But I can call hypocrisy when I see it."

Rick glared. "Strong words."

"Think about it."

"I will. What about you?"

Sam slumped back in his chair. "Ah, Jesus, Cheryl would never go for anything like that, Rick! She'd think I was crazy! Besides, you're right about the pepper, it's pretty strong—"

"Try something milder to start with. Then go from there."

"Like?"

"Shit, you have an imagination."

He nodded. "Yeah. Like you say, Rick. I'll think about it. Even if she went hog-wild over it, it wouldn't solve all my problems, though."

Rick looked at him closely. "Yeah. The girl herself. You're smitten, aren't you?"

"I guess so. It's really painful to think about not seeing her again. She's something else, Rick. Really unique."

"I wouldn't mind meeting her."

"You can forget that shit. I've got enough problems already!"

"Yeah, okay," Rick said, laughing. He looked down at the table. "Sam Leo, who would've believed it. How the mighty are fallen."

Embarrassed again—and wondering if it had been a good idea to pour out so much of himself to Rick—he looked back up at the TV set again. It was still tuned to MTV; the video of George Michael's song "Freedom" was playing. This one, he couldn't help but notice, was filled with erotic images—images which, it seemed to him, had very little to do with the lyrics.

And one of them—quite naturally, the one that caught Sam's attention—showed a young woman either piercing—or allowing someone else to pierce—her fingertip with a large needle of some sort.

He sighed. Sam, he told himself, someone is trying to send you a message.

Twenty-Nine

"AHA!" STEPHANIE SAID sharply. "I've caught you! Playing with that kaleidoscope again when you should be getting things together for the beach!"

At her first word, Art jumped. Turning to face her, he put the little tube down on the table—the place it stayed most of the time now. "I didn't hear you come in," he told her.

"I know. Seems like you never do when you've got that thing stuck on your eye."

"Tell me you don't play with it, Stephanie. Tell me that and I'll feel guilty."

An exaggeration, she told herself, he already feels guilty. Remembering Clarence the Cloud-Watcher, however, she decided it wouldn't be a good idea to push that. "No, I won't tell you that," she replied. "The damn thing is more addicting than a soap opera. I was almost late getting in this morning, again. Because I was playing with it."

He looked around, seemingly realizing for the first time that it was late, that the sky outside was darkening. "Damn!" he muttered. "I really did get into it again, the time has really slipped up on me!" He looked around himself and groaned. "And nothing has been done—not a damn thing—" He rambled on for a few seconds, castigating himself over a long list of household chores that needed attention.

For a while Stephanie just watched and listened. You could play your usual role now, she told herself. Get a slightly pissed look on your face and start doing things yourself, make him feel a little more guilty. That Art was susceptible to guilt was something she'd long known and had never hesitated to use; only since they'd had the kaleidoscope had she started getting some clues about where that susceptibility might be coming from, and knowing them made using it to get her way a little harder.

Besides, she told herself, that really isn't what you want to do right now, is it? You want to talk; you want to ask him what he sees in those carvings on the kaleidoscope tube, you want to talk about Alice Near's murder, you want to tell him about the ritual sacrifice Dave was talking about and the fantasy you had. You want to talk about it.

But she could not, she could not talk to him like that, she couldn't even ask him about the carvings, it seemed to her that the mere fact of asking would somehow give her away, even though she already knew that Cheryl and Jennifer had seen the same thing in them that she did. She did not trust him completely enough to risk exposing this side of herself—she did not trust anyone that much. This was too deep, too dark. Pathological, she was certain of that. Concerning its source she had no questions, but she didn't want to dwell on that right now, either.

But she had to do something. Do something or explode, right here and right now. "Fuck everything we have to do," she said offhandedly. "It'll wait."

He glanced up at her; his expression was first one of wide-eyed surprise, but that was followed by a frown. "What is with you lately?" he asked bluntly. "Has something happened, something I don't know about?"

She put on a startled look, tried to fend off a blush. "Happened? No. Why do you ask?"

"I dunno. You just seem—I don't know, different somehow. Looser. More—playful, maybe, is the best word."

She gave him a mock-angry look. "Are you implying that I'm normally a pedantic and boring workaholic?"

"Oh, no, I—"

"Well, if you were, you'd be right. I am normally a pedantic and boring workaholic. Maybe I'm just getting a little tired of it. Maybe I want to be a beach bunny for a while. I never have been a beach bunny, I think I might like to experience it. You have a problem with that?"

He turned his hands palm-up. "Not a bit."

"You sure? Remember, you married a pedantic and boring workaholic."

"In the hopes of curing her of her pedantism, her tendency to be boring, and most of all, her workaholism. Alas, I fear I have failed dreadfully." He glanced at the little kaleidoscope. "But something has succeeded. I'd say it was this thing, I'd say Jennifer was right—it's magic somehow. But that can't be. Because the first beach-bunny thing you did was to buy it."

She caught her lip with her teeth; her eyes widened, and she rolled them from side to side. "Oh, no, Art, it is magic! I looked in it and it cast a spell on me! I couldn't resist, I was helpless! And now we're cursed with it, cursed! It's from the Twilight Zone, Art!"

Joining in, he stared at it fixedly. "I think you're right," he breathed. "What was it you said Cheryl called it? The kaleidoscope from hell?"

"Yeah, but what does she know? It's from the Twilight Zone, I tell you!"

"I have to agree. I come in here in broad daylight and start looking through it and the next thing I know—twilight!"

Stephanie laughed. "And you always say Sam is quick with a comeback!"

"He is. But hey. I take a back seat to no man."

Her smile changed character. "Well—in some ways, I suppose it's possible that that's true!" Or at least it used to be true, she reminded herself. Her chain of thoughts began to threaten her somewhat lighthearted mood; without effort, she pushed them away.

His mouth dropped open in feigned amazement. "You know all men? You've never told me that! You must've been a busy girl before I met you!"

"Busy enough."

"I'll bet! Some day you ought to tell me all the gory details!"

"You've heard enough gory details. You've heard about Meyer, you've heard about Tim—"

He pointed a mock-accusing finger. "I haven't heard about Sam!"

"Well, I don't know about Sam. Maybe one day I'll find out. No, I can't do that. Cheryl'd kill me for sure."

"She might have to stand in line!"

"You'd kill me, Art? If I had an affair?"

"You'd better believe it! I'd want to yell at you for a while first, though. Make you apologize. I figure all that would take, oh, maybe eighty or ninety years. Then, I'd kill you!"

She laughed again. "A patient man."

"You bet."

"You'd better think about what you say. Someday you might have to back up those words or eat them. Remember, you were the one who just said I was turning into a wild woman."

"I don't think I used exactly those terms."

"Close enough."

"Well, I suppose I'll just have to keep you busy enough around here that you don't have the time to go wandering off."

"That's one solution. Probably a pretty good one. But you can't waste time."

"What, you're feeling a wanderlust right now?"

"Maybe. You never can tell what wild women are going to do or when they're going to do it."

Art's grin was all over his face; Stephanie was smiling back, waiting for him to make a move, to respond to the rather direct suggestion she'd made. Inside, though, she was again wondering about herself. After a long hiatus, they'd made love twice in the days since she'd brought the kaleidoscope home; both times it had been unsatisfying for her, the usual problems remained unresolved. The rational thing, she was telling herself, was to initiate an open discussion about those problems.

But that was not what she was doing. Instead, for the third time, she was teasing him into making an advance, something she hadn't done even back when their sex life had been good—her usual mode then had been a direct "Would you like to make love?"

As always she was quick with rationalizations. The first time was to console Art; the second time was to deflect him from matters she did not want discussed. This time it was merely because she was feeling playful, an uncommon mood for her. She was enjoying it; there wasn't a point in stifling it. To judge from the expression on Art's face, he was enjoying it too.

He reached for her, tugged at her hand gently; she responded, stood up. After pulling her over until she was standing in front of him, he reached down with both hands, touching her knees; then he started caressing her thighs, pushing her skirt up with his fore-arms. His touch was light, delicate, pleasurable.

He nudged her skirt on up just a bit higher. Hooking his fingers into the waistband of her pantyhose, he started pulling them down. Passively, she watched and waited as he took his time roll-ing them down her legs, all the way down to her ankles. One at a time, she stepped out of her shoes and allowed him to slip the hose over each foot. When the pantyhose were gone he started back up her legs, massaging them and caressing them, still taking his time, his touch very sensual. He did not stop until he was near her waist again, but he was limiting his stroking to the fronts and outsides of her legs, staying away—for the moment—from her inner thighs.

Finally—without ever having allowed his hands to wander to those more sensitive areas—he let her skirt fall, and moved his hands to her blouse, undoing the buttons one by one. The snap on her bra was in front; taking care not to open her shirt too much, he reached inside and unhooked it, allowing it to fall open. Then he extracted the sides through her sleeves, still taking his time, maneuvering it carefully to get it off without first removing her blouse.

"Now what, sir?" she asked, putting her hands on her hips and pushing her elbows back to spread the gap in her blouse a little.

"Now you sit down here," he told her, gesturing toward his lap. "Now you kiss me."

"Very well, sir." Matching an action to her words, she lowered herself onto his legs, put her arms around his neck, and pressed her mouth to his. As they kissed his hand sidled inside her open blouse, cupped her breast; his fingers teased the nipple. Very gently, as always. She felt a familiar sharp tingling spreading from it, felt it stiffen under his touch. Against her thighs, he, too, began to stiffen. It was not long until one of his hands slipped in between her knees and snaked along the inside of her thigh until it could go no further. There his fingers encountered the warm dampness she already knew was there, and she began to moan, very softly.

Gradually, over the space of the next ten minutes or so, her skirt and blouse ended up on the floor, in a pile with his clothes. Just as they'd done a few nights earlier, she straddled his legs and impaled herself on his erection, letting herself down slowly, enjoying its slow push up into her. He began moving his hips from side to side while his hands assisted her in moving up and down. His head was resting against her shoulder; his hands moved between her waist and her breasts, and they moved smoothly, rhythmically, pleasantly.

Abruptly, though, her mood started to fade. The verbal teasing preceding their lovemaking had been, for them, something new and different; the foreplay had been longer than normal and hardly unpleasant. But now things were already beginning to settle into the same old molds, the patterns she knew so well and had tired of so thoroughly. From here, it was quite predictable. Art would climax and she might; they'd remain together for a while in silence, after which they'd get up and clean up.

As before, she felt an initial flash of anger at Art for all this; and yet she was not unaware that this style of lovemaking had been her choice from the beginning. She'd communicated her desires in a thousand little ways, and he, eager to please her, had been sensitive enough to pick up on them.

As for his desires—his real desires—she realized that she had no clue. She'd guided their behavior in every area; foreplay, intercourse, oral sex. All her way. Part of her dissatisfaction, almost paradoxically, arose from his reluctance to express any of his own desires, verbally or physically.

No, she told herself firmly. No. You made this bed, and you've gotten very tired of lying in it; you can either get up and leave it or you can change it. Starting right now.

Without any further thought, she dipped her head down to the side of his neck, opened her mouth, and bit down. Rather hard.

"Ow!" he cried, jerking away. He stopped moving. "What are you doing?"

"Being a wild woman," she told him with a sleepy-eyed smile. "Wild women do things like that!"

"Yeah?"

She dug her fingernails into his back a little. "Yeah. All kinds of strange things. You never know what a wild woman is going to do!"

He looked confused. "I have never in my life known you to do anything like that," he said. "Or even talk like this, for that matter."

"Things change."

"I guess so. It's a funny coincidence, though."

"How's that?"

"Before you came home. I was sitting here looking at—I mean, through—the kaleidoscope, and I was fantasizing about making love to you this evening. In my fantasies I was doing some things we've never done before."

She lifted her eyebrows. "Yeah? Like what?"

"Like—"

"Don't tell me! Show me!"

The confusion left his face. "All right," he said. Then his head went down to her chest, and he began nibbling at her breast. She twisted her lip a little. Big deal, Art, she said silently. You have done that before. She looked down at him; he was currently biting around the edge of her nipple. Very lightly. Just the slightest pinching sensation.

As if throwing off another piece of her clothing, she tossed aside a few more of her reservations. "Is that the best you can do?" she demanded challengingly. "I did better than that, didn't I?"

Startled, he looked up at her for an instant. Then his head went back down and he started biting her breasts again—harder. A good deal harder.

"Yeah," she whispered, beginning to move her hips again. "Yeah, that's a lot better!" She dug her fingernails into his back a little more; he kept biting her breasts for a while, then contorted himself so he could reach her sides and bite them too.

This was good, she told herself. This was good. His biting was hard enough to hurt a little, but it was driving her, higher and higher. She turned her head and bit his bicep, hoping it was having the same effect on him.

It surely seemed to; he groaned, bit her harder yet. Then, finally, his teeth caught hold of one of her nipples. She'd been waiting for that, wondering when he'd do it, what he'd do now. Always before, she'd complained if he was even slightly rough with them—she'd always believed that was something she should do—and now she wondered if he'd recognize that this, too, had changed, or if she'd have to tell him. Wrapping her hand around the back of his head, she pulled him hard against her breast, hoping he'd get the message.

He did, though he obviously wasn't sure. He bit down, hard but not nearly so hard as the bites he'd been administering to the outside of her breasts. She cried out softly, pulled his head harder. He bit down even more firmly, and she began moaning loudly. His teeth were now causing her real pain, but, just as it had been in her fantasy, she was able to control it, accept it, transform it. It was driving her toward an erotic plateau she hadn't reached in a very long time. She found herself wishing he'd bite down harder yet, that he'd draw blood.

Suddenly becoming a little frightened by herself, becoming afraid of going too far, she eased up her pressure on his head. He got the message; he let go, leaned back in his chair, looked up at her. He was breathing very heavily, he was making deep grunting sounds. Art never did that. Not the Art she knew.

But she discovered she loved it, she wanted to make him grunt louder. Bouncing on him almost violently and forgetting her fears, she took her hands off his back; taking each of his nipples between a thumb and forefinger, she pinched hard. It clearly drove him onward, and he pinched hers in turn—not quite as hard, but hard enough. At the same time, his movements became even more violent than hers.

"Ah, my God!" he cried. He grabbed her, crushed her torso to his, and she felt him jerking inside her, felt the hotness of his orgasm. Her own came roaring up, enveloping her; she cried out too, clutching wildly at him while her body quivered and trembled.

Then it was over. With a long sigh she laid her head down on his shoulder. On her face was a smile of utter satisfaction. Ah, so much better, she thought. It is repairable, after all. All is not lost.

That didn't last, though. After a few seconds she realized his body was so stiff he might've been in rigor mortis. She raised her head, looked at his face.

He looked downright scared. His eyes wide, he stared at her.

"Are you okay?" she asked.

"Yeah. Fine. Question is, are you?"

He thinks he's hurt me, she told herself. He's afraid I'm going to be mad. He's very far from right. Still smiling, she stretched her arms up over her head and intertwined her hands. "I am more than all right," she answered. "I am, right now, wonderful!"

He touched her nipple, the one he'd bitten, gingerly. "Sure?"

"Oh, yes!" She looked down at it; it was distinctly reddened, as were several other spots on her body. "I'm a little sore, but I sure am all right!"

"That was—that was—"

"Fantastic is the word that comes to mind immediately."

He started to relax. "Uh—yeah—it was, wasn't it?"

She put her hands on his cheeks. "You like me as a wild woman?" she asked.

He hesitated for a few seconds. "After due consideration, I'd have to say, yes, I do. I liked you the other way too, but this—this is something else! I don't know when I've had an orgasm like that!"

"Well, I never have," she declared. "And if this is what you get for being a wild woman—then I, by God, like it!"

Thirty

THE HIGHWAY UP ahead was shimmering in the August heat, waves rising from it and from the cars on it. Comfortable in the air-conditioning of a rented four-wheel-drive Jeep, Sam watched a semitruck in front of him as it appeared to rise right up into the air between two steeply cut cliffs and then, starting from its wheels, vanish. He smiled. He'd seen this effect before, out here on Highway 64 in midsummer. The mirages created by the superheated pavement made it appear, in certain places and at certain times, as if the road weren't there. There were no cliffs and the truck had not vanished; it had merely passed over a small rise.

He glanced over at Cheryl, who was at the moment paying no attention; she was leaning back in her seat, her eyes closed, listening to the music emanating from the Jeep's stereo. She was dressed in her usual tiny shorts, her hands folded in her lap, one leg extended and the other propped up near the center console. He resisted the urge to reach over and touch her knee. If he did, she might well open her eyes and initiate conversation, and right now he wanted to think.

As far as Ken was concerned, Friday had gone smoothly; the programmer had, as promised, given him the laptop, and it was now riding in the back of the Jeep with the rest of their luggage. Ken still wasn't to be trusted, but he had no reason to precipitate things before they got back, especially if he was getting some of his analyses back over the phone—and Sam had every intention of satisfying him in that respect.

Selinde, however, was another matter.

In spite of his intentions, he'd spent his lunch hour—and more —Friday at her apartment, making love with her, playing pepper games with her, for what he kept telling himself was the last time. On the road back, he insisted; that's when he'd tell Cheryl about her. And after that, he couldn't see her again. Just as Rick had had to give up Ann, he would have to give up Selinde.

She had, he was sure, sensed his intentions—she'd sensed something when he told her he'd be gone for two weeks, that he'd be down on the Outer Banks on vacation. She'd asked where he was going, and he'd told her; afterward he'd entertained some vague suspicions about the purpose of that question, but he'd dismissed them. Selinde knew his name and Cheryl's, and he was listed quite plainly in the Raleigh telephone directory. If Selinde wanted to call Cheryl and cause trouble, she didn't have to wait until he was down in Corolla to do it.

He glanced over at Cheryl; her eyes were still closed, her face relaxed. He found himself wondering if she suspected anything. She had not yet asked him directly where he'd been that Saturday night when she'd gone to see Stephanie and Jennifer. There were certain things she had noticed, however; she'd commented repeatedly on his newfound fascination with hot pepper, and she kept remarking that his eyes looked "funky." There was a pattern to this last, a pattern he'd worked out: his eyes looked "funky" when he'd been with Selinde. What, he wondered, was she actually seeing? Shiftiness, evasiveness? Guilt?

Pushing the guilt he without question was feeling away, he ran over in his mind the discussion he'd had with Rick, specifically the recommendation that he involve Cheryl in the pepper games or in something similar but milder. She would never, he was certain, go for it. If he begged? No. Most likely she'd recommend that he get professional help. His mind drifting, the road unrolling monotonously before his eyes, his thoughts wandered back to the things they'd said to each other early in their relationship, all the little clichés: I'd do anything for you, I couldn't live without you, I'd die for you. What, would I suffer some minor pain just because it gives you pleasure? Forget it, you're crazy!

There's a sequence involved in giving yourself to another person, he told himself. First, you trust each other enough to be alone together. Then a touch, a holding of hands, a hug, perhaps. Personal barriers are broken, permission for violations of personal space are given. Overtly erotic touches come next, and more surrenders follow quickly; the woman opens her vagina, her mouth, maybe her anus; the man risks extending himself into the spaces she offers. And there, except perhaps for the many mutual sacrifices involved in the bearing and raising of children, it ends.

But there's more, he told himself, there's more; Selinde had shown him that graphically, and he understood, instinctively. There was pain to be offered, there was blood—and there was more, too. He could see that clearly, very clearly.

Feeling that his fantasies were going off wildly in a dangerous and disturbing direction, he pulled his thoughts up short, forcing himself to be rational. All you were considering, he told himself, were some harmless games—like Selinde's, like Rick's. Maybe even milder and more harmless.

It makes no difference, he snarled mentally. No matter how minor, no matter how harmless, she wouldn't be interested, she'd be appalled at the idea. Besides, your sex life is hardly bad—hardly in the state of collapse that, if you've read correctly the hints Art has dropped, his and Stephanie's is in. True, she's not approached you sexually—nor you her—since the night we made up, but that in itself was not really unusual, not these days.

He sighed softly, stared blankly at the road. There had been a time, early in their relationship, when a missed day—indeed, when a missed opportunity—would have been most unusual, but that had faded with the years, yielding to the pressures of jobs and problems and even such mundane matters as housekeeping. It was just that . . .

His mouth twisted as he recognized his own rationalizations. No, he told himself, no. Those were just excuses—they'd always had jobs, problems. The real reason was the familiarity, the sameness. No matter how attractive the person, no matter how sensual her touch, at least the intensity of the interest was sure to fade if things became patterned and mechanical, if there was no element of surprise or discovery, no dangers, no risks. Maybe that was why Rick kept having affairs; it certainly involved risks, if nothing else. Hadn't Rick said, several times, that he and Jennifer underwent a renewal of sorts during the reconciliation phase of his affair cycle? Glancing at Cheryl again, he wondered if that was to be the case for them—and that thought led him again to fantasies of playing those minor and harmless—trivial, really—games with her. Yes, he told himself, she'd be outraged at first, but maybe—if your timing was good, if you could find the right words—maybe if you approach her with the idea before you tell her about Selinde—

Mercifully—at least it seemed so to him—his almost obsessive chain of thought was cut off by the traffic, which had come to a near-halt up ahead. It was at least ten minutes before he was able to see the cause; as he'd suspected, it was an accident. The police and several emergency vehicles, including a pair of ambulances, were already on the scene. On the shoulder, so mangled it was hardly recognizable, sat one of the vehicles involved. As he approached it, he started thinking about the quite different accident that day on Hillsborough Street, the day he'd first met Selinde.

He could not help but notice that there was one striking similarity between that accident and this one. That day, a large crowd had gathered to watch the luckless pedestrian die; today, the traffic had slowed to a crawl not because the accident and the emergency vehicles presented any obstruction, but merely because the passing drivers wanted to look.

We all find it fascinating, Sam told himself sourly. We may deny it, we may shudder and avert our eyes—but not until after we've seen. We do not slow down our lives for the beauty of a sunset or the scent of a rose, but these red flowers will always command our attention.

Thirty-One

SEVERAL HOURS LATER, Sam found himself guiding the Jeep onto the bridge spanning the Alligator River—which at this point was so wide the far bank was hard to see. Crossings like this one always made him a little nervous; this two-lane bridge was long, and low, close to the water. Far up ahead he could see the small drawbridge section in the center of it, and he knew that beyond that was another span as long as this first one—and more, a few miles on down the road was another bridge, just as long and low, that led to Roanoke Island. It always seemed to him as he drove

onto a bridge of this sort that he was making some sort of commit-
ment, that somehow his life would not be quite the same until he
crossed back. Beyond that, he felt the crossing itself was fraught
with dangers.

He glanced down at his speedometer. Just above sixty-five; a bit
more than ten miles over the speed limit. He backed off a little
and smiled, remembering last year. He'd met a highway patrolman
coming the opposite way. He'd been speeding, but the officer had
had no way of turning his cruiser around to give chase, and had
been forced to content himself with merely pointing ominously at
Sam as they passed. Perhaps the patrolman had turned back, at
the other end of the bridge; maybe at the little store there that
proclaimed LAST CHANCE TO BUY GAS WITHOUT PAYING BEACH PRICES.
Sam didn't know. He hadn't seen the patrolman again, and he
hadn't gotten a speeding ticket. Not that time, anyway.

As he came to the end of the second bridge he breathed a sigh
of relief. There was another bridge to come, the one that would
allow them to cross the Roanoke Sound to Bodie Island, to the
Outer Banks proper. It, too, was low and narrow, but it was not
long. Much more relaxed, he cruised on through the deliberately
picturesque town of Manteo, across the remaining bridge, and into
Nag's Head.

In many places, the Outer Banks are so narrow that from buildings or high dunes the Sound and the Atlantic Ocean are both
visible; the highway runs almost due north, right up the middle of
this strip of sand. As Sam knew, this was fundamentally a giant
sandbar whose nature was to creep inward toward the mainland
or, under other conditions, outward toward the ocean. Currently
its movement was inward, which was noticed by residents and visitors mainly as a loss of beach. Much effort and many dollars were
spent trying to keep the recalcitrant sand in one place.

Here, virtually every available space was developed. Motels and
seafood restaurants abounded, fighting for room with souvenir
shops and stores oriented to the fisherman. They soon reached
their first major landmark—Jockey's Ridge, an enormous sand
dune whose native wildlife was now limited to hang-gliding enthu-
siasts. Occasionally Sam had read in the papers that there was
concern about the future of Jockey's Ridge, since natural forces
plus the stress of many feet were conspiring to tear it down, inch
by inch. As they passed it, he wondered why it mattered. It was
just a hang-gliding theme park now, not a natural feature of the
beach.

Without so much as a mile of open space, without any noticeable change in their surroundings, they entered the next intriguingly named town, Kill Devil Hills. The monotony continued as they passed the Wright Brothers Memorial, left Kill Devil Hills, and entered Kitty Hawk—which passed immediately into another town called Southern Shores. The one that followed that was called Duck; after they'd passed through it, the development, except for a few isolated enclaves of houses and condos, abruptly vanished, replaced by open dunes, small stands of trees, and numerous signs warning visitors about the herds of wild horses that still lived here. Continuing up the same road for another ten miles or so brought them to the town of Corolla, so small as to be almost nonexistent, which would be their formal address for the next couple of weeks. Here the road ended; here the four-wheel drive capabilities of the Jeep would be needed.

After passing the ancient-looking Corolla lighthouse—and the two strips of stores, one old and one new, that constituted Corolla's "business district," they found themselves at the beginning of what could only be called a road by extending the definition of that word considerably. A mix of loose and hard-pack sand, it twisted on northward through yaupon groves and salt marshes, weaving its way past sea-oat-covered dunes and stands of pines. Stopping the Jeep, Sam got out and lowered the pressure on all four tires to give the vehicle some additional flotation, then climbed back in and shifted into four-wheel drive. Driving slowly, they began bouncing their way down the trail, slowing even more whenever he encountered a deep and usually water-filled rut or a section of soft sand.

After they'd put a little over a mile of this road between themselves and Corolla, they came to another, very similar, road that veered off to their left. Forcing the Jeep into a sharp turn, Sam guided it down this road for perhaps two hundred yards before being forced to stop in front of a gate bearing a sign: PRIVATE—NO ADMITTANCE. There was a graded-out area to permit a vehicle that might stray that far to turn around, but the gate itself was fastened with a heavy padlock.

Sam didn't use the turnaround. Instead, he got out of the Jeep and took a key from his pocket, which he then used to remove the padlock. After he'd opened the gate, Cheryl, who had slid behind the wheel of the Jeep, drove it through. Sam relocked it, then climbed back into the Jeep.

The road proceeded on through stands of pine trees for a few hundred yards before turning sharply to the right; only after this turn had been made were they able to see the house up ahead. "Well, here we are," Sam said unnecessarily as he pulled the Jeep up alongside the two other vehicles that were already parked there, an Isuzu Trooper and a Chevrolet pickup. The Isuzu belonged to Rick and Jennifer; the Chevy Sam hadn't seen before, but a placard on the door indicated its owner as CURRITUCK BEACH ASSOCIATES—the company that looked after the house when its owners were not present, and the company that would provide maid service for them during the time they were here. For a few minutes Sam and Cheryl sat gazing at this charming old house, remembering the many pleasant vacations they'd spent in it.

It was two-story, gray clapboard, gambrel-roofed, with the almost obligatory widow's walk atop it and a long narrow balcony off the second story facing the ocean side, fronted by pine forests that served to protect it from the full force of the storms that often swept in off the Atlantic. Studying the rear of the house, Sam cocked his head to one side and frowned.

"It looks different than it did last time," he commented.

"Sure does," Cheryl agreed. She pointed to a finger of water reaching in from the west, from Currituck Sound. "You remember? Jennifer said that the land contour had changed. That inlet wasn't there last year; there were dunes there."

Sam examined it briefly and nodded. "You're right. The Sound itself is well on over, beyond that salt marsh. That water wasn't there at all."

"It looks nice. No salt marsh, just sand. A private swimming pool, maybe?"

"It probably isn't as nice as it looks. I imagine it's really shallow. Next year it'll be a salt marsh for sure."

"Don't be so negative. Maybe it's ten feet deep."

"Wishful thinking. But it's easy enough to find out."

"No, Sam. We're not running down there right now, there's plenty of time for that." She gestured toward the house, toward the cars parked nearby. "Rick and Jenny are already here; we're going to go in first, we're going to unpack our things first."

"You are a cruel taskmaster, Cheryl. You going to put on your black leather, get out your whip?"

She arched an eyebrow. "If necessary."

He opened the car door. "Not necessary. I'm going, I'm going."

"Good," she said. "I'm glad I don't need them. They're packed at the bottom of our bag."

He grinned. "Funny. They're always at the bottom of the bag. Funny how I've never seen them in all these years."

She arched her eyebrow higher. "You never know when you might, Sam."

Thirty-Two

"Now let me make sure I've got your names straight," Sam said. He pointed to one of the two teenagers sitting across the table from him, a small girl with dark hair and a broad face covered with fine freckles. "You're Fran, right?"

She shook her head and laughed. "Wrong. Take another guess, Dr. Leo!"

He looked crestfallen. "Maybe I can get it on the second try. You're Traci."

"Right. Traci Melrose. She's Fran Retton." As she spoke she nodded toward the brown-haired, heavily sun-bronzed—and strikingly attractive—girl sitting on her right.

"And you're going to come twice a week, Mondays and Thursdays, at—what'd you say? Around ten?"

"She said around nine, Sam," Cheryl corrected.

"Oh. Okay."

"That's right," Traci agreed. "And we'll be here—well, as long as it takes, but I expect about four hours or so. If you folks need anything extra, just let us know."

"We will certainly do that," Rick said. He was leaning across the table and staring at Fran, whose eyes were large and mahagony-brown. "You can count on it!" He jumped; quite obviously, Jennifer had kicked him under the table. Sam didn't even try to repress his smile, and neither did Cheryl.

"We have two more coming," Rick said, his own grin more than a little sheepish. "You two might want to wait around until they get here, if you have the time . . ."

"No, we have to go," Fran told him. "We have several other

places out here we have to look after, as well. I tell you, Dr. Mason, George just works us to death!"

"You tell George to take it easy on you," Rick instructed. "Tell him I said so."

"Oh, George isn't so bad," Traci put in, grinning at the other girl. "You can see that Fran's had time to get one truly bad tan this summer!"

"Hey, I had to work for this!" Fran rejoined. "Every spare minute!"

"Hard work, lying out there on that beach. Backbreaking."

Fran poked her lower lip out at her friend. "You're just jealous, Traci! Just because you're all pale and washed-out looking, that's all!"

"I," Traci said with an exaggerated formality, "am not pale. I do not want to get skin cancer. And I don't want to look like an old lady when I'm thirty, either!"

"That's twelve years away for both of us," Fran shot back. "Why worry about it?"

Traci looked back at Sam and Rick, appealed to them. "You're doctors," she said. "Tell her I'm right!"

"She's right, Fran," Rick said sagely. Sam nodded.

Fran's gaze went from one to the other. "Well," she said after a moment, "Okay. Maybe I'll cool it a little next season."

"That'd probably be a good idea," Rick advised. Again, Sam merely nodded.

Traci stood up. She was right, Sam noted; her arms and legs were not nearly as dark as Fran's, but they were hardly pale. Her skin, he thought, was quite different from the other girl's; her limbs had freckled instead of tanning evenly. It was possible that, in truth, she'd gotten almost as much sun this season as her friend.

But Sam didn't say anything about it, and the two girls took their leave, strolling out to the Chevy truck and climbing in. Rick watched them through the kitchen window until the engine started.

"Rick, I can't believe you!" Jennifer said, her tone only half serious. "Coming on to that young girl like that, with me and Cheryl and Sam sitting right here!"

"I was not!" he protested. "I was just being friendly!"

"And besides," Sam put in, "that Fran sure does have gorgeous eyes!"

Rick glared. "You are not being helpful, old buddy. Not a bit."

"Oh, come on, Rick," Cheryl told him. "We all know you, we all know you're an addict. We—"

"Those days are past," he said solemnly. "I've sworn off."

"I hope so," Jennifer commented.

Sam watched her face for a moment, wondering if Rick's last indiscretion, only about two weeks old, was perhaps still too fresh for her to enjoy the banter. She was smiling, her features were relaxed, but she could well be concealing her true feelings.

He decided to change the subject. "So, Paul isn't going to be here this year, eh?" he asked.

There was nothing like a mention of Paul to swerve Jennifer's attention away from whatever else she might have been talking about. "No, he's not," she lamented. "He's up in Norfolk with my parents, he's going to spend this time with them. Mom really wanted him to stay, and he—well, he was torn. He wanted to stay with them but he wanted to come here, too. We wanted him here —I really don't know what I'm going to do, two weeks without seeing him!—but Mom, well, her health is not good, Sam. We really don't know how much longer she's going to be with us."

"Has she had more strokes?"

"No, not since I talked to you last about it, but she's had five now, two of them pretty bad, and her cholesterol's sky-high in spite of everything we've tried to do. And Dad's not in great shape either. He has arthritis, you know, and he had that bout with prostate cancer a couple of years ago. Plus, he worries about Mom all the time, fusses over her, won't let her do anything."

"You sure they can handle Paul all right?" Cheryl asked. "He's a pretty active boy."

She laughed. "He is that, for sure! But I think they'll do fine. Paul's just crazy about them, he minds them a lot better than he does me or Rick."

"Well, I'm sorry to hear they're not doing any better," Sam said. "They're not really all that old . . ."

"No, they aren't. Mom's just sixty-six, and Dad's sixty-eight. They were in great shape until they passed sixty. Then it seemed like they both started falling apart at the same time. Especially after Dad retired."

"Not a nice prospect for the future," Rick mused. "For us, thirty-some years and there we are, too."

"Well, genetics has a lot to do with it," Sam blurted mindlessly. Almost immediately, he wished he could've snatched those words back from the air. Jennifer looked stricken, Cheryl glared.

"So does condition, diet, and a thousand other factors," Rick smoothed gracefully. "But anyway, getting back to Paul. I wish he was here, too. I just have a feeling about this vacation; I think it's going to be the best one yet!"

"It's certainly one of the most needed ones yet," Sam offered.

"What, problems with epidemics, Sam?" Rick asked. "Or more likely, problems with the politics of the Center and the granting agencies?"

He sighed. "Neither one. Problems with Ken Colburn. It'll take a while to fill you in. But now's as good a time as any." He took a deep breath and began telling the story; Ken's "game," the peculiarities of the statistics, his call to Stephanie, Ken's subsequent threats. He told them about Ken's tampering with his data and the menace to his professional reputation; naturally, he did not mention Selinde or the letter to Cheryl.

"It does sound like you got some problems, Sam," Rick agreed. "You can't come up with the original data on those old studies?"

"I doubt it. Most of it was paper reports; a lot of them were probably destroyed after the stuff was archived on the system, and those archives are what Ken's rigged. But if it comes down to it, I'll have to try to get what I can. It's the only defense I have."

"Now, you say he wants you to—"

"Push Stephanie into pumping Dave for details of these killings, the kind of details they withhold so they can check on confessions and things like that. You know I can't ask her to do that. I don't even know if she could."

"You considered just feeding him a pile of bullshit? Details you make up? How's he gonna know?"

Sam considered this for a moment; that idea had not occurred to him. "Well, it wouldn't help his predictions any—in fact, it would probably diminish predictability—"

Rick laughed. "What do you care?"

Sam nodded slowly. "You're right. I don't care, I'd enjoy seeing him lose his game. His buddy in California is probably just as much of a dirtbag as Ken is, but I don't see any way he could be any worse."

"Well, that's your answer," Rick pronounced, waving a hand as if to dismiss the whole affair. It wasn't a bad idea, Sam told himself, but he was, at the same time, sure that it wasn't going to be quite that simple.

"This stuff you were telling me about this 'game,' though," Rick went on, cutting off Sam's ruminations. "Sounds interesting. You say the patterns are like what you'd expect from a carrier?"

"Uh-huh." He explained, in some detail and in rather technical terms, the way Ken's data points tended to spread as they moved eastward, and added the programmer's speculation—and his own initial observation—that the data made it look more like the spread of a disease than the meanderings of a serial killer.

"Sounds like a carrier, all right," Rick agreed. "Maybe you ought to follow up on this, Sam. You could be the first to identify this new virus, this sex-murder virus."

Sam grinned. "You know, that's exactly the term I used the first day I saw that data, talking to Ken. 'Sex-murder virus.' "

"Is that possible?" Jennifer asked them.

Sam glanced over at her, shook his head. "No. It isn't."

"Why not?"

"Well, maybe I should be a little more cautious, maybe I should say I can't see how it'd be possible." He thought about it for a few seconds. "You'd have to have a virus that affects the CNS—the central nervous system—and it'd have to do it in very precise ways —there're just so many variables, and the—"

"Maybe you aren't looking at it right, Sam," Rick said.

"You think it is possible?"

"Not necessarily. But remember, there is such a thing as the general adaptation syndrome, there's already a linkage."

Sam grinned again. "The three Fs."

"What's that mean?" Jennifer asked.

"The three Fs," Sam explained, "stand for Flee, Fight, or Fuck. Your body goes into the same general physiological state—elevated blood pressure and heartrate, changes in blood flow, a lot of things—when you're getting ready to do any of those three. In other words, when you're scared, enraged, or really turned on." He glanced at Rick, almost surreptitiously. "And there are some other connections between sex and violence, too—some pretty well-known ones—"

"Like what?" Jennifer persisted.

"Well, people get turned on at bullfights," Rick said, jumping in quickly. He quickly recited the other two instances Sam had thought about a few days before, the violent demonstrations and the gladiatorial contests, and added in the public executions so common in the Middle Ages, and the Terror in France.

"That's really sick!" Cheryl remarked. "Really sick!"

"No, it's just one aspect of a more general thing," Sam commented. "It doesn't have to be people killing people. Natural disasters are a turn-on, too. Earthquakes, cyclones, volcanoes, tidal waves. The Australians have been able to show a sharp jump in the birth rate nine months after they have a cyclone down there."

"But that doesn't make any sense!"

Sam smiled and shook his head. "No, it makes perfect sense. You consider; you're a member of some ancient tribe, and enemies invade. There's a fight, people are killed left and right. Your tribe wins, but afterward there's gore and severed heads all over. So everybody gets turned on; it sounds weird, but look at it this way—following the disaster, what does that ancient tribe need most?"

"A better defense!" Cheryl cracked with a laugh.

"No, seriously. More people; replacements for the dead. That's what they need. You only get more people one way! And so, for violence and destruction to act as a sexual stimulant is, really, adaptive. Beneficial to the group. It might be a very old thing in human beings."

"You're right, it does sort of make sense," Jennifer put in.

"And if you take that a little further," he went on, "you can see that since violence and bloodshed are, in fact, aphrodisiacs—whether a person chooses to admit it or not—that once that's recognized, at least some people would start using it that way deliberately—the Marquis de Sade is the example everyone's heard of. Since the—shall we say, adaptive value—of this comes in when the other members of your 'tribe' are the victims, it's only a short step to making your own sex partner the victim—particularly if you're deliberately using the violence for its aphrodisiac effect. Now that—"

"So it is possible," Jennifer said, cutting in. "It is."

Sam laughed. "I'd say that's a real jump in logic. There may be a few fine lines here, but most of the time, when we're talking about human psychophysiology, what we call fine lines are pretty hard to cross."

"That might be," Rick put in. "But what if there was something that interfered with that? Drugs like LSD can break up the fine lines between the senses, so you see sounds and hear odors. You could have something that mixed the 'three F' reaction all up, so that there's a general terror, rage, and lust, all three set off by any one; that could easily cause bedroom murders. Or they could just get mixed up, so the reaction to arousal is inappropriate, it comes out as rage."

"Doesn't explain the other part," Sam argued. "The passive victims."

"Hey! Give me a chance! I just got going with this!"

"And you're already stretching it beyond all reason—"

Sam's words were cut off by the sound of a vehicle approaching the house; all four turned to look out the window, to watch a rather grubby-looking Jeep Comanche pull up beside the other two cars.

"I believe our remaining third is here," Rick said. "Shall we go greet them?"

"Might as well," Sam agreed.

Thirty-Three

"WE'RE LATE," ART was saying as he turned off the ignition. "We're the last ones here. We're never the last ones here. Sam and Cheryl always get here after we do." He sat still for a moment, watching the other four as they emerged from the house.

"Art, it really isn't a problem, is it?" Stephanie asked in a slightly exasperated voice. "We're going to be here for two weeks, after all. A couple of hours doesn't matter. Besides, nobody else is even going to notice." She opened her door, swiveled in her seat, and hopped out.

Rick rushed up to her, gave her a huge bear hug. "Ah, Stephanie, good to see you!" he enthused. Still holding her, he turned and looked at Art. "And who are you, sir?" he asked. "Didn't you see the sign on the gate, the one that says 'No admittance'?"

"Never could read worth a damn," Art answered.

"You pick this guy up on the road?" Rick asked Stephanie. "I tell you, I really have to wonder about your taste!"

"I've always wondered about Jennifer's," Art shot back.

Rick finally let Stephanie go. "You guys are late," he pointed out. "You always get here early."

A sour expression on his face, Art hooked a thumb at Stephanie. "Her doing. We're coming up through Nag's Head and she decides last year's swimsuits aren't worth a damn, she had to stop and get a new one. It's August and they're all on sale, but that also means the selections are poor. The stop turned into three stops and a couple of hours."

Rick leered at her. "A tiny bikini, I trust?"

"You'll just have to wait and see," she replied with a smile.

"Oh. Well, I can hope. I've never once seen you in anything but a one-piece."

"That's what Jennifer usually wears too, isn't it?" Art noted.

"I do not!" Jennifer cried indignantly. "A lot of times I wear a two-piece! And this year, I—"

"Biiiig two-pieces," Art interrupted. "Oh, well. At least Cheryl knows how to dress on the beach."

"Yeah, there is that," Rick agreed. "Okay, Now. Down to business." He rubbed his palms together. "You brought a hoe, I take it?"

Art reached into the back of the truck and extracted the garden implement. "I sure did," he replied, brandishing it.

"Good, good. Where shall we put it?"

"Same place as last year. Same place as the year before that."

Side by side, they walked off across the grounds to a site near the back of the house. Sam and the women, knowing it was expected of them, trailed along behind.

"Here, right?" Art asked, pointing to a spot.

"Right! Proceed, Counselor Dixon!"

Art put the hoe head into the sand and began digging a little trench, an almost-straight line. After he'd extended it about six feet, he gave the hoe to Rick. "And now you, Doctor Mason?"

Taking it, Rick vigorously hoed out another six-foot section. Then he leaned on the hoe, and both men looked down at the little trench with satisfaction. "I proclaim that this is this year's Mason-Dixon line," Rick said with a flourish.

Reaching over, Art poked his belly. "Where you, Doctor Mason, will suffer a terrible humiliation. You're putting on the flab. I have been working out!"

"We shall see. Last year you did not fare so well, Counselor Dixon."

"The South will rise again!" Art cried. Then he looked back at the others. "Dixon was South, wasn't it?" he asked.

"Of course, ninny," Jennifer answered. "They call the South Dixie, not Masie!"

"A preliminary test, Counselor Dixon?" Rick challenged. Standing on one side of the line, he planted his feet and put out a hand.

"Absolutely not! You've been sitting around here relaxing, I just got off the road. You'd have an advantage."

"Do I detect a hint of fear, Counselor Dixon?"

"No! You detect reason. I know this is an unfamiliar concept to you, Dr. Mason!"

Smiling, Stephanie began to tune them out as they continued to banter, as Rick continued to issue challenges that Art kept ducking—for the moment. He would not, she knew, do that for long. Periodically during the vacation they would be out here struggling and sweating, arm-wresting in a standing position or pulling at ropes, challenging each other over this line in the sand. Art sometimes insisted it only took place because of the coincidence of their names, but Stephanie knew better. They'd find a way to test each other physically if their names were Schwartz and Sanchez, they simply wouldn't have created a Schwartz-Sanchez line.

Stephanie's mind wandered back to the last couple of days. Friday had been almost a carbon copy of Thursday; she'd gotten up, spent a good deal of time with the kaleidoscope glued to her eye, then finally gone to work. On coming home, she'd found Art sitting there as before, playing with the kaleidoscope. They'd waited until after dinner this time, but they had made love, in the same near-violent style as Thursday. If anything, they'd been even rougher with each other—as Stephanie's currently sore nipples proved.

In the bright light of day, her behavior—she recognized quite clearly that she'd been the one to initiate all this, that Art was merely following her lead, as always—seemed very strange to her. Certainly she felt she understood where the impulses came from, why she enjoyed such things; where her newfound freedom to express her interest was coming from she didn't know, and that was worrying her. Each morning, while still satiated from the previous night, she told herself it wouldn't happen again for a while; then, as the day wore on and the hungers increased, her determination melted slowly away. By nightfall she'd begun to feel almost frenzied, her mouth dry and her stomach nervous, eager to get back to these new delights.

Without thinking about it, she pursed her lips and shook her head. It isn't a big deal, Stephanie, she told herself. All you've done is loosened up a little, in other ways as well as this one.

That's a positive change, isn't it? Your bedroom problems with Art are certainly well on their way toward being solved, aren't they? There's nothing to fear, there's nothing to be worried about; you're in command, not your impulses. Tonight, you'll prove it; there'll be no such activities tonight, there'll be sedate lovemaking or none at all.

"You're on vacation, Stephanie," a voice from beside her, unrecognized at first, said. "You aren't working, you don't have to stand here and solve all the world's problems!"

She looked around, stared at Jennifer blankly for a moment. "Huh?"

The blond woman laughed. "That's what I mean!" she said. "You don't even know where you are, you don't know who I am!"

Stephanie blinked and looked around. Art and Rick had finished their games and were standing a few yards away with Sam, discussing something. Jennifer and Cheryl were standing with her; both were obviously amused. It really wasn't rare for Stephanie to wander off into the depths of her own mind on occasion.

"The boys are going to walk down and take a look at the new inlet," Jennifer told her. "They want to know if we're coming. We thought maybe we ought to get you out of the ozone first."

"Oh—yes, that'd be fine." She flashed a quick frown. "New inlet?"

"Uh-huh. There was, as they say, a contour change—of the land down here. We seem to have a piece of the Sound in the back-yard."

"Oh?"

"Come on, Stephanie," Cheryl said patiently. "Let's go with them, otherwise we'll have to listen to them describing it, and that'll take hours. You want me to hold your hand?"

Stephanie laughed too. "No. I'm fine. Lead on!"

In two distinct ranks—the three men in front and the three women behind—they crossed what remained of the backyard to the water. Some of the pines had evidently stopped the shifting sand from moving so much that the house would be threatened; a little patch of them stood near the water's edge on what was now a small hill.

The inlet itself was perhaps a hundred feet wide and stretched off in the distance to merge with Currituck Sound. It seemed to have formed between two now-collapsed dunes, the remains of which formed sandy beaches that were fairly wide on the far side but only spanned about five feet on the near, where they were backed up by the trees. The water was clear, very blue; nowhere was there evidence of the grasses that might signal its conversion into a salt marsh, the usual status of the fingers of water that were thrust in here and there from the Sound.

"Damn, it looks really nice," Art commented.

"Yeah. It's probably six inches deep in the middle, too," Sam grumbled pessimistically.

"Maybe not," Rick offered. "Shifting sand around here can be pretty dramatic at times. I wouldn't be surprised if it was oh, two or three feet deep out there, even at low tide. In which case it'd be a great fishing hole."

"I was hoping for a swimming hole," Cheryl put in.

"That's not likely," Rick told her. "Wading hole, maybe. That's the best you're gonna get."

Cheryl kicked off her shoes. "There's only one way to find out," she told them. She stepped into the water. "Oooh, nice," she commented. "Cool but not cold." She began wading on out; Jennifer, who was also wearing shorts, took off her shoes as well and went out to join her. Stephanie, clad in a summer dress that fell to her knees, decided to wait.

Cheryl and Jennifer went on while the others watched them; they went almost knee-deep immediately, then plodded on out another ten feet without encountering any greater depth.

"Like I said," Rick almost crowed. "Good for fishing, piss-poor for swimming."

He'd hardly gotten the words out of his mouth when Cheryl, taking another step, abruptly went deeper. Another step and the water had risen to the middle of her thigh; two more and it was up near the lower edges of her brief shorts. Smiling broadly, she turned and started back, Jennifer accompanying her.

"It keeps on going down," she said happily as she came. "I'd bet on at least five feet of water out there. Deep enough for swimming, that's for sure! Does anybody know where we are in the tide cycle?"

Rick glanced at his watch. "Real close to extreme low. This's about as shallow as it's gonna get. It doesn't matter much anyway; the tide shift in the Sound is only a few inches."

Cheryl laughed. "See? No faith! We do have a swimming hole, right here at the house! This is great! Nice early morning or late afternoon swims without having to go all the way over to the beach side . . ."

"Nice early morning or late afternoon fishing without having to go over to the beach side . . ." Art echoed rapturously.

"You can have the fishing, I'll take the swimming," Stephanie told him.

"Maybe," Jennifer suggested, "we ought to designate one side for swimming, one for fishing."

"Fine," Rick agreed. He pointed to the far side. "That side'll be for—"

"Fishing!" Jennifer yelled.

He scowled. "No, I was going to say—"

"I know what you were going to say! But I got it out first!"

"That doesn't matter! We'll vote on it. All right?"

"No, I—"

"I say we vote," Art said.

Jennifer wilted a little. "All right. All in favor of this side being designated swimming, raise your hand." All three women raised a hand; Rick started to sigh, seeing a tie vote. But then Sam rather slowly raised his too.

"Traitor!" Rick snarled. "You shall pay for that!"

Jennifer went over and put her arms around him theatrically. "Don't worry, Sam. We'll protect you. We love you."

"You're right, Rick," Sam said, smiling. "I am paying for it!"

Thirty-Four

"YOU GET THAT thing away from me, Sam Leo!" Cheryl said, her eyes wide. She scooted backwards on the bed a little. "Have you gone completely crazy?"

Sam looked down at the object in his hand. "But it's just a jalapeño pepper . . ."

"Just! I know what those things do, and I know you, too, Sam. You've just developed a taste for those things and now you're obsessed with them, and you want me to share them with you. Listen to this, Sam: No. No, no, no."

"I don't know why you have to act like that about it," he complained. "I'm not stuffing them into your mouth, Cheryl." He gestured to the late-night snack they'd brought to their bedroom, the smoked oysters, cheese, and crackers. They'd brought them up here after Stephanie had broken out the kaleidoscope, and after, to all appearances, Rick had fallen victim to it as much as the other three had. Sam had looked through it too, but his reaction had been the same as Cheryl's—it was a very nice kaleidoscope, a very beautiful and interesting kaleidoscope, but, as far as he was concerned, nothing more. After a while he and Cheryl had excused themselves, leaving the others to sit and stare through the little tube. Now, he waved the pepper again, and again Cheryl shrank from it. "All I was saying was—"

"No. I know you. I'm trying to be firm with you because I know you. It'll come up, again and again."

"But how do you know if you haven't—"

"Tried them? I have. Not like that, not the whole pepper, but in things, on pizzas. Those things are pure fire, Sam. If I wanted that experience I'd go stick my tongue in a candle flame."

"No, it really isn't the same thing. These things make your mouth more sensitive to certain flavors and all, and—"

She picked up one of the fondue forks they always used for this purpose, speared a smoked oyster, and wiped it onto a Ritz cracker. "Are you suggesting," she asked with mock hostility, "that my mouth lacks sensitivity?" With exaggerated movements, she slipped the cracker and oyster between her lips.

He speared his own oyster and mimicked all her movements, except that he took a small nibble of the pepper along with it. "I don't know," he told her. He leaned toward her. "Let's see!" She moved her face to his; they kissed, and he pushed his tongue into her mouth.

She jerked back suddenly, as the pepper from his tongue was transferred to hers. "Oh, you son of a bitch!" she cried. She grabbed for her glass of wine, took a gulp. "Damn you!"

He laughed. "You see?" he asked. "See how much better that wine tastes?"

"It does not! That's like showing me how good it feels when you stop beating me in the head with a hammer!" She shook her head, sipped the wine now. "Damn it, it still burns!"

He leaned toward her again. "Let me see what I can do about that," he offered.

She pushed him away. "No way! I'm not kissing you again! What do you think I am, stupid?"

"No, really. I've swallowed it. Trust me."

She turned her head to one side and looked at him suspiciously. "Well, all right," she agreed finally. "But if you do that to me again, Sam Leo—!"

They kissed once more, and this time she did not pull away. This one went on for quite a while; Sam was getting the distinct impression that the late-night snack might be over.

But then, abruptly, he was given cause to wonder. Cheryl broke the kiss, slipped out of his grasp, and got up. "I just want to set a mood," she explained, answering his unasked question. "You have any matches?"

"Sure." He dug in his pocket, extracted a book, and tossed them to her.

Since power failures during summer thunderstorms were hardly an uncommon occurrence out here, all the main rooms in the house were provided with at least one hurricane lamp and several candles in holders; Cheryl went around lighting a few, bringing a pair back to sit on the bedside table beside the remains of the snack. Then, after switching off the light, she sat down on the bed again.

"See?" she asked him.

He reached for her again. "Uh-huh. Nice." She kissed him again, and as she did her hands found the buttons of his shirt, undoing them rapidly, expertly, then pushing the shirt back and off. He wriggled out of it; she stopped kissing him and put her head down on his chest, licking his nipples lightly. He reached for her breasts, but she pushed his hands away and pushed him back, licking all over his chest. Leaning back at a slight angle, he closed his eyes. Later, he realized she'd known, from long experience, that he'd do both those things: lean back and close his eyes.

Because the next thing he knew, she'd stopped licking and fiery hot flashes were dancing over his chest. His eyes popped open; she was grinning broadly, and she was holding one of the candles over him, allowing the hot candlewax to drip on him.

"Gotcha back," she gloated.

He was so startled, so confused, that for several seconds he didn't do anything at all. He was aware of one instinct, one that derived from a perfectly natural desire to avoid pain: to yell at her, to jump up, to knock the candle away. There was another pain, too, a mental one that derived from the fact that this was the type

of game he'd hoped to interest her in when he'd pushed pepper
into her mouth. The problem was, her attitude was all wrong.

Or at least he thought it was. In any case, he didn't want to let
the moment pass without being sure.

Putting his hands behind his head, he grinned. "Why, Cheryl,"
he said, just enough tease in his voice to let her take it either way.
"I didn't know you were into this sort of thing!"

She raised one eyebrow, kept smiling. "Oh, so you're getting off
on it, huh?" she teased back. She let another couple of drops fall.
"You want me to get some rope and tie you to the bedposts too?"

He let the hot flare of the latest droplets fade down before
trusting himself to answer her. "Not necessary," he answered
coolly. "I've always told you, Cheryl, that as far as anything erotic
goes, I'm at your disposal. Do with me as you will." It wasn't yet
like the games he'd played with Selinde, not yet. But it could be,
he was sure of that; it could be, if Cheryl got into it. Anxiety
chewing a knot in his stomach and perversely adding to the thrill,
he waited, he hoped. She bent closer to him, let another drop fall,
watched it strike his chest, saw his muscles tense. Then she looked
back up at his eyes; he was already watching hers.

In the space of the next fraction of a second, something passed
wordlessly between them. As something had passed between them
the first time they'd looked at each other, each realizing the
other's attraction; as something had passed between them the first
time they'd realized that they were about to go to bed together,
realized and understood with no words spoken at all.

Her smile faded; her expression became soft, serious. Putting
the candle back on the nighttable, she reached for his pants, undoing his belt and pulling the zipper down. Once she'd gotten them
halfway down over his hips, she left him to finish that job himself.
Standing up by the bed, she slowly unbuttoned her blouse and
slipped it off; then she squirmed out of her shorts, perhaps wrig-
gling a little more than was necessary. By that time, he'd finished
removing his pants and shorts. Naked, she climbed back onto the
bed and sat down between his legs, stretching hers across his. He
brought his hands from behind his head, began stroking her calves
and the backs of her knees. She in turn began caressing his penis
gently with her fingers; it rose quickly in response.

Finally, she picked up the candle again. His breath caught in his
throat; something inside him began pulling tight, like a guitar
string wound beyond its normal pitch.

Again, she tipped the holder over his chest; two drops of wax fell, two sharp hot flares ignited and slowly died on his chest. He could not help but notice that the character of the experience was changing rapidly. Now that his hands were on Cheryl's legs and her fingers were massaging his erection, the pain itself was becoming positively pleasurable. It was the same as it had been with Selinde and yet it was different, different perhaps only in that he was not so distracted, in that Cheryl's familiarity allowed him to see what was happening a little more clearly. It seemed that somehow the pain was lowering the threshold on the nerve endings throughout his body, amplifying other unrelated sensations. Cheryl's thighs had never felt so smooth, so sensual, to his fingertips before; from the point where her hand was gripping his erection an amazing warmness and tingling was spreading throughout his lower body, concentrating itself in his abdomen.

"You really are getting off on this, aren't you?" Cheryl asked, letting another drop fall.

Again, he waited until the initial intense burning subsided before speaking. "Aren't you?" he countered.

She didn't answer immediately either; just stared into his eyes. In the darkness of her pupils he thought for a moment that he could see kaleidoscopic patterns, deep down, far away. Suggestion, he told himself. Just suggestion, just a touch of déjà vu.

But he didn't want to think about Selinde, not now, and at this moment it really was pretty easy not to. Cheryl had gotten up on her knees; balancing the candleholder carefully, she turned herself around in the bed, lying down on her side so that her knees were close to Sam's face, her cheek resting on his thigh.

Then, once again holding the candle over his chest, she lowered her head onto his erection, allowing it to slip softly between her lips. As it went she looked back up toward his chest and carefully allowed another drop of wax to fall on his skin.

The bright pain was like an exclamation point to what she was doing with her lips; the two stimuli, the soft dark wetness of her mouth and the hard metallic brilliance of the burning pain, roared toward each other, the first being intensified by the second while at the same time altering it, transforming it. The set of converging sensations seemed to meet, to concentrate, somewhere between his navel and his groin. It was as if something were beginning to open in there, as if a flower was starting to bloom in there, as if some sort of a spectral rose, springing from the fertile soil of her lips and tongue, was being driven upward by the hot solar flare of the wax.

There was another component to all this as well, a component more purely psychological—the wildness of it, the abandonment, the quest for sensual pleasure without regard to the possible costs. Though all Cheryl's actions had been very methodical, though there'd been no suggestion of frenzy whatsoever, he still, if he closed his eyes, could see her as a dancing maenad, one of those wild devotees of the Greek god Dionysus who tore wild animals—or people—apart in their unbridled passion. Opening them, looking at her eyes, he felt sure that that sort of frenzy was there: it just hadn't been released yet.

And the notion of her frenzy, the notion of her utterly beyond any sort of restraints or controls—no matter what manner of price he might have to pay for that frenzy—was very, very erotic.

Then—just when he was beginning to feel he could take little more—she abruptly stopped. With the candle still in her hand, she swiveled around in the bed, lying down beside him. He turned to stare at her, wondering for a moment if she planned to leave him hanging on this cliff. She smiled softly, kissed him lightly, and offered him the candle.

"You do me now," she whispered, her voice husky.

He stared at her blankly for a few seconds. This was, without a doubt, the last thing he would've expected her to say. He wasn't going to try to convince himself he hadn't hoped; but he had been sure that, at the very least, it would've taken weeks or months, a slow and careful approach, many long discussions, much soul-searching—and no certainty of success even then. He hesitated, still staring at her, wondering.

"Well?" she prompted, offering him the candle insistently. "You want to, don't you?"

His eyes widened almost imperceptibly. Oh yes, he replied silently. Yes, I do. But still, he did not act; he was too uncertain about her motivations, this was too unlike the Cheryl he'd always known. He was quite sure she was putting on no act; her eyelids were a little swollen, they'd taken on that sleepy-sexy look he knew meant she was very aroused.

Seeing his hesitation, she squirmed a little on the bed. "Come on, Sam," she urged, running her free hand down over his body and pulling him closer.

That was all it took. Raising himself up, he took the candle from her, lifted it over her chest, let a drop of wax fall.

She gasped, stiffened, and arched her body slightly as the droplet struck her breast, spread, and began to cool and harden, but her expression did not indicate displeasure and she did not ask him to stop. Sam felt almost like crying. He felt an overwhelming tenderness toward her, much the same as he'd felt the first time they'd made love—like she was giving him some priceless gift, like he was some sort of a god and she was sacrificing herself to him. He didn't really know, couldn't really tell, if she was enjoying it or not; all he did know was that her willingness to venture into these exotic and perhaps even potentially dangerous realms with him spoke reams about her feelings toward him. For Sam, it was producing an almost overwhelming rush of emotions; he wasn't openly crying, but his eyes were moist, his breath was catching in his chest.

He continued to hold the candle over her, continued to let the drops of wax fall onto her breasts, one after another. As each one struck her she went rigid; it was amazing to him, she really did look the same whether reacting to pain or experiencing orgasm. He moved his legs between hers; she grabbed at him, stuffing him inside herself, almost roughly. He began to move inside her gently as he allowed a few more drops to fall. Within seconds her body went stiff once more and stayed that way for a moment, trembling violently; a little cry escaped her throat. Seconds later, the rose that had been budding inside Sam's abdomen erupted in full bloom; his orgasm was so intense that it was almost painful. For a few seconds he felt as if he were wavering on the edge of losing consciousness. When his senses returned he laid his hand on her abdomen, just below her navel, and felt the muscles there fluttering—as if she, too, had had a flower blooming inside.

Fading but not even thinking about withdrawing, he almost tossed the candle onto the bedside table and held her body tightly against his own. They remained like that, silent, for a long time. "Oh, Christ!" she muttered as he finally slipped out of her. "Jesus Christ! I wouldn't've believed that!"

Remaining in close contact with her, he moved himself over until he was lying beside her. "I know what you mean," he agreed, thinking that his words hardly expressed his feelings.

She turned toward him, her face so close he could not quite focus on it, and offered him a rather fragile smile. "Pretty kinky, Sam Leo. Pretty kinky."

"Yeah, I guess so. Are you sure you're comfortable with this sort of thing, Cheryl?"

She laughed a little. "Look," she told him, "I know what you're gearing up to here. But let's not analyze it too much, okay? Right

now I'm fine with it; we did it, we both got a kick out of it, fine."
She reached down and peeled a chunk of wax off her skin. "We
can do it again sometime, as far as I'm concerned. But I don't
want to lie here and study it too much." He nodded agreement
and fell silent again, just lying there with her in his arms, enjoying
the afterglow.

It was then that he first heard the odd sound, from somewhere
else in the house. A distinct slapping noise. Faint, indistinct. At
first, Sam thought he'd imagined it, but then he heard it again.

Cheryl raised her head. "What's that?"

"I don't know. Wind making a loose board or shingle bang,
maybe?"

"I don't think there's any wind to speak of."

He glanced at the window. She was right; there wasn't. "I don't
know," he said with a shrug.

"Maybe you'd better go see."

"I don't think that's necessary. As far as I know, the others are
still up, playing with that damn kaleidoscope."

"Maybe not. It's late, Sam."

Reaching over, he picked up his watch from the somewhat
crowded bedside table. After midnight; she was right about that,
too.

"I really think you should go check it out, Sam. You never know,
someone might be trying to break in or something."

Sam sighed, but he grinned; this was Cheryl, classic. Pulling
himself up from the bed, he dragged on his pants. He wasn't planning to put a shirt on, but the hair on his chest was still matted
with wax; there wasn't a way he was going to get it off quickly, and
he surely didn't want to have to try to explain it if he ran into any
of the others. He retrieved his shirt, put it on too. Then he went
out into the hallway.

The bedrooms—the three they were using, the old house had a
total of six—were all on the second floor. Long ago they'd planned
this so that no couple had direct neighbors, so that none had a
wall in common. The bedroom Sam and Cheryl were using was
nearest the stair, on the ocean side; the next one on that side of
the hall was vacant, and across from it was the one occupied by the
Dixons. On down, on the same side as Sam and Cheryl's, was the
one the Masons used. Alongside it was a door giving access to the
balcony, and across from that was a bathroom.

Standing with his back to his own door, facing the stairs, Sam
listened for a moment. Out here, the slapping was substantially

more distinct, and it was pretty clear that it was coming from somewhere down at the end of this hall, not from downstairs. Turning his head from side to side, Sam moved slowly down that way, reviewing the layout. At the end of the hall was a linen closet; if the sound represented someone trying to break in, then the reasonable possibilities were the unused bedroom, the bathroom, and the balcony access. Though why someone would go to the trouble of breaking in on the second story, Sam didn't know. From downstairs, entry would be simple—in any number of places.

Headed for the unused bedroom first, Sam moved on down the hall and prepared himself to open the door, wondering what he was going to do if he found himself actually confronting an intruder. He took a deep breath, reached for the doorknob, and as he did he heard a new noise from behind him.

He whirled around. But it was merely Art, emerging from the Dixons' bedroom. "Shit!" Sam whispered hoarsely. "Don't do that!"

Art grinned. "Sorry," he whispered back. "We heard a noise."

"Yeah. That's why I'm out here, too."

"Oh. Figured it out yet?"

"Uh-uh. Sounds like someone clapping hands or something."

"Yeah." The sound came again, following Art's word immediately. He turned, pointed. "There. Rick and Jennifer's room."

The first thing that popped into Sam's mind he rejected. "Can't be." He hooked a thumb at the spare room. "Here or the balcony door."

"Let's check them out."

Again, Sam reached for the knob, feeling a little better now that he had a backup. He pushed the door open; he could see nothing except darkness and diffuse moonlight through the window. His hand snaked around the doorframe and he snapped on the light.

There was nothing. Nothing except the minimal furnishings of a spare bedroom for which no immediate use was planned. He turned off the light, started to close the door, and as he did they heard another slap.

Now it was obvious. There was no need to check the balcony door, the sound was coming from Rick and Jennifer's room.

The two men looked at each other for a moment, then tiptoed down the hall to that door and stood there for a few seconds. There was another slap, and this time a very soft feminine moan could be heard following it.

Art looked around at Sam, widened his eyes, drew his lips in. Silently, the two crept back up the hall to the stair.

"Now I know what that sounds like!" Art whispered. "It sounds like someone getting spanked!"

Sam felt he was expected to chuckle; he chuckled. "Yeah. I guess so." He's done it, Sam told himself. He's involved Jennifer in his games.

"We gonna ask ol' Rick about this?"

"Jesus, I don't know," he temporized. "How can we?"

"I dunno. But we gotta, Sam. Some way. Can't let him get away with this! Not without a little ragging."

You rag him, Art, Sam said silently. Me, I'm in no position to. "I'm just not sure how to approach it, that's all."

"We'll get him drunk. How about that? He's got a weakness there. I can't drink, and you drink like a goddamn fish and never get drunk."

"Uh, yeah, I suppose—I guess I could run out and get us some booze."

"Sounds real good to me." Frowning, he leaned forward, peering into the open collar of Sam's shirt. "What's this?" he asked, reaching forward boldly and pulling out a chunk of wax.

Sam felt his cheeks go hot. "Uh, uh, well, Cheryl wanted some candles lit—romantic mood, all that—I was, uhm, carrying one and I stumbled. I guess some wax splashed on me."

"Oh," Art said. To Sam's relief, he didn't pursue it. "Well, I'd better get back to Stephanie," he said. "She's gonna love this!"

"Uh-huh. So's Cheryl." He had to tell her. Art would tell Stephanie, she'd say something to Cheryl, Cheryl would want to know why he hadn't told her. Complicated. He really didn't want to reveal that he'd known about Rick's propensities for years and had never mentioned it to her. Distracted—and feeling a little responsible in the event that any problems developed between Rick and Jennifer over this—he started wandering back toward his room. This clustering of events, he told himself, was truly amazing.

"Well, g'night," Art called from behind him.

"Oh, yeah," he answered abstractedly. " 'Night, Art."

Thirty-Five

SITTING ON THE side of the bed, Art held his head in his hands while Stephanie modeled in front of the mirror. "I can't believe this," he was saying. "I just can't."

She looked around at him. "I told you I was going to be a beach bunny when we got here," she reminded him. "Told you I was going to put on my swimsuit when I got up in the morning and never take it off except to shower and come back to bed. That's what I'm doing. I talked to Cheryl, and she's going to do the same thing."

"Cheryl," he pointed out, "always wears little tiny bikinis. You never have. And this! It's just so—so—"

"You don't like it?"

"Wrong! I love it! Rick and Sam will too, I can goddamn well guarantee that! No, don't get me wrong, I'm not objecting! I'm just amazed, that's all!"

She pirouetted in front of the mirror again, examining the suit. It was black; the top consisted of two equilateral triangles, not more than five inches on each side at most, and two thin strings, one that passed around her back and one that went around her neck. The bottom was the "thong" design; small in front, high-cut over the hips. In back, nothing more than a slender strap passing down between her buttocks.

She grinned. "It is daring, isn't it?"

"You can only get more daring with a topless one!"

She patted her almost-bare rear end. "I'm going to have to use a lot of sunscreen here," she mused. "This hasn't ever seen much sun. I'm going to have one fried ass if I'm not careful."

"That's true. But remember, you got the tree side of the new inlet for swimming. Mornings, that's going to be shaded."

"I'll still have to be careful." She turned back to him. "Well.

Shall we go downstairs? I want to get some coffee and get out there to the water."

Art almost jumped up. "You bet. I can't wait!" He went to the door, opened it. "Is that the only suit you bought?"

"No," she said as she stepped through. "I got four, they were on sale, they only cost twenty dollars apiece. They're all this cut, though. Just different colors." Behind her, Art closed the door, and she could hear him chuckling as he did.

Facing away from him, her smile faded a little. She'd bought these suits on a whim—or perhaps to express her new attitude toward things sexual—and now she was determined to wear them, in spite of the razzing she knew she was going to get, especially from Rick.

But earlier, she hadn't even been sure she'd wanted to follow her plan of wearing a swimsuit at all times. On waking, she'd been more than a little upset with herself, since she had not been able to control their lovemaking the previous night, and it had, once again, been quite rough. Art was worrying about it too, she could tell, though as yet he'd said nothing—and probably would not. The roughness was her idea; she'd initiated it in the first place, she was the one who continued to instigate it in their now-frequent sexual encounters.

She hadn't said anything to him, either. Getting up before he did, she'd gone to sit by the window, watching the morning sunshine over the pines and the dunes, listening to the raucous symphony of the gulls. After a while—as had also become her habit—she'd picked up the kaleidoscope, she'd watched it create patterns that seemed increasingly sexually suggestive. It's just where your head is, she'd insisted; and in any case, why are you worrying about it? It's solved the problem you've been having with him, hasn't it? The urge to go back to bed and rouse him for another bout of lovemaking had been strong, but in the morning light she'd resisted successfully. It wasn't that she hadn't wanted to. It was just that she was too sore, in too many places.

Finally she'd done what she'd planned. She'd torn herself away from the kaleidoscope, put on one of the new suits. At this point Art had returned to consciousness; at first he'd been rendered speechless. She knew why. No one who knew Stephanie would have imagined that she would've so much as gotten near a swimsuit like this.

But why not? she told herself, looking down at herself as she started down the stairs. She was still young, she had the body for it, it looked good on her. Lots of women wore swimsuits like this now. At the moment—in fact, not since she'd gone into the first shop at Nag's Head—she couldn't understand why she'd always insisted on the overly modest suits she'd worn previously. When she packed for this trip they'd looked downright ugly to her. Maybe she'd been making a mistake all these years, buying swimsuits for herself, maybe she should've encouraged Art to do it for her. Cheryl, she knew, never bought a single piece of her own swimwear; all her suits were gifts from Sam. And that meant they were all small, all revealing.

She was still thinking about this when she crossed the large living room and entered the kitchen. She and Art were the last ones down; Rick and Jennifer, early risers, were seated at the table with half-empty cups of coffee. Sam and Cheryl's were full and steaming.

Sam's back was to her as she walked in, but Rick could see her immediately. His eyes grew huge. "Oh, my God!" he cried. "I can't believe what I'm seeing! I must've died and gone to heaven!"

Sam swiveled around in his chair, and he stared too. "Oh, yes. I see what you mean."

Cheryl, dressed in a beach coverup as Jennifer was, grinned and shook her head. "Let me guess. A gift from Art, and he threatened you with bodily harm if you didn't wear it."

No, the thought flashed through Stephanie's mind. If that had been the way it was I probably would've refused and dared him to carry out his threat. "No. My choice. I just felt like a change."

"Well, I think it's one hell of a fine change!" Rick roared. He squinted at the bottom of the suit. "Wait a minute, wait a minute! I don't think we know the full story here, not yet! Turn around, Stephanie!"

She hesitated, but she did; they were going to see it sooner or later anyhow.

"Aiiieee!" Rick screeched. "A thong! Jesus!"

"Yes, I think we've gotten to the bottom of this matter now," Sam noted with a broad grin.

Rick turned to his wife, who had so far made no comment. "Well, sweetheart, I've got to agree. There's just no explaining it any other way, there's something in the stars!" He looked closely at her, then back at Stephanie. "Unless she knew all about this. Unless you two cooked it up between you."

Stephanie looked bewildered. "Rick, I don't know what you're talking about," she replied sincerely. "I bought this on—uhm—on impulse, on our way down. Nobody knew about it, not even Art. Not until a few minutes ago."

He looked back at Jennifer again. "True?" he demanded.

"True," she answered innocently.

He shook his head. "I guess I'm gonna have to start studying astrology," he observed. "Why don't you show them, Jenny?"

"Now?"

"Why not?"

She stood up; all eyes were on her now. Turning her back on them, she undid the belt on her coverup and let it fall from her shoulders.

"No!" Art breathed from behind Stephanie. "No, it isn't possible!"

Jennifer's suit was not a thong; it covered more of her bottom than Stephanie's did, although not much more. But, from Stephanie and Art's viewpoint, she didn't appear to be wearing a top at all; her slender back was quite bare.

"Dare we ask her to turn around?" Sam queried.

Slowly, Jennifer started to turn, and though both men goggled, she was not bare-breasted. A thin strap, concealed from behind by her hair, dropped from each side of her neck and was connected by a snap to the bottom of the suit; on its way it managed to somehow cover at least the center of each of her breasts—though the inner and outer margins of them were, indeed, exposed. Additionally, the bottom was cut in a deep V in the front, exposing all but the center of her pubis. She must've trimmed her pubic hair, Stephanie thought. Otherwise half of it would be in plain view.

"How in God's name," Art asked when he'd caught his breath, "do those straps stay in place?"

"With any kind of luck," Sam put in, "they don't."

Jennifer touched one of them. "No, they do," she informed them. "At least they're supposed to. I've worn it for a while around the house already, and I haven't fallen out yet."

"Sounds like we can only hope," Art said. He glanced at Rick. "I see what you mean about the stars. The odds of them both doing this at once, well, they've got to be phenomenal."

"A P of ten to the minus-nine, at least," Sam commented.

Jennifer picked up her coverup as if to put it back on, but, seeing that Stephanie had none, apparently decided against it. Hanging it on the back of her chair, she sat back down. Art and Stephanie moved toward the coffeemaker. Feeling Rick's eyes on her as she walked, she had an urge to wriggle her rear at him, but she refrained. He might well take it the wrong way, or just as bad, Jennifer might.

"I guess nobody's interested in my swimsuit," Cheryl sniffed plaintively.

Rick turned toward her. "No, that's not so. But we know you, Cheryl. You wear knockout bikinis every year. These two, well, they don't, you know, they practically wear Mother Hubbards. We're just all—startled. That's the word, *startled.*" He paused. "And pleased, too, yes, *pleased,* that's the other word!"

"I'm too predictable," Cheryl said to Sam. "That's my problem. And now nobody cares."

Stephanie put a hand on her friend's shoulder. "I'd love to see your suit, Cheryl," she said.

The dark-haired woman folded her arms; the leg came up, the ankle rested on the knee. "Later," she said. "When we go swimming. It's just a bikini anyway. Just what everybody expects from old reliable Cheryl."

There wasn't a person in the room who didn't know that it was best to leave Cheryl alone for a few minutes; even so, Stephanie made one more request to see her swimsuit. When it, too, was rebuffed—as she'd known it would be—she turned away, got her coffee, and sat down at the table. Sipping it, she glanced around at the three men in turn, wondering if any of them was going to make the sacrifice. It was from them that Cheryl was awaiting the request to view her suit; but, after having committed the crime of failing to ask her without prompting, whoever did ask was sure to be verbally assaulted. Still, if one of them didn't, Cheryl's mood was apt to be less than pleasant for much of the day.

We play such stylized games with each other, Stephanie told herself as she waited, as the somewhat awkward silence over the breakfast table stretched on. You make this move and now I'll make this one in response, the exact move you knew I was going to make. Absolute locks; Cheryl and Jennifer are your girlfriends, you do this with them, you talk to them about these things. Art is husband and lover, a whole different set, and may never the twain meet. Sam and Rick are husbands of girlfriends first and professional colleagues second, and let none of us forget that, even as we banter about the swimsuits.

All of us, it seems, are individual people dead last. Rick is carrying on but he doesn't really know how to talk to you while you're wearing a swimsuit that bares your ass, and Art doesn't know what to do with Jennifer either, he wants to look at her tits but he's scared to.

Sam, however, is just a little different. A little less locked into patterns, a little more independent. He is, blatantly, staring at Jennifer's tits. And he doesn't feel the least bit guilty about it; he won't, either, even if he gets jumped on about it by Cheryl or Rick. Most likely, he'll go right on doing it—maybe a bit surreptitiously.

"Well!" Rick said suddenly, breaking the now-long silence. "Are we all ready to head out to the water, see how it is this morning?"

"Do we all have to go?" Cheryl demanded. "Maybe some of us don't want to go yet. Maybe some of us would like to lounge around for a while and drink coffee. We don't have to do every-thing together, do we? That's what I dislike about these vacations. Got to get up, hurry up and have fun, rush around, can't miss a minute of the fun. Some of us might like to use some of this time to relax a little." The ankle moved up a little more.

"No," Rick admitted, obviously chastened. "But I want to go out and drop a line, see what's biting. How about you, Art?"

Art gave Stephanie a quick glance. "Uh, yeah, sounds good to me. Let me get my stuff, and we'll go. Sam, you coming?"

"Not yet," he answered. "I'll be out there in a little while."

"How about you and me going and trying the swimming beach, Stephanie?" Jennifer proposed.

She nodded. "Sure." She gave a quick glance toward Sam and Cheryl. "You two know where we'll be. Whenever you want to come . . ."

Cheryl dismissed them all with a wave of her hand. "Go," she said. "We'll manage fine."

Stephanie, Art, and the Masons rose from the table; Sam and Cheryl remained. While the men went to get their fishing tackle, Jennifer sidled up to Stephanie.

"Uh—look," she asked, her manner very little-girl. "Can we get that kaleidoscope and take it down to the beach? I'd really like to see what the sunlight does to it!"

Thirty-Six

"THEY'RE GOING TO go blind looking through that thing," Cheryl said as soon as the others had left. "I can't believe they're so obsessed with it." Her mood seemed to have lightened considerably now that the others were gone.

"Are you really upset with them?" Sam asked carefully, hoping not to reinstate it.

She turned to him, uncrossed her legs; he breathed a sigh of relief. "No, I'm just a little irritated. It's hard for me to believe that Jennifer and Stephanie both made a sudden about-face in their taste in swimsuits without having talked about it. Me, I'm stuck with the same old thing."

He'd watched her dress; he knew that, under the coverup, she was wearing one of the thin white bikinis he'd bought her, one of the ones that became somewhat translucent when it was wet. It was a brief suit, a sexy suit; it really wasn't much larger than either Stephanie's or Jennifer's. But it wasn't a new suit, it was one of the suits she'd worn last year.

"I tell you," she went on, "I am tempted to take off my top and go down there like that. See what they have to say then!"

Sam grinned. "God knows, don't let me stop you."

She waved her hand impatiently, as she'd done before; he doubted she'd carry out her threat. "Anyway, it isn't important. I'm sort of glad it happened, in a way. It gives us a minute to talk before we charge off to have fun, fun, fun."

"About what?" he asked.

"About last night. I don't understand what happened, Sam."

He shook his head. "I don't either, really." He touched his chest, lowered his voice. "And I suffered for it, too! You know how long it took to get that stuff off of my chest? How much hair comes off with it? That isn't a problem you have, you can just peel it off painlessly!"

"I certainly do know," she reminded him. "I was lying right there, listening to you go 'shit' and 'fuck' and 'damn' every time you pulled a piece off!"

He pursed his lips. "Well, it wasn't quite the same without the other stimulation!"

"No, I'm sure it wasn't. I don't know, Sam. That wax really did hurt! But I did get into it, too. There's no denying that."

He nodded. "Yeah. So did I."

She propped her elbow on the table, raised a finger. "I don't want you to get the idea that that kind of stuff is going to become a regular part of our sex life," she said firmly.

"Hey!" he replied, a little taken aback. "I didn't suggest that! You were the one who started it!"

"I was not! You did, when you stuck your pepper-tongue in my mouth!"

"So you liked that too, huh?"

She frowned. "No, I didn't. I—"

"Come on, Cheryl. Sure?"

"Real sure. I want no more of your hot peppers and no more of your hot wax, Sam Leo!"

He felt himself beginning to get angry. She was laying all this squarely on him, and as he remembered things she'd been a pretty eager participant. "It wasn't my hot wax," he told her. "I am not the one who got the candles out. I'm not the one who dripped the first drips. I didn't even ask you to do it to me. You decided I was liking it. You were right, but that's beside the point. Am I right?"

Her expression softened a little. "Yeah, I suppose you are," she admitted. "But I just want to make it really clear, I don't want to do that kind of thing anymore."

He hesitated a moment before saying anything else, selecting his words carefully. "We don't have to," he told her finally. "But I want to ask a question—why not? The wax is harmless, we're not even blistered. If you enjoyed it, then—"

"Because," she cut in, "it's weird."

He frowned deeply. "Weird? You don't want to do it because it's weird?" He turned his head, looked out the window for a moment. "Who am I talking to? Can't be the former Cheryl Connor, the girl who wasn't afraid of anything, who always said we should share our desires and fantasies, no matter how strange they were! You don't believe that anymore?"

"No. I still believe that."

"Then it doesn't make any sense for you to say you don't want to do it again because it's weird! It's perfectly legitimate for you to say you don't want to do it because you didn't like it, but—"

"No, Sam. I don't want to do it again because I did like it. I feel like I liked it too much. I was lying there afterward thinking I wanted more. What's more? The flame itself, third-degree burns?" She stopped, stared down at the table for a few minutes. "This morning I don't want more. I don't know if I much liked the side of myself I got a glimpse of last night. I enjoyed hurting you, and I enjoyed being hurt by you." She raised her eyes. "I'm not sure that's not kinda sick."

Sam watched her closely. "Maybe so," he allowed. "But, in one way, so what? We're consenting adults. Not too many years ago oral sex was considered 'sick.' It's a matter of perspective. Besides, Rick has told me that it's a lot more common than—"

He stopped, bit his lip. He hadn't meant to say that, hadn't meant to mention Rick. Unless Cheryl missed it, it was surely going to pop the lid right off a rather old can of worms. At first he thought she had; there was no particular surprise in her eyes.

But then she dispelled that illusion. "So you know about Rick," she said bluntly. "About Rick and his—hell, what is the best word? Let's say his exotic tastes. You could've discussed it with me, Sam. How long have you known?"

Sam stared at her. "You know about it too?"

She shrugged. "Uh-huh. So does Stephanie. It sort of came up, I guess you'd say peripherally, in our conversations. Never directly, but it isn't hard to put two and two together and get four."

"Rick doesn't know that Jennifer knows! They don't—"

Cheryl laughed. "I know they don't do it together." She hesitated. "Or didn't—I mean—if you were right about what you and Art heard last night, if he was spanking her—" She shook her head. "But she's known about it for a long time. I don't really know how, maybe she just put pieces together too. Rick isn't always careful, as you know. He gets overheard on the phone and things like that." She went on for a while, and gradually Sam realized that she and Stephanie knew just about as much about Rick's proclivities as he did; all she lacked were some of the procedural details.

Cheryl fell silent for a moment, staring out the window toward the Sound. "I hope they know what they're doing," she allowed finally. "As you said, Jenny's never been involved with this stuff before. And she's always hinted that there's some reason why she couldn't be. Stephanie and I have no idea what that reason might be."

"Things changed, evidently." He started to tell her about his direct suggestion to Rick that he approach Jennifer with such ideas, but in the end decided to leave that one lie—more possible complications were lurking in those bushes.

"I think," Cheryl mused, "that maybe Art's idea—about getting Rick drunk and talking—is a good one. If for no other reason than to clue him in about this. He's the only one who doesn't know." She shook her head. "But that depends on Rick cooperating . . ."

"Rick cannot resist good Kentucky bourbon. A bottle of Maker's Mark spells his doom. Tomorrow's Monday, the ABC stores'll be open, I could go get it then, I guess."

Cheryl nodded. "It's worth a try, anyway." There was a distant look in her eyes. "As far as we're concerned . . . Maybe you're right, maybe I shouldn't rule that sort of stuff out altogether. I do want to cool it for a while, though, at the very least."

"We can cool it or eliminate it, hon. I'm not pushing."

She leaned over and kissed him. "You never do," she said. "You remind and you bring up and you suggest, but you don't push. I do appreciate that." She stretched her arms, looked out the window again. "Maybe we ought to go on outside," she suggested. Her moodiness seemed to have evaporated. "It's starting out to be a great day."

"Starting out to be a great vacation, if you ask me," Sam agreed.

Thirty-Seven

THE BRIGHT BLUE waters of the inlet rippled around Jennifer's legs as she came back up toward the beach. Stephanie, already there, finished toweling her hair and watched her friend as she slowly and languidly made her way back. A short while earlier, both had been swimming some twenty yards out from this bank, and they'd

discovered that the inlet was at least seven or eight feet deep out
there—they'd had no problem finding places where they could not
touch bottom. Putting her towel down, Stephanie crossed her legs
and waited for her more slowly moving friend. Jennifer's hair,
thoroughly soaked and matted tightly, was streaked with dark
gold. The new swimsuit, now wet, looked almost metallic in the
sunlight.

"They do stay in place," Stephanie observed, nodding toward
the two straps on the suit. "I'm amazed."

Turning her head, Jennifer glanced back at Art and Rick, just
now settling in to a spot on the far side to try a little fishing.
They'd delayed for a long time, hanging around, "enjoying the
wonderful scenery," as Rick said—repeatedly. They'd only left
when the two women went swimming, when suits and bodies were
concealed in the water.

"They didn't think they would either," she noted. "I think
maybe they're disappointed."

"Art is. That's for sure."

"Well, Rick may've seen all this before, but he's sure getting a
kick out of yours!" She sat down on her towel and used a smaller
one to rub some of the excess water out of her hair. "He's just
stunned. To be honest, so am I. I never expected to see you in a
suit like that."

Stephanie grinned from under a stray lock of hair. "Likewise,
pal. Likewise." She looked thoughtful for a moment. "You said,
back up there at the house, that you'd tried yours on at home
before you came down here. How long have you had it?"

"Not long. You remember the night we got together to look at
your new kaleidoscope?"

"Uh-huh."

"Next day. I was out shopping and I saw these wild things, and,
well, I just decided I wanted one, just decided I wanted to see
everybody's reaction to it. I bought two, in the end." She laughed.
"You can't know how stunned I was when you did the same sort of
thing!"

"Yeah," Stephanie mused. "Yeah. When I went into that store
at Nag's Head I was thinking maybe, for once, a two-piece—something like what Cheryl wears but not even quite that—uh—revealing." She paused, shook her head. "Then I saw these. There
was a photo there of a girl wearing one, and she had the same
general sort of body type I do—the model, I mean—and, well, it

just seemed like a really good idea at the time. It was kind of hard to come downstairs wearing it this morning, though."

"Mm-hmm. I almost chickened out too."

"But you didn't."

"Neither did you."

"No." She paused again, looked across the water, watched Art cast a line far out, watched Rick try to exceed his distance and fail. "That's like them," she commented. "That's the way they've always been, since they've known each other, they compete with everything. This isn't like us, Jenny."

"No, it isn't."

"Then why'd we do it?"

Jennifer leaned down and brushed sand from her calves. "I'm not sure. Not sure why I did it, I mean. I have no idea about you!" She laughed, but then her voice became quite soft. "I've been doing a lot of things lately I haven't done before. I can't say why."

"Like what things?" Stephanie asked.

Jennifer's voice was still very soft. "I'm not quite sure I'm ready to talk about it." She looked down, idly brushed a few more grains of sand from her legs.

"Naturally," Stephanie said carefully, "I don't want to pry or anything like that. But we've talked to each other about almost everything over the last few years, Jenny. Let me just ask this: is everything all right with you?"

"Uh-huh." There was a silence. "Uh, I think so."

"You sure you don't want to talk about it?"

She looked up; she looked very fragile, very childlike. "No, I'm not sure," she replied. "But I'm not sure I do, either. I—"

"You might as well hold it off for a few seconds, anyway," Stephanie said, cutting her off. "Because if you say anything important, you'll just have to repeat it." She pointed; Jennifer turned and looked, saw Cheryl coming toward them from the house. "Here comes our other third."

"Mmm. I hope our other third is over her snit."

Stephanie chuckled. "She doesn't have snits. Just ask her."

"I wouldn't dare!"

By that time, Cheryl was close enough to hear them. "You wouldn't dare what, Jennifer?" she asked.

The blond woman looked up, her expression one of utter innocence. "Ask you if you were over your snit."

"I don't have snits," Cheryl said. She put down a towel and sat down, still wearing her coverup.

"You see?" Stephanie said.

"Well, she seems to be, anyhow," Jennifer commented.

"Uh-huh."

"It wasn't a snit!" Cheryl protested. "But you two could've told me you were going to do this, instead of springing it on me too!"

"Neither one of us," Stephanie insisted, "had any idea about the other. I assure you."

Now it was Cheryl who was looking off across the water, watching Sam as he joined Rick and Art. "Even so," she mused, "I'm the one who's stuck here with last year's suits." She took off the coverup at last, revealing a white bikini with thin brown straps. "See? Same old suit."

"It looked good on you last year and it still does," Stephanie told her. "Last year, I don't think any of the men so much as glanced at me or Jennifer while you were on the beach."

"Oh, that's ridiculous! Sam stares at your legs all the time! He did last year, when you were wearing the one-piece!"

Stephanie started to answer but hesitated. Cheryl's comment might have been true and it might not have been; she might well never have noticed Sam staring at her friend's legs. It was just a comment, it was not meant, Stephanie was sure, to be profound, to be laden with meaning.

But she was discovering that it was having a very strong effect. She was delighted, that was the only descriptive word, delighted at the thought that Sam Leo might enjoy looking at her legs. And it came to her, almost like an explosion inside her head, that Sam was a very attractive man. At the same time, she realized that she'd always known that, she'd simply never, because of the closeness and complexity of the relationships among the six of them, allowed herself to think of Sam in that way.

And now, suddenly, it seemed she couldn't think of him in any other way. She had a momentary fantasy of catching Sam alone while she was wearing this suit, of him staring at her legs and her bare rear end, of him losing a little of his reserve, kneeling down, beginning to run his hands over her thighs, higher and higher . . .

No, Stephanie, she told herself firmly. No, stop this. This is not healthy. She called on the mental discipline she'd cultivated over the years, tried to expel this newly sexual Sam from her thoughts. To her chagrin, she discovered that she could not do it, not completely. Almost in desperation she turned her attention back to her friends, focusing on what they were saying.

Neither of the other women had really noticed her lapse in

conversation. Jennifer was telling Cheryl how she'd come to buy her suit. And—as Stephanie saw it, significantly—she reiterated her statement about "doing things she'd never done before."

"It sounds to me," Stephanie pointed out bluntly, "as if you really do want to talk to us about this, regardless of what you told me a few minutes ago."

Jennifer sighed, very long and slow. "You're right," she answered. "But—well—" She picked up a handful of sand, let it drain from her fist like sand running through an hourglass. She glanced over at Cheryl, chewed her lower lip for a few moments. "Sam," she opened tentatively, "had that talk with Rick one night when he was—uh, just before he ended—this last, uh, affair, I guess you'd say. Did he tell you what they talked about?"

Cheryl looked concerned, but she shook her head. "Uhm, no, not really," she replied. "He never does. No, wait, he mentioned that Rick was, ah, fascinated with the girl's eyes. That's about all. Why? Rick isn't still seeing the girl, is he?"

"Oh, no, no. No, I'm pretty sure he's not."

"What, then?"

Jennifer was silent for a long time. "Well—we've never really talked about it, not right out, but—you know, that, well, a lot of these girls that Rick has had his, uhm, flings with, are, well, they're—"

"Kinky?" Stephanie supplied, almost too quickly. There was only a little catch in her voice; she couldn't quite prevent it.

Jennifer didn't notice. "Uh-huh." She sighed, sifted some more sand idly. "They, uh, they played some games—Rick told me—"

Cheryl's eyes flashed. "Rubbing your nose in it? That—"

"No, no, I asked, it was my doing, he isn't like that." She sighed again, very hard. She rolled her eyes, stared fixedly at the white-puffed blue of the Carolina summer sky. "So he told me, anyhow. About their games—with handcuffs—"

Stephanie arched her eyebrows. "Handcuffs? Who's the cuffer and who's the cuffee?"

"I don't know. Both ways. Mostly, he talked about handcuffing her." There was a moment of silence; then Jennifer looked intensely at each of her friends in turn. "What do you think about that?" she asked, her voice again little-girl. "Really sick, huh?"

Stephanie touched a finger to her lips. Clinical, Stephanie, she told herself. Purely clinical, and you don't need to give away a thing. "Well, no, it isn't 'sick,' not in any medical sense. I've read some papers that show that things like that are—well, they're a lot more common than most people think." She stopped, squinted at her friend for a moment. "But, Jenny—if I've read things right over the years, you've known about this—taste—of Rick's forever. Why is it a problem now?"

Jennifer bit her lower lip again, hard this time. "Well—I'm not sure—it's just that, just that, well, Rick and I, we talked about it a lot, and we—well, we sort of decided that—"

She ran down when she realized that both Cheryl and Stephanie were staring at her. "Wait a minute!" Cheryl cried, waving her hand dramatically, as if wiping a blackboard. "Wait a minute! You're not telling us that—!"

Her cheeks flaming, Jennifer nodded.

"You're kidding!" Cheryl blurted.

Jennifer spread her hands helplessly. "No, no I'm not! Like I said, we talked about it, and he said—well, he said pretty much the same thing you just said, Stephanie." She sighed yet again, as deeply as before. "Then—it was just one day after I'd bought this suit, it was the day I told you about, when I was trying it on around the house while I was alone. I was cleaning up Paul's room, and, well, he has these handcuffs—I don't know if they're toys or real, but they're metal, they work. I decided—I don't know why I did this, I just don't. But you two know, I guess, how it's been with me and Rick over the past few years. We're never really close, physically, except when he ends one of his affairs. It was like that, then. It's still like that."

"So what'd you do, Jennifer?" Cheryl asked. "With the handcuffs?"

"I put them on our pillow. And when we went to bed, I said, 'If you like that so much, there they are.'" She closed her eyes for a moment and raised her hands toward her face as if she were about to cover it, but did not. "I don't know why I did it. I shouldn't've, there're reasons, there're reasons why I shouldn't've, but I did, maybe I was just trying to—"

"Yes, we know," Cheryl pointed out. "What you try to do is do everything better than the competition, try to make him see what a fool he'd be if he lost you! I've told you before, that just rewards him for his escapades, it just makes him more likely to go out and—"

"She knows, Cheryl," Stephanie cut in. "God knows, we've told her often enough. But that isn't the point, not just now." She looked back at Jennifer. "So. What'd Rick say?"

"He got real serious about it. He said, Are you sure? He said he wasn't."

"Why would he say that?"

Jennifer threw her a quick but somehow pungent glance. "He knows me," she said flatly.

Stephanie frowned. "What does that mean?"

The blond woman waved a hand impatiently. "It doesn't matter," she almost snapped. "The point is, I sort of insisted. You like it, I said. We both know that. We've never done anything like this together, I said, and I'm not sure that hasn't caused us a lot of problems. So let's quit screwing around, let's do it!"

"So he agreed," Cheryl put in, resting her chin on her hand.

"Uh-huh."

"And he put them on your wrists."

"Uh-huh."

"And then?"

"And then, then nothing. We made love, he took them off, we went to sleep."

"There's more to this, Jennifer," Stephanie told her.

Jennifer's cheeks were redder than ever. "Well—I kinda—I sorta—"

"Liked it?" Cheryl supplied.

"Uh-huh—and besides—"

"Besides what?"

Abruptly, Jennifer jumped up. "Oh, nothing! I just thought it was sick, that's all! If you don't think so, then what's the big deal? It was just a game; let's go swimming!" With that she ran out into the water; when she was almost waist-deep, she threw herself in and swam on out a bit farther.

Sitting on the sand, Cheryl and Stephanie looked at each other. Just a game, Stephanie was thinking; exactly her mental description of the new forms of sexuality that had developed between her and Art. It seemed to her that her cheeks, too, might've been a little red, that her eyes might have been evasive.

Concerned again about giving herself away, it took her several minutes to notice that Cheryl, too, had pink cheeks and shifty eyes.

Thirty-Eight

As HE CAME down the highway from Duck toward Kill Devil Hills, Sam was not paying much attention to his driving. At times he had to jerk himself back to awareness, usually when he realized he was overtaking the car in front of him so fast that there was a risk of driving the Jeep squarely into the back of it.

His mind was not on his ostensible mission of acquiring liquor to loosen Rick's tongue. In his thoughts he could see and feel Cheryl, sitting on his crossed legs, the two of them coupled; he could see the candle in her hand, so close to his skin that he could feel the heat of the flame, the drops of wax falling from it much hotter than the night before. He could see that same candle in his own hand, now dripping the wax on her skin, and he could feel the unfamiliar and exciting new wildness in their lovemaking.

And he could see Cheryl this morning, examining the two tiny blisters the wax had made on her breasts. He could see her almost haunted-looking eyes, her repeated protestations that she could not understand how they'd gotten into it again when she'd been so determined that they would not.

Yet they had—and she, again, had initiated it. He remembered the way she'd lit the candles before they'd started, the way she'd put two of them on the bedside table within her reach, even as she was insisting that they would not be using them that way tonight. And he could remember the way she'd picked up the candle after they were well into their foreplay; almost automatically, almost with an air of desperate surrender. He could also remember his own eagerness to feel those bright hot flashes, and his equal eagerness to see her experience them again.

This wasn't like Cheryl and it wasn't like Sam. This morning they'd agreed that there'd be no more of this, at least for a while. They'd agreed that tonight the lovemaking—if any—would be by electric light or in darkness. But Sam could not be certain; Cheryl certainly hadn't lacked any determination the previous day, either. It just seemed that, once the sun had gone, their determination had somehow gone with it.

Worse, it wasn't just the two of them. Cheryl had told him about Jennifer's admissions; this had caused him a few pangs of guilt and self-doubt, as he could remember only too well his suggestions to Rick that he involve Jennifer in his games, and at the same time he could well remember Rick's repeated statements over the years to the effect that there was some mysterious reason that such games were not suitable for Jennifer. He'd pressed Cheryl a little, but she'd insisted that Jennifer had said no more; he could well recall, though, the slapping sounds and the soft moans, and he was quite sure there was more.

Things were changing, he told himself. How or why, he wasn't sure, but they were changing. Neither Jennifer nor Stephanie, as he'd known them, were the sort of women to wear the swimsuits they'd both suddenly—and, according to them, independently—chosen to buy.

Until now, apparently.

A car coming toward him in the other lane blasted its horn; Sam saw it, realized he was allowing the Jeep to meander into the other lane, and jerked it back over to the right as the other car whizzed by, its driver yelling insults. Annoyed with himself, Sam pounded on the wheel with his fist. Pay attention, he demanded; it sure won't help anything if you get killed out here on the highway.

Thinking about death on the highway brought Selinde back to his mind, brought that first enigmatic conversation back, the words they'd exchanged while a stranger lay dying on Hillsborough Road.

Trying—again—not to think about Selinde, he forced himself to look around. He sighed and cursed; he wasn't even really sure where he was, where the local liquor store was. All he saw was the welter of souvenir shops and hotels that made up most of these towns. He could have been in Kill Devil Hills or as far south as Nag's Head. Up ahead, a Blazer with a small boat on a trailer chugged along; he couldn't even remember seeing that vehicle before, the last one he'd almost collided with had been an Olds station wagon. He glanced in his mirror. Behind him, four or five car lengths back, was a white Corvette. That car, at least, was familiar; it had fallen in behind him somewhere above Duck, and had stayed there since. At the moment, it gave him an odd sense of stability, it proved he hadn't fallen off the edge of the world somehow.

Driving on, he began forcing himself to look for the familiar ABC logo, the emblem of North Carolina's state-owned retail liquor stores. By state edict they were never placed too closely together, but even so there was more than one out here; if he'd passed one, there should soon be another. There was; he hadn't driven many more miles before he saw one on his right. He pulled the Jeep in, parked it, and hopped out.

Inside the store, he moved through the aisles, collecting bottles. Maker's Mark for himself and Rick, two fifths was overkill but that's what he picked up anyway. For the women, Bacardi light and mixers for piña coladas. Art he didn't have to shop for, there was already a plentiful stock of soft drinks up at the house. Balancing the bottles, he started for the checkout, which at that moment was empty. Before he got there, though, a young woman carrying a single bottle of Kahlúa stepped up to the counter. At first, trying to hold all his bottles without dropping any, he hardly looked at her.

But, once he'd put them down on the rear part of the checkout counter, he did—and he froze.

White top, abbreviated white shorts exposing spectacular dark legs. Thick straight black hair falling to the middle of her back. The middle-aged male clerk was staring fixedly at a face Sam could not yet see.

It can't be, Sam told himself. It isn't possible. There just isn't any way.

Then, having paid for her Kahlúa, the woman turned. "Hello, Sam," Selinde said softly.

Sam couldn't say anything, not for a moment. Mechanically he pushed his bottles forward toward the clerk; the man was still staring at Selinde, and he just as mechanically checked them through and bagged them. He asked Sam for an amount of money and he paid it, not knowing if it was correct.

"Well?" Selinde asked as he picked up the bags. "Aren't you even going to say hello?"

"Yeah," he mumbled. "Hello. Selinde, what the fuck are you doing here?"

She laughed. "That's quite a greeting!" She turned, moved toward the door. "Come on," she instructed. "We can talk as we walk, there's no need in you standing there holding all that!" He followed her, she held the door for him, they went outside. "In answer to your question," she said as she headed unerringly toward his Jeep, "is that, well, I just decided to come down, it sounded nice. You don't have to be concerned, Sam. I'm not staying anywhere near Corolla. I'm staying in Nag's Head, at a motel called the Blue Heron."

He opened the back of the Jeep, put the packages inside. "I just can't believe," he told her, "that you just happened to be here, at this particular liquor store, at the same time I was. That just stretches the limits of coincidence all out of any reason!"

She laughed again. "It does, doesn't it? Come on, Sam. Walk with me, let me put this in my car." After closing the back of the Jeep, he did; she led him to the white Corvette, and she opened the door and put the bottle inside.

He sighed. "This is insane," he told her, shaking his head. "What have you been doing, sitting up there by the roadside waiting for me? How'd you know I'd come into town, anyway?"

"Oh, I didn't. There was some luck to that, Sam. I admit I was driving around up there, wondering how I was going to let you know I was in the area. And I saw you, driving along staring straight ahead, not seeing anything. I made a U-turn and followed you."

Visions of *Fatal Attraction* leaped to his mind. "Why?" he demanded. "Why did you want to let me know you were here?"

She leaned against the Corvette. "Because all the choices are yours, Sam. I've told you that before. And you cannot make choices if you do not know all the facts! Not intelligent ones, anyway."

He tried to glare at her, but her impact on him was too strong for him to do that, he merely ended up gazing hungrily. "I still don't understand you," he said slowly. "What do you want from me, Selinde?"

"Nothing." She smiled engagingly. "You are perfectly welcome to return to the house at Corolla and stay there. I won't call; I have no plans to come by. I plan to enjoy the beach for a while, that's all. But I did want you to know I was here."

"Why?"

"So you could make choices, Sam."

His suspicion, if anything, intensified. "What choices? Choices between you and Cheryl? I don't think—"

"No. I am not available to you as Cheryl is, Sam. You can, if you wish, choose a life with her; you cannot choose a life with me. You have other choices involving her as well, or you will soon, I think. Choices you do not have with me."

"What choices do I have with you?"

"You can choose to see me, or not. You can choose to talk to me, or not. You can choose to listen to my words, or not. You can choose to make love with me, or not. To swim in the ocean with me, or not; to ride in my car with me, or not."

"And you don't care, one way or another?"

"Oh, no. I didn't say that, Sam! I would prefer that you did all those things! But only for a time, only for a time. I will not be here much longer."

"In Nag's Head?"

"In your world, Sam. I have already moved out of my apartment in Raleigh; I will not be returning there. That's one of the reasons I wanted you to know I was here."

In spite of his suspicions he felt a sick sinking feeling in his stomach. "Where—where are you going?" he asked her.

She waved a hand carelessly. "I'm not sure yet. Away. I have not yet decided."

"When you do—will you tell me where?"

"No, Sam. I won't."

He frowned, shuffled his feet on the pavement, tried to find words to express his confused feelings. Just a few seconds ago he'd thought she was pursuing him with an intensity that might turn dangerous. Now he was trying to find something to say to her to keep her, as she'd just put it, "in his world." You watch too many goddamn movies, he told himself.

"I don't understand you at all," he told her finally. "You have got to be the strangest person I've ever met in my life. And that is saying something, Selinde!"

She smiled and shrugged slightly. "That may well be, Sam," she responded. "But, considering what you do, it would be a surprise to me if you had in your lifetime met any people that might be considered 'strange.'"

Thinking particularly of Ken, he laughed. "You don't know. Maybe I'll tell you about some of them sometime."

"Now," she said softly, "would be fine. The Blue Heron is not far." Her eyes, her expression, were very distinctly seductive.

He chewed his lip. "Don't think I wouldn't like to," he told her. "But I have to get back. I'm expected."

She shrugged again and she opened the Corvette's door. "Very well," she said. "You know where I am. I will be here almost as long as you are. My room is number two twenty-three; if I am not there, look for me on the beach, or perhaps at the pool inside."

"I don't know if I can. I don't know if I can get away, if I can come and see you . . ."

"You are in no way required to, Sam."

"I want to, you know . . ."

She sat down behind the wheel, her legs still out of the car; Sam could not help but stare at them. "I know you do, Sam." She swung her legs in, closed the door, started the engine. He took a step back; she backed the car up, drove out of the parking lot. He watched until the bright white sports car was out of sight.

Finally he climbed back into the Jeep and started it. He knew, generally, where the Blue Heron was; it was farther south, back toward Manteo, the direction the Corvette had taken. It was all he could do not to turn his own wheels that way, but he managed to swing out to the left, to head back north toward Corolla.

Thirty-Nine

"I REMEMBER READING about a case—I think it was maybe out in California. Yes, it was, I'm sure of it." Art rolled onto his back; there was a smile on his face, but his eyes remained closed. "A very interesting case. A man was charged with murder; he'd murdered his girlfriend, beat her to death with a baseball bat. The cops asked him why; you want to know why?"

Stephanie, seated on the side of the bed, looked down at him. "Why?"

"He said it was because he was trying to sleep. He was trying to sleep and she wouldn't stop talking."

Stephanie laughed quietly. "I'm sorry, I'm keeping you awake, I know. Maybe I'd better shut up, huh? I surely don't want to be beaten to death with a baseball bat!"

"You're lucky. We don't have a baseball bat down here."

She leaned over and kissed his cheek affectionately. "I am

lucky. In more ways than one." For a moment she hovered over him, smiling down at him. Things have sure changed, she told herself; two sessions of near-violent lovemaking after they'd come upstairs, as her sore and aching body attested, as Art's pretty much total exhaustion confirmed. Not even in the heady beginning of their sex life, she told herself—those days when she could hardly keep her hands off him—had things been this good. It was, truly, amazing. Like a phoenix rising from the violence of its own funeral pyre, stronger and better than ever.

His eyes flickered open as she fell silent. "Look," he said gently, "I know you're fascinated with what Rick and Jennifer have been up to; I'm interested myself. But we've about talked it to death; until and unless we get some new information, there really isn't a whole lot left to say." He grinned broadly. "Maybe, when we get back to Raleigh, we can buy some handcuffs ourselves. See what happens."

She rolled her eyes. "Forget it, Art! Besides, you haven't had to handcuff me to have your way with me, have you?"

"No; sure haven't. Still, it might be fun. A new twist on things. Just another game, Stephanie."

She fell silent again, thinking about it. The overriding question in her mind was—why? What was the point? Handcuffs—or the idea of having one's hands restrained—didn't seem particularly erotic. Art's theory that Jennifer was being spanked by Rick was a little more interesting, but not much; she tried to visualize herself lying across Art's lap while he slapped her rear with his hand or with some instrument like a hairbrush, and found the image unappealing. Besides, she felt it a bit degrading, playing the role of the child while Art portrayed the adult. That might be all right between Rick and Jennifer, but it wasn't the way things were between them, they should be standing face to face, as equals.

No, she thought, a bit sadly. No, she'd never allowed things to be quite that way. In their relationship, just as in Rick and Jennifer's, there was an adult and a child—but here, Stephanie was the adult. For a moment she felt intensely envious of Sam and Cheryl—they alone seemed to have achieved a sort of a balance, even if it did require periodic warfare to maintain. Maybe they should reverse it; maybe she should put Art across her knee and spank him. She visualized that, found it utterly distasteful, dismissed it. Having sorted out her thoughts somewhat, she turned back to Art, planning to reinitiate the conversation in spite of his desire to sleep—and discovered that he'd already faded out on her.

For a moment, a bit of the old Stephanie reemerged; how dare he, she wasn't through talking! She reached for his shoulder to shake him awake but caught herself in time. No, Stephanie, she told herself firmly. No, the man has every right to sleep. Besides, you don't want to be beaten, do you?

Well . . .

Angry with herself, she stood up. Go downstairs, she told herself; get yourself a glass of wine or something. That you don't feel like sleeping right now is your problem, not his. She reached for her swimsuit to put it back on, decided that was too much trouble. Instead, she dressed in a short housecoat, belted it at her waist, and padded quietly downstairs to the kitchen.

Forty-five minutes later, still feeling restless, she sat at the kitchen table staring blankly at an empty glass. She really wished that someone else was up—anyone—so that she'd have someone to talk to. You really are changing, Stephanie, she said silently. It never used to bother you to be alone. Her eyes wandered—as they'd wandered before—toward the kaleidoscope, which was lying invitingly in sight, resting on the living-room mantlepiece, visible through the kitchen doorway.

Again, she commanded herself not to do that—the kaleidoscope could not be used without a light, and she didn't want to turn one on, since it would be noticed by anyone upstairs who got up to go to the bathroom. Sort of silly, she told herself—you want company but you don't want the others to think you were so obsessed you came down here just to play with that thing.

But maybe there was another way. The small kitchen nightlight didn't provide sufficient illumination, but outside, the moonlight was very bright; it might be interesting to see what that sort of light did to the images.

Having made her decision, she hurried off to the downstairs bathroom and sprayed her arms and legs with insect repellent—the Outer Banks mosquitoes could be vicious—then quickly retrieved the kaleidoscope from the mantle. Mere seconds later she was in the backyard, trying to locate the gibbous moon.

I can't see it from here, she mused silently. It's still too early, it's only around eleven; it hasn't cleared the house yet. Determined, she went around to the front, but discovered that she could get no clear view there, either—the trees were in the way. For the next fifteen minutes she wandered around, even walking a hundred yards down the driveway, trying to get an unobstructed view. There was not one to be had.

From the ground, anyhow. Her gaze roamed upward, to the second-story balcony that stretched out across the bedrooms the Leos and the Masons used, and to the widow's walk high atop the house.

The widow's walk would be best but it wouldn't do, she told herself. Access to it was through the attic, and one could not get to the attic except via a disappearing stair in the ceiling of the hall-way between the bedrooms. She'd been up there, and she knew how much racket that disappearing stair made when it was pulled down; it would wake everyone, draw everyone into the hallway.

It was the balcony or nothing. There was a risk there, too; if one of the Leos or one of the Masons decided to sit at the window—and Stephanie knew, from casual comments, that Sam often did that—she might well be seen.

Well, what the hell, she thought. If you're caught you're caught. It isn't a crime. Having made her decision, she reentered the house, went upstairs, and went down the narrow side hall along-side the Masons' bedroom that gave access to the balcony.

For a moment she stood by the door, inspecting the balcony. Immediately to her right were the windows of the Masons' bed-room, from which a soft light spilled. Beyond, the spare room, which was of course dark; lastly, the Leos' room, from which an even softer light—candlelight, perhaps—emerged. Damn, she said mentally. They're probably all still up, Art's most likely the only person around here sleeping.

Still, there was only one obstacle—the Masons' room. Once past it, she could sit by the spare room's windows and run almost no risk of being seen. She had two choices; dash by and hope, or creep by under the sill on her hands and knees.

She chose creeping. She wasn't really afraid of being caught, but it would be embarrassing. The others would, she knew, tease her about it unmercifully. Feeling like some sort of cat burglar, she dropped down and began crawling, being careful not to allow her head to poke up above the sill and trying to be equally careful not to bash the precious kaleidoscope against the floor.

Her concerns were unwarranted, though; she cleared the Ma-sons' room without incident, and she heard no cry from within that might have suggested that either of them had seen her. Feeling rather proud of herself now, she sat down and lifted the kaleido-scope to her eye, aiming it at the now easily visible moon.

And discovered, to her immense disappointment, that the moon did not provide enough light for her to see the crystal patterns.

For a moment, she sat cursing silently. All this for nothing; and there was nothing she could do now except go back, the same way she had come.

Again she dropped to her hands and knees and started crawling, again wary about the position of her head and the position of the kaleidoscope in her hand. She was not so nervous this time; having done it once successfully, she was quite sure she could do it again.

She was still thinking that when, without warning, something large, dark, and furry sprang up from the shadows, striking her right in the face.

Startled, she slapped at it and rose halfway up; but it only took her a second to realize that her assailant was merely a large moth, disturbed from its resting place. Again, she swore mentally; by the time she understood that she'd already gotten up, she was in full view of the Masons' still-lit window. She sighed, waiting for them to call out to her, to begin the inevitable razzing.

Several seconds passed; no call came. She turned her head, looked in the window.

She was indeed in Rick's and Jennifer's sight; if they'd been looking, which they were not. She was seeing them in profile, Rick on his back on the bed, Jennifer astride his hips and bouncing up and down. Embarrassed—feeling like a peeping tom even though this had been the purest of accidents—Stephanie started to turn away.

And found that she couldn't, not immediately.

It was the look on Jennifer's face that trapped her, that kept her frozen there on the balcony for a few seconds. Stephanie could not have said that she'd actually seen very many women in the act of love; she'd seen a few X-rated videos—in Art's company and in the company of other, former, lovers—and she'd seen herself, in a mirror, once when she and Art had stayed in a motel near Charlotte that had mounted mirrors on the ceiling.

The expression on Jennifer's face was not even remotely close to the one Stephanie herself had worn at that time—and that had been a time when she and Art had been very passionate with each other. The comparisons were like the comparisons she'd made, not too long ago, among kaleidoscopes—the X-rated actresses matched the dime-store version, her own was like the other high-quality scopes she'd seen in the Dancing Moon. And Jennifer's—right now, as she watched—was like the kaleidoscope in her hand.

Most women, she was sure, never reached heights like that in their lives; and she knew quite well, from various discussions with Jennifer, that her sex life with Rick had not always been this good. But what she was seeing now stunned her; she could almost feel, physically, the force of the other woman's emotion. She felt herself begin to tremble as waves of feeling swept over her: first an erotic flush, then something like fear or anger, then intense envy, then all of them, all jumbled up together. If this was what handcuffs could do, she wanted handcuffs. Whatever could do this, she wanted. She had no doubt whatsoever.

Still feeling dazed, she nevertheless managed to break free of her paralysis; not noticing or caring if she was seen, she careened back to the door leading into the hallway. From there it was only a few steps to her room, but even so she had to restrain herself, had to force herself not to run. Art was, as a matter of fact, going to wake up. She wanted to talk; and she wanted something else, as well.

Forty

"TWO WHOLE DAYS now," Cheryl said in a slightly disgruntled tone. Lying on her stomach on an air mattress that was floating gently on the waters of the inlet, she folded her hands and propped her chin on them. "I'd bet they haven't spent an hour, total, in the water. Nobody's sunbathed—except me. Nobody's dropped in a serious fishing line—except you. What's the matter with them, anyhow?"

Sam, half standing on the bottom alongside the raft and half hanging onto its edge, shook his head. They'd been like this when he'd returned from his trip into town—almost exactly like this, in fact, Cheryl out floating on her raft alone. The planned drinking party hadn't gotten under way, and it didn't look like a good bet for tonight either—Sam simply could not command Art's attention long enough to lay any plans. He gazed over at his friends on the bank, who were, as had now become usual, fighting over the kaleidoscope, over whose turn it now was to sit and stare through it for a while. Watching them, Sam was reminded of college marijuana parties, the well-stoned participants staring vacantly into space for hours.

"Maybe it's just our age," he mused. "We're all, all six of us, within three years of thirty-five; maybe there's something telling us to have our high times now, to play our childish games now, because tomorrow will be too late."

"Doesn't make sense," Cheryl answered. "Why all of us at once? This has all developed over maybe the last two or three weeks. If it were age, it'd be scattered out. You and Rick are thirty-seven, you should've had your crisis two years ago. Stephanie's thirty-three, Jenny and I are thirty-two; we've got a while to go. Art's the only one right on the nose."

"I'm not sure it works like that, everybody doesn't have his crisis right at thirty or forty or whatever. Still, it is odd that we'd all hit at exactly the same time; you're right about that."

She turned her face toward him; her green eyes were extremely bright in the sunshine. "So what's the answer, Sam?"

He grinned. "I don't think I have one."

"You, Sam? You don't have an answer? This is a red-letter day. This one we have to mark down on the calendar!"

He laughed and suddenly flipped the raft over, dumping Cheryl unceremoniously into the water. She came up sputtering, splashed water at him; for a few minutes they churned the inlet furiously, hurling spray at each other and giggling like children. As the moment of playfulness ended, Sam noticed that Rick was standing up on the shore, yelling at them. Sam couldn't hear the words, but he could see Rick motioning for them to come in.

"What's going on?" Cheryl asked as she clambered back up onto the raft.

"I don't know," he replied. Grabbing the string on her raft, he started half-swimming, half-walking toward them, towing the raft along. "But we'll soon see." He glanced up at the sky. "It's getting kind of late anyway. About time to be thinking about what we're going to do about dinner tonight."

"Oh, we planned all that while you were off fishing," Cheryl told him. "We're going to make some sauces and fire up the fondue pots, we've got a lot of goodies we can stick in them. But you are right, it's time we should be getting to it."

The others were waiting for them on the bank. "Sam," Rick said as they came close, "we need you, we need your ingenuity. We have something we want to rig up."

"Rig up? What?"

"Well, we understand that you and Cheryl aren't all that interested, but we're just fascinated with this thing!" He held up the kaleidoscope and laughed. "But you know that, I guess . . . Anyway, we've been sitting here for a long time with each one of us saying, 'God, I wish you could see this one!' We want to rig up some way so we can."

Sam looked blank. "Can what?"

"Can all see it at the same time!"

"How're you planning to do that?"

"Well, you remember the slide projector we have stored away? Art and I were wondering if we could figure out a way to set it up so that the images from the kaleidoscope were projected. You used to screw around with cameras a lot; we figured you'd know how to do it."

Sam scowled as he considered the problem. "Let me see that thing for a minute," he asked. Rick handed it to him, he looked through it, up at the late afternoon sky, at the really lovely patterns inside. He still didn't feel drawn to them as the others were; he was still able to view them more or less objectively. The lens was a slight magnifier, he told himself, not intended for projection. Examining it closely, he saw that the eyepiece looked as if it was designed to screw out. He tested it with a gentle turning effort; it was.

"I think we can do it," Sam said finally, handing it back to Rick. "You mind?"

He shrugged. "I guess not. Maybe after dinner—"

"The ladies are going to make the food tonight. We've got some free time. How about now?"

"Right now?"

"Sure! As soon as you get dried off."

Sam considered it; he wasn't himself really that interested, but it was obvious Rick was, and so were the others. It'll be a challenge, he told himself, and it'll take your mind off things for a while. "Yeah," he said finally. "I see no reason why not."

It was just beginning to get dark by the time the women had finished making their sauces and preparing various tidbits to dip into them. At about that same time, Sam had finished his project, mounting the little kaleidoscope in the slide projector and fixing the lens in front of it so that the image could be focused. While Rick and Art watched over his shoulder, he tested it, firing a multicolored beam of light at the projection screen. A few minor distance adjustments and the image was bright and sharp.

"That's great," Art breathed. "Just great!"

"I fixed it so you could turn it, too," Sam told them, demonstrating. As the tube turned, the image fractured and reformed, completely different than before. Proud of himself, he held out his hand. "Now all we need is music and popcorn, and the show can begin!"

"Or music and fondue?" Rick suggested.

"Sure," Art agreed. "Why not?"

Cheryl and Sam had little to say about it; they were outvoted by enthusiastic responses from both Jennifer and Stephanie. A low table was moved into the living room, the fondue pots and the stubby candles that had been placed under them were moved; wine was poured into five glasses and Coke into a sixth. Cushions were moved from the chairs and the couch onto the floor, and the group, all of them still in their swimsuits, settled down to dinner— and to a kaleidoscope show. Rick put on music as well, old classics; a "greatest hits" CD featuring the songs of Steely Dan.

The patterns were beautiful, Sam told himself once again as Rick turned the tube periodically, evoking admiring comments from the others. Beautiful, but after a while, almost boring to himself and Cheryl. More and more, he found it difficult to understand his friends' near-obsession with the thing.

"Have you tied into the system back at the Center yet, Sam?" Stephanie asked abruptly.

A little startled, he held a shrimp over one of the fondue pots and allowed it to drip. "No," he told her. "Not yet. I guess I'm going to have to pretty soon—tomorrow, probably—or that asshole Ken'll start getting impatient. Why'd you ask?"

Colored patterns in reds and whites streamed down Stephanie's face, reflected from the screen. "Oh, I don't know. Something just made me think of all those weird cases, that's all. I wondered if you'd found out anything new."

"That's weird," Rick commented. He left the pattern as it was and speared a piece of beef tenderloin with his fork. "I was just thinking about the same thing!"

"So was I," Art chimed in.

"The kaleidoscope," Jennifer put in. "Something in one of those images, just a few seconds ago. That's what suggested it!"

Sam's fondue fork reached out to the plate of steak. He speared one, watching the twin prongs sink into the meat, noticing how their penetration was limited by the division of the prongs. The fork was of exceptional quality, the tines very thin and sharp, surgical steel; they pierced the piece of beef effortlessly. A little blood flowed from it, and he watched that too. Then he dipped it into a pot of hot spiced oil. "I didn't see anything like that," he said as it cooked. "All I'm seeing are colors."

Stephanie turned, looked back at them. "It really doesn't affect you two at all, does it?" she asked. Both Sam and Cheryl shook their heads, and she sighed. "I wish I could explain the effect it has on me," she continued, her voice soft. "Those patterns make me think about things I haven't thought about in years . . . They make me think of things I've never thought about, too. . . ."

Sam leaned forward a little. "What sorts of things, Stephanie?" he asked her.

A frown crossed her face, only to vanish almost immediately. "Oh, I don't know. Things." Her eyes were again evasive.

"A lot of times," Art put in, "those patterns seem sort of— erotic—to me. I'll be damned if I could explain why, though."

"They're like Rorschach patterns," Stephanie observed.

"Yeah, that's what it is," Rick agreed. He turned the tube again, produced an all-new mandala. "That's why they do what they do. I wonder if whoever made this thing understood that, if it was intentional or just a happy accident?"

"If they're Rorschachs," Cheryl noted, "they should suggest all sorts of things. Not just erotica."

"They do, Cheryl," Jennifer told her. "It just seems like—well, I have to agree—there's a lot of—uhm—erotica—"

Sam grinned. "Hell, that's easy to explain," he said.

"What's your idea, Sam?" Stephanie asked.

"It's simple enough. Just look at this group; three attractive women sitting around in miniature bathing suits, and three—well, I won't say anything about the men, but you get the idea, I'm sure."

"No, that's not it," Stephanie protested. "Well, it's not all of it, anyway. I'd sit around in the morning, at the breakfast table, all alone, and those patterns would have the same sort of effect on me." She glanced at Art and colored slightly. "Of course," she admitted, "we have been—uhm—well—"

"More active than usual lately," Art supplied blandly.

Stephanie was smiling, but she was squirming just a little too;

she turned her face back toward the table, speared a shrimp with her fondue fork, and watched it closely while it cooked.

Sam watched her do it, thinking about what she'd just said. He'd not failed to notice, from the first time he'd met Stephanie Dixon, how attractive she was; now—probably because of the suit, he told himself, probably because of that—she seemed to almost radiate sexuality. She was twisted slightly to one side as she cooked her shrimp, rolled a little onto one hip, her exposed rear lifted. Sam felt an almost overwhelming urge to crawl forward and caress it, kiss it. Naturally, he resisted this urge; it seemed to him he'd been resisting a lot of urges lately. Jennifer was saying something; Sam used the distraction to tear his eyes away from Stephanie, look over toward her. When he did, he discovered that he was having almost exactly the same reaction to her, the same urges, although they were more focused on her almost-bare chest.

"I know what you mean," she was saying. "I really do have to sit down and do a chart with all the progressions. There's something going on, that's for sure! The swimsuits are part of it, that kaleidoscope is part of it, and what Rick and I have been doing with the— uh, the, uh, uhm—" She faded down, her cheeks turning red once again, her gaze moving to her lap.

For a few seconds no one said anything. Of the six of them, only Art could harbor any real doubts as to what she was referring to.

It was he who broke the silence. "You know," he said mildly, "we've all known each other for a long time. And still, for all that, there's a lot of pretense, a lot of posturing. You three women, you all know that Rick and Sam and I talk pretty bluntly among ourselves, and we know that you three do the same thing. We also know that spouses share secrets with their spouses; maybe not quite all, but a lot. I, for one, certainly wouldn't tell Stephanie anything that I didn't want Rick to know—not without swearing her to silence, on pain of death, first. But for the most part, we all know a great deal about each other's private lives. Yet we pretend, all the time, that we don't."

There was another short silence; Rick had fixed his wife with a piercing stare. "I take it," he said finally, "that you told the ladies about our little games." He glanced at Stephanie. "And I further take it that you told Art." Both Stephanie and Jennifer nodded, a little sheepishly. Rick turned his attention to Cheryl. "You told Sam, too, didn't you?"

The dark-haired woman caught her lower lip with her teeth. "Uh-huh."

He sighed, rubbed his hand down over his face. "All right. So everybody knows all about it. I—"

"Not all about it, Rick!" Jennifer cried, drawing stares from everyone.

Art's head swiveled around. "What don't we know, Rick?" he asked with a sly grin.

Rick broke into a grin, too, but his was close to wolfish. "I don't know. But there's some things I do know. Don't forget, I'm a doctor; now I know that doesn't make me special in this group, but I have a daily practice, I run into things, I've learned to observe—"

"That doesn't make you special either, Rick!" Stephanie pointed out.

"Maybe not. But I'm not blind. I know the games people play in bed; sometimes folks get carried away. Then they need my services, and I hear about it." He looked squarely at Art. "Human teeth are pretty septic, old buddy," he said directly. "Even nice, pretty, straight ones like Stephanie's. When you bite nipples with them you make little lesions and infections set in. They usually aren't dangerous, but their effects are sort of obvious!" He looked over at Stephanie. "If yours are the same," he went on, "relief from the trauma and a little Neosporin will clear them up. But then, you know that, don't you?"

"Now, wait just a minute," Art snapped heatedly. "There might be other reasons—"

Stephanie, like Jennifer, was looking down at her lap. "I don't think that's going to do any good, Art," she said quietly. Squaring her shoulders, she looked back up at Rick. "All right," she said challengingly. "So we've been a little rough with each other lately, a little wild. So what?"

Rick shrugged. "So nothing. It's your business. Just like the games Jennifer and I are playing are our business."

"No one ever said they weren't," Stephanie pointed out, her voice cold.

"Now wait a minute," Sam cut in. "Let's not let this thing get all out of hand here. Rick, I think what Art was doing was trying to save Jennifer some embarrassment. The fact is, he was right. We all know you two have been playing handcuff games. You're right about it being your business, but it surely isn't something for us to have some huge falling out over. Art's right, too. We do know a lot about each other's private lives, and it's kind of ridiculous for us to sit around pretending that we don't."

Rick glared for a moment, but then his features softened and he shrugged. "Yeah. I suppose that's true. It just, well, it just isn't the kind of thing you issue a press release about."

"No. But talking about these things among the six of us isn't releasing it to the general public. Information runs around this circle like wildfire, but it stays in the circle."

"Yeah." He looked over at Stephanie and Art. "Sorry, guys," he said. "You know I love you, don't you?"

"You did lay our laundry out on the table for everybody to see," Stephanie answered. But she followed her statement with a smile. "But I suppose I would've talked about it with Jennifer and Cheryl at some point, and by the next day you guys would've known all about it."

"I don't know why," Jennifer put in, "you didn't mention it when I was telling you about the handcuffs!"

"I was embarrassed, okay?"

"Well, so was I, Stephanie! But I told you anyway! I wanted to hear your opinion! You don't care about mine? I guess not. I'm just a housewife, everybody else here is an expert on something!"

"Oh, you know that isn't true! It's just that—it's just—"

"It's just what?"

"A little hard to talk about, okay?"

"You don't think it was hard for me to talk about the handcuffs?"

Sam was not sorry that Stephanie and Art were in the hot seat. It could just as easily have been himself and Cheryl, and he was hoping against hope that Art wasn't going to remember the wax and start putting things together.

Again, Stephanie squared her shoulders. "All right. All right, Jennifer. You're right, I owe you." She glanced at Art; he said nothing. "What we've been into isn't—I don't know, as structured as handcuffs. All that's happened with us is, we've taken the usual —uh, nibbling—during loveplay another step."

"In other words, biting," Jennifer observed. She smiled.

Stephanie's manner was very formal, very stiff. "Yes. We've found that the, uh, uhm, the stimulation of—I mean, it just seems to—" She stopped, slapped the floor beside her cushion. "God damn it! It's a turn-on, okay? We just discovered that, okay?"

Jennifer's eyes were quite wide; Sam was having no trouble identifying a phony "oh, I am so shocked!" look. "So what have you two been doing?" she persisted. "Exactly, I mean?"

"I told you. Biting."

"Where, I mean?"

Stephanie ground her teeth audibly. "Lots of different places. Arms, legs."

"I haven't seen any bite marks on your arms and legs." In exaggerated fashion, she looked over Stephanie's still-exposed limbs. "And I still don't."

"I think," Rick observed, "that I've already identified the primary site!"

Jennifer looked back at him. "The nipples."

"Uh-huh."

She rose from where she was sitting, went over and knelt beside Art. Leaning her head down, she studied his chest closely. "Yes," she announced. "You're right. They are red." Art didn't even look up at her.

"I have apologized," Stephanie begged almost desperately. "You don't have to milk this for all it's worth!" Everyone erupted in giggling, but it was a few seconds before Stephanie herself became aware of her unintended pun. She groaned, passed a hand over her face.

"I think," Rick commented, "that you should let me examine your nipples, Stephanie. Real closely. Professionally, you understand. Make sure there's no infection."

To this Stephanie didn't reply. Red-faced, she and Art sat and took Jennifer's and Rick's jokes stoically, without protest. Cheryl had scooted over close to Sam; he knew she, too, was hoping that nothing would come up that would cause them to end up in the Dixons' place.

But the conversation was, in fact, beginning to turn him on—and the onrush of the night outside seemed to be intensifying that. Cheryl was not unaffected either; her hand had stolen over to his thigh, and her fingers were very active. He moved toward her, too, put an arm around her, slipped a single finger inside the top of her swimsuit.

Eventually Cheryl stood up. "Well," she said, cutting into the continuing teasing, "don't get me wrong—all of this is very interesting—but I think Sam and I are going to head on upstairs."

"Oh, don't go, Cheryl!" Jennifer cried.

"Have to," she said, grinning and tousling her hair. "Nature calls!"

Forty-One

HER EMOTIONS IN turmoil, Stephanie watched Sam and Cheryl as they left the room; when they'd disappeared up the stairs, she breathed a sigh of relief. Her position relative to that of Rick and Jennifer was not too bad, but she'd been terribly embarrassed about having her sexual peculiarities laid bare in front of Sam and Cheryl—who, if they had any, were still successfully concealing them.

With lowered brows, she turned on Rick. "Okay, Dr. Mason," she said ominously. "For the last half hour you've been ragging us without mercy. Now, it's time to turn things around! You know what we've been into, and you know a lot about it! How about you and Jennifer? We haven't heard a thing, except that you've been playing with handcuffs! Are you still using Paul's toys? Or have you gone out and bought yourself some brass ones, maybe some encrusted with rhinestones? What about leathers, leather outfits? You can't do bondage right without leather outfits, can you? And do you have one of those little balls to stuff in Jennifer's mouth so she can't scream?"

Rick idly turned the kaleidoscope, and everyone was distracted for a few seconds by the new pattern that appeared. "I suppose," he mused, "that we'll have to answer all those questions, even though the answers are going to disappoint you. But I still have a problem here."

"What's that?"

He laughed. "You still haven't let me examine your nipples! As I said, my only interest, I swear, is purely professional, and—"

Stephanie, determined to take control of this conversation, glared at Rick as he spoke. Then, after an instant's hesitation, she reached around behind her back and untied the top of her swimsuit. With a flourish, she threw it aside. "Here they are," she announced. "Examine."

Several seconds of absolute silence ensued. Both Art and Jennifer stared at her in disbelief.

"Uh, Stephanie," Rick said finally, "uh, gee, I was only kidding around—"

"You kidded around too much," Stephanie told him, her hands on her hips. "Now you come here and examine them! That's what you said you wanted to do!"

"Ah—come on, Stephanie, gee whiz, I can't do that!" Rick's manner had reverted to boyish—his last-line defense, as Stephanie knew. "I mean, Jennifer and Art—!"

"You asked, Rick," Jennifer said. "More than once."

"That's right," Art agreed, grinning. "Now I think you have to do it!"

Looking even more confused, he stared at each one of them in turn. "All right," he said finally, though his voice quavered a little. "All right, all right. You think this is going to be hard? You're wrong. I have no problems with this." He started to get up, lost his balance, had to try again. Jennifer giggled; Stephanie kept her hands on her hips and her gaze steady.

Taking more time than it really required, he came over to Stephanie and knelt down beside her. He took a deep breath, then leaned forward; Stephanie sat rigidly while he looked closely at each of her breasts in turn.

"They don't look bad," he said eventually. "A little red, but not bad."

Stephanie decided to push a little more. "Is that the way you do examinations in your office, Doctor?" she demanded. "That wasn't the procedure when I was there!"

"I was checking for infection," Rick said through clenched teeth. "Not for tumors or fibroids!"

"As I recall," she persisted, "the procedure for checking a possible infection is—"

"Damn it, I know the procedure, Stephanie! How far are you going to push this?"

She knew that this had a potential for getting out of hand, but right now, she really wanted to push on. Somewhere deep in her mind, a small and almost-unheard voice tried to council caution. She looked over at Jennifer, then at Art; neither seemed upset, so she continued. "So now, Doctor, I think you should proceed with a proper examination!"

"Damn," Rick muttered. "I didn't think I'd ever see this day, and I sure didn't think I'd be embarrassed if it ever came!" With his jaw set, he raised his hands, put them on Stephanie's breasts. Watching the nipples, he squeezed them gently; then he moved his thumbs and forefingers down to the nipples themselves, squeezing them too, very lightly. Promptly, they completed the erection they'd begun a few moments before.

Stephanie caught the inside of her lower lip between her teeth as he rolled her nipples between his fingers. It had been a very long time since any man—other than Art—had touched her like this, even professionally; her gynecologist was female. It was sending little shocks all through her; her whole body was beginning to react to Rick's touches.

Then, abruptly, he took his hands away. "There's no exudate," he told her. "There's no major infection." He started to rise to his feet but stopped halfway up. Maintaining a bent-over posture as if he had severe abdominal cramps, he returned to his own cushion. His effort was in vain, Stephanie was sure; no one missed the fact that he had an erection.

Stephanie took her hands off her hips and looked around for her top; she'd thrown it quite far away, and it seemed ridiculous to get up and go after it. Letting it go, she drained the last of her wine. "Okay, Rick," she said when she'd finished. "Now, you've done your examination. Now, you can answer my questions!"

"I've forgotten what they were," he grumbled, spinning the kaleidoscope once again, changing the long-static pattern and staring at it blankly for a moment.

Stephanie looked too, and was momentarily distracted. The crystals were taking their time about settling into a new position; even though Rick wasn't moving the tube, the images kept shifting, changing. Four distinct circles formed at the corners of the array, drew attention to themselves by developing multiple borders. A sort of a twelve-pointed star in creamed-coffee brown appeared in each circle, the two points at the bottom being squarely blunted and much thicker than the others. After a moment the upper ten points grew long, slim, pointed; pale red ovals tinged their tips. Then a ribbon of bright silver wound itself around the two thicker points. Behind the star a long band of darkness developed, spilling rapidly across the circle and vanishing; bright flecks of a brilliant scarlet remained in its wake.

Stephanie could not have said why, but she could not help but notice the erotic appeal of this particular pattern.

"Oh, yeah," Rick continued, drawing her attention back to the conversation. "No, I bought us some handcuffs, I—" He stopped speaking, looked directly at Stephanie. "Well, shit. If you're so damn curious, maybe we ought to just show you! What do you think about that, Jennifer? Should we just take them upstairs and show them?"

"Yeah, that'd be fine!" Art said jokingly. "Then I could decide if either of you has grounds for a suit against the other!"

Stephanie was not about to allow Rick to recapture the initiative. "That's a very good idea, Rick," she said coolly. "If you can, that is!"

"Oh, I can, all right!" he blustered. "You'd better believe it!" He smiled at Jennifer. He knows she'll put an end to this, Stephanie told herself, he knows she'll rescue him. And that's all right; as long as I don't have to take him off the hook.

"I have no problem with that," Jennifer said unexpectedly.

Art's and Stephanie's heads swiveled toward her. She, too, was smiling; she, too, was obviously enjoying Rick's discomfort.

Rick was staring at his wife with almost goggle eyes. "Uh—uh, are you sure, Jenny? I mean, I mean, I was—"

"We don't have to," Stephanie said magnanimously. "Since you obviously aren't comfortable with it, Rick—"

He turned back to her, and his jaw was more set than ever. "All right," he said, and from the tone of his voice Stephanie knew she'd pushed too hard. He flipped the slide projector off and stood up. "Let's go. Let's go upstairs, to our room." A little more slowly, Jennifer stood up, too.

Art, who'd been lounging against the table, suddenly sat up straight. Clearly he'd hadn't seen how serious this was getting. "Let's go?" he echoed. "Upstairs?"

But Stephanie was already getting to her feet. Not only did she feel she had no choice—she couldn't be the one to back down— she was also feeling an intense surge of excitement. "Yes, let's," she told him. "Come on, Art."

"Uh—really?"

"Really." By then, Rick and Jennifer had already started moving toward the stair; Stephanie took Art's hand, pulled him to his feet. He was so dazed he stumbled along behind her; she was by then so excited that she'd forgotten she was wearing only half her swimsuit.

Stiff-backed, Rick marched down the hall past Sam and Cheryl's room, followed closely by the others. Stephanie thought about knocking on their door to tell them what was happening, invite them to witness as well, but she decided against it; it'd be overkill,

she told herself, especially if this whole thing went very far—and
she could not foresee, at the moment, exactly how far it might go.

Rick, certainly, seemed intent on backing up his boasts, no matter what the outcome. He opened the door to his and Jennifer's
room, showed everyone inside, closed it behind them. Stephanie
and Art took seats; Stephanie on a chair that stood in front of the
vanity, Art on the floor beside her. The bed, significantly, remained vacant.

Standing in the middle of the room, Rick put his hands on
Jennifer's shoulders. "You serious about this?" he asked, his eyes
moving rapidly from one of hers to the other.

"Sure," she said, her voice almost inaudible. "Sooner or later
I'll talk about it with Stephanie, we've decided that. And she'll tell
Art about it. So why not?"

He looked like he was going to choke. "All right, then," he said.
"Let's do it!" He went to the dresser, opened the bottom drawer,
rummaged around in it.

And, while he was doing that, Jennifer quietly began removing
her swimsuit, pushing the straps over her shoulders and revealing
the remainder of her breasts, then rolling the tight fabric down
over slim hips. Art watched her carefully; Stephanie saw his eyes
fix on her breasts, then move downward as her pubic hair was
exposed. To Stephanie's surprise, she seemed quite unselfconscious about this; she even met Art's gaze and smiled at him.

She held out her hands as Rick returned from the dresser carrying an assortment of items. First, he wrapped each of her wrists in
foam rubber, then secured it with Velcro straps, the type used on
blood-pressure cuffs. The handcuffs followed, bright shining steel
glinting in the moderate light of the bedroom. He snapped them
on, snugged them up, tested their fit by tugging on the links of
chain that connected them.

Then he turned away again, first picking up a stool from the
floor near the closet. Another trip to the dresser followed, and this
time he came back holding a length of yellow polypropylene rope
with a hook at each end.

"What's that for?" Stephanie asked.

"You'll see," Rick replied, stepping up on the stool. As he
reached up toward the ceiling, she noticed for the first time the
hook that had been mounted there, right in the center of the
room. After looping the rope over the hook he stepped back down
and fastened the hook at the other end to a ring that had been
screwed into the wall. Then he helped Jennifer to step up on the

stool. After a quick glance at Stephanie, she raised her arms, and Rick engaged the remaining hook in the handcuff chain.

Then he pulled the stool away, leaving Jennifer hanging naked from the handcuffs, her feet swinging a few inches off the floor. Wide-eyed, Stephanie and Art watched in silence.

"Go on," Jennifer whispered. "Go on."

With a nod, Rick left her and went to the closet. The door opened, closed. When he came back, Stephanie's mouth dropped open; in his hand was a black leather belt, gold slip-buckle, no holes. She knew, now, where this was headed.

Rick glanced over at the two of them; then, a look of absolute determination on his face, he drew the belt back and swung it, hard. It struck Jennifer's bare buttocks with a resounding crack.

"Ah!" she cried in muted tones. "Yes, God, yes!" Rick hit her again, across the front of her thighs, making her body swing back and forth in a rather wide arc.

"Jesus Christ!" Art muttered. "And I thought we'd gotten kinky!"

Rick lashed out with the belt again, and the leather smacked hard against her stomach; she cried out and began to moan. The next blow was across her breasts, causing them to bounce. Like a wild animal he circled her dangling and swinging body, and the belt kept snaking out, kept pounding against her skin—which quickly reddened.

After he'd delivered perhaps ten or twelve strokes, Jennifer told him that she'd had enough; to Stephanie's considerable surprise, his response was to hit her again, harder than before. Once more she told him to stop, and instead received another lash across her breasts.

But then, after giving her one more, Rick lowered the belt. Both of them were coated by a fine gloss of sweat, both seemed to be really getting into it, both seemed to have forgotten that Art and Stephanie were there. Putting the belt down, Rick struggled out of his swim trunks; his erection bounced up. He then wrapped his arms around Jennifer's body, kissing her passionately, all over. Kneeling down, he pushed his head between her legs and she started moaning louder than ever. After an extremely brief interval, she cried out again and shuddered with a violent orgasm.

Moving quickly, Rick put the stool back; she stepped up on it, he unhooked the rope from the cuffs, helped her down to the floor, and unlocked the cuffs and took them off her wrists. Still holding them, he offered her his own hands; she removed the

Velcro straps and the foam pads from her own wrists and put them on his. The cuffs followed, and after a very few seconds, it was Rick who was dangling and it was Jennifer who stalked around him, lashing him repeatedly and violently with the leather belt. He didn't take as many as she had before calling for a halt; as if following an agreed-upon pattern, Jennifer dealt him three more —the hardest yet—before stopping.

Kneeling in front of him, Jennifer used her tongue to sweep his rigid erection into her mouth. She began moving her head back and forth, but Rick was obviously highly stimulated; after only a few minutes he stiffened and sprayed his ejaculate into Jennifer's mouth. She swallowed most, but not quite all; a little trickle of white fluid ran from her lips onto her chin.

Moving much more slowly than Rick had, she replaced the stool, let him down, unlocked the cuffs. He kissed her deeply, held her tightly for a few seconds, then, as if finally remembering that they'd had an audience, turned to Stephanie and Art. His eyes were still wild, his erection had not yet completely disappeared. "So," he said, his voice breathy. "That's it, now you've seen it. You want to take a turn up there, Stephanie?"

Stephanie didn't hesitate, not even for an instant; she felt like she was on fire. "Yes," she said, standing up and tugging at the bottom of her swimsuit. "Yes, I do!"

Art looked up at her as if he simply could not believe what he was hearing. "Stephanie, are you out of your mind?" he cried.

"Maybe," she told him carelessly as she stepped out of her suit. "What's the difference, Art? They know what we've been doing, and now we know what they've been doing. Come on! Aren't you turned on? I am, I don't mind saying that!"

"Well, yes, I am, but Jesus Christ! I can't believe—!"

She extended her hands toward Rick. "We can't do this in our room," she pointed out logically. "We don't have the stuff. Come on!"

Rick was hesitating, watching Art; when the lawyer finally shrugged and stood up—revealing, through his trunks, his own erection—Rick started wrapping the foam around Stephanie's wrists, and a few seconds later she found herself dangling by her wrists, swinging lazily in the air.

Rick offered Art the belt, but he drew back his hands. "No way!" he protested. "I don't know what I'm doing, I'm afraid I'd hurt her! You do this, I'll do the other part!"

"Hurting her," Rick said quietly, "is the idea!"

"No, I can't. Do it, Rick. She wants to try it, do it."

"Somebody do it!" Stephanie begged.

Still holding the belt, Rick turned back to her, watched her face for a second or two, let his eyes wander down her nude body. Then he stepped around behind her. There was a sharp crack and a sudden violent pain in her rear end.

Stephanie could not restrain a little cry, small but louder than any noise Jennifer or Rick had given voice to. Following the same pattern he'd used with Jennifer, he circled her, lashing her thighs, her belly, her breasts. It's good, she told herself, feeling her passions rise. It hurts but I can handle it, I can take more. It could be better, it isn't focused enough, it's too diffuse. The belt struck her again, though, and with that stroke it quite utterly drove such logical thoughts from her mind completely.

She wasn't able to count the strokes, but she was aware, perhaps a bit vaguely, that she was allowing things to go on longer than the others had. Eventually the pain of the belt became rather extreme; she could take more, she knew that, but she felt she needed more direct stimulation now, and she, like the others, called for a halt. But she was not surprised when Rick lashed her again, even harder than before. Unlike Rick and Jennifer, she now fell silent. She would not ask again, she told herself silently. No matter what he did to her, she could take it and she would take it.

It didn't matter; he delivered the remainder of what seemed to be the obligatory three, then stopped. Immediately she felt lips on her breast, and she looked down to see Art holding her, nuzzling her. Following their own pattern he bit her, hard but not nearly so hard as was now usual for them. Following Rick's example he moved his head down; under direct stimulation, Stephanie's climax erupted even more quickly than Jennifer's had.

She felt dazed as they took her down; hazily, she realized they were putting Art up there in her place. He was protesting, he was saying he wasn't sure, but they were pushing and he wasn't really resisting them. When he was hanging, Jennifer offered her the belt, but she merely stared at it blankly; with a smile, her friend took up a position behind Art and began lashing him savagely. Chewing her lower lip, Stephanie waited and watched; Art's continued erection was her best evidence that he was finding this as erotic as she had.

Compared to the other three, Art took very few strokes before requesting a halt. After he'd gotten three more—three more hard ones—Jennifer stopped. Stephanie moved to him quickly, imitating what he'd done to her, biting his nipples and letting her tongue glide down over his body until she reached his erection. Now, she told herself, it'll become more normal. Certainly, having an audience wasn't normal, but in ways she was hardly aware of that circumstance at all.

She was wrong, however. Things did not become more normal.

Forty-Two

CHERYL PICKED UP one of the fondue pots, looked at the sticky and hardened mass of cheese sauce inside. "Ich!" she exclaimed, making a face at it. "I cannot believe that Stephanie and Jennifer left things like this last night!"

"The liquor hasn't been opened," Sam commented, glancing around the mess of a living room. All the fondue pots remained; the candles that had been placed beneath them had burned down, and there were streams of white wax like glaciers, running across the table and in one place, down onto the rug. Dried-up chunks of steak and shrimp that were just beginning to smell remained on the plates. "But you'd think it had. This is pretty extreme, even for Art and Rick."

"Oh, men are capable of anything!" Cheryl declared. "You could leave this mess, Sam. And you know it."

"Yes, under a circumstance or two I guess I could. But Art? He's pretty meticulous, Cheryl."

"Yeah, he is. I can't imagine what happened last night."

"Well, they ought to be down shortly, it's pushing nine o'clock already. We'll probably find out then." He walked over to the slide projector; the kaleidoscope remained in place, but the power switch had been turned off. "This they paid attention to," he grunted. "And it looks like that's all they paid attention to. I guess we can sort of piece together what happened here."

"What's that?"

"This damn thing!" He pointed to the kaleidoscope accusingly. "It's like some kind of a drug! I don't know how or why, but it is!"

Cheryl laughed. "That's sort of silly, Sam," she said. "It doesn't do anything to us, does it?"

"No. But we've been going through some of the same sorts of changes they have, you can't deny that."

She rubbed her breasts through her coverup and swimsuit. "No, I can't," she admitted. She glanced through the doorway, checked to make sure they were still alone. They were, but she lowered her voice anyway. "Damn, my nipples are sore as hell! You really bit the shit out of them last night, Sam!"

"Did I do anything you didn't want me to do? Anything you didn't ask me to do? Let's try it out, you said, instead of playing with the candles. And then we played with the candles, too!"

She turned to him, put her hands on her hips; the eyebrow went up a little. "Well, I sure didn't hear you arguing, Sam!"

He scowled at her darkly. "And that makes it my fault, I suppose. I go along with what you wanted to do, and—"

"Wait a minute, wait a minute! What I wanted to do? Who started all this, Sam Leo?"

"You did! With the candles, the night that—"

"I did not! You did! You and your damn jalapeño peppers!"

"You never did try the peppers! You never had a thing to do with the peppers, you've never shown any interest in them!"

"Because if I did, there'd never be an end to it—"

"I'm not seeing an end to this, to the wax! And now we've added the Dixons' biting games, and that'll probably go on and on, too! And you talk about me being obsessive!"

"You are!"

"Maybe so. But so are you, Cheryl!"

"I am not! I never had an interest in things like this before you —before you—"

He pointed a finger at her. "Before I what?"

"Get that finger out of my face," she snarled. When he did, she visibly wilted a little. "Before you something, Sam. I don't know what. Shit. What's happening to us, anyway?"

"I don't know," he said quietly. "I don't know. Maybe nothing, really. Maybe our lovemaking just got a little too pat, maybe there was just a little too much sameness. So when we discovered, pretty much by accident, a new stimulus—"

"I don't think so. I don't feel like we had a problem with our sex life. Did you?"

"Well, no, not really, but—"

"Not really?" she demanded challengingly. "You haven't been satisfied, Sam?"

He put out his hands defensively. "No, no, you're taking that wrong. No, I haven't been dissatisfied! I'm just saying, this stuff is new, different—"

Again, she did not maintain her threatened anger. "Yeah, I guess," she agreed. "It's weird, though. Right now, the last thing in the world I want is for you to start chomping on my nipples or pouring hot wax on me. It seems like I'd feel that way tonight, too, but the problem is, I felt this way yesterday morning, too! Then, when it started getting dark—"

"I know what you mean. The same thing happens to me. I can't explain it, Cheryl. Not any better than I just did."

"That worries me. And it scares me, too, I'm not too proud to admit that. Every night since we've been here we've taken things a little farther. How far does it go, Sam? Where does it stop?"

"I'm not sure. But I don't think there's a reason to be scared, Cheryl. We're not doing anything that's likely to seriously injure us."

"I don't want to lose a nipple," Cheryl muttered. "I don't want you to bite one of them off!"

"I'm sure. I don't want a brush fire in my chest hair either!" He rubbed his own chest ruefully. "Although I guess there won't be much of a risk of that soon. I'm losing it all getting the wax off!"

That provoked a smile from her. "We have a new theme song, Sam."

"What's that?" Cheryl, as he well knew, attached considerable significance to the lyrics of popular songs; they'd had several "theme songs" over the years.

"You know, the Blue Oyster Cult? 'I'm Burning For You'?" She laughed; he joined her, but even as he did, he couldn't help thinking that that could, just as well, be a theme song for himself and Selinde. And that, in turn, started him thinking about ways he could get away for a few hours, ways he could find time to run down to Nag's Head.

"Well," she sighed, "I suppose we ought to get busy cleaning this mess up. The girls aren't going to be in until tomorrow, and we did leave it too, as much as anybody else did."

"Not in this condition, we didn't."

She patted his arm. "Come on, Sam. Let's get it done."

He sighed too, but he started picking up the dishes and pots from the table, carrying them into the kitchen. Among the now-spoiled food he discovered a little half-pint container of cream; after a moment he remembered that Jennifer had been using it in the sauce she'd made, stirring it in after they'd moved into the living room and started the kaleidoscope show. He pushed the lip open and sniffed it; a strong sour odor assailed his nostrils.

He carried it to the sink, where Cheryl was now in full concentration, scraping gluelike residue out of the fondue pots. He intended, at first, to pour it down the sink, to toss the little paper container in the trash.

On the way he stopped, staring at it, an idea forming in his mind. He could use it, he told himself; use it to inoculate the milk in the refrigerator. It would sour, and then someone would have to go into town for more milk. No one, he knew, would want to volunteer. Except, of course, Sam.

No, he decided; there was a Food Lion in Corolla, entirely too close. To account for his time, he'd have to claim he got the Jeep stuck in the sand or something similar. "This stuff is shot," he said, stepping up beside Cheryl and pouring the remainder of the cream into the sink.

She crinkled her nose. "Sure is!"

Crossing to the trash can, he tossed the carton in. There has to be a better way, he told himself as he walked back into the living room to collect more of the dirty dishes, there has to be. Still trying to come up with one, he began gathering up the dishes; as he did, his gaze fell on a small piece of black cloth lying on the floor. Reaching down, he picked it up.

He frowned at it. The top of Stephanie's swimsuit, without a question. But what was it doing down here? He went back into the kitchen, showed it to Cheryl.

She laughed. "Well, now we know who to blame for the mess!" she exclaimed. "Art and Stephanie!"

"How do you figure?"

"It's obvious, isn't it? Rick and Jenny went up to their room first. Art and Stephanie got into it down here. She sure as hell wouldn't take that off with Rick Mason in the room! Not Stephanie!"

"No, I don't suppose she would," Sam agreed while mentally imagining her doing just that. He found the image highly charged, found himself wishing that she'd do it when Sam Leo was in the room. Externally, he grinned at Cheryl. "Would you?" he asked.

"No way! Not Rick! You know he'd take it too seriously!" She waggled her head back and forth a few times, smiling impishly. "Now Art, I wouldn't really object."

That image was not without its effect, either. "You find Art sexy, huh?"

"I've told you that before. Rick too; but Rick, Rick's too much the riverboat gambler, the cad. He'd try to follow it up, we all know that. It'd turn into a problem."

Sam started to say something else, but was distracted by noises from the stairway. Still holding Stephanie's top, he peeked back in. "We have company," he said.

"Two or all?"

"All." He stepped back, stood close to Cheryl, spoke directly into her ear. "And let me tell you, they look like they've had a much rougher night than we did!"

Forty-Three

FOR SEVERAL LONG minutes Stephanie sat and watched Cheryl as she floated around on her air mattress out in the inlet. She glanced at Art; he was lying on his back and slowly turning the kaleidoscope in front of his eye, a look of complete contentment on his face.

She felt anything but contented. The events of the previous evening kept racing through her mind, over and over—not just the hot sting of the belt, but what had taken place afterward. As she'd knelt before her suspended husband, prepared to satisfy him orally, she'd become aware of Jennifer, who had knelt by her side and who was very tentatively touching Art's legs. Releasing Art, she'd turned her head, she'd looked at her friend. Jennifer's blue eyes had been very wide, questioning; Stephanie had stared into them for a moment, understanding very clearly, without any words being passed between them, what her friend was suggesting.

For a fraction of an instant, her reaction had been one of shock and of rising anger, but those emotions had dissipated even before she was fully aware of them. Jennifer was one of her two closest friends, a person who was, in spite of her foibles, very dear to her —a person, she realized, that she truly loved. Why, she'd asked herself at the time, shouldn't we do this?

And she'd made her decision; without speaking, she'd pushed Art's erection to the side, directing it toward Jennifer's face. Keeping her eyes on Stephanie's, the blond woman had leaned forward hesitantly, had touched the tip of it with her tongue; when she'd seen Stephanie smile she'd moved on, engulfing it completely.

From there things had progressed very rapidly. While she knelt watching Jennifer and Art, she'd felt Rick's hands come around her body, cupping her breasts; she'd found his touch welcome, and at that point she'd abandoned all her restraints. Moments later, when his rejuvenated erection had touched her buttocks, she'd wriggled against it welcomingly, and she'd gasped with pleasure when he'd pushed it inside her.

There were more gasps to come; gasps when the belt lashed down across her back again, even though Rick was using shorter and softer strokes than before. Gasps when, during a brief lucid moment a short while later, she realized that she, controlled and rigid Stephanie, was between two men—Art's penis in her mouth, Rick's in her vagina—while Jennifer whipped them all indiscriminantly with the belt. Before it had ended all variations had been tried, each man with both women and each woman with both men, while the fourth wielded the belt, the—for Stephanie—wonderfully stimulating, inhibition-destroying belt. Toward the end of the evening—before they'd all more or less passed out as if drunk— she'd felt it a symbol of freedom, she'd felt like running it up a flagpole and saluting it.

She did not feel that way now. In the bright light of the morning, her overwhelming emotion was one of embarrassment; she was still having considerable trouble believing that she'd actually done the things she'd done. Turning to Rick and Jennifer, she spoke in a hoarse whisper. "That was a one-time thing, okay?" she insisted. "That is not going to happen again, that can't happen again!"

Rick wouldn't meet her eyes. "Don't make it sound like it was all our doing," he protested. "You were right in the middle of it too! You were the one who threw off your clothes and demanded that I come and examine—"

"I know, I know! I have no idea what got into me! Look, I'm not trying to throw it all off on you two, I am more than aware that I share in the responsibility, okay? All I'm saying is, that's the end of it! We aren't going to do it again, we aren't going to talk about it, and I don't want Sam and Cheryl to hear a word of it! Okay?"

"I," Art put in in a dreamy voice, "had a great time. A great, magnificent, fucking goddamn shit-eating fan-damn-tastic time. You guys can sit around and fret about it if you want to. Not me. That's a time I'm always going to remember with great fondness." He paused. "What I can remember of it, that is. How it ended is a little hazy in my mind . . ."

"Yeah, it is, lots of times," Rick ruminated. "Endorphins."

Art looked blank. "Endorphins?"

"Compounds that act like drugs," Stephanie explained, "that are produced by the body under stress. Rick's probably right about that. They act like opiates; they dull pain and after a while they make you sleepy—like, well, like a drug."

"So we just all sort of fell asleep, and—"

"Woke up in a pile of bodies this morning like a bunch of drunks!" Stephanie snapped.

"Nice bodies," Art murmured. "Nice, nice, bodies."

Stephanie whirled around to glare at him. "Will you stop that! This is serious, Art!"

"Don't you think you're overreacting a little, Stephanie?" Jennifer asked.

Turning back, she pursed her lips angrily. "Are you telling me you're comfortable with all that, Jennifer? Don't you feel this sort of thing complicates the—"

"What I felt," Jennifer interrupted, "was like we'd all become one. For a while there I truly forgot who I was, I felt like I was all four of us at once. I don't know, Stephanie. I guess I'd have to say I feel the same way Art does. There was such a closeness, such a caring. I wouldn't go back and undo it even if I could."

Hearing at first only an echo of Jennifer's "New Age" ideas, Stephanie started to snarl at her, to tell her that that stuff was all claptrap, garbage, silliness.

But she held her tongue. There was a certain familiar ring to Jennifer's words; she'd felt pretty much the same way, and she couldn't deny it. During that time, she'd been madly, passionately, in love with both Art and Rick. She could remember, quite clearly, the moment when she'd passed Art's erection to Jennifer, the moment that had initiated the four-way interaction; she'd felt so close to the other woman then that there'd been practically no difference between them. She didn't feel that way now, and there was a certain sadness in that knowledge, in knowing that the wall that separated her from her friend was once again in place.

"Maybe you're right," she said finally. "Maybe I am being a little extreme. But that doesn't mean that I want to go back and do it again tonight!" She shook herself. "I am sore all over! There're places that're sore that've never been sore before!" She looked down at herself. Her body, all of it that the thong revealed—which was most of it—was unmarked. "I can't understand why we're not all bruised up, as a matter of fact—"

"I selected the belt for that," Rick told her with a grin. "As I guess everyone now knows, I do have some experience with this. A thicker one would've bruised. A thinner one wouldn't've had any pizzazz."

"He shaved it," Jennifer said, giggling. "With a razor. Until it was just right!"

Stephanie shook her head and allowed herself to smile for the first time that day. "Well, you did get it right," she admitted. "I'll have to give you that. The only thing was—"

Rick was watching her intently. "What?"

It wasn't sharp enough, she told herself, not quite. Feeling her cheeks get hot again, she waved off Rick's question. They weren't going to be doing this again, she assured herself, this business had to stop for a while. Get things back to normal for a few weeks or months, then maybe she and Art—and only herself and her husband—could play a few kinky games. Right now, she had no interest whatever in being beaten with a belt or being bitten; nor did she have any desire to bite anyone or beat anyone. More, she had no desire to have intercourse with Rick or watch Jennifer and Art together—even though she remained aware of the pull both Rick and Sam were exerting on her. You are not a swinger, she told herself. You are not. You are a monogamous woman. This is not you. Tonight, things'll be different. Things'll be normal.

The problem was, she was not unaware that she'd told herself similar things repeatedly, over the last few days. After dark—or maybe just after her libido had had time to build itself up again—she had not been able to maintain her resolve.

That concerned her. Seriously.

Forty-Four

WITH A SIGH, Sam looked out the window at his friends, at Cheryl floating on her mattress while the others, as usual, remained on the bank with the kaleidoscope, breaking away occasionally for usually brief swims. It all looked very inviting; the bright sun, the clear water, the three women in their more than brief suits.

"And I'm stuck in here," he told the laptop on the table in front of him. From the computer, a thin clear wire ran to the telephone jack in the wall. "With you." He tapped a few keys, listened to the little relay inside the machine convert the phone number he'd assigned it to the older rotary system the house's telephone service was wired to. "Actually," he went on as the screen blanked, "it isn't your fault. You're a perfectly nice little Mitsubishi. It's that son of a bitch Ken."

Falling silent, he watched the screen blank to a pale bluish white and flicker a few times; undoubtedly the system was threading its way through the elaborate security Ken had set up. At last, however, the uniform blue-white was interrupted by a message; it requested his social security number. He gave it; it asked for his driver's license. Snarling, he put that in too. It still wasn't satisfied. Now it wanted the exact date his employment at the center began. He put that in and five huge letters popped up: ERROR. Then it blanked and started all over.

"Ken," he said as he typed all the numbers in again, "I am going to murder you. No jury would ever convict me, not once they'd heard the facts."

This time the computer accepted the information he gave it; the first thing that came up, though, was a memo from Ken:

"It's about time," he read. "You're getting slack, Sammy boy, not thinking. Now that you've logged on, I know the number down there; I can call your foxy wife any old time. Don't forget. Now get to work! I expect results, and soon!" It concluded with, "your friend, Ken. Use F8 to clear this screen and proceed."

"Shouldn't be an *R* in that word," Sam growled. "You can't spell worth a shit, either!" He touched the suggested key, and the screen cleared again; when it came back he was in the dataset, ready to begin work.

To start with, he ran the best predictors he currently had, asking the software for probabilities. They came up after a brief delay, scrolling down the screen: Raleigh, 12.8 percent. Cary, 12.4 percent. Durham, 11.9 percent. Smithfield, 7.9 percent. And so on, lower and lower as it proceeded on down its reference list. Raleigh was the highest, but 12.8 percent likelihood of a correct guess was, he told himself, piss-poor; especially when the next one down was 12.4. Surely, he told himself, there were predictors not properly weighted in the statistics that could do better than that.

Trying to get a new idea, he recalled the file on one of the victims, choosing the most recent, Alice Near of Morrisville. There was all sorts of information there; age, occupation, income, marital status, and so on. Nothing looked too likely. He pulled Bill Near's file, checked the information on him—not relevant, of course, if the cause of these events was really a serial killer.

Staring at the screen, he drummed his fingers on the table. Not relevant if a serial killer, true. But Art had assured him that Bill Near was almost certainly the killer. Still, every instinct Sam had told him there was some relationship among these killings, some pattern. And Alice Near's death sure looked like part of it.

At random, he pulled up another file, stared at it. Joan Simms, Oklahoma City. Age at the time of her death, twenty-three. Single. Occupation, research tech at the University of Oklahoma. Income, 17K per year. Height, five-three. Weight, one-oh-five. Hair black, eyes brown. Body discovered in open field near campus. Nude, evidence of recent intercourse. Stabbed twenty-one times with a long narrow knife, wounds in all areas of the torso except the vicinity of the heart. No injuries to the neck area. Cause of death, penetration of both lungs; Joan Simms drowned in her own blood. No defensive wounds. No evidence of a struggle. No evidence that the victim was tied or drugged. No arrests, no suspects. This one was still open.

Pushing away a fantasy Sam could not deny was erotic—a fantasy in which the luckless Joan Simms looked a lot like Selinde and was accepting the killer's blade in the same way Cheryl accepted the candlewax and his bites—he forced himself to concentrate on the business at hand. Most of that information, he told himself doggedly, was already in, already weighted. Maybe a different viewpoint was needed, maybe there's something here we're all overlooking. Almost idly, he called up the weightings on such factors as occupation, age, and income. To his considerable surprise, they weren't in at all.

It took a little while, but he put them in, using a test weighting just to see what might pop up. This might not be truly valid, from a purely statistical viewpoint, but he didn't care; he wasn't planning a publication from this. Once he was finished he ran the statistics again and waited impatiently to see the results.

As they started to come up, his eyes widened in surprise. Age, a high correlation; all victims between eighteen and thirty-nine, centered on twenty-nine. That wasn't a shock. What was, was that there was just as high an occupational correlation, and a fairly high income correlation.

Interested now, he called up a sort on the occupations; as they came up, he scowled at the screen. They surely didn't look like they'd be correlated; they were all over the map, everything from housewives to hookers to lawyers. He didn't understand; the computer had no list of occupations like its list of cities, not unless Ken had put in something special—and he doubted that, since Ken hadn't made an effort to use this data. All the computer knew were matches—simple word matches. A housewife here is the same as a housewife there. If "homemaker" was entered, the machine would pitch it into a different category.

Determined to get to the bottom of this mystery, Sam tapped more keys, looked at this data in several different ways. It took quite a while before he stumbled onto the answers.

The income correlation was, generally speaking, a sawtooth; moreover, there was a pretty high correlation within the clusters. In one killing a cluster was centered on low-income victims, like Alice Near, the next was centered on high-income victims. A sawtooth: up and down, up and down.

Next, the occupations; here, the results were even more surprising. There was a very high consistency within the clusters; all the victims in Oklahoma City, four total, were technical types associated with the University or local industry—the word *tech* or *technician* occurred in each job title. In Memphis, the computer noted three clusters it considered unrelated, but Sam knew better at a glance. Three listed as dancers. Two as prostitutes. Two, "no visible means." Those were probably not unrelated—even though a dancer could be a stripper or a ballerina.

The amount of work it would take to tie all these up into something like real groups was intimidating, but not insurmountable; there weren't that many data points. He started experimenting, putting such occupations as "prostitute" and "no visible means" in the same category; the levels of correlation started to rise dramatically. And, soon enough, a new one popped up. Another sawtooth, another up-down, but now multilevel. As the pattern progressed across the country, it focused first on blue-collar workers—waitresses and so on—then on housewives, then on groups like dancers, hookers, and showgirls, then on professional and technical types. Regular, as if planned.

Coming back to North Carolina, he could easily observe that the pattern was holding. In Winston-Salem, all the victims except one were housewives—and that one could've been, she was a "no visible means." In Greensboro and Burlington, dancers and hookers—then there was a jump to Morrisville, where Alice Near also fitted into this category. That seemed to him strange, until he looked back over some of the other data and saw that such jumps were fairly common.

"So we can add a prediction," he told himself, working intently. "The next group is one or the other—a continuation of our showgirls or professionals. Waitresses and housewives are safe." Again, it took a while to do it, but he managed to ask the computer's statistics program this question.

The answer: professional/technical, likelihood of a correct guess, 79.2 percent.

Sam whistled softly. That was good, that was very good. Now, he told himself. Now weight that and put it back in the whole package.

He did that too, watched the location and date information scroll down. There'd been big changes. Cary's odds were down, but Raleigh's likelihood was far higher; 38.7 percent. So was the date—the odds for two days from the current date were up to almost 50 percent.

"That's good," he said aloud. "That's good. And I haven't even gotten all the occupational and income groupings done yet! We can get it higher than that, Ken; higher than that! That ought to satisfy you for a while, you bastard!" He glanced up at the clock; almost four, he'd been at this for three hours. Enough, he told himself, was enough. He disconnected, switched off the computer, closed the lid, packed it in its case. Then he went outside to join the others, never giving another thought to Ken's data.

Forty-Five

THAT NIGHT'S DINNER was, in general, an almost exact reprise of the night before. This time, the men had cooked; six sirloins had been prepared on the grills outside, even one for Jennifer, who did not normally eat red meat. Once again, the living room was prepared for dining; once again, the food was placed on the low table and the cushions scattered about for seating. The remainder of the scene was to be the same, as well; as Stephanie and the other women came in, Rick was in the process of putting the kaleidoscope back in the slide projector. Art pointed out her steak to her and she sat down. At the next place was Sam's, which was extremely rare; red blood oozed from it, spreading over part of his plate. She found herself staring at it fixedly, and she took her eyes away only when Rick turned on the projector. Dinner tonight was being held a bit earlier; there was more light, and the images were fainter, the colors less saturated. But they were there, they were visible. And they were as fascinating to her as ever.

"That doesn't interest you at all, Sam?" Art asked, pointing toward the flowing images on the screen.

"Well, sure it does," Sam answered, cutting off a piece of his steak and spearing it with his fork. "It's very pretty. I have no problems with it as dinnertime entertainment. But it doesn't draw me to lie here and watch it all night; and I'd rather swim or fish than sit out there by the inlet and look through it."

"I guess it just touched a chord in me," Art told him. "It keeps bringing up things from the past for me. Making me think about things that happened when I was just a kid."

"Like what?" Sam asked idly. Stephanie paused in her eating, peering at her husband, wondering if he was going to share the story of Clarence the Cloud-Watcher with the whole group. If he broke down in tears in front of them he'd be terribly upset about it later, she knew that.

"Oh, lots of different things," he said noncommittally. "There was one just a minute ago that made me think of a time when I was, oh, maybe fifteen or sixteen. I couldn't tell you why. You know how sometimes a certain odor, a food smell or something, will set off a memory, bring it back clearly? It's like that."

"You still haven't told us what it made you remember," Rick pointed out.

Art looked a little embarrassed. "Oh, it isn't worth the telling," he said. "Just a time with a girl . . ."

"Come on, Art!" Cheryl chided. "Let's hear this!"

He grinned at her boyishly. "It isn't a big deal. I was just remembering a time when I was young and inexperienced. Sitting in a movie theater with a date and—uh—feeling her up. You know what I mean. That's so damn exciting when you're fifteen. For some reason those colors just brought it back. With a taste of that old excitement. It's funny how it recalls the emotions. I've noticed that before."

"It does that sort of thing to me, too," Stephanie commented. "Makes me think about the past, makes me—feel it again. Sometimes I watch those patterns and I feel—I feel like I was a very little girl again—the way I felt before—before—" She stopped speaking, put her fork down, put her fingers against her temples and rubbed.

"Before what, Stephanie?" Cheryl asked gently.

She sighed. In ways, she didn't even feel like she was talking to her husband and her friends, she felt like she was reviewing these things in her own mind, trying—for the first time in quite a few years—to come to terms with them instead of merely burying them. "Before Daddy lost his business," she went on, her voice soft and small.

"I didn't know your dad ever had a business," Sam said conversationally. "All you ever said was that your family was very poor."

"Well, he did, and we weren't poor then. He ran an automobile dealership, but it went bankrupt. I don't know why. That happened when I was, oh, maybe four. I don't really remember it. All I remember is that things weren't always—the way they became."

"How'd they become?" Jennifer asked.

"You sure you want to talk about this, honey?" Art queried, concern in his eyes.

She didn't really hear him. "I guess," she went on, her eyes fixed on the kaleidoscopic patterns, "looking back on it, that Daddy must've gotten really depressed over the business. But what it came down to was that he just wouldn't even try to get another job. He just kept saying, over and over, that he'd get back to where he was, sooner or later. That everything'd be all right. He kept saying that when we lost our home, our car, lost everything. He wouldn't take welfare, he said that was for bums—and we became those bums." She sighed. "So Mama went to work, she got a job in an office. We rented a little house in—they called them the slums. And Daddy—Daddy changed. He changed a lot."

"What happened?" Cheryl prompted.

She frowned deeply. "He became—abusive. He used to sit around at night and say he was, quote, 'a goddamn piss-poor excuse for a man.' Then he'd get up and he'd find one of us—Mama or me—to hit."

Everyone was silent for a moment. "For no reason?" Jennifer asked.

"For no reason at all. I remember walking through the living room carrying my doll, one of the few toys I had left; I think I was six. I said, 'Hi, Daddy.' He jumped up and punched me, with his fist, knocked me across the room. Then he picked up the doll and tore her head off." Tears formed at the corners of Stephanie's eyes, began rolling down her cheeks. "He wanted to do that to me, I knew he did. . . ."

"Jesus Christ," Rick whispered.

Stephanie brushed away the tears. "He'd do the same thing to Mama, too; she was all bruised up, all the time. Then he got into the thing about the food."

"About the food?" Cheryl prompted.

"Uh-huh. God, that went on for years! Mama didn't make much money, like I said, and there was never really enough food. So Daddy decided one day that we had to ration the food we did have. Tighten our belts, he said. But what it meant, in the end, was that he got what he wanted and Mama and I got almost nothing. We were hungry all the time after that. For me, a crust of bread with some mold on it was a treasure."

"My God, that's horrible!" Rick exclaimed. "I can't believe—I mean, I can believe it, but—didn't your mother ever say anything?"

Stephanie laughed shortly. "Sure. And when she did she lost a tooth, or she got her nose broken. I don't know how many times I saw him back her up against a wall and punch her right in the face, over and over. I'd be running around screaming, but he'd just go on and on. Then, when she was almost unconscious, he'd tell her he loved her, he'd start kissing her, and he'd carry her off to the bedroom. She got pregnant that way three times. Every time she did he'd hit her in the stomach until she had a miscarriage."

"Good God, it's a miracle he didn't kill her!" Sam put in.

She turned her head, looked at him directly. "He did," she said flatly, without noticeable emotion. "One night it went that way, just like I told you, he beat her up and then carried her into the bedroom. I was ten, then. Afterward, he went out. I went in to see if she needed any help. She didn't. She was dead."

"Oh, my God . . ." Art breathed. "You never told me . . ."

Stephanie pushed her hair back from her face. She looked quite calm, perfectly under control. "I can still see her, right now," she said quietly. "Lying there on the bed, a sheet over her, bloodstains on the sheet. Her eyes were closed, she looked so—so peaceful. I thought maybe it wasn't so bad this time, thought she was sleeping. 'Mama?' I asked. 'Mama, are you okay? Wake up, Mama. Mama, Mama, Mommie, please, it's Stephanie, open your eyes, Mama.' I touched her shoulder, it felt like wax—like wax—not like skin—and then—then I started to realize that things weren't right, I understood that things weren't ever going to be right, not ever again, not ever ever again." Little by little, as she spoke, Stephanie's calm demeanor had begun to fracture, fragment by fragment. Her voice had risen in pitch and volume, its tone passing gradually into that of a panicked child, her eyes filling up. "It wasn't ever going to be right again, Mama wasn't ever going to wake up and they were going to come and take my daddy away somebody was going to come and take him away Mama was gone I was going to be left behind all alone, all alone, oh, God, Daddy, Mama, nooooo . . . !" She stopped speaking, her hands coming up in front of her face, her fingers like claws, ready to rip at her own eyes like a modern-day Oedipus. But her eyes were tightly closed and her whole face was twisted into a mask of impossible agony.

After a moment of shocked paralysis, Art sprang from his place on the floor and went to her, trying to put his arms around her. For a moment she fought him, but then she collapsed into his arms like a rag doll, her whole body going limp abruptly.

She was only vaguely aware of it, but the others had gathered around her too. She opened her eyes, blinked; everyone was crying, even Rick! Even Sam! Crying for her, crying for her pain! She felt like something inside her chest had suddenly torn itself in half. She let herself go, great sobs pouring out, all the pain of the years after her father had gone to prison and died there, the years when she'd been a ward of the state, when she'd sworn, like Scarlett O'Hara, that this would never happen to her again.

And it never had. Now, surrounded by her husband and her friends, she felt like she could face it for the first time in her life. Her feelings were weirdly mixed; in one way, having more or less relived those times, she felt terrible. But in another, she felt so strongly loved, so strongly supported, that if these were the last moments of her life it wouldn't really matter much. She cried more, overwhelmed by these people, overwhelmed by their love for her and her love for them.

"I can't imagine how," Sam said after things had calmed down a little, "you could've chosen a career in pathology after that sort of a childhood experience."

"I don't know that they're not connected," she told him. Her face was still tearstained. "I think I had something to prove to myself. That I could confront it and not flinch, something like that. The first few were hard, really hard!" She clenched a fist, shook it. "But I did it! By God, I did it!"

Art squeezed her arm tightly. "Yes, you did," he said. "It's incredible to me that you could've lived through something like that and come out as normal as you are!" He shook his head. "And never let on, never talk about it, even with me . . ."

She leaned her head over against his shoulder. "You can see," she murmured, "why I never did want to talk about it."

"Yeah," he answered. "Yeah, I sure can." He turned to her plate, cut a small piece of her steak, offered it to her lips on a fork.

"I'm not sure I'm really hungry anymore . . ."

"Eat," he said gently.

Obediently, she opened her mouth and allowed him to place the piece of meat on her tongue; gradually everyone began to return to their dinners and Rick began again to turn the kaleidoscope, which by now had been exhibiting a static pattern for quite a long while. The new pattern was just forming when abruptly, the screen went dark.

"Damn!" he said. "Lost the bulb!"

"Well, those things do have a limited life," Sam pointed out. "You have a spare?"

"No. Shit."

"We can probably find one in town."

"Yeah. Next time we have to go in for some other reason."

Sam didn't say anything more; Rick got up and turned on a lamp, and as dinner was completed the conversation had turned to lighter topics, to quiet banter. After the postdinner cleanup, Jennifer suggested soft music and dancing; that was done, too, continuing until the couples began drifting away to their bedrooms.

In the Dixons' room, Art and Stephanie sat on the bed for quite a long while, just looking at each other, saying nothing. Finally, by mutual agreement, they rose and went across the hall, knocked on the door softly.

Jennifer opened it. She was nude; she hadn't bothered with a robe. "We were hoping you'd come," she whispered, pulling the door all the way open.

Forty-Six

IT HAD WORKED out perfectly, Sam told himself as he once again drove the Jeep south through Kitty Hawk. Just perfectly. He hadn't had to do a thing; the burnout of the slide projector bulb had provided a perfect opportunity. By volunteering to go get another, he'd gained not only his window of free time—who could say how long it might take to find a type ELH projector bulb on the Outer Banks?—but additionally, the gratitude of the others.

Gratitude that from Cheryl, at least, would hardly last if she were to ever discover what he was doing with that free time.

He didn't think he had to worry about that, though. Not even Ken could suspect that Selinde was here, in Nag's Head; even if the letter were to be sent, there'd be no suspicion that he'd gone to meet her here. The question would never even come up, he wouldn't even have to try to lie. He was here to find a projector bulb and that was it.

Coming into Nag's Head, he began trying to jog his memory, trying to remember where the Blue Heron was. Not on this road, he reminded himself; over on the beach side. Numerous little side streets connected the bypass with that beach road; choosing one at random, he turned left, bumped down the short narrow street, then turned south again on the beach road. The Blue Heron, he remembered, was beachfront, that'd put it on his left. It wasn't far, either. He hadn't gone two blocks before he saw the sign. Swinging into the parking lot, he almost immediately spotted the white Corvette and pulled the Jeep in beside it.

The motel's indoor pool was straight ahead; he went there first, took his sunglasses off, peered through one of the windows. Inside, a few couples and one or two children were splashing around in the water or sitting in lawn chairs; the hot tub at the far right corner was unoccupied. At a glance, he knew none of the women there was Selinde; none was strikingly dark, none had her spectacular hair. Leaving the pool, he walked up the stairway and back down to number 223, where he knocked briskly. There was no immediate response. Probably not here, he told himself, probably on the beach. It's too nice a day to be inside.

Then, just as he was about to turn away, Selinde, wearing a white terrycloth robe that barely reached the tops of her thighs, opened the door. "Sam!" she greeted. "I'm glad you came! I must say, I really didn't expect you so soon! Come on in!"

He did, following her through the short narrow corridor between the bathroom on the left and the small stove and refrigerator on the right. Once he'd cleared it, once he'd entered the main room, he stopped cold.

There was a young man just in the process of rising from the bed. He was nude, he had an erection; glaring at Sam, he grabbed for a pair of ragged cutoffs and began dragging them on.

"Sam, this is Jack," Selinde said nonchalantly. "He runs a fishing boat out of Manteo. Jack, this is—"

"An asshole who butts in where nobody wants 'im!" the man growled. "An asshole who better get the fuck out of here if he knows what's good for 'im!" Zipping up the cutoffs he started moving toward Sam; he wasn't as large or as heavy as the epidemiologist, but his torso was lean, wiry, muscular. You may have a real problem here, Sam told himself.

But, without any hesitation, Selinde stepped between them. "I don't care for your attitude, Jack," she said, her voice cold. "I think you should be the one to leave. For now."

"I ain't goin' noplace," the fisherman said, taking another step forward. "I—"

Sam couldn't see Selinde's face, but he did see her straighten her head and shoulders. "Jack," she repeated, very calmly. "Go. Now. And don't come back. You aren't welcome here, not any longer."

He glared at her menacingly, and now it was Sam who took a step forward; the tension in the air was almost palpable.

But the fisherman didn't follow through. He scowled at Selinde, his expression that of a man whose best judgments were running counter to his desires. "Well, fuck you anyhow, lady!" he spat. He walked past her, walked past Sam. "Fucker," he added, throwing a glance filled with venom at him. Then he was out the door and gone.

Still calm, Selinde walked over and closed it. "I'm sorry about that, Sam," she said, turning. "He really was rude, wasn't he?"

"Rude! I thought he was going to break me in half! I thought he was going to slap you around and force me to get into it! What in the holy hell was he doing here anyway?" He shook a finger at her. "You were in bed with him, weren't you? Were you about to fuck him or were you right in the middle of it? Damn it, Selinde, tell me the truth!"

She gave him a quizzical open-mouthed look, then burst into peals of laughter. "Sam, Sam," she said, walking toward him. "I'm not your wife, Sam! I'm not your mistress, either! Don't get me wrong—I'm not angry with you—but really, Sam! What gives you the right to ask me questions like that?"

His face tight, he turned away, looked out the window, watched the ocean waves pound the beach. "You're quite correct," he replied stiffly. "I have no right. I just thought there was a little more between us than this, that's all."

"You thought I'd given you exclusive rights to my body? I don't recall saying that, Sam. I don't recall your asking, either. And I don't recall your offering to leave your wife."

"No. You're correct. You didn't and I didn't."

"Then what is the matter with you? Jack's gone. Here we are. Where's the problem?"

He turned back. "It just bothers me, all right? For one thing, that guy is such a—a—"

"That guy is a workingman," she finished for him. "At times, he can be quite nice. He is not you, his life and his feelings run on automatic, he reacts, he does not act. He has no choices, none. He is not you."

"He's not like you, either!" Sam raged. "He's—!"

"I've told you. I am a student. Would I not be a poor one, Sam, if the only people I studied were the highly educated, the very intelligent?"

"I study viruses and bacteria in my work! I don't sleep with them!"

"I do. It's a matter of approach, Sam."

He groaned, turned his back on her again. "You make no sense to me at all," he told her. "No sense at all. I shouldn't've come here. I wish I hadn't. I wish I'd never met you!"

"That isn't true. Not really. Is it, Sam?"

He couldn't help looking at her again. She was half-smiling; her face, he told himself, was so beautiful, so charming, that it made him glad to be alive at this particular moment, just so he could see it. "No," he admitted. "It isn't true." He cleared his throat. "It—it isn't easy for me to see you with other men. And it's less easy for me to face the prospect of you going away, of never seeing you again."

Her expression became serious. "But it's a prospect you must face, Sam. I'm sorry, but that's the way it must be."

He shook his head. "If you say so."

"I do." She came to him, took his hand. "You should not be this way, Sam; so sad. Everything ends. Not even the mountains and the seas last forever."

"I really will miss you. I feel like I've known you for years."

She stepped closer to him, tipped her face up. "And I'll miss you, too, Sam."

He could not resist, it was absolutely impossible. He put his arms around her, pulled her to himself, kissed her. "You know," he said when they finally broke the kiss, "when I first called you, I kept telling myself that I wanted to talk to you about the sort of things we'd started discussing that first day, the day we met. You remember?"

She smiled up at him. "Of course. We were talking about death."

"Yeah, in a nutshell, I guess so. You seemed to have an unusual attitude toward it."

"It's not a subject," she pointed out, "that we can explore in depth now. You'll be expected back at the beach house too soon for that, Sam!" She pulled gently away from him and went to sit on the side of the bed, facing the window; he joined her. Outside, the sun was pushing toward its zenith; it sparkled brilliantly on the crests of the incoming waves. Far off in the distance, the water's surface at the horizon seemed to dance, as if it were boiling. Temperature inversions, Sam told himself.

"I told you most of it that day," Selinde went on. "It's just that most people have such a terrible fear of death, they fight so hard to avoid it. Yet it's a natural thing, like eating, like sex, like childbirth. In Mexico, you often hear it said that one's death sits on one's left shoulder, always. Sometimes they play with death, they tease death, they have a holiday they dedicate to death and the dead."

"Still, it's only natural to put it off as long as you can."

"Perhaps. And yet there is something to be said for choosing the time and the place of your death. That gives you a power over it, you see; you choose, not death, and you can, if you wish, choose the exact best moment. That man we watched die that day did not choose, he waited. Waited until death selected him. Then, even when he knew he was selected, he fought. And he suffered, terribly. Not from the physical pain, but from his fear."

"I guess I can see that. But that poor guy, I doubt if his physical pain was insignificant!"

"That sort of pain can always be controlled," she told him. "It's just a matter of approach; with a correct approach it can even be pleasurable. But you know that already, Sam!"

He frowned, just for a second, as the sharp but very distinctly pleasurable pains from the wax and from Cheryl's teeth came to his mind. He had not, he knew, even hinted at any of that in his discussions with Selinde.

Then it occurred to him. The hot peppers, of course. She was talking about the peppers.

"Yeah," he admitted. "I guess I do. I still don't understand what you mean by choosing the moment, though. It sounds to me like you're talking about suicide."

"That's one way, of course."

"That's usually an act of desperation. What you do when there's nothing left, no way out."

"It doesn't have to be. Not if the exact best moment is chosen."

"I can't see how you would know that exact best moment."

She laughed. "That, of course, is the hard part!" She shook her head. "I think most people do know, though. They can recognize it, they just don't admit that to themselves." She looked away from him, back out at the rolling surf. "There's a moment," she went on, "in each person's life, a moment when you can say to yourself, this is the peak, I stand now at the top of my existence. My life has never been better than this, nor will it ever be this good again. That, Sam, is the time. As that moment passes away."

He laughed a little, a slightly incredulous look on his face. "But, Selinde, that moment could occur when you're nineteen!"

"And it could occur when you're eighty."

"I don't think I can agree with you. Most people can't even recognize that peak moment until it's long past, anyway."

"That's true too. I didn't say it was easy, Sam. One must listen to one's instincts; one must listen to death. Death sits on your left shoulder, as I said. And Death is not silent; Death speaks."

Sam studied her profile carefully. It seemed to him that this was no abstract discussion, that this was something she herself took very seriously. A thought crossed his mind, a possible scenario about who Selinde was and what she was doing. He decided to take a stab at it, see how she might react.

"Is that what you're doing, Selinde?" he asked bluntly. "Is that what you are? A disaffected girl from a rich family looking for a peak experience, after which you plan to end your own life?"

She turned back to him again. Her eyes were very soft. "No, Sam. I can see why you might think that, but that isn't so. I am, as I've told you, a student. I seek only to learn. And I have learned much from you, Sam Leo! I hope you, too, have learned something from me!"

"I have. But I'm concerned about you, Selinde."

"Concerned that I might kill myself?"

"Well, frankly, yes."

"If I did—if I were to do that this afternoon—it would be my choice, Sam. Just as who I make love with is my choice."

"That's true. But it would make me very unhappy, Selinde."

"Why? After I leave Nag's Head you cannot really expect to ever see me again. What does it matter, to you, if I am dead or alive?"

"I care about you. It's that simple. I wouldn't be here if that wasn't so."

She leaned over against him. "Yes. And I care about you, too, Sam Leo. And I suppose that does make each of our fates the other's business, so let me set your mind at ease. I plan to remain alive for quite a long while, Sam. I have no plan to commit suicide."

Uncertain, he started to question her further, but did not; even as he opened his mouth to speak, it seemed to him that her words were perfectly sincere, that there was no reason whatever to doubt them.

"And," she went on, "because I care about you, I want to remind you again that for you, the choices are your own. Don't forget that, Sam."

He laughed. "I couldn't possibly. You've told me often enough."

She rather suddenly pulled away from him and stood up. "I want to give you something," she said. Crossing the room quickly, she lifted a small bag onto the dresser and unzipped it. After digging around in it for a moment, she came up with some small object; he couldn't tell, immediately, what it was. Returning to the bed, she sat down again and handed it to him.

He took it, looked at it. It was a knife; the blade was encased in a finely-tooled leather sheath, and the exposed hilt seemed to be made of bronze or some similar metal. It was covered with artistic reliefs: images of a stylized nude woman, a snake, a tree; familiar images somehow, but Sam couldn't place them at the moment and didn't try. The finger guards and the rounded pommel looked as if they might be made of some material like ivory or even bone. Carefully, he pulled it out of its sheath. The blade was dark and slightly reddish, not shiny like steel. Double-edged, it was six or seven inches long but less than an inch wide at its widest point, and very thin from top to bottom. He tested the edges; they were as sharp as any scalpel.

"It's sort of a family heirloom," she told him as he examined it. "It's quite old."

He slid it back in its sheath. "It's beautiful," he said. "But I don't quite understand why you'd give me something like this."

"Because it is mine," she replied. "Because it has been mine for a very long time. Because it has been close to me for a very long time."

He moved his gaze between the knife and her face several times. There was a possible meaning here, he told himself. They'd just been talking about his suspicions that she might have been planning a suicide; was this what she'd planned to kill herself with, was she giving it to him as a way of saying that she'd given up those plans? That was, he told himself, possible. But it might not be prudent to address it; it would be best, he was sure, to simply accept the gift and thank her for it.

As he did, a series of images sprang up in his mind. Selinde in a motel like this one. Lying back on the bed, nude, this dagger in her hand. She is propped up on pillows, moonlight plays on her dark skin. She holds the dagger with its blade pointed downward, she brings it down so that it touches her body, under her breast on the left. She does not lack for courage, she holds the hilt with both hands and she begins to push it into herself. It is so sharp it slides in quite easily; bright red blood wells up around it, runs onto the white sheets she's lying on. Her lips part and her eyelids flutter but she does not stop, she pushes it right on in, as deep as possible. She leaves it standing in her body, folds her hands over her stomach, and lies quite still while her life flows out of her.

Sam blinked; the images vanished. Aware of discomfort, he glanced down at himself and saw that he had a raging erection.

Selinde, though he was sure she was unaware of the direct provocation, did not fail to notice it. With a slight smile, she reached over with one hand and caressed it lightly through his pants. With the other hand, she pulled the knot loose on the belt of her terrycloth robe. It fell open; as he'd suspected all along, she wasn't wearing anything underneath it. The sleek brown body he'd just been visualizing was revealed to his view once again. He stuffed the knife into his pants pocket and left it there while his hands went to her breasts and thighs.

When he finally left, a couple of hours later, he was scrupulous to take that knife with him. After that he didn't really think about it for a while; he located a photo shop in Nag's Head, bought a bulb—just one, another burnout would give him another excuse to drive into town—and drove back through Corolla and back onto the trail leading to the house. Not until he was on that trail did he realize where he'd seen the patterns emblazoned on the knife's hilt before—and when he did, he was so startled he stopped the vehicle and pulled the thing out again, examining it carefully once more. This he'd have to ask Selinde about, he told himself, the next time he saw her; he had to force himself not to turn the Jeep around and go back. This concerned him; this was no coincidence.

There was no difference, none. The images on the knife's hilt were the same as those on the kaleidoscope. Exactly the same.

Forty-Seven

YOU'VE SURRENDERED, STEPHANIE told herself as she avidly consumed the stuffed clams she and the other women had fixed for tonight's dinner. You've just surrendered, and things'll never be the same for you again. That morning, she'd again started making claims that the events of the previous night—events very similar to the night before—could never take place again. But her words, she could tell, were not being taken seriously by any of the others, and even to her they sounded hollow. Finally she gave it up. The old supercontrolled Stephanie seemed to have died, and now that the fears that had created that woman had been confronted and shared, it seemed to her no great loss. Once they returned to Raleigh she'd have to take a long hard look at her career. Being in pathology might itself be pathology; she didn't know, right now, if she'd stay there or not.

More on her mind, as she sat watching the lovely kaleidoscopic patterns on the screen, were Sam and Cheryl. So far, neither she nor Jennifer had said a word to Cheryl about their nocturnal activities; she doubted very much if Art or Rick had mentioned it to Sam, either, particularly since Sam had spent an incredible amount of time in town that day, surrendering the pleasures of the water, selflessly searching out a bulb for the slide projector—when he himself wasn't even especially interested.

For Stephanie, there were several issues here. First and foremost was the simple fact that Sam and Cheryl were fully a part of this group, and they were being excluded; to her, it didn't seem right, they should at least be told, should be given a choice. Most likely, she assumed, they'd decline; that didn't matter. The offer should be made.

Secondly, there were matters playing in that were much more basic. Stephanie was feeling a near-hunger for Sam, a strong desire to be physical with him, a desire quite as powerful as her desires for Rick and Art. She and Art had discussed this briefly, he'd expressed the same sort of interest in Cheryl, and she presumed that Rick and Jennifer had much the same feelings.

The question, of course, was how to present it to them. She could not simply sit down with Cheryl, tell her what they've been doing, and ask her if she'd like to dangle by her wrists while the others beat her with a belt. She was only too aware how she herself would've reacted to such a suggestion if it had been made in any context other than the way it had actually happened.

So that's the way it'd have to be done, she told herself with a secret smile. Initiate some graphic discussion, set up a challenge. Sam and Cheryl, as much as herself, Art, and Rick, could be counted on not to back away. Jennifer was the only one in their group who in any sense behaved in a noncompetitive way—and Stephanie suspected that she merely concealed it, not that she lacked such urges.

Continuing to smile, she glanced around at her husband and at the Masons in turn. Would she have to make them aware of her little plot? No, she decided. Not necessary. Once she started playing games, she was sure they'd understand where she was going and fall in with her, nobody in this group was stupid.

Rick turned the kaleidoscope in the holder Sam had rigged for it, and a new pattern appeared; slightly disturbing to Stephanie's line of thinking. It made her remember the way she'd felt this morning, out by the inlet, when she'd been trying to tell the others that these strange sexual practices had to stop. Then, her predominant emotion had been fear; fear that things were getting completely out of hand, confusion as to what exactly was happening to them, why they were changing so much, so fast. As the day had gone on, the fear remained, but her response to it had shifted subtly. The fear itself became exciting; by late afternoon, positively delectable. That, she was sure, was part of the appeal here; none of them knew exactly where they were headed, and that was both exciting and frightening.

"That one's interesting," Rick commented, lowering his fork to his plate as the kaleidoscope's crystals settled into their final position. "It's—uh—"

"Sort of scary," Jennifer filled in.

"That's the way I see it, too," Art added.

"This just doesn't make a lot of sense to me," Sam commented. "All I see is a pretty pattern. Blues and violets, mostly. I don't understand why two of you would see something frightening in it."

"Make that three," Stephanie said.

"Four," Rick nodded. "But scary in an—interesting way. Like a good horror flick. I'm not sure I can explain that to you, Sam. Not if you can't see it."

"Well, I certainly can't. Like I said, to me it's just an abstract."

"Me too," Cheryl chimed in.

"Change it, Rick," Jennifer asked. He did, and a totally new pattern rolled up, this one dominated by reds and earth-tone browns. Jennifer was the first to note that this one was sexy, and the other three agreed.

"I think you're putting me on," Sam chided. "One of you says something and the others just follow suit."

There was a chorus of protests to this, a chorus of denials. Sam's expression clearly said he wasn't convinced. "No," Rick said, jumping up and walking over to the screen. "No, and I'm not sure it is just suggestion, I'm not sure that whoever made this thing didn't cut the crystals in certain ways to create patterns like this." He pointed to the screen, to one of eight softly rounded light brown shapes. "Doesn't this look like a torso?" he asked. "A female torso? I mean, there aren't any details, but . . ."

"If you stretch it," Sam agreed. "You could also say it looks like an hourglass."

Like a lecturer instructing a recalcitrant student, Rick pointed again. "No, look here, do hourglasses have these nice—uh, these bulges up here? And look at these, on both sides! Faces, right? Male faces, looking up at the torso?"

Sam laughed. "Rick, you're really pushing it here—"

"No," Stephanie put in. "No, I can see what he means. It's just suggested, it's generalized. Your mind fills in the blanks, makes it more than it is."

"Makes a little movie out of it sometimes," Jennifer added, leaning forward. As she did, she touched the projector, just slightly, but enough that a new spill of shapes appeared. Long, thin, pointed shapes in metallic reddish-brown and thicker leaf shapes in jet black, slipping in from the perimeters, surrounding the still-extant forms Rick had said were torsos and faces. Stephanie felt a jolt, halfway between arousal and sheer terror; frowning, she asked Jennifer to turn the tube, and she did. A whole new set of forms appeared now; among them series of bright red rings in pairs, each pair linked along the perimeter by a high and sinuous chocolate arc. Much better, Stephanie told herself with another secret smile. A golden opportunity to steer this conversation into potentially more fruitful areas.

"Oh, Sam!" she cried, "surely you can see those rings!" She pointed them out. "They look just like—like handcuffs! Don't you think so?"

Art picked it up immediately. "Yeah. They do, don't they?"

She looked up at Rick, saw his apparent confusion. Scraping out the last bit of her last clam, she turned her face so that Sam and Cheryl would not see and winked broadly.

Rick's expression did not change for a moment. Then his face took on a look of dismay—a totally phony look, as Stephanie saw it. "Oh, come on!" he protested. "Let's not get into that again!"

"No, we'd better not, not right now anyway," Cheryl said unexpectedly. "The last time that was the topic of conversation the dinner dishes got left all night. Come on, gentlemen; we were the cooks tonight!"

There was some grumbling—particularly from Sam—but they did get up. Rick turned off the slide projector, the room lights were turned on, the table was cleared, and the dishes started getting done. While the men worked, the women lounged around the living room, studiously doing nothing whatever.

"It's good to watch this," Cheryl said as Sam wiped up crumbs and a few small spills from the table. "They are good for something after all, aren't they?"

Stephanie was determined. "Oh, they're good for more than that! You have to admit it, Cheryl!"

"Well, yes," the dark-haired woman replied. "Sometimes. A lot of times, lately!"

"Dancing with them last night was nice, too," Jennifer commented.

"Yes, it was," Cheryl agreed. "We don't do enough of that these days. I enjoyed that."

"We should do it again tonight," the blond declared. "Put on music, turn on the projector, and dance the night away. Maybe have a few glasses of wine, too."

Cheryl was nodding; Stephanie sighed, seeing that her plans for a conversation that hopefully would turn explicitly erotic were being thwarted. She shrugged. There was time, the vacation was not even half over yet. "We can start on that right now," she observed. "Allow me. I shall return momentarily, bearing glasses and bottle."

"Three only," Cheryl said. "Let the guys get their own."

"Naturally," Stephanie agreed as she got to her feet. "Why don't you go ahead and put on some music? Your choice."

The music was already playing by the time Stephanie returned with the wine jug and the glasses. Cheryl, as was her preference, had loaded tapes bearing classic rock of the sixties and seventies. At the moment, the song was "Don't Fear the Reaper," by the Blue Oyster Cult, and Cheryl was quietly singing the words along with the tape, her shoulders moving to the rhythm.

Sitting back down, Stephanie poured each glass half full; the women toasted each other, drank. "Those straps on your suit," Stephanie told Jennifer, "have done an admirable job of staying in place out there on the inlet. I'm not too sure, though, that they're going to fare as well if you start trying to dance to this music!"

Jennifer looked down at them, adjusted one slightly. "I guess," she said nonchalantly, "we'll just have to see. I'm sure not going to go up and change!" She gave Stephanie one of her innocent looks. "Maybe I should just take them off now. On this suit they unsnap from the bottom. Get rid of the problem."

Cheryl laughed. "It'd be worth it, just to see the looks on Art's and Sam's faces when they came back in here!"

"If you want to do that," Stephanie said, almost too eagerly, "I'll take my top off too! Both of us, that'll really wipe them out!"

"Oh, come on!" Cheryl scoffed. "You two? Never happen. Don't think I don't know what's going on here, ladies!"

Stephanie frowned at her. "What do you mean?"

"The suits! The wearing them all the time, day and night! It's get Cheryl week, isn't it? Payback for all the times I've worn string bikinis while you two were in one-pieces!"

"No, it isn't like that, Cheryl," Stephanie protested.

"Besides," Jennifer pointed out, "you're in your suit, too. Just like we are."

"Hey! I'd feel overdressed otherwise! But I know where it stops, too. So don't try to put old Cheryl on here, all right?"

"She doesn't believe we'd do it," Jennifer said.

"No," Stephanie agreed. "She doesn't."

"She knows you too well," Cheryl said, nodding and smiling.

"Stephanie, love," Jennifer said, turning around, "would you undo the snaps at the back there?"

"Surely," Stephanie answered, reaching for them. As Cheryl's amused smile started to fade, she undid them. Jennifer pulled them back over her shoulders, freeing her breasts, and unhooked the front snaps. As she cast the straps aside, Stephanie untied her top and took it off.

"I don't believe this," Cheryl said slowly, looking from one to the other. "The guys could walk back in here any second!"

"That's the point," Stephanie told her, leaning back and taking a long sip of her wine. "This is for them, isn't it? Although I must admit, it is comfortable, too."

Cheryl started to say something else, but at that moment Art came back through the doorway. He stopped, staring; Rick, trying to follow him, bumped into him. They remained there for a moment, blocking the doorway.

"Well, come on in, guys," Jennifer said. She grinned broadly and winked at them. "We aren't going to bite you!"

Again, Art and Rick both took their cues; both acted terribly surprised—which they probably were—and terribly shocked—which Stephanie knew full well they were not. Dutifully they also stared at each other's wife's breasts as if for the first time.

"Where's Sam?" Stephanie asked after the other two men had come in and seated themselves. She felt like they'd committed themselves to this now, but she wasn't sure about how to proceed. If she or Jennifer made any overtly sexual moves toward Sam, they risked Cheryl's wrath. Likewise—at least she presumed likewise— if Rick or Art were to move on Cheryl, Sam was apt to get angry.

"I think he went off to the bathroom. He ought to be back in a minute or two," Art said.

"He's sure as hell in for a big surprise when he does come back," Cheryl observed.

Forty-Eight

SAM WAS STARTLED when he came back in to find Stephanie and Jennifer lounging around topless, but he was hardly shocked, and he was not nearly so surprised as Cheryl had been, or as the two other women had assumed he might be. Considering the swimsuits they'd been wearing since their arrival, and considering the fact that things seemed to be getting looser and looser with every passing day, it wasn't an illogical next step.

As he entered the room, he stopped, just as Art had, and his eyes, he knew, widened a little. But, determined to remain cool, he got himself under way again quickly. "I do love your evening attire, ladies," he said smoothly. "Although you look a bit overdressed for the occasion, Cheryl!"

Cheryl was still looking at her friends in disbelief. "Yeah," she answered, nodding. "It seems like I'm finding myself overdressed a lot lately." Her hands were resting on her knees, she made no move to take off her own top.

Sam sat down beside her. "Well," he said. "Do I take it there's something planned for the evening? More dancing, maybe, if I can judge by the music?" As he spoke he kept glancing over at Jennifer and Stephanie. Both, he told himself, looked really lovely. And they seemed quite unselfconscious about this; that was really the biggest surprise of all.

"We thought so," Jennifer told him. "But, maybe, just some conversation first. Rick, you want to turn on the projector there?"

"Addicts," Cheryl sniffed as the room lights dimmed and the patterns reappeared on the screen. "I'm not sure that thing isn't a conversation killer anyway!"

"It hasn't been so far," Stephanie pointed out. "It's been much more of a conversation stimulator."

But, for a few minutes, Cheryl was proven correct; the talk faded away as the other four watched a few mandalas develop and vanish. Sam was hardly bored, however. The way the reflected colors washed over the women's bare bodies was most interesting, most appealing.

Especially, he noticed after a while, the reds . . .

The significance of that did not escape him. Almost frantically he tried to push those thoughts back, but he failed; the vision of Selinde lying in bed and committing suicide came back, passed relentlessly through his mind. Once again, even though he'd already had a sexual encounter that day, he felt himself becoming erect.

Still trying to get himself under control, he tore his eyes away from the women and looked out the window. Darkness, he told himself; darkness was falling out there, the daylight was fading. And, as before, his own self-control seemed to be fading with it.

Turning his head back, he focused his eyes on Stephanie and

rested his chin on a closed fist. For quite some time he sat immersed in thought. Why are you fighting this? he asked himself. Every night you struggle and lose, every night Cheryl struggles and loses. Every night, in the end, you have a wonderful time. What is the problem? Why don't you just let go a little?

He leaned close to her ear. "I think," he whispered, "that you ought to take your top off too! This isn't fair to Rick and Art. Don't you think so?"

She looked up at him. Confusion clouded the green eyes; he saw the kaleidoscopic patterns whirling in her pupils, and for an instant they didn't look the same as those coming from the projector. "You think I should?" she echoed.

"Uh-huh."

"You want me to?"

"Uh-huh."

"Really?"

"Uh-huh."

The confusion seemed to clear up abruptly. She smiled her impish smile and stood up. "Sam," she announced loudly, "thinks I should take my top off, too. He thinks I'm overdressed for the occasion—I have to agree." She reached behind her back, untied her top, ripped it off. Showgirllike, she whirled it around her head a couple of times and tossed it; Sam didn't see where it landed. Rick and Art burst into applause. "There!" she said, looking down at her bare chest for a moment. "Now I'm in style! But I'm used to being the trendsetter in this group, not the follower!"

With that she pushed the bottom of the suit down over her hips, stepped out of it, whirled, and tossed it too. Completely naked, she turned around and bounced her rear end at Rick and Art. Then she sat down, not even bothering to keep her knees together.

Art pursed his lips and nodded. "I like it," he said. "I like your new fashion, I like it a lot!"

"You do?" Stephanie asked. "What do you think, Rick?"

"Oh, I like it, too. I think it's really fine!"

Nodding, Stephanie stood up and began pushing the bottom of her suit down; almost immediately, Jennifer joined her. Within a few seconds, all three women were nude.

"You see?" Cheryl asked, turning to Sam. "You see how fast they copy my new fashion trends?"

"Yeah. I have to tell you, I'm with Rick and Art. I like it!"

"Good!" she said. "I'm glad you do! But you three men, frankly, you look like a bunch of beach bums to me, sitting around here in your rumpled swimming trunks!"

"What do you want us to do, Cheryl?" Art asked. "Go put on tuxedos?"

Boldly, she drew up one of her legs while leaving the other extended, exposing her genitals completely. She grinned at Art. "That'd be nice," she replied. "But you guys don't have any tuxedos down here, do you? I guess you'll just have to think of something else!" She swung her head around, fixed her gaze on Sam. "You have any ideas?" she demanded.

Smiling, Sam shook his head. It was, in reality, less out of character for Cheryl to strip nude than for the other women, even though her performance had certainly startled him. This, however, was typical. There was no way her egalitarian nature was going to permit the three men to remain dressed while the women were naked.

"All I can do," he answered, "is follow your lead, my dear!" A bit awkwardly, without getting up as the women had, he stripped off his trunks. Imitating her, he spun them and tossed them. Everyone laughed, but Sam's attention was on himself. To his delight, he was less than half erect. Hopefully, he'd stay that way. For a while, anyway.

A little less speedily, Art and Rick did the same; Art was in the same condition as Sam, but Rick was not so fortunate, he was already in full bloom.

He accepted it well, though. "I have to tell you all, dancing while I'm like this isn't going to be easy!"

To Sam's absolute amazement, Cheryl rose from her seat and went to him, reached down for his hand. "Oh, it won't be that bad, Rick!" she teased. "Come on, let me show you!"

By that time a slow tune was playing on the stereo; without any hesitation at all, Cheryl pulled the protesting Rick up from the floor and pressed her nude body against his. His erection poked her belly; she quite casually used her hand to push it upward, after which it remained clamped between their bodies as they began to dance.

At first Sam was astounded; but as he thought about it, he began to realize that even this was not out of character for Cheryl. He'd expected more initial resistance from her, but she tended to go to extremes; once into it, she might well go further than anyone else. Circumspectly, he looked over at Jennifer, wondering if she was going to get upset. She showed no sign of it whatever; and, as if to underscore that, she rose to her feet and went to Art, pulling him up to dance, resting her head on his shoulder, her bare breasts pressed tightly against his chest.

"Looks like that leaves you and me," Stephanie told him.

He was on his feet almost instantly. "Sounds good to me," he told her. He went to her but he'd decided to let her set the tone. She did, holding him tightly against herself, nuzzling her lips against his neck.

Jesus Christ, he told himself. Things really are moving fast here.

The slow song was not even a third of the way over before Sam's erection had returned; Stephanie dealt with it in almost the same way Cheryl had dealt with Rick's, except that she pushed it down, not up. As they danced he felt the tip of it encounter wetness, move back to dry hair, encounter wetness again. Almost involuntarily, he moved his hand up along her side toward her breast. He managed to stop short, but she hooked her arm under his elbow and pushed him onward. He took the hint, laid his hand directly on her breast, felt her nipple harden under his palm.

Much too soon for him, the song ended and a much faster tune took its place. With Stephanie still in his arms, he looked around at the others; no one was dancing. Cheryl was still pressed tightly against Rick, her face turned toward him, her eyes sleepy looking because her eyelids were a little swollen. Sam knew that look. Your wife, he told himself, is seriously turned on.

"We need to tell them," Jennifer mumbled, her voice thick. "I can't take much more of this. We need to tell them, straight out."

Sam pulled away from Stephanie a little; he could not concentrate at all while the glans of his penis was resting where it was, just between the folds of her labia. "You talking about us?" he asked. "Tell us what?"

Stephanie moved a little so that her thigh pressed hard against his. "Tell you that we've—tell you that the four of us—Rick and Jennifer and Art and I—have spent the last two nights together." She was breathing very hard. "In bed."

"We wanted to know if you wanted to join us," Jennifer added. "But we didn't know how to ask you."

"Why not straight out?" Sam asked. "Like this?"

"There's a little more to it than that," Rick said. "We've been, uh, uhm, playing games, too. My games, Sam."

"Your games? You mean—" Rick was nodding; Sam looked back at Stephanie. "You too?"

She smiled, but she turned a little red as well. "Me too," she admitted.

"We've talked," Rick went on, "a lot about this over the years. I think it's time that you learned something about it, old buddy. The same way Art and Stephanie learned."

"How's that?"

"By watching."

He looked at Cheryl, raised his eyebrows slightly. Almost imperceptibly, she nodded; and as she did, her hand moved to Rick's erection, her fingers coiled around it. There wasn't a question as to her preferences, and Sam already knew his.

Thirty minutes later they were all upstairs in the large master bedroom, Sam and Cheryl watching with mouths agape while first Jennifer, then all three of the others, took a turn dangling from the ceiling hook and being beaten with the belt. They had more or less explicitly invited Sam and Cheryl to join in the oral sex that followed the floggings; they, however, hadn't moved, hadn't accepted or declined. They merely watched. Sam was finding this almost impossible to believe, he wondered if he was awake. That Rick enjoyed these variations was hardly a surprise; that the other three people would be such enthusiastic participants had been, quite literally, beyond imagining.

But then, the idea of himself and Cheryl pouring hot wax on each other was pretty farfetched too. Or at least it would've been a month ago.

Sam continued to watch as they took a smiling and obviously happy Art—the final participant—down from the apparatus and freed him from the cuffs. In a dreamlike state, he heard Rick ask Cheryl if she wanted to be put up there. He waited for her to refuse.

And knew that he had to be dreaming when he heard her accept the offer eagerly.

Once she'd been suspended, he saw Rick handing him the belt, saw his own hand reaching out to take it. Holding it, he looked up at Cheryl. "Honey, are you sure?" he asked.

"Yes," she told him firmly. "Yes, I am. Do it, Sam!" He drew the belt back, swiped it halfheartedly across her buttocks. "Oh, come on!" she cried. "Can't you do any better than that?"

His inhibition broke free, and the next one was really hard. Cheryl cried out, but she urged him on nevertheless. He moved around in front, struck her across her thighs, across her belly, across each breast in turn, making sure he covered all the sites that Rick and Art had covered in whipping Jennifer and Stephanie. She took perhaps a dozen before crying "Enough"; Sam quit instantly, dropping the belt to the floor.

Rick grabbed it up, pushed it back into his hands. "No," he said firmly. "You don't quit when she says enough. Push it on, a little further. Three strokes."

Sam hesitated; Cheryl said nothing, and after a moment he hit her again, very hard, across her buttocks. Like Stephanie, she groaned but didn't ask again; he whipped her thighs and her belly once more each before stopping again. He almost sprang on her then, hardly able to wait to begin stimulating her body with his lips and tongue. Art and Rick stood by, clearly waiting for an invitation; after a moment, Sam issued it. Under the pressure of three mouths and six hands, Cheryl was pushed into a shattering orgasm within minutes.

Then it was reversed, Sam dangling, Cheryl wielding the belt—with some trepidation at first but with increasing enthusiasm and vigor. Sam found that he couldn't've said whether he himself was truly enjoying this as much as he'd enjoyed the wax, but he was certainly caught up in the moment, and he did not call a halt until he'd taken a few more lashes than Cheryl had. Now knowing the rules, she went right on; by the time she did stop, he'd been much more severely whipped than any of the previous five. He did not object, especially when lips whose touch was unfamiliar drew his penis in, when six feminine hands were caressing every part of him.

By the time they got him down, Rick was ready for more, and Art wasn't far behind; Sam's head was spinning as he watched Cheryl avidly tonguing Art's erection, as he saw her lie back and pull herself open for Rick, her face a study in passion. He knew his own looked little different as his own erection returned, for the third time that day, inside Stephanie's mouth. Almost always, someone was swinging the belt, whipping any and all of the bodies in sight; Sam was in a daze, hardly knowing where he was or what he was doing, sometimes not even sure which of the three women he was coupled with.

It could not go on forever, though. Eventually everyone was pretty much forced, by sheer fatigue, to take a break. Even then, as they lay about the floor with their hands still on each others' bodies, Sam's head was buzzing. He had a distinct feeling of unreality, as if this could not be really happening. There was a slight fear, too, but he ignored that. He was enjoying himself far too much to pay any attention to it.

It was Stephanie who finally broke the long silence. "It just isn't quite right," she mused, lying flat on her back with one knee propped up, Sam's hand on her lower belly, her own hand cradling Art's now limp penis. "It's close, but it isn't quite right."

"What's not right?" Rick asked her. "It all seems goddamn perfect to me!"

"Oh, it is, don't get me wrong! No, well, really, it's close. The belt; the—well, the kind of pain it causes—it just isn't quite right. Neither is the biting, really. They're both close, but they aren't quite right."

Cheryl lifted her head from Rick's upper thigh, where she'd been nuzzling his penis with her lips. "I know what you mean," she agreed. "It isn't. Neither is the candle wax."

Stephanie and Jennifer raised their heads simultaneously. "Candle wax?" they asked in almost perfect unison. Nonchalantly, Cheryl began explaining what she and Sam had been doing with the wax.

And immediately began suffering a terrible verbal beating from the other two women, the basis of which was her failure to mention any of this when they were suffering the embarrassment of having their own foibles exposed.

Eventually, however, the discussion reverted to the problem with the belt, with teeth, with wax. Sam alone did not participate. He lay on his back while the others sat up talking, his eyes closed, his mind working. He understood exactly what they meant, he found he agreed with them fully. Some of the events of the last few days passed through his mind, fast-forward; he picked one out. That, he told himself, might be a solution. Might be perfect. The others might think he was crazy, but so what? If they'd told him about this before, he would have called them crazy, too.

"I have an idea," he told them finally as he got to his feet. "I'll be back in a few minutes."

Leaving the others, he went downstairs, located one of the fondue pots in the kitchen, filled it half full of water and put it on the stove. When the water was boiling he removed it, put it on its stand with a candle under it, and, after picking up the other items his plan required, went back to the Masons' bedroom, carrying the still mildly boiling water carefully.

"We've been waiting for you, Sam," Stephanie said as he came in. She looked at the fondue pot. "What've you got there?"

He put it down on the dresser. "Sterilizer," he replied. "For safety's sake." With a little flourish, he put six fondue forks in the pot.

Everyone gathered around, looked. He waited for someone to say he was crazy before they'd even heard the details of his idea.

He was only mildly surprised when no one did. This group, he told himself, is ready to accept just about anything right now, or at least they're ready to talk about it.

"What're we going to do with the forks, Sam?" Cheryl asked. "I mean, I can see one possibility, but—"

There! he told himself. One sort-of objection. Now he could explain. "I was thinking about what you were saying, Stephanie," he told them. "About the belt and everything not being quite right. These may do better—they're real sharp, and if we just press on the skin with them, we may be able to get a perfect balance."

"Why the sterilizer, then?" she asked. "And why not just use a kitchen knife?"

"Safety. See, we're safe with these things two ways—if the skin gets accidentally broken. One, they're sterile now. Two, they're self-limiting." He took one out, indicated the V between the tines. "They can't go in far, even under the worst circumstance. Maybe three-quarters of an inch or so."

"I," Rick observed, "do not care to be the subject of the first experiment!"

"I do!" Jennifer said eagerly. "It sounds interesting to me!"

"I was going to say you could try it on me first," Sam said when Rick threw Jennifer a look he could only interpret as warning. "It was my idea, after all . . ."

"Let's all try it!" Cheryl enthused. "Like Sam says, what can it hurt? You can say stop at any time, can't you?" She giggled. "And if you do, it'll stop, sooner or later . . ."

Cheryl's excitement was contagious; it was agreed, although Rick looked distinctly worried and made some rather halfhearted protests, that since Jennifer had asked first, that she should be the first subject. With Art leading her by the hand, they took her to the bed, stretched her out. Her eyes were dancing with excitement as they organized themselves around her.

"I think maybe we should hold her down," Rick said, stroking his chin and looking down at his wife. "Hold her hands. So she doesn't jump around." He still looked doubtful, but he looked terribly excited, too.

"You can tie me up if you want to," Jennifer told them. "Use the handcuffs."

"Isn't necessary," Art observed, taking hold of one of her slender ankles and running a hand sensually up her leg. "There's five of us; one for each arm and each leg plus our surgeon!"

Smiling, Jennifer spread-eagled herself; still holding her ankle, Art put his head down between her thighs and began nuzzling around. Taking their cues, Stephanie held the other ankle, Rick one wrist and Cheryl the other.

Holding a fork, Sam knelt beside the bed. Jennifer, gasping as Art's tongue teased her clitoris and Rick's mouth found one of her nipples, stared fixedly at Sam as he carefully located the fork's tines on her other breast, just below the nipple, standing it upright. He paused for a moment, considering what he was about to do. Then, for a little extra margin of safety, he lowered the handle, eventually holding the fork so that its blade was nearly parallel to her chest. He pushed gently, indenting her skin.

"You tell me how hard," he advised. "On this I'll stop as soon as you say so. You can judge it a lot better than I can!"

"Harder," she breathed.

He did; she repeated the word, he pressed even more.

Her eyes widened a little. "Oh, yes, Sam!" she breathed. "Yes! You were right, this is perfect, perfect—after the belt, this is perfect—push harder! Harder!"

He kissed her and followed her instructions—and abruptly felt a release in the pressure. There was a quick forward movement of the fork. A bead of blood, brilliant red, welled up and hid the points.

"Oh, shit," Sam muttered, momentarily paralyzed. "Damn, I'm sorry, it—"

"No!" Jennifer cried. "No, keep going! Harder! Push harder!"

She was looking right at the blood; she wasn't unaware of what had happened. She squirmed on the bed. "Please, everybody go on! Please, oh God, please!"

Everyone did, Sam included. He felt the tines of the fork move on into her flesh, saw more blood well out, saw it begin to draw a thin red line down toward the bed. Still she urged him on, and in the end he'd forced the fork into her until the division of the tines, as predicted, had stopped him.

She exploded into orgasm, thrashing on the bed; Sam held the fork's handle very lightly so she would not tear her flesh with it. As her climax faded he pulled it free; more of her blood flowed then, adding to the red line. Impulsively, Sam bent down and licked it away; more replaced it, and this time Cheryl licked it. Panting, Jennifer laid still and allowed them to do whatever they wanted.

"Ah, God, that feels good," she sighed as Stephanie, her eyes shining, sucked up some of the blood. "Feels wonderful, wonderful, just wonderful . . . !"

She remained on the bed for a long time, until the bleeding had pretty much stopped. Sam examined the wound with a professional eye; it wasn't serious at all. Everything had worked exactly as he'd presumed it would, except that he hadn't imagined that it would go quite this far. At least not quite so soon.

But it was perfectly evident that the sight of the blood had inflamed everyone; all the men had raging erections once more. Jennifer sat on the side of the bed swaying as if in a trance, blood still trickling from her breast, an expression of absolute satisfaction on her face.

"Do me now!" Cheryl demanded. "Do me! Just like you did her, do me!"

"Uh-uh," Rick argued. "That isn't fair. Woman-man-woman-man. It should be one of us now."

"Me," Art said with a broad grin. "Hell, the fringe benefits are bound to make it worthwhile!"

Rick argued with him too, and eventually they settled the matter in very juvenile fashion, hammer-scissors-paper. Art was the winner; he plopped down on the bed, readied himself. Stephanie went to the pot, took out another fork, began blowing on it to cool it. Her eyes looked utterly feral. Cheryl, meanwhile, climbed onto the bed and straddled him, letting herself down slowly on his erection.

Then, while Jennifer kissed his face and chest and while the men held his wrists and ankles, Stephanie drove the fork into his chest, angling it upward but keeping it shallow, following the method Sam had already established. Art yelled, lifting his hips and Cheryl's whole body with them as he climaxed into her. Stephanie, not waiting for him to say "enough!" pulled the fork free before he was finished; then everyone tasted the flowing blood.

For Sam, the evening terminated in a haze; at some point he lost consciousness—maybe fell asleep, maybe passed out, he didn't know. But that wasn't until he, too, had experienced the bright white pain of the fork, until each one of them had been pierced, until each one of them had allowed their blood to flow free.

Forty-Nine

"WE HAVE TO face it," Stephanie was saying, her face tight and drawn. "We just have to face it. Something is wrong with us, something is really, seriously, wrong!" This morning, she was dressed in a bathrobe as she sat at the kitchen table trying to drink coffee, her hands shaking so badly she could hardly hold the cup. With red-rimmed eyes, she looked around at the others. Sam, like herself, looked haunted. He was even more fully dressed, a shirt and slacks. He nodded as she spoke; unlike her he threw down the coffee, emptying his cup in two or three drafts and refilling it immediately.

"Yeah," Jennifer agreed. "Yeah, we did get a little carried away last night, didn't we?" She giggled; she did not seem to be upset at all. She was already in her swimsuit, the narrow straps that covered her breasts also covering the small puncture wound. Cheryl, too, was dressed for the beach, and her injury could not be seen either.

Rick and Art, though, were bare-chested as always, and she could see at a glance what their play last night had produced. Each man showed the evidence of the piercing on his chest, a little red line less than half an inch wide, a mark Stephanie herself possessed as well. Both of them were refusing to meet her gaze; they both sat staring fixedly at the table, as if embarrassed.

"Yeah, we did," Rick agreed. He looked up and he managed to grin, but it looked forced, phony; his eyes remained evasive. "But damn, none of us are really hurt, are we? My old buddy Sam here was right on the money, those forks can't—"

"I didn't really think," Sam cut in, "that we'd actually start sticking them in each other like that! I just didn't imagine that!" Studying the black liquid in his half-full coffee cup, he shook his head. "I had milder things in mind. I just thought, safety. In case somebody slips. In case somebody jerks at the wrong time. Safety." He looked up. "Last night somebody said why not kitchen knives. Christ, what if we'd done that instead?"

"Wouldn't have worked," Rick answered firmly. "It just wouldn't have. We all have confidence in what you say, Sam. You said the forks were safe, so we just sort of—let go. You wouldn't've said that kitchen knives were safe."

"We're letting go of everything!" Stephanie cried. "God damn, I'm not accusing anybody here, I was right there with everybody else at the time, but I don't mind saying, here and now, that I am fucking well scared to death! Okay?"

"I don't think there's a thing in the world to be scared of," Jennifer insisted. Her voice was rather dreamy, like Art's had been a few days earlier; there was a smile on her face and a distant look in her eyes. She leaned her head against Rick's shoulder. "Not a thing."

Art looked around at her. "I don't know how you can say that," he told her, frowning. "We up the ante every time, every night. I don't know, once we get into it it doesn't seem to matter a lot. Right now, I just can't believe we were doing that! Sticking fondue forks into each other, for God's sake! If one of my clients told me that I'd ask for a psychiatric exam!"

"That's exactly," Cheryl put in, "what we all need right now. Badly. I thought Sam and I were pushing things pretty far, but I don't know. Sitting here right now, I just can't believe we actually did—what we did. We just went so far, so far. I'm like Stephanie; I'm scared, I'm really scared. Of myself, more than any of you. Of what I might do when I'm like that. I've never been like that, never!"

"Look," Jennifer said. She sounded almost desperate. "Look, we're just getting started, we're just beginning to explore these things. Three of you are doctors, Cheryl's a nurse—surely you can take care of whatever comes up. I think that . . ."

"We can't deal with anything when we're like that," Stephanie insisted. "Nothing! At least I can't; I'm completely caught up, all I want is more and more and more. My mind just goes away, that's all there is to it!"

"The big question," Sam said, "is why." He looked around at the members of the group. "Anybody here—besides you, Rick—ever been involved in anything like this before? Any hints, hidden fantasies?" He turned his gaze toward Jennifer. "I don't mean to be—ah—don't mean to be insulting, but you seem—I don't know—enthusiastic? And—I don't want to create a problem here, but . . ." He paused, cleared his throat. "Uh—Rick's said, at times—in the past—that there was some—uhm—reason why— why you shouldn't play games like these . . ."

Jennifer laughed, a childlike peal. "I suppose," she said with a glance at an uncomfortable-looking Rick, "that I should have realized that you'd know all about this stuff, Sam! Should've known he'd've talked to you. He never told you why? Why I—in his opinion, I might add—shouldn't play his games?"

"No. Not a hint."

She gave Rick an affectionate pat on the shoulder. "He can keep some secrets, I guess." She stirred her cooling coffee with her spoon; slowly the amusement faded from her eyes. "In a way," she continued finally, her voice so soft Stephanie had to listen closely to catch her words, "what happened last night might've been my fault." She glanced at Sam, bit her lip, then plowed on, the words spilling out rapidly: "I knew what I wanted as soon as you brought those forks in. I was just afraid you wouldn't do it, that you wouldn't make me bleed. Rick knew about all this—as for me, I guess I didn't really want to face it. For me, blood is—well, it's a turn-on. My own especially." She stood up, put one foot up on a chair, pointed out some extremely faint, almost invisible, white scars on her calves and thighs. "When I was a teenager, I used to deliberately have 'accidents,' I used to cut my legs. The blood running out turned me on. At first I wasn't aware of that, and when I finally did figure it out I thought I was really sick."

Art ran his palm over her thigh, traced one of the scars with a fingertip, one that ran from inside her leg around to the back near her knee, covering perhaps four inches. "You can't even see them," he noted, "unless you really look close. What'd you cut yourself with?"

"Broken glass, mostly," she answered. "I'd drop a Coke bottle and break it, and then I'd 'trip' and fall on it." She laughed shortly. "It was funny, my mom and dad used to always say how lucky I was. You're so clumsy, Dad used to say. One day you'll fall on a big piece and it'll go in way deep. You only get these little shallow cuts. I can't understand how you always manage to fall down so you only get these little shallow cuts." Pausing, she shook her head. "Some of those falls were so contrived, anybody who'd been watching would've known it was deliberate, but somehow I managed to keep telling myself they were accidents." Her eyes took on a faraway look. "Then things sort of changed. I think I was about fifteen; I was trying to do it, but I couldn't seem to make it work by falling down. That was the first time I deliberately cut myself, a long cut down the inside of my thigh. I told myself I deserved it for being so clumsy. Then I went home like always, with blood running down my leg. If I could, I'd go in the bathroom and stand in the tub until the bleeding stopped on its own, telling myself that the bleeding was good, that it'd clean out the cut. And I'd—uh—touch myself." She sighed again. "No, let's be honest, I'd masturbate. And tell myself that there was no relationship between the two things." She pushed her hair up, wound her fingers in it. "It kinda went on from there. By the time I was eighteen I always had a cut healing up somewhere. One of my boyfriends—I couldn't hide it from boyfriends—convinced me to go see a doctor. I did, but the problem was, I didn't really want to stop; it made me feel good, it made me feel special—if I quit, I'd be just like everybody else." She looked up at Stephanie, then at Cheryl. "You remember, that day when you were talking about those 'borderlines,' those 'carvers?' You were talking about me . . ."

Stephanie looked around at Rick. "So those little pills she's been taking . . ."

He sighed. "Uh-huh. Lithium, I've been using it as a mood stabilizer, she has terribly violent ups and downs—but of course, you can see, I was afraid of what might happen if we got into—well, if we got into what we got into."

"In other words," Jennifer added, addressing herself to Sam, "he never trusted me. I did suggest this, more than once. But I never insisted, not until recently." She looked back at Rick. "And now, look what did happen. Last night was a dream come true for me, to be able to share this, these things that've been bottled up for so long. I don't know if any of you can understand that . . ."

"I think I can," Stephanie said. "I mean, everybody has quirks. But, for some reason, we're just losing it here, losing all control. I think we need to cut the vacation short, head back to Raleigh. Separate for a little while. Get our heads straightened out."

Looking around the table, Stephanie didn't have any problems reading the faces. Sam was nodding agreement; he seemed to be in her corner completely. Art looked unhappy, but he didn't look like he was about to argue. Rick seemed unsure, and Stephanie had little trouble understanding that—he surely did not want to give up the "games," but at the same time he had to be concerned about their effect on Jennifer—whose expression was unequivocally one of dismay. No surprise there.

Where there was a surprise was in Cheryl's reaction. The fear she'd expressed earlier was still there, but there was clearly, unmistakeably, a hint of Jennifer's dismay mixed into it.

She wondered if she, too, was communicating such an ambivalence. In spite of all her fears, all her misgivings, there was definitely a part of her that wanted to stay, wanted to do it all again—a part that kept throwing up objections to her carefully reasoned plan.

"There's no reason for us to go home, the place isn't doing it!" Jennifer protested, echoing one of those objections. "We've been here before, this hasn't happened! It's us, and it isn't going away just because we go home!"

"No," Stephanie argued. "I agree. But we're feeding off each other on this. We need to be apart for a while."

"You're right," Cheryl commented. "We are losing it. Even before—before we all got into it together, I mean—Sam and I were having trouble controlling things—and it's harder now. But I have to say it, in a way I don't really want to."

"Neither do I," Art grumbled. "But—"

"No, I think Stephanie's right," Sam interrupted. "It'd be best for all of us. Don't get me wrong, it isn't that I'm not enjoying it too. I just don't think we can keep this up, we're going to burn ourselves out." He hesitated. "Or maybe up."

Rick sighed deeply. "Well, it looks like it's decided—and I agree, we should get some distance, should think about all this objectively for a while." He twisted his mouth. "Never thought I'd say that in this situation." He glanced at Cheryl. "I'm with you; in a lot of ways, I don't want to."

"We have to, Rick," Stephanie said earnestly. "We just have to. I can't handle any more of this right now, that's all there is to it." She drained her coffee cup. "There's no real reason for you and Jennifer not to stay on, though. Like you said, it isn't the house, it isn't the beach."

"Do you think," Jennifer asked, her voice small, "that it might be the kaleidoscope?"

Now Stephanie sighed. "No, Jennifer," she said patiently. "No, you've just told us about something that might make this sort of thing attractive to you; I'm no different. I still have enough of my wits about me to see that being beaten up as a child by a father you loved and being whipped by the people you love now might just be connected somehow!" Nobody was about to speak, but she held up her hands defensively anyhow, closing her eyes and turning her head as if to stop any objection. "No, it might be," she protested, "Daddy never made love to Mama except when he beat her up, he'd beat her up and then he'd take her in and make love to her, he used to make love with her while she was beaten all bloody while she had broken bones while she was having a miscarriage while she was while she was he might've he I don't know if he did he did he make love to her while she was dying the night he dying made love dying while oh my God, my God, my God, my God, my . . . !' "

Feeling Art's strong hands on her shoulders, she stopped speaking and, opening her eyes very wide, looked around at the others. Her mind was whirling, she felt like she was spinning down some long tunnel with who could say what at the bottom. Oh, yes, she told herself, you have dealt with this perfectly. You're all under control. That's perfectly obvious, isn't it? One night of tell-all wipes away twenty-five years of agony. What a laugh.

"This isn't an explanation," Sam observed after Stephanie had calmed down a little. "Unfortunately, there are lots of people around—please don't take this the wrong way, Stephanie, I don't mean in any way to belittle your experiences, you lived through a horror I can't even imagine—but there are, in fact, lots of people whose parents were abusive." He sighed, spread his hands on the table and looked down at his fingers. "I don't know. I've had some —fantasies lately, fantasies about doing things, well—things like the things we've been doing." Pausing, he looked around at the others. "For me, there's no background I can hang it on." He fixed his gaze on Rick. "I'll admit it, I've always been—I guess the best word is *fascinated*—by the stuff you've always done, but I never could see myself doing it." He cradled his cup in both hands, turned it slowly. "So, the question is, why now?"

"The more important one," Stephanie interjected, "is how do we get it to stop!"

"Why do we have to stop?" Jennifer asked plaintively. "We don't have to, we don't. We haven't really hurt each other; damn it, Stephanie, I've never felt so free, so satisfied, in my whole life! I don't mind saying it, I don't want to stop!"

Watching her, listening to her words—and hearing the passion behind them—Stephanie found herself wavering. Jennifer has a point, she told herself. Your own sex life with Art was in the toilet until you started these games, and now you've experienced heights of passion you hadn't known existed. It's worth it, part of her insisted. No matter what happens, it's worth it.

"Maybe we don't have to stop," she heard Art suggesting again. "Maybe we don't. Maybe we just have to set some limits."

Frantically pushing down the part of herself that wanted to shout out an enthusiastic agreement, Stephanie shook her head. "What limits?" she demanded. "And who's going to enforce them? Not me, not when I'm like I was last night, I just want more and more! No, I'd say that maybe—"

"Maybe what we need to control," Jennifer suggested, "is the kaleidoscope."

Stephanie scowled in frustration. "Jenny, please. It doesn't have anything to do with it—except that maybe something in the, I don't know, the Rorschach patterns, they suggest things and we start thinking about them, and—"

"No. There's more to it than that. Look at it logically," Jennifer insisted. "Look at when it all started. It started when you bought it; I got out Paul's toy handcuffs the same night I first looked through it! It seems to me that—"

"It doesn't do a thing to me," Cheryl cut in. "Not a thing."

"Then what did?" Jennifer demanded, wheeling around to face her. "What caused a sedate nurse to let herself be hung up by her wrists and whipped, to have hot candle wax dripped on her? What caused her to beg her husband to stick a fondue fork into her tit? Answer me that, Cheryl!"

Cheryl's eyebrow hopped up, and instantly her ankle was on her knee. "I never was a 'sedate nurse,'" she snapped back. "It was just—it was just—" she looked bewildered for a second, then swung around to look at Sam. "Because you wanted me to, Sam," she went on. "Because—" She stopped speaking, shook her head as if to clear it, lowered her foot to the floor. "Jesus! Just because you wanted me to?"

Sam's eyes rolled heavenward. "Oh, come on!" he cried. "Don't make this out to be all my fault! You've never done anything in your life just because I wanted you to! Besides, I didn't ask you—!"

Cheryl's head was moving back and forth steadily. "No, you're wrong. On both counts, you're wrong. You did ask, you asked me to take my top off. That's all you asked, but I heard more, I felt more. You said, 'Cheryl, be wild. Cheryl, let it all go, do whatever you feel like doing. Cheryl, there're no tomorrows, do it now, Cheryl. So I did, I did. Ah, God, and I loved it, too!" She blinked furiously; a tear ran from each eye. "You think you know me very well, Sam, but you don't, you don't. I always needed you; I never really felt like you needed me. You like strong and independent women, and I tried to be that for you, I tried to be everything you wanted me to be, so you'd love me, so you wouldn't leave me, like Dad left me—"

"Your father didn't leave you, Cheryl," Sam pointed out, frowning. "Your parents were divorced, that's all—"

"How do you think it feels to a six-year-old, Sam? You've heard it a million times; it's trite because it's so goddamn common!" She counted on her fingers: "He left because of me. If I'd been better he wouldn't've left. It was all my fault, if he'd really loved me he wouldn't've left." She waved her hands in the air as if to dispel the memories. "You don't know what I've been thinking, Sam. Years ago I had fantasies about dying young, about dying of some nice clean disease like the one that wiped out Ali McGraw in *Love Story*. Now I know better, I know that cancer isn't like that, but it didn't really change anything, it just changed the nature of the fantasies." Her voice dropped to a near-whisper. "You changed the nature of my fantasies too, Sam. Now, they involve us getting killed. Oh, sometimes it's just me, sometimes I see myself dying in your arms; because I was hit by a truck, because a burglar shot me, it doesn't really matter. But the best ones are where we're doing it together. Like in a thousand old movies where the hero and heroine would endure anything, any amount of pain, when they'd rather die than be separated by whatever's forcing them apart. Like that."

Sam was staring at her, amazed. "We're not about to separate, Cheryl," he said. "Nothing's forcing us apart. And besides—"

She burst into full-blown tears. "Time was forcing us apart, Sam!" she sobbed. "Just time, just years, just our jobs, just plain old living! Romeo and Juliet, Tristan and Isolde, they had it right, they knew, they understood! You have a great love and you have to die for it, one way or another, if you don't die the love dies, it crumbles, it rots, it always does, always! They had one thing wrong, just one thing, they didn't do it together! That's all!" She pounded her fist on the table; coffee cups jumped. "We've got ours back now, Sam, and I by God want to keep it back! I've got a love with Art and with Rick, and with Jennifer and Stephanie, and I by God want to keep it! I'd rather you guys take me upstairs and cut off my fucking head right now than to see that go away, see it crumble, see it rot! You hear me, Sam? I'd rather go all the way than see that happen!" She was shrieking now, her tears pouring out. "You hear me?"

Sam wasn't saying anything; he was on his feet, standing beside her, pulling her toward him. She fought him weakly, flailing her arms, before collapsing against his chest, sobbing bitterly. Jennifer was up, too, stroking Cheryl's hair while Sam held her.

"I know how you feel," Jennifer was whispering. "I feel that way myself; I just didn't know it, not until right now, not until you made it so clear, so clear . . ."

Stephanie could only shake her head. God in heaven, she told herself, we are such a bizarre crew. Who could ever have guessed it?

"I guess," Rick said, very slowly, "that it's pretty obvious, isn't it? Stephanie, you're right. We need to get back to Raleigh; we all need, like Cheryl says, some sessions with a good shrink. There's just too much going on, just too much." He picked up his napkin, wiped up some coffee that had spilled. "Today," he went on, "we'll spend some quiet time on the beach. I don't think the kaleidoscope has one damn thing to do with what's been going on, but just to be on the safe side we're not going to touch it, not today. Tonight we'll pack up. And tomorrow, first thing, we'll all leave." He looked around at the others, resting his gaze on each face in turn. Art nodded; so did Jennifer. Cheryl had her face buried in Sam's shoulder, and he looked doubtful.

"I think we should go today . . ." Stephanie said hesitantly, voicing what she hoped were Sam's feelings as well.

Art, in particular, looking crestfallen. "No, tomorrow's soon enough!" he insisted. "One more day, what can it hurt?"

Again Stephanie found herself wavering; she understood, quite well. No one, herself included, really wanted to go. Eventually, she agreed; eventually, Sam did too. It sounds okay, she told herself. Tomorrow sounds okay. The only problem is, we still have to make it through another night.

Somehow.

Fifty

"IT'S OUR LAST day here!" Cheryl complained. "You shouldn't be doing that, not now! Come on out to the beach, Sam! Everybody else is already out there!"

Sam looked up from the laptop. "I'm going to, I'm going to," he replied. "I just want to look at a few things here first. An hour, maybe, no more. You go ahead. I'll join you."

She leaned down toward him, looking concerned. "You sure, Sam? An hour, that's it?"

"I promise."

She kissed him, ran her fingers through his hair. "I want you close to me today," she said with a slightly bittersweet but most appealing smile. "After what we went through last night and this morning, I don't want to be away from you for a minute!"

He grinned. "I know what you mean. You're welcome to sit here with me if you wish. Like I said, this won't take long."

"Well," she said hesitantly, "I want to get out there to the water, too . . ."

Laughing, he waved a hand. "Like I said, go. I'll be out there with you, very shortly."

She nodded, squeezed his arm, rose, and headed for the door. He watched her go, then turned back to the laptop, started going through the rigmarole required to link up with the system back at the Research Triangle. This time it wasn't quite as difficult as before—he did not get the ERROR signal even once, and the dataset came up without comment from Ken—and a short while later he was engrossed in the data once more. It really was interesting, he told himself; the apparent predictability of the data was already unusually high, especially for so small a sample. Besides that, he was finding it hard to shake a nagging suspicion he'd developed that there was somehow a connection between the deaths he'd been studying and what was happening to them at the beach house.

No, he told himself as he watched his variable categories come scrolling down the screen. No. Certainly, with predictabilities this high, that there was a connection among the deaths in the database was almost without question. But to presume that it had anything to do with their recent behavior was, he insisted mentally, irrational. Yes, there was a possibility that some of the victims had engaged in sex-play similar to what they'd done with the fondue forks, but that proved nothing. None of them had been killed, for one thing; by now, if anyone in the group had any connection with any group that might be practicing this sort of thing in an organized way—some sort of club or whatever—then Sam would've expected at least some hint of that to have come up in the very open and blunt conversations they'd been having.

That left only the hypothetical sex-murder virus—and the notion that they'd contracted it—as a possible connector. And Sam was hardly ready to consider that as a real possibility. Even though, he told himself, there are diseases—like rabies, as only one of several examples—that produce behavioral changes. And there were large numbers of drugs that could produce such changes, many of those changes quite specific. Add to that the well-known fact that the symptoms produced by disease-causing organisms are frequently the direct result of some chemical the organism releases—chemicals called exotoxins and endotoxins— and maybe, just maybe, the idea was not so totally outlandish after all.

No, he told himself once again. No. Pseudoscientific, as silly in its own way as Jennifer's attribution of their behavior to the kaleidoscope. No, there was a simpler explanation, and that had come out this morning over coffee. Several of them had factors in their backgrounds that made this sort of thing attractive to them; it had been set off by Rick's recent affair and by Sam's newfound affection for jalapeño peppers, and from there it had taken root quickly, the soil being more than fertile. No other explanation was required.

Giving his full attention to the dataset, he started changing the weightings once again, applying tests to throw out some more outliers, cut the variance. Recalling what Stephanie had said Dave Brennan had told her—that there were cases in North Carolina with male victims as well, cases that fitted the model—he checked to see if by any chance Ken had scanned those in as well, if those cases existed in the data he had access to.

When they began popping up, one after another, Sam grinned. You're thorough, Ken, he told himself. You never sorted them but they are here.

After a few seconds his grin began fading. They hadn't stopped popping up; there weren't just cases in North Carolina, there were cases in Tennessee, in Arkansas, in Oklahoma, Texas, New Mexico, Arizona. All along the same pathway. After a few long seconds of calculation, the software informed him that the sample size of his analysis group had almost doubled.

Without bothering to do any more weightings, he applied a query that would sort the new cases into the categories he'd already set up. Noting some obvious outliers, he checked on a few of them quickly.

Outliers by occupation, each and every one. And, in almost each and every case, using the occupation of the victim's spouse caused the case to drop right into line.

Incredulous, Sam stared at the orderly way the computer was now able to organize the dataset. Some outliers remained; he'd be willing to bet, now, that those were cases where the victim's spouse's occupation was not mentioned in the news reports or where the victim had a boyfriend or girlfriend whose occupation would fit. Using a couple of additional dependent variables, he ran the statistics again; and he was even more incredulous when the answers came up.

Raleigh, 91.3 percent likelihood. The current date, 69.7 percent; tomorrow, 88.9 percent, the following day 71.4. The victims, doctors or lawyers or their spouses, 82.1 percent.

That, Sam told himself as he stared at the screen, was far too close for any sort of comfort whatsoever.

Leaning back in his chair, he tugged at his beard and frowned. The first question was, whether to tell the others about it; and the next question was, what should they do? Stay here and continue what they'd been doing? Or, as they'd agreed, return to Raleigh tomorrow and thereby run a risk of being the target of whatever it was that had caused all those deaths?

And there were more problems than that, too. Should he tell Stephanie and only Stephanie, have her call Dave Brennan and alert him? But even if Dave took these computer analyses—admittedly esoteric programs—seriously, what could he do? He hardly had the manpower to keep watch over all the doctors and lawyers in Raleigh. If he merely posted officers in the hospitals and court-houses—not to mention the state capitol, a place crawling with lawyers—he'd stretch the department thin doing it. Should he call his other physician friends? What about Rick's associates, the others in the Medical Examiner's Office, Art's partners, the people Cheryl worked with? All their wives and husbands?

He pulled at his beard harder, worrying about it, almost wishing, in a way, that he didn't possess this information. He did not know how he could possibly use it in any constructive manner, and yet he was hardly unaware that if a friend of his turned up dead—especially one of the people here—he'd be driven almost mad with guilt.

Best to tell them, he decided. Best to talk to them about it, make sure they were all aware of it, make sure no one took any unnecessary chances. That's what he'd do, tonight, over dinner. There was no need to distract everyone's attention from the pleasures of the sun and water during their last day there. Having made his decision, he started to close the files, exit the analysis software, and log off the system.

But he stopped himself, his fingers poised over the keys. "Ken," he said to the screen, as if it was itself the obnoxious programmer's face, "I wonder if you thought of everything. You put this system together rather fast—did you cover all your bases? You did, probably, you asshole. But let's just see. Let's just find out." He didn't go through the usual sequence of closing the files and exiting via the menu; instead, his fingertip moved to the upper left of the keyboard and touched the ESCAPE key. When he saw the results, he grinned broadly.

A long while—well over an hour—later, he turned off the laptop and reconnected the telephone to the wall jack. He had a phone call to make, to the Institute; he did, and the results, to him, were more than satisfactory. Afterward, feeling like dancing or whooping with pure pleasure, he nevertheless disciplined himself enough to disconnect the phone again, to reconnect the line to the computer. Ken, once he figured out what Sam had just done to him, would be calling—there wasn't a doubt of that, and he certainly didn't want to take a chance on Ken talking to Cheryl. He'd send the letter, certainly, but that had been pretty much inevitable anyway; by the time he did Sam should have been able to make his confession, clear the air on that point. Once he did, now, the programmer would have no further hold on him.

Feeling freer than he had in quite a while, Sam walked to the window, looked out. Today, the kaleidoscope remained in the slide projector; no one was sitting on the beach with it stuck to his or her eye. He saw flashes of tanned bodies in the water and on the beach and grinned; evidently the swimsuits had been discarded. That wasn't unreasonable, there was no one around to see them except each other; Fran and Traci were not due until Monday— when they'd find an empty house. Sam didn't wait any longer, he started unbuttoning his shirt. He wanted to get out there too. Make the most of this final day on the beach.

Fifty-One

"It's not that I don't believe what you've come up with, Sam," Stephanie was saying. She wasn't particularly interested in her dinner, was merely picking at it, and she was using the topic Sam had brought up—his computer analyses—to distract herself. They were having dinner early tonight, to give everyone plenty of time to get packed up and ready to leave. Already, as far as she was concerned, things were not going especially well. They had managed to leave the kaleidoscope alone, but they'd also been running around stark naked all day; hardly conducive, she told herself sourly, to keeping their impulses in check. Now, as they ate dinner —in the kitchen tonight—they'd all redonned, at least, their swimsuits. Stephanie had led the way in insisting on this, and for a while she didn't think she was going to succeed. She herself hadn't wanted to put anything on, she'd been perfectly comfortable in the nude. But she'd forced herself, and the issue; she was quite sure she knew where things would go if they all remained nude in the house. It was hard enough for her to keep her hands off Rick and Sam as it was.

"It's just that I don't understand, that's all," she went on doggedly. "How in the hell could the predictability be that high? I mean, you don't even have a working hypothesis to go on!"

"Well, I do and I don't," he told her. "Originally Ken was using stats developed by the animal-behavior folk, predator-prey dynamics. That actually does fit the data somewhat, and it made his idea of a serial killer plausible; we know—or at least, he tells me there's research that shows—that a serial killer behaves a lot like a predator; focusing on one victim, stalking, all that. I changed that, I used a disease-carrier paradigm."

"I still don't understand how that lets the computer make predictions as specific as doctors and lawyers."

"It doesn't, not automatically. The software just sniffed out a pattern, that's all. Say we had a Typhoid Mary, and she moves from city to city, leaving outbreaks in her wake. Here, she works selling Tupperware; the typhoid victims are primarily housewives. Next city, she takes a job in a restaurant that caters to blue-collar workers; the victims are blue-collar. Next, a maid on a cleaning service that cleans the offices of doctors and lawyers. She sets up patterns, she keeps going back to the same type of jobs over and over. Pretty soon the predictability of what she'll do next gets pretty good, pretty tight. And so do the predictions about where you're going to see the next outbreak of typhoid fever."

Jennifer toyed with the food on her plate. "Does that mean," she asked, moving her shoulders up and down uncomfortably as if the straps on her suit were bothering her, "that this—what was it, sex-murder virus?—that you talked about is real?"

Sam laughed. "No, not at all. It's just a working model, that's all." He frowned. "To tell you the truth I really can't imagine what might be causing all this." He looked over at Stephanie. "Maybe Dave Brennan is right. Maybe it is some satanic cult."

She snorted rudely. "No, that's just Dave's favorite thing, he sees them everywhere and never can find one. You'd have to be talking about a cult that has hundreds—no, hundreds wouldn't do, it'd have to be thousands or tens of thousands of members—to get this many cases."

"Why?" Jennifer interrupted. "A cult of just a few people could kidnap hundreds if they weren't caught—"

"That's so," Stephanie agreed. "But you couldn't get all those kidnap victims to sit still for being killed like so many lambs!"

"Maybe they were drugged."

"Not Alice Near, anyway. Not with anything that's even close to ordinary. We did some really exhaustive bloods on her."

"Aren't you the husband's attorney, Art?" Jennifer asked. "Didn't I hear something like that?"

He nodded. "Yep. Sure am. And I'd have to agree with Stephanie. Bill Near isn't a cult member, I'd bet on that, although I can't doubt that he and Alice did some drugs now and then. What he is, is a nut. Apparently, so was his wife. That's going to be my defense strategy for him; insanity."

"Can you tell us about it?" Jennifer asked, her eyes maybe a little too bright, a little too interested. Stephanie glanced at the window; it wasn't dark yet, but the sunset was beginning to touch the western sky with red. She felt an ominous twinge in her abdomen. She, too, wanted to hear this story, in detail.

But she couldn't help but think that there was a risk. "No, he can't," she blurted. "It'd violate the lawyer-client ethic, it'd—"

Art laughed, waved a hand, pushed his plate aside. "Oh, that's ridiculous, Stephanie! Yes, it does, technically. But none of you are going to be sitting on that jury, the prosecutor would never allow it! Besides, we talk about things among ourselves that violate confidentiality all the time!"

Stephanie tried to insist. "I still don't think—"

But Art had his audience and the floor, and he ignored her warnings completely. "Well," he began, "what Bill tells me is that he and Alice were playing some—uh—sex games, I guess you'd say." He glanced around at the others almost furtively. "With a, uhm, a knife. Playing around with it while they were making love. I suppose you can figure out where it went from there."

Jennifer's fingertips were on her lower lip. She leaned forward. "No," she breathed. "Where? What'd they do?"

Art shrugged. His manner was casual and so was his speech, but his eyes gave away his own excitement. "Well, maybe Stephanie can give you some of the details, she did the autopsy on Alice Near. All I know is what Bill said, that they started sticking each other with it. Just nicking the skin a little at first, then pushing it in deeper. They were really getting off on the blood, he told me, there was blood all over. . . . Anyway, they just kept urging each other on, and before he knew what was happening, he says, Alice started choking and died. By then he was in pretty bad shape himself. He says he wanted to die too, but he staggered outside their trailer and a neighbor hauled him off to the hospital. He still says he wants to die."

Stephanie found herself lost in the images. She remembered what Alice Near had looked like; petite, blond, pretty. She could see the woman on a bed, gasping and shaking while a man—who in her vision looked a lot like Art, she had no notion what Bill

Near might look like—was carefully and gently pushing a knife into her belly. She could see the knife coming out, the blood flowing. He handing it to her, she taking it and with a trembling hand pushing it into his broad chest. More blood. More gasps.

She came back to the present with a start; someone was asking her a question. She didn't really know who, but she knew what the question was. "Yeah," she answered, glancing at several faces in turn. "Yeah, that's entirely consistent with what we found on autopsy. It might've been that way." She glanced at Jennifer and Cheryl in turn, her eyes narrowed. They'd been running the same fantasy, she was sure of it.

"I suppose," Cheryl noted, "that everyone has noticed that there may be, just possibly, a little similarity between that and what we were doing last night? Just a little? Just a tiny bit?"

"Not really," Rick said casually. "We took precautions. My old buddy Sam here saw to that! Besides, we—"

"That still," Cheryl insisted, "doesn't make it different! It's just a different approach, because we're medical people, we don't slip up and do something we don't mean to do! I'd have to say this: you said Bill Near was a nut, Art. If he is, so are we!"

Art laughed good-naturedly. "I never said we weren't! But you're such a nice nut, Cheryl!" He let his eyes roam boldly up and down her body. "Such a nice, nice, nut . . . in every way. . . ."

"Beautiful green eyes," Rick added.

Stephanie was hearing their words, and at the same time she was still seeing the images of Alice and Bill Near; superimposed on them she saw the others hanging by their wrists, being whipped, saw the fondue forks piercing their chests, the bright red of the blood. Her mouth was dry, her stomach tight, her labia wet; she could literally feel the tension in the room rising, and it wasn't even dark yet! You have to stop this, she told herself. Nobody else even can, it has to be you. You know how to control yourself, now do it!

"Well," she said, raising her voice a little to be heard above the generally erotic banter that was beginning to fly around the table, "I don't think the risk in going back to Raleigh tomorrow is particularly high. Even if you're right, Sam, there're hundreds of people in Raleigh who fit the description, the risk for any one of us isn't high. Besides, these things don't develop overnight, at least I wouldn't think they would, would you?" She ran on, tripping over her words at times, trying to pull them back down to where they'd been that morning, at least.

"No, you're probably right," Sam agreed. "Who knows, maybe I'm subconsciously juggling that data because I really don't want to go either. We have to, I know that. But it just seems a shame. We surely did achieve some wonderful things down here this time." He shook his head. "We got so close, so close."

"Yes," Cheryl added. "I'm afraid if we go we'll lose that. I'm afraid that once we get back to Raleigh, back to our jobs and our everyday lives, it'll go back like it was. Six people. Six people, each one with their walls and their defenses. Down here, nobody's had walls. Nobody's worried about defenses much. We've all been open to each other, open, completely . . ." She looked back up, and there were new tears in her eyes. "I don't want to lose this . . . I said that this morning. I'm scared too, I'm scared to death, but I don't want to lose this . . ."

I don't either, Stephanie said silently. I've never even been close to this with anyone, I didn't know how it could be. "We don't have to lose it," she said strongly. "We don't have to. We can have this in Raleigh too, there's no reason in the world why we can't, no reason!" As she finished she looked around at the others, one by one. "Is there?" she finished plaintively.

"It's hard to say," Sam answered. "Here, there's just us. No other influences, nobody else to worry about. None of us have cared how things looked. None of us have been embarrassed, not for long, and we sure have let some wild and kinky things hang out! We make love with each other's wives and husbands as if they were our own, and it isn't like wife-swapping; we all love each other, deeply and passionately. We've turned into a tribe, I think, in the oldest and purest sense. There aren't real differences between us anymore, we've melted into each other, blended together."

"There may be something to that, Sam," Rick put in. "Your idea that we've turned into a tribe. The sorts of things we've been doing—they're pretty common in societies we call 'primitive.' There aren't very many that haven't practiced things like this— piercings, tattooing, scarification, what the anthropologists call 'self-mutilations' of all sorts—like the American Indian sun dance. Not always openly sexually related, but often enough."

"They practiced human sacrifice often enough, too . . ." Jennifer muttered, so low Stephanie barely heard her.

"I had a dream about that recently," Cheryl commented, a faraway look in her eyes. "Remember, Sam? The one where you and I were Celtic warriors? Maybe we weren't Celts. Maybe we were Aztecs. Did they have swords?"

Stephanie started to ask for further details, but Sam, as if he didn't want that discussed, hurried on. "The problem is, the society we live in isn't like that and doesn't understand that. Can we hold on to it when we're in a day-to-day life where we know that almost anybody who knew what we'd been doing would call us sick, certifiable? I don't know. And you know they would. We would've, three weeks ago."

"None of us knew," Jennifer said softly.

"How could we?" Art asked rhetorically. "Every message we get from our society tells us to push the other person down to get what we want. Dominate your wife, manipulate your husband. Rub that prosecutor's face in the dirt, who cares whether the person in the dock is guilty or not, winning is what counts—no, no, wait. That isn't right. It's not winning that counts."

"What is it, then?" Stephanie asked sadly.

"Winning doesn't matter. It's making the other guy lose that really counts. Turning the other guy into a loser. You can't stomp on his face if he's a winner, even if you're a winner too."

"And down here . . ." Jennifer began.

"We were all winners. Nobody wanted to humiliate anybody, so nobody was afraid of being humiliated. We could let go, open up, really know what it meant to love and be loved, for the first time in our lives."

Sam was nodding steadily as Art spoke; his eyes were misty—or perhaps, Stephanie thought, smoky. "I think you're right. We managed, for a little while, to dump all the bullshit our society loads onto us, all the behavioral rules. Mother Nature came back—with a vengeance. But people like us—doctors, scientists—we're used to thinking we understand her, that we can bend her to our will. That's the problem, we don't know how to to interact with her anymore—we've been 'civilized' too long."

"Maybe we should just let her have her way," Cheryl offered, her voice small and tentative.

"If we do," Sam said, "She'll consume us. She always does. She gives us life but she always reclaims us in the end."

There was a long silence, which Jennifer eventually broke by beginning to cry. "I know you all think I'm silly," she sobbed, "but I still think that the kaleidoscope had something to do with it, that it showed us the way somehow—"

"No," Cheryl argued. "We showed each other the way." She touched Jennifer's hand. "But even so, we don't think you're silly."

Jennifer's fingers coiled around Cheryl's. "But you just have to look at it, at the outside of it, to see how special it is—"

"Not quite true," Sam said. "And that, I can prove. Let me show you something." He rose from the table, went into the other room; through the doorway Stephanie could see him taking something from the laptop's case. Returning, he laid it on the table.

Stephanie, along with everyone else, stared at it. A knife—a dagger, really—in a leather case, the handle carvings an almost exact match to those on the surface of the kaleidoscope.

She picked it up with shaking hands, withdrew it from its case partially, looked at the dark metal blade. "Where in the world," she asked, "did you get this?"

"Uh—from a gift shop in Nag's Head," Sam said, literally reeling the words off after the initial "uh." "I went in to ask the manager where I might find a photo shop," he babbled, "and I saw that lying there in display case and so naturally I bought it because it was just like the kaleidoscope ha ha . . ."

He's lying, Stephanie realized. Every instinct she had confirmed it; she knew it beyond any sort of reasonable doubt. Glancing at the other four faces, she knew that they knew it too. And yet, no one, not even Cheryl—who normally could be counted upon never to let such a thing go by—was challenging him.

So, why don't you? Stephanie asked herself as Rick took the knife from her, withdrew it completely, examined it closely.

Even as she formulated the question, she knew the answer: because it would put him on the spot. He was lying, but Sam was not a man to lie for no reason; sooner or later, he'd tell them the truth and along with that truth, the reasons for his lie. There was no need to push, no need to corner him.

In fact, her instinct was to go to him and hug him, let him know that he had no need to feel uncomfortable—no matter where he'd actually gotten it.

She didn't have to decide whether to do that or not. Jennifer, apparently feeling the same, beat her to it. From the expression on Sam's face, there was little question that he understood. He hugged Jennifer back, and their hands began gliding over each other's bodies tenderly.

Stephanie watched them for a moment, then looked at the window again, at the gathering darkness outside. Her hungers were rising too, and they were rapidly growing harder and harder to deny.

"We have to pack," she said shakily. "Have to get ready. Have to leave in the morning, bright and early . . ."

With obvious reluctance, Jennifer pulled away from Sam. He ran his hands through his hair, leaving it wild. "Yes, yes," he agreed. "Pack, pack. Gotta pack."

"Pack and then come back here for a glass of wine, a toast to a great if too short vacation?" Rick asked. "Or maybe just a taste of that fine Kentucky bourbon Sam brought back?"

"Me, too," Art said. "I can control it now, I'm sure I can. I don't think I have a problem with alcohol anymore; that's all gone, all gone."

Stephanie stood up suddenly. "Yeah, fine," she said, fighting for her own control, not even paying any particular attention to what Art had just said. "Let's just get packed, okay, God damn it?"

A little over two hours later, they had all gathered around that same table once again. By then, they'd all packed; other than the clothes they were planning to travel in and the swimsuits they were still wearing, everything was in bags and all the bags were lined up by the door. It was dark outside, completely, utterly dark, the only light that from a nearly full moon. On the table sat the bottle of Maker's Mark and a bottle of wine, along with six glasses. The kaleidoscope was in Stephanie's bag; they'd all watched her put it away, and they'd watched Sam replace the matching knife in the laptop's carrying case.

They sat in silence for a long while, all six of them, just watching the two bottles as if they expected them to move on their own.

"We were going to have a drink," Rick said at last. "We were going to have a drink, we were going to toast what we'd accomplished here. We were going to toast each other."

"There's no reason we shouldn't," Stephanie agreed. "Alcohol hasn't played any role in this. Nobody's been drunk. It has nothing to do with anything."

"Right," Sam put in. He was staring down at the surface of the table blankly. "No reason we shouldn't have a drink."

"Shit," Rick muttered. He reached for the bottle of Mark, unwound the red wax from the cap, popped it open. "You too, Art?" he asked, and the lawyer nodded. He poured it, a little over an inch deep, in each of three glasses. "Any of you ladies want a taste of this?"

"No," Cheryl answered, and the other two nodded concurrence. "No, we'll have the wine." Looking determined, she opened the wine and filled the remaining glasses half full while Rick fetched ice cubes for the whiskies.

Rick held up his glass. "A toast, to all of us," he said. "May we never be separated."

"Never," Cheryl agreed, lifting hers. The others did the same, glasses clinked. Kentucky bourbon flowed into the men's mouths, German wine into the women's. More or less simultaneously, the glasses came back to the table, landing in a series of soft thuds. To Stephanie the sounds seemed to echo throughout the room, as if the house were totally empty, as if they'd all already gone.

A heavy silence settled over the room as the sounds drifted away. Stephanie looked at each of the faces around the table in turn, realized that all of them were doing the same. The tightness in her abdomen seemed to increase as the stillness dragged on.

"I feel like," Cheryl said, her voice sounding very loud as she broke the silence, "something is about to jump out and get me. Like there's something here besides the six of us."

Stephanie shook her head. "There's just us," she said. "But God knows, that's enough! What's the matter with us, anyway? We've made our decision, we're all scared to death—and we're still sitting here fighting it! At least I am!"

"I'm not scared," Jennifer said. "And I don't want to fight it. Why don't we—"

"We've spent the whole day trying to figure this out," Sam noted hurriedly, cutting Jennifer off. "So far, no luck; and I'd say that means that trying to work it out tonight isn't going to do any good. We need an outsider, an objective viewpoint—like a psychiatrist— before we go on. But I've got enough objectivity left to say this, though—if we want to get through this night without—uh, getting into trouble—it probably isn't a good idea for us to stay together. In the same room, I mean."

"So what're you suggesting?" Rick asked.

"Well, we're leaving tomorrow," Art put in, his manner a little too hearty, a little too jovial, a little too forced. "Maybe we should all turn in a little early. Maybe we should try to get back in the groove with our spouses—without the group, without biting or wax or belts or forks. Maybe that's what we should do."

"That sounds like a very good idea," Stephanie agreed. She felt like crying. Even to herself, the enthusiasm she tried to put into her statement sounded flat.

"Fine," Cheryl said, her tone lifeless. "Whatever." She stood up. "Let's go, Sam." Obediently, Sam rose as well; the other four watched them disappear up the stairs. As they passed from sight, Stephanie felt that she'd lost a part of her body.

But the die had been cast; Art was up too, reaching out to her. She took his hand, and they, too, moved on up to their room.

——————— Fifty-Two ———————

"I WANT TO go downstairs," Cheryl was saying. "Or maybe outside. Yeah, that's what I want to do. Let's go outside, Sam. Let's go outside and sit and stare at the moon."

"I can see the moon," Sam answered. "From here. Outside, the mosquitoes will eat us alive." He turned himself in his chair, looked over at Cheryl; she presented, he thought, an extremely beautiful picture. She was lying on the bed, naked, staring up at the ceiling, her arms up beside her head, one leg propped up and the other extended. He sighed, shook himself; he felt uncomfortable, anxious, somehow bedraggled. He'd tried to make love with Cheryl. She'd tried too, but it just hadn't worked out; it had ended with him lying between her legs, his erection incomplete, and both of them staring at the unlit candles on the nightstand.

At that point, he'd surrendered; he'd climbed out of the bed, seated himself in the chair by the window. She'd remained in bed and they'd both been silent for at least an hour. He glanced at his watch: a little after three, and for him, at least, there was no possibility of sleep, he was far too keyed up. This was, he told himself sourly, turning into one of the longest and most unpleasant nights he could remember.

"Maybe," Cheryl answered finally, "I want to be eaten alive. You said earlier we had problems because we fought against nature. Well, it's natural to be eaten. I want to go out."

"You'll end up with welts all over. They'll itch. You'll complain, all the way back to Raleigh."

"I don't care." She sat up, swung her legs off the bed. "You coming, Sam?"

"Maybe we should try again."

Her green eyes were blank. "Why? What makes you think it'll be any different now?"

"Well, shit! Are we totally dependent on the others for our sex life now? We can't do without them?"

"That's not it, and you know it. We'd reached a peak, Sam. I'm not sure we made the right decision. You get to a peak like that, I'm not sure you can go back."

"We have to. Somehow."

"You tell me how."

He sighed, very deeply. "Damn, I don't know. I do know I've been sitting here going over last night again and again in my head; I do know how badly I want to do all those things again. I also know we can't. Not right now."

She gave him a look a small girl might give to a parent who'd just taken away her favorite toy. "I want to go out," she repeated. "I'm going out. You coming?"

He scowled, fidgited. "Yeah, okay, I guess. Let me get some pants on, and I'll—"

"Screw the pants. I'm going like this."

"Bad idea. What if we run into some of the others?"

"We won't. They're sleeping. Come on, Sam! Don't be so goddamn stodgy!" Crossing the room on bare feet, she opened the door and plunged into the hall. Quickly, Sam followed.

"Stodgy people," he said in a low voice as they approached the stairs, "do not get themselves into things like this! Stodgy people do not have these problems! Stodgy people—"

"Will you shut up, Sam?" Cheryl asked as she started down. "If you wake the others they're going to come out here to see what we're up to. We may yet get into trouble tonight."

"Can't. Not now. I'm too damn beat."

"A few minutes ago you wanted to try again."

"Wishful thinking."

Over her shoulder, she smiled at him—the first one of those, he told himself, that he'd seen today. Maybe things are smoothing out, he thought hopefully. Smiling too—if hesitantly—he followed her on through the darkened kitchen and out into the yard.

Outside, it was a little less dark; the full moon was casting considerable light over the yard and the inlet beyond, glinting brightly on the quiet waters. Cheryl stopped, gazing up at it fixedly; the skies were mostly clear, but as they watched a ragged dark cloud, driven by evidently violent winds aloft, zoomed across the moon's face.

"Somewhere," Cheryl murmured, "a storm's raging. I sort of wish it was here."

"If it was," Sam pointed out logically, "we certainly wouldn't want to be standing outside. What makes you think there's a storm somewhere, anyhow?"

"I dunno. That little cloud. The night's like us, Sam. All around here it's so calm, so peaceful, so quiet. But there're other things going on, things we can't see." She lowered her head, looked at him; a mosquito landed on her arm, he shooed it away, it didn't come back. "Let's walk," she suggested, "down to the inlet. Where we've been swimming."

"The mosquitoes are liable to be worse by the water."

"I don't care." She turned away, started walking; again, Sam followed her lead. They hadn't gone very far at all before he realized that there were already two people down there, sitting under the pines.

"Do I take it," Rick asked before Sam and Cheryl had gotten close enough to see anything more than silhouettes, "that you two couldn't sleep—or do anything else—either?"

Sighing—it seemed to him he'd been doing a lot of that lately— Sam nodded. A few steps closer and he could see that Rick had managed to get some pants on; Jennifer, like himself and Cheryl, was nude. "Cheryl thought it might help if we came out for some air. Or, as she put it, to stare at the moon."

"No," the dark-haired woman put in. "I didn't think it would help. It was just something to do, I just got tired of lying on the bed and staring at the ceiling."

"I have never felt like this in my life," Rick said. "Never. I feel like the ancient mariner—'water water everywhere, but not a drop to drink.' I'm all turned-on, all hyped-up; I can't seem to force myself to calm down. All I can do is keep telling myself no. And keep sitting here waiting for daylight."

"It isn't going to come," Jennifer moaned. "It isn't, not ever! The earth has stopped turning, the night is going to go on and on and on and the rats inside me are going to keep gnawing and chewing at my insides! Forever, forever . . . !"

Sam stood looking down at her as she lowered her head and sobbed. There were tear-streaks down her face that were visible even in this light; she sat on the sand with her knees drawn up hard against her chest and her arms wrapped tightly around her shins.

"This is ridiculous," Sam said slowly. "Ridiculous. We're all just falling apart! Shit, I know I am! I mean, everybody needs sex, but good God! We're acting like we can't survive one night without it!"

"It's not the sex," Cheryl told him. She sat down beside Jennifer, stroked her friend's hair gently. "Not that it wasn't good, but it's not that—if it was we'd've been able to make love a few hours ago and get to sleep. It's the feeling, it's the freedom, the intensity of the love and the amount of it. It's like a drug; I remember a heroin addict we had on the ward once telling me that he wasn't unaware that the drugs he bought on the street might be too strong or cut with something lethal; it just didn't matter to him, he needed the stuff too badly. I didn't understand him, then. I do now."

"I just can't understand," Jennifer wept, "what all of you were so afraid of! I can't understand why we're putting ourselves through this! It was so wonderful, so wonderful! . . ."

Crouching beside her, Cheryl continued to stroke her hair. "I'm not sure," she murmured, "that I can either . . . anymore . . ."

"Don't do this," Rick begged. "Don't, Cheryl. Jenny's been like this all night, don't you start too. I don't think I'd be able to take it!"

Cheryl nodded, slowly; reluctantly. Gazing at the two nude women, the moonlight casting soft shadows on their smooth skin, Sam found himself agreeing with Rick.

Passionately.

Fifty-Three

RAISING HER HANDS from the sink counter in front of the kitchen window, Stephanie looked down at her palms. Each one showed four little crescent moons, marks she'd made there by clenching her fists so tightly, by digging her fingernails into her own hands.

"They're just sitting there. That's all," she told Art. "Just sitting there, doing nothing. Well, they're talking, probably."

Across the kitchen, Art faced away from her, his hands clasped behind his head, his body rigid. At her request, he wore a pair of cutoffs; Stephanie had, by force, resisted her own urge to wander downstairs nude: she was clad in the sundress she'd planned to wear on the ride home. For them, there hadn't even been an attempt at lovemaking. Once in their room, they'd removed their swimsuits as if to try; but Art had not approached her and she hadn't pushed the issue, she'd rolled over on the bed to try—entirely without any sort of success—to sleep. They hadn't been downstairs long before she'd spotted movement out by the inlet. A few moments of observation through the window had shown her four figures out there; she hardly suspected them of being trespassers.

"I don't see why we don't go out there and join them," Art griped. "We aren't going to do anything, that's been decided. At least we can talk to them."

"A few minutes ago," Stephanie pointed out, "you were almost in a rage at the idea that they might be doing something behind our backs. That hardly suggests to me that you're under control. No, we should stay here. We really should go back to our room before they come up here."

Art ran his hands through his hair and turned around. "Look, Stephanie," he said, "I'm not waffling on you here but—it's already past four in the morning. Neither of us has slept at all, and I'd bet that no one else has, either. I don't think anybody's going to be leaving here tomorrow."

"We have to!" she snapped, her arm coming down hard in a gesture of finality. "We just have to! If you can't drive then I will! Damn it, we've pulled all-nighters before—"

"Not like this. Not all-nighters under continual stress. I don't want to die out there on the highway, Stephanie. Do you?"

She turned back to the window. "No, but I think— Damn! One of them's coming back up here! Come on, Art, let's get back upstairs!"

"We have every right to be down here—"

"That's not the point! Come on, damn it!"

Art sighed loudly, he waved his arms in frustration, but he followed her as she hurried back up the stairs—at a more leisurely pace, one that irritated her. She decided, much earlier, that she didn't want any of the others to know—at least not until tomorrow

—that they, too, had been unable to sleep. Everyone's control was tenuous, and she was no exception—she felt they were all balanced on a razor's edge, ready to topple over if the right stimulus was applied, if the proper word was said.

You've tasted true ecstasy, Stephanie, she told herself—the forbidden fruit. You've tasted it; now you know, and it's damn hard to leave it behind. Maybe whoever did the engravings on that damn kaleidoscope knew exactly what he was doing.

Stopping in the hallway—she and Art were by then well out of sight of whoever had come back in—she closed her eyes for a moment. Stupid, Stephanie, she reminded herself mentally. The kaleidoscope has nothing to do with it, nothing. That's Jennifer's notion, and it's silly—you know better. Again trying to control her wildly swirling and in reality hardly controllable thoughts, she listened, wondering if the person downstairs would come up. One footstep on the stair and she'd herd Art into their room; there was plenty of time for that.

Instead, she heard the bathroom door close, heard the bolt locking the door slide into place. She breathed a sigh of relief; the idea of seeing any of the others was close to terrifying. And then she heard another sound, very clearly, very distinctly.

The sound of glass breaking. In the bathroom.

She and Art stared at each other, both of them wide-eyed, neither failing to understand. "Jennifer," Stephanie breathed. "Come on, damn it!"

Seconds later, they stood in front of the bathroom door. "Jenny!" Stephanie cried. "Jenny, we know what you're doing! Open the door!" From inside there was no sound, no response; Art did not wait any longer, he motioned Stephanie aside and threw his shoulder against the door. The first time it merely groaned; the second, the bolt splintered away from the wood and the door flew open.

What they were seeing came as no surprise to Stephanie. Jennifer, her eyes wild, was standing by the shower, one foot up on the edge of the tub; in her hand was a piece of a broken Listerine bottle, savage sharp edges clearly visible. She smiled at them, but her lower lip trembled violently.

"Come and do it for me, Art," she whispered, holding up the piece of glass.

"Put the bottle down, Jenny," Stephanie said firmly. "Come on, now. You don't really want to do this . . ."

"Yes I do!" she shrieked. "Yes I do! It's the only way to get it to stop, the only way!"

Stephanie moved toward her carefully. "No, let's talk about it. Come on, Jenny."

"You can't tell me not to! I want to, Stephanie! I need to!"

"She's right," Art said unexpectedly. "We can't, as a matter of fact, tell her not to. It's her body. If she wants to cut it, we can't say no."

Stephanie whirled on him. "How can you say that? She isn't in control, she's—"

"We can't make that judgment. If she were about to have an abortion and you didn't believe in it, would you think you had a right to stop her? If she were going to have cosmetic surgery, would you have the right to stop her?"

"No, of course not! But—"

"This is the same. It's her body." He looked past her, at Jennifer. "I'm sorry," he told her, "that we broke in on you like that. We'll go now; if you need us we'll be right outside. All I want to say is that I, personally, feel you're violating agreements we made earlier this evening. In a way, I think you're betraying a trust; I don't know if the others would agree, but if you do this, I'd feel betrayed. That's all I have to say." Taking Stephanie's arm, he steered her out of the bathroom quickly, almost pushing her back toward the living room.

"Are you crazy?" she hissed. "She's going to—"

"Stephanie?" Jennifer called from behind them. "Art?" Stephanie turned; Jennifer was following them, and she'd left the broken glass behind. She began to cry again; Art moved forward quickly, took her in his arms. Over her shoulder, he winked at Stephanie.

She nodded as the others, attracted by the crashing and the shouting, came hurrying through the kitchen door. There were quick explanations, after which Art handed Jennifer over to her husband.

"Smart man," Stephanie whispered to Art as the others clustered around Jennifer. "Smart man."

"Smart, hell," he said sourly. "What I really wanted to do was exactly what she was asking me to do!"

Fifty-Four

IT WAS AFTER three when Stephanie's consciousness finally returned. At first she felt disoriented, confused, out-of-sorts—all of which changed to dismay bordering on terror when she realized how late it was.

Art had been right; no one was going to want to drive home today. She could try to insist—she would at least try, she promised herself—but she knew she was going to encounter intense resistance. No one really wanted to leave; even for her, it was a matter of forcing her reason to keep her impulses in check, something that was becoming more and more difficult all the time.

That things had gone this way really wasn't surprising. Not one of the six of them had slept at all the previous night, they'd spent the whole evening fighting themselves, wearing themselves out in the process. The tension had eased a bit when dawn broke out over the Atlantic, but even so it was after ten before the first of them—Sam—began dozing in the living-room chair. After that, sleep came to the others relatively quickly.

Sitting up, her sundress bunched up around her waist and her hair hanging in disarray, she looked around. Rick, evidently, was up; Stephanie didn't see him, but Jennifer was still curled up on the couch asleep. Sam and Cheryl were sleeping too, crowded together naked in the chair; Art's head was on a cushion on the floor beside her, and he, too, was still sleeping peacefully.

Without waking him, she got up, staggered into the kitchen. The aroma of coffee welcomed her; Rick, seated at the table, looked up.

"I think," he opened, "that we've fucked up."

"Because we slept so late. How long have you been up, Rick?"

"Oh, maybe fifteen minutes. Just long enough to get the coffee going." He paused to drink some while she poured herself a cup.

"We aren't going to get everybody out of here today. That should be obvious."

She sat down. "We have to!" she told him urgently, not forgetting that she'd already been through this same conversation with Art. "We have to, and we have to be gone before dark! I can't go through another night like last night!"

He waved his hands helplessly. "I didn't have any more fun than you did, Stephanie! But it's too late to go now. That ought to be obvious. There's no way we could get on the road before about five, no way."

"What's wrong with that?"

"You feel up to it? You feel like you could get out there on that road for five hours or more?"

"Yes, I could!"

His cheeks flushed slightly; he looked uncomfortable. "Well. I don't feel up it. That's all I can say. And I don't think—"

"That's just an excuse! And you know it!" She leaned across the table. "Look, Rick—I'm convinced that the only reason we got through last night without breaking down was because everyone was just worn out by the time we all got together again. It isn't going to be that way tonight! We've all slept past the middle of the afternoon, we're all going to be wide awake and ready to go—and you're right, no one is going to want a repeat of last night! We have to use that energy to get ourselves out of here, we just have to!"

Rick tried to argue with her further, but not convincingly; he knew that his "reasons" were pure excuses, he wasn't really able to defend them. After a while, Stephanie began to feel she was about to convince him; but, at that point, the others began waking up— Art first, then Jennifer, then Cheryl. As each one wandered into the kitchen, they echoed, almost as if it had been planned, Rick's objections. Frantically Stephanie tried to hold the line—and all the while the one person she felt sure would back her kept right on sleeping in the chair.

Sam didn't come in until well after four, and even then he didn't speak at all for a while—like a zombie he clumped over to the coffee, poured himself a cup, sat down, and started drinking it. The discussions went on, and, even though Sam did eventually join in—on her side—Stephanie became aware that they were losing— simply because the others were succeeding in stalling them. "Can't get under way until five" shifted to "Can't get under way until six," then "seven." By that time, the clear blue sky outside had begun to lose some of its brightness; as always, Stephanie began to feel her resolve fading with the sunlight.

ı   "We're past the worst of it, Stephanie," Art assured her. "I think we beat it, last night. Like kicking a drug habit cold turkey."

"You don't get over an addiction that fast," she said sadly. She closed her eyes for a moment, then waved a hand. "Look, I know I've lost this; even I have to agree it's ridiculous to talk about leaving now. But we should do the same thing we did yesterday. Make a pact, agree that we aren't going to do anything tonight, that we're going to go tomorrow." Sam agreed readily; Art, Rick, and Cheryl were a bit slower but they did too. Jennifer was the only holdout, insisting repeatedly that there wasn't a problem, that they should feel free to do whatever they desired—and making it quite clear what she, at least, desired.

From that point onward, the evening began to develop into a near-duplicate of the previous one. Cooperatively they prepared a meal—by time of day a dinner—cleaned up, unpacked fresh clothes for the drive home. After everything was done, Rick suggested another toast, and the whiskey and the wine were brought out again. The conversation over the drinks was light, good-natured; quickly it became tinged with the erotic, and even more quickly the tinge turned to saturation. As before, Stephanie began playing fantasies in her head; she tried to expel them but they would not go. Still, the anxiety this caused her did not prevent her from joining in, from bantering freely with the others—and, after a while, some of the anxiety began to fade. She discovered that she'd begun to feel quite good, almost exhilarated; like the feeling she'd gotten in her college days, when she'd been a competitive diver, soaring free off a high board into an Olympic pool.

That there might not be any water in this particular pool did not seem to dampen her enthusiasm.

There was little question that the others were feeling the same way, but, as usual, Jennifer was the first to address it directly: "I don't want to be sitting here drinking," she said abruptly, her fingers still wrapped around her wineglass. She drank most of it, then held it by the stem. For a moment Stephanie believed she was about to break it against the table edge, but she merely put it down. "That's not what I want to be doing."

"Me neither," Cheryl agreed, but she took another gulp of hers anyway.

Stephanie felt no need whatever to ask either of them what they'd rather be doing; she was feeling exactly the same herself.

Desperately she looked over at Sam, her ally yesterday, her ally this afternoon.

He'd drained his glass; he sat gazing into it, shaking his head, not looking at any of them. "We can't do this," he said, to Stephanie's gratification. "We can't. We promised ourselves."

"We're leaving tomorrow," Art pointed out. "Definitely."

"Last chance," Rick added.

Stephanie began squirming in her chair. Without thinking about it, she gulped her wine. "No, Sam's right," she said shakily. "Look, I'm about scared to death of us—of me, of all of us. We could get together tomorrow night, back in Raleigh, maybe. But we can't do anything tonight! If we do, we're lost, we're just lost, we'll never get back to—"

"Get back to what?" Rick demanded, leaning forward and raising his voice. "Back to where we were? You want to go back, Stephanie? You want to give all this up?"

She felt, for a moment, like he'd hit her. No, she told herself, no. You'd like it if he hit you. But his disapproval was like acid, flowing over her skin and burning it off.

"No," she almost whimpered. "No, Rick. You know what I want, too. No less than anyone else!"

"I don't understand," Art said, "why we are sitting here and fighting it. Yes, I know we promised ourselves we wouldn't. But God damn it, so what? So we changed our minds! Is that a fucking crime?"

"I feel," Stephanie said doggedly, "that if we give in, we're going to reach a point of no return, a point—"

"And I think," Jennifer interrupted, "that we already have!"

Again Stephanie looked to Sam for support. "Sam, tell them," she begged. "Please, I'm losing myself here, I just can't—"

Sam didn't say anything immediately. All eyes turned to him, as if he had the final say-so. Even Stephanie felt that way, she realized; if Sam failed to support her all her resolve would go right down the drain. Jennifer, she noticed, was giving Sam The Look. He couldn't even see it, he wasn't watching her, he was staring into his empty whiskey glass as if searching there for answers.

The silence stretched on, long and pregnant.

"Maybe," Sam said, his voice very soft, "maybe just one more time wouldn't matter that much . . . At least we'd get some sleep . . . afterward. . . ."

His words were like a trigger, like a detonator cap attached to dynamite. Stephanie felt a sudden release flood through her; she sighed and shook almost as if she were having an orgasm right then. Jennifer smiled richly and stretched her arms up above her head, intertwining her fingers.

"Should we go upstairs?" Cheryl asked. Her breathing was already heavy.

"No point," Rick informed her. "We took the stuff down, packed it up."

"We can put it back," Jennifer pointed out.

Rick stood up suddenly. "Yeah," he said. "We can put it back up down here, where we've got more room!"

A quick welter of activity followed; Rick dug the hook, the ring, and the other paraphernalia out of the luggage, Art located a ceiling joist and a stud to mount them to in the living room. At Jennifer's urging, Stephanie got the kaleidoscope back out, Sam remounted it in the slide projector, and soon the patterns were once again appearing on the screen. The fondue pot and the forks were gotten out, the water was set to boiling. Cheryl and Stephanie moved the low table back in, put the wine and whiskey on it; everyone, Stephanie observed, looked excited but perhaps more than a little frightened. This time, obviously, there was more urgency, more need.

And less control, Stephanie told herself. Definitely less control.

Fifty-Five

"THERE'S NO NEED to rush this," Sam said as he sat down on a cushion in front of the low table. "We shouldn't rush it. We're all a little too eager, I think. We should sit here and finish our drinks." He looked at his own glass, saw that it was empty, poured a little more of the bourbon into it.

Art picked up his, took a tiny sip. "You know, it wasn't long ago that I'd be emptying this for the fifth or sixth time," he mused. "Once I tasted it, it'd be gone and I'd be pouring more, I just couldn't wait to start feeling drunk. Good stuff like this was wasted on me, I didn't care, as long as it was alcohol. Now, I don't seem to need it, I don't really even want it. I was right, I was right. That's how I figured it'd be."

"I don't want this wine, either," Jennifer said. She turned to Sam. "You say wait, finish our drinks, we're too eager. But the longer we wait, the more tense I'm getting, the more eager I am! We can at least get our clothes off, can't we? Put on some music again, dance like before? I loved that . . ."

When Sam made no protest, Cheryl jumped up. "I'll turn on the stereo," she said, almost running over toward it. In a moment, the music of Blue Oyster Cult filled the room. On her way back she discarded her swimsuit; she paused and posed prettily for a moment before sitting back down.

The other swimsuits followed quickly, tossed into the corners. "Is anybody else scared to death?" Cheryl asked, shivering visibly. All three men nodded, as did Stephanie; Jennifer was the only holdout. "It's nice, though," she went on, "to be scared to death like this. I don't think I've ever enjoyed being scared before." She looked around aimlessly for a moment. "I want to dance. Dance with me, Art."

Moments later, all the couples were up, dancing; the song was rather up-tempo but everybody ignored that and danced close, half speed. This time Sam found himself dancing with Jennifer, holding her almost fragile body close, comparing and thoroughly enjoying the contrast between her and the more robust Stephanie. He pushed his face into her fine blond hair, felt her hands drop down to his waist and then lower. He became erect, she pushed his penis down and trapped it between them, just as Stephanie had done before—and just as, he noticed, Stephanie was now doing with Rick.

They danced through the remainder of this song and about half of the next; by that time no one, Sam included, could wait any longer. The handcuffs came out, Stephanie's wrists were extended —how it had been decided she'd go first Sam didn't know, but it didn't really matter—and soon she was suspended, each of the men taking turns in lashing her with the belt. The kaleidoscopic patterns on the screen—someone kept rotating it periodically— seemed to be adding to everyone's frenzy, although they still didn't affect him much.

The mood was different, though, he couldn't question that. He wasn't feeling the liquor at all—and neither Rick nor Art had even finished their first drinks—but the music and the lighting, plus the eagerness of their anticipation, seemed to be pushing them all harder than before. Stephanie, dangling from the newly installed ceiling hook, was enduring and quite obviously enjoying a severe beating from all three of the men, a substantially more serious thrashing than the previous one—in part because she did not call for a halt to it nearly so soon.

She had at least two orgasms, as near as Sam could tell, before they took her down and put Rick up in her place. As before, it continued, all of them taking a turn, Art this time being last. After he was taken down there was a brief, but warm and pleasant, interlude, during which all six of them remained in a tight little knot in the middle of the floor, their hands continuously on each other's bodies, their lips active.

No one questioned what was to come next, and it was Cheryl who volunteered—claimed the right, really—to go first. After pushing Art down on the floor on his back, she crouched over his hips and allowed herself to descend slowly onto him; then, pulling Rick close and licking at his new erection, she asked Sam to get one of the fondue forks. He positioned the tines against the outer margin of her as yet unpierced left breast. Keeping the angle acute so it could not go deep even if it slipped, he began pushing.

Sighing, moaning, and bouncing on Art's erection, she urged him on, begging for more and more. Kissing her ear and neck and cupping her breast with his left hand, he did as she asked. As before, he rather suddenly felt the resistance of her skin disappear.

This time, for whatever reason—perhaps because he was trying to do it too quickly, because he was not quite so controlled, or because he was not so tentative—the division of the tines did not stop the fork's progress as it sank into her breast. It went right on in, just under her nipple, and the skin on the far side failed to stop it, as well. It emerged, bloody; twin streams of blood began running from her breast as she trembled and cried out in orgasm.

Sam felt an initial chagrin, exactly as he'd felt before, when he believed he'd accidentally pierced Jennifer. But Cheryl, with the fondue fork transfixing her breast horizontally, grabbed his face and kissed him passionately, telling him how wonderful it was, how wonderful he was. He started to remove it but, telling him to leave it where it was, she turned her attention back to Art, who was still inside her. She watched closely as Jennifer brought a fork down to his chest, touched his skin with the tines. He wasn't nearly as enthusiastic as Cheryl—he tried to call a halt after she'd made a very shallow puncture.

But Jennifer followed the pattern she had Rick had established with the belt, she pushed on—and in the end she'd followed Sam's example, she'd skewered him with it, passing it through the pectoral muscle. He didn't appear to mind. His blood began flowing out too; he and Cheryl experienced another orgasm almost simultaneously.

After that, things got a little hazy for Sam as the orgy of blood and sex pushed relentlessly onward. He'd set the tone; the others seemed to believe that he'd made an active choice to pierce Cheryl's breast all the way through, and that now became the standard procedure, each one of them experiencing it, Sam included. The pain, he was able to observe, was severe, hot, persistent; but that didn't seem to matter, it seemed to set every nerve on fire, it acted the same way the jalapeño peppers acted but a hundredfold more powerfully. Just as they could activate taste sensors in such a way as to make everything taste better, so the pain seemed to activate virtually all other nerves in his body, and somehow the flowing blood heightened that even more. A caress became a magnificent, sensual experience; a kiss was more exquisite than it had been when he'd first been kissed as a young teenager. Direct sexual contact shot him to heights he'd never even imagined, much less experienced. It had never been like this, he told himself, not even on the previous nights.

After the last person—Rick—had been pierced, after each man had had his second orgasm of the evening—Sam could not even conceive how many the women had had—they again found themselves clustered in a knot, carefully extracting the fondue forks from each other, spilling even more of their blood as the steel instruments came out. There was now a substantial amount of blood splattered around the room; each person's body was flecked with it, his or her own plus more. In spite of the two climaxes, Sam's excitement remained at a fever pitch, he wanted something more but could not decide exactly what that was. As he looked at the other faces he was sure they felt the same. His thought processes had become even more vague; somewhere down deep inside him there was some little voice, almost like a tiny and lost man waving a red flag, trying to scream out a warning. He couldn't hear it. All he could hear was the music and the driving rhythm of Jennifer's heartbeat as he laid his head on her bloodied chest. He couldn't see anything now except the bodies, the blood, and the incessant kaleidoscope patterns, so much like those he thought he'd seen in Selinde's eyes. . . .

There was going to be more tonight, he realized as he felt Jennifer begin to play with his now-flaccid penis. He didn't have the strength, but somehow, there was going to be more. He felt a bright flash of raw terror, very unlike the delicate and delectable fears he'd been feeling earlier. Think, Sam, he demanded—something about today, about this group, it's important, think! Work it out!

But Jennifer kept playing with him, and the thoughts were driven from his mind along with the terror. He wanted more, there had to be more, somehow there had to be! They just had to find the way, that was all. Just find the way. He glanced around at the others; at the moment Cheryl was involved with Art, Stephanie with Rick, both women working hard to resurrect the men. Their eyes would have frightened him if he hadn't been sure that his looked the same; wild, devoid of any trace of intellectual control. His thoughts were hazy, tumultuous, and the few lucid ones he did have seemed distant from his conscious self, from what he was doing.

He focused for a few seconds on Stephanie and Rick. The surgeon was pretty much erect again; he'd picked up one of the fondue forks they'd used previously and he was teasing her with it, pricking her nipples, slipping the tips back into the puncture they'd already made. Stephanie was clearly enjoying it, her face a study in passionate abandonment. Sam watched him push it against her breast in a new place, watched a droplet of new blood appear; he wanted to call out to him, to warn him that the fork was no longer sterile and that he was pushing it straight in, that he was not using a safe angle, that if it broke free it might sink right on into Stephanie's lungs. But he couldn't seem to make his voice work, couldn't seem to make a sound. He just watched, holding his breath, wondering how far Rick would go.

Cheryl had been watching too, and she sighed audibly when Rick withdrew the fork after allowing only a very shallow penetration. "None of us can really, truly, let go," she said, more to herself than to anybody else. "Not really, not really. Not all the way."

Jennifer had also seen what Rick and Stephanie had been doing; now she turned her face toward Cheryl, her eyes unreadable. Then, suddenly, she jumped up, went to Rick, began whispering in his ear. At first, he looked at her as if he thought she was mad. But she kept talking, her manner urgent, and Sam could see his expression shift, by degrees. At last he nodded, if perhaps a bit reluctantly; Jennifer, looking feverish with excitement, came back to Sam and set to work on him again.

"What's going on?" he managed to ask her.

She chewed her lip. "An idea I had," she told him. "You'll see, Sam. You'll see!"

Stephanie, left alone momentarily, came to them too, echoed Sam's question, received the same answer. They were both speaking haltingly, as if it were an effort. Sam knew how they felt, it wasn't easy for him to string words together into an intelligible sentence. He felt like he was drugged.

But when Rick came back—came back carrying the little slender-bladed knife he'd taken from the laptop case—Sam was so shocked and terrified he almost snapped out of it.

Almost. Not quite.

Once the moment had passed, he sank back down into the sensual mire he'd been immersed in all night. Even so, he knew vaguely that this wasn't at all a good idea, and he did succeed in croaking out a word of protest. At least he thought he did; he really wasn't sure.

Jennifer seemed to understand in any event. "It'll be okay, Sam," she said reassuringly. She was chewing her lower lip again. "I just have to feel it, just a little, that's all. It's so pretty, just like the kaleidoscope . . ."

Stephanie didn't say anything; Art and Cheryl, having become aware that something new was going on, had moved to a position close to them, but neither of them commented either, they just watched eagerly, expectantly.

Sam's erection had returned by then; Jennifer pulled herself up over him and sank down on it, her eyelids fluttering, while Rick, the knife in his hand, knelt down beside them. Her legs were folded at her knees; Sam stroked her smooth and slender thighs, thinking about what she'd said, about how she used to cut them. He felt as if he could see the lacerations now, the flowing blood.

No words were spoken; Rick, too, evidently was thinking the same thoughts Sam was. While Stephanie reached around his waist to stroke his now raging erection, he brought the knife close to one of Jennifer's thighs.

Holding her lower lip tightly with her teeth, she brushed her hair back and put her hands on her legs. Starting at her groin, she ran them down the upper surfaces of her thighs, all the way to her knees, then came back up, her palms touching the inner surfaces. She glanced up at Rick, her eyes half-closed, and nodded.

He brought the knife closer, touching it to her thigh, a couple of inches down from her hip. He looked at her face again; she pleaded with her eyes. Not too hard, he pushed.

Sam knew how sharp it was. It sank right in, an inch deep, the skin and muscle of her leg offering almost no resistance. Blood welled up and out instantly.

"Yes!" she screamed, twisting her hands into her hair, her body rigidly erect and quivering. "God, yes! Oh, Rick, oh God, yes!"

Smiling like a happy child, Rick pulled the little blade out of her leg. Sam could not take his eyes off the flowing blood; the multicolored images from the kaleidoscopic display washed over her skin, casting patterns, changing the colors. The music seemed to be booming out incredibly loudly, and Jennifer kept writhing atop him; he could not focus any of his thoughts now, everything had become utterly surreal.

It became even more intense when Rick stabbed the knife into her other leg, piercing her more deeply this time, provoking more bleeding. A tiny remaining kernel of lucidity in Sam's mind wanted to warn them that this was dangerous, that Rick might accidentally cut a major blood vessel, but that kernel could not find a voice. Worse, the kernel seemed to be getting smaller and fainter with every passing second. He felt overwhelmed by the incredible eroticism of all this. In spite of his previous orgasms, he felt as if his penis might literally explode.

Jennifer, apparently, wasn't satisfied. "You have to do more," she told Rick, her voice thick. "More, you have to do more . . . !" She lifted her breasts with her hands, offering them.

Whatever misgivings Rick might've once had seemed to be gone. He didn't hesitate; he brought the knife up, held her right breast with his hand. Carefully, delicately, he located the point against her skin, just over her nipple. Their eyes met; he pressed on it and it slipped quietly in, an inch deep perhaps.

Sam had some vague idea about protesting again, but Jennifer was far from objecting; she went into an orgasm almost immediately, quivering violently, holding Rick's hand so he could not immediately withdraw the blade. Again, the little voice inside Sam began howling; he still could not hear, he was too involved in watching Rick slowly withdraw the knife from Jennifer's breast, in watching the blood running down from this new puncture.

"Do it again," Jennifer whispered. "Let it go, Rick! Let it go, let's go all the way!"

"All the way?" he echoed dumbly.

"Yes, all the way!" Cheryl cried, adding her voice to it. Within seconds it had become a frenzied chant, all of them yelling it out, even Sam. Rick still seemed hesitant; screaming "all the way!" in his face, Jennifer grabbed his hand and brought the knife toward herself, toward her abdomen.

He didn't have to make an active decision, all he had to do was keep moving his hand in the same direction. Driven by the chant, he touched her belly with the point, just a little below her navel. Her skin indented for an instant before the knife broke through; Rick continued to push and it sank right on into her, the entire blade passing softly into her body.

There were sighs and moans from all the onlookers; Jennifer's mouth dropped open, her eyes closing at the same time. She shook violently with another orgasm, one that seemed to go on and on. Rick pulled the knife out and blood spurted, splashing on Sam's chest. Again, everyone began chanting "all the way!" and by now Rick had abandoned any reservations he might've once had. Joining in the chant, he relocated the blade against her left side, between two of her ribs. She made no sound, she simply wound her fingers in her hair and arched her trembling body back, her eyelids fluttering, while Rick buried the blade in her chest.

Everyone yelled their approval; Rick jerked the knife out, and, not waiting now for a further invitation, pierced her again, under her ribs on the right this time. Her orgasm seemed to be continuous; if she was experiencing any of this as pain her face never showed a trace of it.

She showed every sign of wanting more, as well. Chanting "all the way!" with the others, she directed Rick's hand to her side, right at her waistline; as the blade passed into her body again, Sam began his own orgasm, a wrenching and tearing experience that he'd later remember as the most intense of his life. He felt as if his whole being were spraying upward into Jennifer's trembling body.

After that, he could not keep his eyes open for long, and things became very vague for him. He was dimly aware of Rick driving the knife into Jennifer yet again, of Rick screaming as he himself climaxed into Stephanie's mouth. Even fainter was his memory of Jennifer rolling off of him and folding herself into Rick's arms, of the two of them settling into what looked like a peaceful sleep—even though blood was still flowing from her wounds. He felt Stephanie curl herself up beside him, saw that Art and Cheryl had apparently fallen out together a few feet away. Foggily, he thought about endorphins—about their pain-killing and sleep-inducing effects. From there, though, his consciousness gradually slipped away. Even as he drifted into sleep it never occurred to him that Jennifer was other than all right, not even once.

———— Fifty-Six ————

STEPHANIE WOKE TO the sounds of soft laughter—or perhaps sobs, she wasn't quite sure which, not at first. For a few minutes she could not even pry her eyes open; she had never been on a two-week drunk, but she assumed this might well be what one would feel like at the end of one. Her mouth was filled with something that tasted incredibly foul, she even thought she could smell it, wafting up from her lips. Where her breasts had been pierced there was a dull but persistent heavy aching; her skin felt sticky and clammy.

Slowly she raised her head. Some biological clock told her it should be morning, but there was only a faint—and somewhat strange—light at the windows. She looked around; it seemed to her she'd awakened in a charnel house. There was blood everywhere, splattered all over the place—and all over her own body, as well.

Sam was still sleeping, his head on her thighs; she moved him gently and started to sit up. Her head didn't hurt, but still she felt like she had a terrible hangover; none of her muscles wanted to work, her arms and legs almost refused to move and when they did they were sluggish.

She managed to rise, though, managed to turn around and look in the direction from which she was hearing the sounds. When she did, she saw Rick, fully awake, sitting up. Jennifer was lying across his lap, and he was cradling her head, whispering something to her, making sounds that seemed like simultaneous mirth and weeping.

It did not take Stephanie long to realize that Jennifer's body was considerably more bloody than her own. Or to see that she was not responding to whatever it was that Rick was whispering in her ear. Then, and only then, did she begin to remember, in bits and fragments, the events of the previous night.

She turned her head away, her eyes growing large. "Oh, God," she muttered aloud, her voice rising in both volume and pitch. "Oh God, oh God, oh God!" She saw Sam's eyes flutter open, but by then she was getting to her feet, moving as quickly as she could toward Rick and Jennifer, almost falling over one of Cheryl's outstretched legs.

She half knelt and half fell beside them, staring at her friend's relaxed face. Rick looked up at her; his eyes were like tunnels, she felt as if she could see for miles down in there. As if there were nothing at all left, as if everything that had once existed behind them was gone.

"She's so happy," he said, his voice little-boy, singsong. "Just look at her. So peaceful. She's never been so happy." Ignoring him, Stephanie put her hand on the other woman's shoulder, started to speak to her.

She knew instantly that there was no point. Her skin was little warmer than room temperature, it felt like wax—very familiar, both from her profession and from her past. Even so, Stephanie pulled up one of her eyelids, stared at the enlarged and unresponsive pupil. She pressed her head to Jennifer's chest, listened for a heartbeat, tried to find a pulse in her neck.

But she knew, she knew. There was, indeed, no point. Jennifer Mason was quite dead, had been dead for some hours now.

"Nooooooo . . . !" Stephanie started to moan. "No, no, she can't be, she can't, it isn't possible!"

"What?" Sam demanded, up now and by her side. "What, what?" He looked at Jennifer, and instantly he knew. Even so he went through all the same steps, came up with the same answer. He pulled back, eyes wild, hair standing out in all directions, his beard bristling as if charged with electricity, echoing Stephanie's chant of "no, no." Cheryl was up too, by then; her response was an animallike cry of pure agony, a cry that brought Art shooting up off the floor. She then came rushing over to Jennifer, doing all the same things that Sam and Stephanie had already done, shaking her head the whole time as if to dispel the reality.

"No, it's all right," Rick said soothingly. "It's all right. You just don't understand, that's all."

"She's dead, Rick!" Art howled. "Dead! God damn, we all understand that! Jesus H. Christ, how could this've—how—!"

Smiling down at her, Rick stroked her cheek. "Yes, she's dead," he agreed. "But isn't she beautiful? She died so happy, she died in the middle of the greatest love she or I had ever known, there couldn't have been a better way for her to die, she'll never have to grow old . . ." He paused, his face twisted, he sobbed bitterly a few times. Then, abruptly, his sadness vanished. He moon-smiled, kissed the dead woman's lips.

Stephanie turned to the others. "She's dead, dead!" she cried, yelling in Sam's face. "Dead, dead! We killed her, killed her!"

"What're we going to do?" Art babbled. "What're we going to do now, what're we going to do?"

"God damn it!" Cheryl shrieked at him. "She's dead, don't you care?" She moved toward him as if she were about to physically attack him. Sam grabbed her arm to restrain her; she jerked loose and whirled on him. "And you!" she yelled, her face crimson. "You! You were the one who said it was okay, one last time wouldn't hurt! You were the one who brought out the forks, it was your knife! You were supposed to keep things under control! What the fuck happened, Sam? How could this have happened, how? You were supposed to keep things under control, God damn you, you son of a bitch! How could you have let this happen?"

"Now just a goddamn minute!" he roared back. "You were right there, weren't you? You watched the whole thing, didn't you? Did you say anything, did you try to stop it? No, you sat there chanting 'all the way!' like a fucking idiot! That's where it came from, you and your goddamn 'all the way!' "

"I didn't mean it like that!"

"Then what did you mean? How were we supposed to take it? You meant it exactly like that, Cheryl!"

She clenched her fists. "Sam, you know goddamn well—!"

"Oh, come on," Rick put in, his voice quiet and reasoned compared to Sam's bellows and Cheryl's shrieks. "Don't—"

"Just shut the fuck up, Rick!" Cheryl screamed, turning on him now. "Just shut up! If you wanted to murder your wife, I don't know why you couldn't've done it in the privacy of your own home, I don't know why you had to involve all of us anyway!"

"I didn't murder her," Rick protested mildly.

"Yes you did!" Art argued, pointed accusatorily. "You did. You. You."

"And you had nothing to do with it, Art?" Rick rejoined, still not raising his voice. "Nothing?"

"He's right," Stephanie said. "We were all right there, we all saw what he was doing. It doesn't take much to figure out that if you stab somebody and you just keep stabbing her, she's going to die! We all watched that, we didn't do a thing, we all watched and then we just went to sleep we didn't even try to help her, oh God, we didn't even try and now she's dead, she's dead, she's dead . . . !"

Cheryl's rage seemed to have dissipated as quickly as it had arisen. She began sobbing bitterly. "You were supposed to have kept things under control, Sam. That was your responsibility, to keep things under control. You didn't do it, you didn't do it, you just didn't!"

"How in God's name did it get to be my responsibility? What am I, a God? Christ, the whole idea was to get ourselves out of control!" He turned to Rick. "Isn't that right? Isn't that the whole point? Out of control? Isn't that what you said?"

By this time, Stephanie had drawn a curtain of control around her rampaging emotions; a thin and ragged curtain, but a shield nevertheless. "This is what I was worried about," she said stiffly. "Exactly what I was worried about. Exactly why I said we needed to go home. If we had, Jennifer'd be alive right now. You all should have listened to me. If you'd listened to me this never would've happened." She, too, turned on Sam, echoing Cheryl's words. "You, you were supposed to support me. You weren't supposed to say, 'one more time will be okay.' Your one more time, Sam—your one more time has killed Jennifer! You feel good about that, Sam? You okay with that?"

"Oh, shit," Sam moaned, throwing his hands up in a gesture of utter frustration. "I don't know how I got appointed as everyone's keeper! I sure didn't volunteer!"

"We didn't appoint you our keeper, old buddy," Rick said. Throughout, as the accusations raged, he remained where he was, softly stroking Jennifer's hair. "We gave Jenny what she wanted. We gave her the greatest pleasure of her life. If she was here, she'd tell you it was worth it."

"How can you know that?" Art demanded. "You dumb fuck, that's just a goddamn rationalization, I hear crap like that from my fucking clients all the time! 'T'aint my fault, Judge. I wouldn't of kilt that storekeeper if he hadn't tried to stop me from robbin' im. 'S'is fault he's dead, not mine.' "

"This isn't real," Cheryl mumbled, her mood evidently shifting again. "It isn't. Can't be."

"It is," Art advised her. "It sucks, but it is." He wiped his eyes. "Look, I don't mean to be cold, but she's dead, we can't help her now. We have to think about what we're going to do!"

"I don't think I care what we do," Cheryl replied.

"No, he's right," Sam said firmly. "We're all grieving over Jennifer, but we've got to get a grip, we've got to stop trying to blame each other! We've got to decide—we've got to—Jesus! The computer, the predictions! Right on the nose, right on the fucking nose!"

Cheryl turned on him again, her rage again building. "What are you raving about now? Who gives a shit about the computer and the—"

"The predictions, God damn it! Right on the money! A doctor's wife, a Raleigh resident, the exact day!" He started babbling, he didn't seem able to control it. "Jennifer died just like all the others, she was stabbed over and over I saw it happening I didn't think I didn't think didn't think she didn't lift a finger to stop it she just took it and took it and finally she died! We're part of the sample now, it's happened to us!" He turned to Stephanie. "This is what happened to Alice Near! Exactly!"

They were all staring at him. "The virus," Art mumbled. "The virus you were talking about, we've caught it . . ."

"There's no virus," Stephanie said sadly. She broke down, and her tears started to flow. "No virus. Just us. Just twisted, sick, insane us."

"I don't know," Rick said after a while, "why you are all carrying on like this. If you'll just stop and think for a moment, you'll understand what we have to do. It's very simple, really."

"I don't understand," Stephanie whimpered.

"We have to go with her," Rick said. "Didn't we all say that, last night? That we'd never be separated? If you think about it you'll see, it makes sense. It's best if you quit when you're at the top of your game, go out winning. That's where we are, right now, that's what this has all been about, it's so obvious! We aren't going home. Not now, not ever. We're going to stay, we're going to keep on doing what we've been doing. And we're all going to die." He looked down at his wife's body. "Like she did. She showed us the way. All we have to do now is follow her."

"I heard somebody else," Sam said, looking confused, "say something just like that, just recently, going out at the top of your game, that it was—it was—"

Initially, Cheryl was staring at Rick as if she believed he'd lost his mind utterly. But then, as he continued to speak, her expression changed, quite dramatically. For a few seconds her features flipped back and forth between horrified incredulity and something that resembled excited acceptance.

She settled on the latter. "Yes," she breathed finally, her eyes growing bright. "Yes, you're right, that's what we have to do! That's the only way, that's what we have to do, just like she did!" As she spoke her excitement seemed to increase. "She went all the way; she understood, she knew, that's what I was talking about, it's the only way we can preserve this!"

Stephanie herself wasn't so sure. When Rick had first made his suggestion, she'd seen it as lunatic; but now, especially since Cheryl had chimed in so vigorously, she was finding herself taking it quite seriously indeed. She began thinking about Sam's knife, the one Rick had used on Jennifer, imagining how it would feel when it slid into her own body; the whole idea, she discovered, was exciting her to the point where she could almost forget her grief for her dead friend. Such a penultimate act! To accept it, to accept the knife and the death it would be bringing, to give herself over so completely to sensuality that even her instinct for survival was discarded! To accept death the way she'd accepted the bites, the belt, and the fork—without hesitation, without reserve. Her choice. Her strength. Just as she'd fantasized it after she'd done the autopsy on Alice Near.

But she was not unaware of the finality of the act, either. For Jennifer, there was no longer any way to turn back, no opportunity for second thoughts.

"No," she said, forcing herself to pronounce the syllable and hoping that Sam and Art would support her. Desperately she pushed her excitement aside, tried to be rational. "No, we have to talk about this, this is crazy, we can't—!"

She was cut off by a sound none of them expected: a knock at the door.

As one, they turned to look in that general direction, even though they could not see the door from where they were. "Jesus, it's the middle of the fucking night!" Art hissed. "Who in the hell could that be?"

"No," Stephanie said, pointing to the kitchen clock, visible through the doorway. "It's morning, it's after nine, I don't know why it's so dark out. But still, I can't imagine who that is!"

"Whoever is just going to have to go away," Sam said in a rough whisper. "We sure as fuck can't answer it!"

"Yeah," Art agreed, looking nervous. "We'll just sit here and wait them out."

They did wait, but whoever was at the door was persistent, the knocks kept coming. Go away, Stephanie said silently. Whoever you are, go away. You sure don't want to be here, not now.

At last the knocks ceased. But, moments later, they all heard, very clearly, the sound of a key being turned in the lock, the sound of the door opening, the sound of footsteps coming through the kitchen. They stared at each other, more wild-eyed than ever; Rick gently moved Jennifer's head and shoulders from his lap and got to his feet.

"Hey!" a voice called loudly. "Hey, everybody, you have to wake up now!"

Less than a second after they'd heard the voice, Traci walked around the corner into the room, followed closely by Fran. As they came in they were smiling; as they saw what was before them, five naked and bloody people and a dead woman, they froze in their tracks. Even their smiles froze. To Stephanie it seemed that even the bounce of Traci's hair froze.

"You don't understand," Art said lamely.

His words broke the spell. Both girls gave voice to ear-splitting shrieks and turned on their heels, headed for the door.

Rick reacted like some sort of jungle cat; he sprang toward them, catching Traci's shirt before she could even complete her turn. Art and Sam were just a little slower, but they raced into the kitchen as Fran, by then in full flight, disappeared from Stephanie's view.

Traci was fighting furiously, screaming and trying to get away from Rick. "The cuffs!" he shouted. "Get the cuffs!"

Without thinking, Stephanie jumped up, grabbed them; while Cheryl helped to control the girl's flailing arms, she managed to get them clamped in place. By then Art and Sam had succeeded in dragging the struggling Fran back into the living room. At Art's suggestion they used the pieces of the women's swimsuits to tie both girls' ankles and Fran's wrists. The men then put them on the couch, where they continued to shriek and howl incoherently until finally Rick used two of the men's suits to gag them.

"Oh, this is just wonderful," Art said after a degree of calm had been restored. "Just great!" He glared at the girls. "What the fuck did you do that for, anyway? You don't normally come in when the door is locked, God damn it! Why didn't you just go away?"

"Don't yell at them," Cheryl complained. "It isn't their fault, they just blundered into this."

"We all just blundered into this! Shit! It isn't like we planned for any of this to happen!" He stopped, stared at the two terrified girls. "And this, this really does make things perfect, just goddamn fucking perfect!"

"It doesn't," Rick observed, "really matter very much." His voice was still quite calm. Stephanie saw Traci and Fran look toward him as if he were the voice of reason around here. Little did they know, she told herself.

"Rick," Stephanie said, her tone low and urgent, "it seems to me it does matter, and it matters a lot! We cannot expect them to understand; try to imagine how you would have seen this six months ago! Damn, I know what my reaction would've been!"

"Yes," he agreed. "Right now they're seeing horrors, they're scared to death. And you're probably right, we may not be able to make them understand—but I'm saying it really doesn't make much difference for us."

"I can't see how you can say that!" Art raged. "God damn it, the two of them showing up here and barging in here like this has just —it's just—it just takes away all our choices, that's all!" He turned to glare at them. "Why the hell did you come, anyway?"

Fran was still squirming on the couch, but Traci had calmed down somewhat; she looked down at the makeshift gag eloquently. Sam went over, removed both gags. Fran gasped and Traci sighed deeply.

"We tried to call," she said in a trembling voice. "We tried. Didn't you notice the storm coming up? It's a tropical storm, it's going to hit here soon! We took a big chance to come out and warn you, we've been trying and trying to call . . ." She ran down, looked around the room again. "What's happened here?" she asked, her voice rising to a squeak. "Is Mrs. Mason dead? She looks dead!"

"She is dead," Sam said grimly. He squeezed his eyes closed for a moment in frustration. "It's my fault you couldn't call," he told them. "My fault. No, it's that goddamn shit Ken Colburn, calling down here, I left the phone disconnected . . ." He sighed, shook his head. "And as to what happened here," he went on, "I think it'd be for the best if we didn't talk about—"

"You might say," Art cut in, his manner suddenly jovial, "that we all went crazy. We all went crazy, we did all this ourselves, we killed Jennifer." He looked at Sam, who was grimacing and shaking his head. "It doesn't matter!" he said firmly, his voice strong but his eyes betraying fear and doubt. "It doesn't matter, not now! We don't have any choices anymore, we have to do it like Rick said, we might as well tell them the truth!"

Sam glared for a moment. "We can talk about that later," he said coldly. "The question now is, what in the hell are we going to do with them? We can't just let them go, not now! The sheriff'd be up here fifteen minutes after they got back!"

"When they told him what they'd seen he would've come anyway, regardless of what we told them. Look, Sam; we just keep them here, keep them tied up. Like I said, it doesn't matter, we don't have choices. In a few days we'll all be dead; the last one can let them go. Okay?"

Sam started to argue, but Traci cut him off. "Why are you all going to be dead?" she demanded, her voice edging close to panic.

"Because," Cheryl answered, very clearly, "the men are going to kill Stephanie and me, and we're going to kill them. One by one, until only one person is left." She smiled and made a helpless gesture, looking very lucid as she pronounced these words.

"But why?" Traci almost screamed.

"Because we love each other," Cheryl answered simply.

Fifty-Seven

THOUGH CHERYL HAD spoken as if the issue had been decided, Sam didn't agree—and he was pretty sure Stephanie didn't either, was sure she'd been about to object when she'd been interrupted by the girls' arrival. Immediately he started trying to get everyone back together so that these obviously profound matters could be further discussed, but no one cooperated; Stephanie and Art insisted on going off to shower while Cheryl joined Rick in talking to Jennifer's corpse. She then engaged him in a lively but macabre discussion about how they wanted to die—a discussion that Sam overheard a good deal of, and one that he found, in spite of everything, intensely exciting. His own dark fantasies reified; but he was determined to prevent it somehow, regardless of how appealing it might be.

By the time Art and Stephanie had returned from their showers, though, he'd realized that their idea was a good one; get cleaned up, take care of the wounds received in last night's wars, behave as if there's a tomorrow. He suggested the same to Rick and Cheryl, and they agreed without argument. After he'd taken his own shower—and dragged on a pair of swim trunks, even though everyone else remained nude—he helped Rick and Stephanie to clean the mess off Jennifer's body and lay it out with some semblance of dignity. They put her on the floor, on a folded chaircover, folded her hands across her pierced abdomen; Sam could not help but observe that she did, indeed, look both contented and beautiful in death. He was reminded of the rash of suicides in Paris early in the twentieth century after the very peaceful-looking corpse of a lovely young woman was found floating in the Seine. He was also reminded of King Priam's observation, in the Iliad, that Hector's corpse, that of a strong young man, would be beautiful while his own, that of an aged king, would be ugly.

And of course, he was reminded of what Selinde had said. Again.

Eventually, though, he managed to bring such dangerous thoughts as these under control. Looking around, he was a little startled to find himself alone with Jennifer and the captive girls; Stephanie, as it turned out, had succeeded in herding the others off to the kitchen to resume the discussions. Feeling a bit left out but realizing they had probably not wished to disturb his meditations over Jennifer, he hurried to join them.

Stephanie, he discovered, was already presenting his point of view. "Rick," she was saying, her voice low but intense, "this is crazy, can't you see that? It's just crazy! We've had one tragedy already, we can't just—"

"What else can we do?" he shot back. He shook a finger at her. "This is where we've been going; I think we can all see that now. You want to just stop, wait for the police, spend the rest of your life in jail or in a mental hospital, all alone? Ask your husband what's going to happen to us!"

"No, maybe we can—"

"No, we can't," Art put in. "We can't. Legally, the best we could hope for is a finding of insanity. Practically, the only option we have is to kill those two girls, sink all the bodies in the Sound, and hope they don't wash up on some shore. There's no way I could be a party to that. Could you?"

"No—no—of course not! We aren't murderers, we—"

"In the eyes of the law we are." His voice shattered, his face seemed to fold in on itself. "And besides, I just can't do it—I can't go on, I can't, not after we've—not after what we've done!" He pressed his fingers to his eyes, and when he took them away his face had smoothed. "We have no choice," he repeated doggedly. "No choice."

She started to say something else, couldn't seem to find the words, and looked desperately to Sam for help.

He rolled his lips in momentarily as they all focused on him. For the problems Rick and Art were addressing, he had no ready answers. "I don't know what we're going to do about our legal situation," he said frankly, after a moment's hesitation. "But no, I have to agree with Stephanie, I don't think the answer is to—"

Rick did not let him finish. "You saw how things were last night, Sam," he said, an urgent undertone in his voice. "You saw how Jennifer was. I didn't know, then, that we were killing her, but I think that even if we had known we'd've gone right on. You saw her eyes, you saw her face, those were the best moments of her life. You know it and so do I." He gestured toward Stephanie and Cheryl. "You think about it, Sam. You want to deny them that moment? Look at them! You want to condemn them to growing old in a prison or a nuthouse? Well, do you?"

Sam held his head in his hands. "There has to be some other answer!" he insisted. "There has to be!" He did look at the two women, as Rick had demanded. Both were still nude; both looked incredibly, spectacularly, beautiful to him. A sudden fantasy came roaring up in his mind, a fantasy about holding Stephanie close and watching her eyes while he slipped the knife into her, about how she'd let him do it and even beg him to do it. As that one faded, it was replaced by another in which Cheryl was doing exactly the same to him. He ran the images again, reversing the two women's roles, and in the end could not decide which of the four was the more erotic. Far from shying away from them, he was finding that he regretted that he could not play through them all in reality.

Rick laughed. Too late, Sam realized that his fantasies were not private, that they were being reflected in his face—and elsewhere. He sighed, hoping his lapse hadn't had much of an effect on them. A single glance at Stephanie, though, told him that such a hope was futile. She was wavering, he could see it in her eyes.

"You do understand, old buddy," Rick said quietly. "And you might as well stop trying to fight it. This is the way it's going to be for me, for Cheryl, for Art. It's right, we all know that. You and Stephanie can't be leftovers."

"They won't be," Cheryl said, speaking for the first time. She reached over and took Sam's hands, looked into his eyes. "Sam," she went on, "maybe you think I've lost it, but I agree with Rick— all the way. I really want to do this, I want to experience what Jenny experienced last night!" She was squirming with excitement, but she seemed quite rational. Her eyes implored him. "I don't want to leave you behind . . ."

She was swaying him; he was close to a breaking point. He'd never denied Cheryl anything she truly wanted, and it was hideously difficult to start now—since this, quite obviously, would be the last request she'd ever make, presuming he agreed to it. Desperately, he looked to Stephanie for support—only to discover that Art was doing exactly the same thing with her. She was still wavering; her resolve hadn't yet cracked, but it was close. As for Sam, it was just not possible to give Cheryl a flat refusal.

"We need to settle down here," he said shakily. "This morning has just been crazy, crazy. We need to think. Need to be sure." He was merely stalling, he knew that, but it was all he could think of doing—other than giving in, both to them and to his own raging emotions.

"I am sure, Sam," Cheryl said softly. "Very sure."

"No, Sam's right," Stephanie said, her voice cracking. "Give it a little time. Right now we're overwhelmed. Jenny's death, the girls coming into it, all that . . ." she trailed away lamely.

"There is one more factor we haven't considered, too," Sam said, looking over at Rick. "A very significant factor."

Rick's smile was knowing, self-confident. "What's that?"

"Paul. What about Paul?"

As Sam watched, the surgeon's self-satisfied expression began to break up, finally shattering into a thousand fragments like droplets of oil on water. The wildness in his eyes faded away; tears welled up quickly, his hands started shaking.

Sam did not hesitate to pursue his advantage. "He'll be left alone," he continued. "Like Stephanie was. You remember the agreements we made, the agreements that're on file in Art's office? That if anything ever happened to you and Jennifer, that we'd adopt Paul, and that if anything happened to us, the Dixons would? Did you plan another level, Rick? If the Masons and the Leos and the Dixons are all dead, who's left for Paul? Who's left to help him grow up?"

"But I can't tell him!" Rick howled. "I can't explain this to him, he's only eight years old! God damn, Jenny's dead already! What am I going to tell him? Ah, Jesus, ah, God, ah—!"

"Rick's right," Cheryl said swiftly. "The last thing in the world I'd want to do is try to explain this to Paul! He has his grandparents, Sam—they love him, they'll—"

"They're old. They're not well. We talked about this."

"Well, fine," Art grumbled. "We can all stay alive for Paul's sake. He can come visit us in prison or in the loony bin—whichever one we end up in. We can guide him in growing up from the wrong side of a piece of shatterproof glass. It'll work out fine."

"We can't," Rick moaned. "We'll just have to leave him with Jenny's parents and hope for the best, it's all we can do, they're good people, they'll find a way." He fixed Sam with a hard stare; the wildness was beginning to return. "It's just one more reason," he snapped, "why we have to go through with it! If we're all gone he'll never really know, he won't have anyone to ask! It'll be a shock but he'll get over it. He's strong, he'll be okay."

"But he'll be alone," Stephanie whispered. "Like Sam said, like I was . . ."

"Well, maybe he will!" Rick cried, waving his arms. "Maybe he will! It can't be helped! Besides, look at you! You did just fine, didn't you?" Without giving her a chance to answer, he got up so suddenly he overturned his chair and stormed back into the living room, where he sat down again with Jennifer's corpse, talking to her about Paul, explaining himself to her, and promising that he'd be joining her very soon, that they wouldn't be apart long. The rest of the little conference broke up at that point; but for a while Sam remained in the kitchen, cursing himself for having lost the advantage and wondering whether this was in any way a card he could still play. When he rejoined the others, he found Rick still talking to Jennifer. Cheryl, however, had by then engaged Art in a graphic

discussion about what they were going to do—just as she'd discussed it with Rick earlier. At first the lawyer's manner was one of
resignation rather than excited enthusiasm, but that began to
change as Cheryl pointed out various body sites—her breasts and
lower abdomen, primarily—that she wanted pierced when it came
her turn to die. Stephanie, looking lost and hungry, sat nearby and
listened silently.

Feeling that he just could not listen to any more such talk and
maintain any trace of self-control, Sam withdrew, moved away;
eventually he went back to the kitchen and got himself a cup of
coffee. He'd tried to draw Stephanie off too, but she'd failed to
respond; he'd felt a brief rage toward her, a sense of betrayal, but
it passed quickly. He understood, quite well, the problems she was
having. He was having those same problems.

Adding to the complications was the storm, which continued to
build as the day went on. By midafternoon, the sky outside was
still almost as dark as night; the rain was falling in sheets, and the
wind, while less than hurricane force, was still sufficient to bend
the pines outside halfway over, to rattle the windows, and at times
to shake the entire house violently. Twice windows exploded inward in the upstairs rooms, collapsing with gunshotlike reports,
allowing gallons of rainwater to pour in. Each time this happened
they went to investigate, but no one seemed concerned, no one
took any action until the power failed. Even then, all that was
done was to light the hurricane lamps, to maintain illumination in
the downstairs rooms that were still being used. During his increasingly rare periods of lucidity, Sam believed, perhaps irratio-
nally, that if the sun had been shining outside, if this day had been
like the others, they would all be more under control.

But the storm seemed to be driving them, lashing them with its
wildness, making things more insane, more dreamlike, more surreal than ever. At around five o'clock Sam was in the kitchen, his
face near the window that looked out over the new inlet; it was
pretty dark out there and he could see little. He couldn't even tell,
at the moment, where the inlet began and the layer of rainwater
on the ground ended; it looked as if the inlet had migrated right
up to the foundations of the house. A series of closely spaced
lightning flashes illuminated the yard, and he watched one of the
pine trees that had backed their swimming beach break loose and,
with a great shuddering of branches, fall forward into the water. It
didn't even stay in one place long; the whole dune where the trees
stood was being undermined, and as the roots tore loose, another

lightning bolt showed him the tree drifting away, floating westward into Currituck Sound.

Stephanie, padding up behind him on bare feet, patted his shoulder affectionately. "Enjoying the storm, Sam?" she asked.

He looked around at her as she fumbled around in the dark refrigerator. She was still naked—except for Sam, they all had been, all day—and his view of her legs and rear end as she bent over sent a thrill through him.

But what bothered him was her manner; she seemed at ease, as if her conflicts had been resolved. "Yes and no," he replied conversationally. "It looks to me like the inlet is getting bigger, I'm not sure it won't threaten the house eventually, especially if we get a storm surge from Currituck Sound. What're you guys up to?"

"Art's hungry. So am I, so's Cheryl. You want to join us?"

He went to the refrigerator, leaned against it; it was still cool inside, although Stephanie was fumbling in darkness, searching out cheese and coldcuts. "Maybe," he answered. "What's happening, Stephanie? You haven't—"

She looked up at him, her eyes large and round. "No," she told him, dragging the word out. "No, I haven't agreed to the pact. I've kind of—put it out of my mind, I guess." She frowned, looked down at the floor. "No, that's a lie. I've put it off." She raised her eyes again, gave him a quick smile; she looked incredibly fragile, impossibly innocent—and terribly sexy. "Sam, I want to," she admitted. "I'm fighting it, but I want to. Art's determined—he says he wants to go 'all the way' tonight. I'm scared—I don't want to be left alone again, Sam . . ." Her eyes began filling with tears.

He took her in his arms, hugged her. "I know, I know. Keep on fighting, that's all I can say."

She smiled again, wistfully. "I'm trying, Sam. I need help . . ."

"I'm working on it." He took some of the food from her and followed her back into the living room. Cheryl and Art were lying together on the bloodstained cushions, her head on his stomach, her fingers wrapped around his partially erect penis. Rick was sitting on the couch with the two girls, talking to them.

"You just don't know," he was saying, his voice intense, "how beautiful all this is! You can't, if you haven't experienced it!"

Traci was trying to reason with him. "Dr. Mason, I don't know what's been going on here," she said in an urgent tone, "but I know your wife is dead! Doesn't that mean anything to you? And you sit there and tell me you're planning to kill each other! I can't believe you're serious, I just can't!"

"You just don't know," he repeated. "But I think you'll see. And you're welcome to join us, at any time, if you want to. I'm sure you'll want to, once you understand, I'm sure of it!"

Sam didn't much like the sound of that; he hadn't heard the beginning of this conversation, but it sounded to him as if Rick were not just offering but actively trying to push the two girls into becoming a part of whatever was happening to them. He went over there, crouched down on his heels in front of them. He was not unaware that, even though he was wearing swim trunks, he probably looked more like a wild man than the naked Rick did.

"You have to understand," he said firmly, looking at Traci but actually speaking more to Rick, "that you don't have to be a part of what's happening here. Nobody's requiring it of you, and we don't mean to hurt you; we plan to let you go soon. In fact, you don't even have to be in here while these things are going on—if anything goes on. We can move you to—"

"I don't think that's a good idea, old buddy," Rick said. "What if they get loose? We need to keep them where we can—"

"God damn it, Rick, where are they going to go?" Sam demanded, exasperated. "Have you looked outside? We're in the middle of a tropical storm!"

"I just don't want to take chances! What if they try to escape and one of them gets hurt?"

"They aren't going to get hurt! Even if they get away clean and bring all the goddamn law enforcement in the state down on our heads, they aren't going to get hurt! They aren't part of this!"

Rick looked a little belligerent, but he backed down. "All right," he said. "I guess you're right." He glanced back at Traci and Fran. "Just remember what I told you. You want to join in, you just say so."

"They aren't going to be in here if we—"

"They should be. They should watch. That's how Stephanie and Art got into it, wasn't it? That's how you and Cheryl got involved! You should give them that chance, Sam!" That was his last word on the subject; he rose quickly from the couch and went to join the others, across the room.

"What does he mean?" Traci asked. "About you getting involved by watching?"

"Just that," Sam told her, fighting a feeling that what Rick had just said did, in fact, make perfect sense. His control was beginning to go again, he could feel it slipping away as memories of his wife and his friends dangling from the handcuffs flashed through his mind. "He may have a point," he admitted finally. "We'll have to see. But remember, the only question is whether you stay in here with us or not. That's it."

Fran seemed to find her voice at last. "You really aren't going to hurt us?" she asked, her first coherent words all day.

"No," he assured her. "Absolutely not." He hesitated. "Like Rick said, not unless you ask us to."

He looked back at the others; sex games with the food were in progress, and he felt a sudden and intense desire to be a part of them. "Just remember," he told the girls, "whatever you see here, nobody's being forced to do anything. Okay?"

"Okay," Traci agreed, her voice soft and shaky. Sam stood up, looked down at them for a moment, shook his head, and turned back to join the others. On the way he paused to step out of the swim trunks; he simply couldn't tolerate them any longer.

At least for a while, Fran and Traci followed Sam's advice—but his halfhearted counsel to the others, that they confine themselves to sex only for a while, fell on deaf ears. He heard horrified gasps from the two girls when they handcuffed Cheryl, when they hung her from the ceiling hook and began lashing her with the belt; by the time Rick had taken her place the shock had evidently worn off, and they made little sound when Rick was put up there in her place, even less when it was Stephanie's turn.

Art was next, and after he was taken down there was a little pause. Rick turned, looked over at the two girls. "You sure one of you wouldn't like to try this?" he asked, his tone wheedling, his manner suggesting that there might be something wrong with them if they did not. Both, however, just shook their heads. He seemed as if he meant to pursue the matter further, but Sam, justifying himself with the excuse that perhaps the lashings could take the edge off their desires for more dangerous pastimes, asked to take his turn. Over Rick's complaints that two men should not go up in a row, he did; he kept urging them on and took a terrible beating, but as soon as he was down he knew he'd been deluding himself, the tension was higher than ever.

There were a couple of seemingly involuntary protests from the girls when the fondue forks were brought out a little later, again attracting Rick's attention to them. He appeared determined, as far as Sam could see, to involve them—perhaps just because they were now missing a female player, perhaps because he himself felt like an extra. Or possibly, Sam told himself, simply because they were attractive girls and they were there.

"They aren't interested, Rick," Sam said after Rick had again issued his invitation. "Just leave them alone, will you?"

Rick stared at Fran hungrily. "No, one of them ought to try the belt, at least. Damn it, they just can't know—"

"They can see what we're doing!" Sam shot back savagely. "If they want to try it, let them say so! If they don't, then leave them the fuck alone!"

"Yeah, forget about them," Art agreed. He plucked a fondue fork from the boiling water. "Can we just get on with this?"

Cheryl leaned over against him, arching her body over his. "Yes," she purred, looking down at the fork. "Yes, let's!" He raised the fork's points toward her; she sank down on it, moaning as her weight drove it slowly but deeply upward, into her breast. Even before he'd withdrawn it Stephanie was pulling out another. She sat staring at it for a moment, apparently struggling with herself, but at last she approached Art with it; he grinned welcomingly, and she carefully pierced his chest with it.

It was simply too exciting, too erotic, for Sam to resist for long either. The forks kept coming out of the boiling water, kept sliding into flesh; arms, legs, and hips now became legitimate targets, and new blood kept soaking into the cushions. The sexual couplings kept shifting; at one point Sam caught sight of the girls' faces. He knew what they were seeing, but he could hardly imagine what they were feeling, the absolute terror they must be experiencing, wondering—as they had to be—if they were going to be dragged into this.

But there was no stopping it, no more so tonight than any previous night. Each evening the pitch had risen higher, each evening the participants had been wilder; tonight, with only the red glow of the hurricane lamps and candles to illuminate the room and the terrible fury of the storm raging outside the house, it seemed destined to reach that new level they'd talked about all day, a level from which Sam was sure there'd be no return—even if one had been possible before. Last night they'd killed Jennifer, but none of them had really known they were doing that, it hadn't been intentional. Tonight, if they did it, it would be planned, they'd know exactly what they were doing. If they did do it, Sam believed, the die would be absolutely cast, there could be no turning back. They'd be forced to carry through to the end.

And at last, after the games with the handcuffs and the fondue forks had been played and the players were again blood-splattered, after there'd been time for the three men to recover sufficiently to regain their erections—the slender dark-bladed knife Selinde had so conveniently provided made its appearance. As it did—in Rick's hand, no one else had been willing to touch it, not yet—Sam watched beads of water drip from it, marking the ruined carpet. Rick had sterilized it—why, Sam wasn't sure. Infection wasn't a problem if you were dead.

They were all watching it; for several minutes, no one said a word. "Rick," Sam said at last, "I think maybe we'd better—"

Rick ignored him utterly. He reached out, took Cheryl's wrist. She threw a glance at Sam, then she looked back at the knife in Rick's hand, her hunger apparent in her eyes. Still, she resisted him a little—for a moment, at least.

"No," Sam breathed as she relaxed into Rick's arms, her eyes closed, her face smooth, her breathing very heavy. "No, Rick, you can't, you can't . . ." He leaned forward, fighting himself, wondering what he was going to do, whether he would attack Rick to stop him or simply be paralyzed by the incredible sensuality of the moment.

"You're right," Rick answered, surprising him. He kissed Cheryl passionately. "We can't do you right now, Green Eyes," he told her. "That'd leave only one woman. It's gotta be Sam or Art. Man woman man woman, the way we've been doing it."

Again, for a moment, there was silence. Tearing his gaze away from the knife, Art stared fixedly at Sam for a while. "Me, then," he said hesitantly. "Sam's not ready yet . . ."

Stephanie grabbed his arm. "Art, no . . ."

He shook himself, all over, and turned to her. "Let's just see," he suggested, "how it goes." He began stroking her body; his erection, which had wilted somewhat, started to rise again. Cheryl, seemingly not upset about the selection, pulled herself away from Rick and went to Art as well. Sam, encouraged by the doubts he was sure he was seeing, joined in quickly, caressing both of the women. Perhaps, he told himself, if they could get up to and over this peak quickly . . .

But that, to the dismay of that part of his mind that remained rational, didn't seem to be happening. All the men had had orgasms; all were at least a little tired by the hours of sex play that had preceded this. It didn't stop the tension from rising, but it made it rise slowly—and whatever modicum of control there might've been was fading quickly. Twice Rick attempted to initiate the chant of "all the way!" The first time, no one would take it up;

the second time, Cheryl joined in and so did Art. Finally, perhaps a little halfheartedly at first, Stephanie added her voice.

At that point Art was atop his wife, missionary position. "Give it to her, Rick," he panted, his hips moving vigorously. "Give it to her now!"

Rick immediately offered it to her, but she refused to take it. "I can't do it, Art," she told him, her lips close to his ear. "I can't, I know you want me to but I just can't, I can't . . . !"

He looked up at Rick. "Give it to Cheryl, then!" he cried urgently, desperation in his voice and fear in his eyes. "God damn it, it's now or never!"

Cheryl's eyes went wide, and she slid backward on the carpet a little, holding up her hands as if surrendering. "No!" she almost hissed. "No, I can't do this either, no!"

It's breaking down, Sam told himself, it's breaking down. All day we talked big, but now the moment is here and it's all breaking down. The almost blinding pitch of excitement he himself had felt was beginning to fade back a little, just a little, as he sensed the hesitancy in the others. Art looked at Stephanie and then at Cheryl, and he looked perhaps a bit disappointed, but he seemed to be losing the edge of his intensity too. He turned his attention fully to his wife, to their lovemaking, as if he were dismissing the whole plan from his mind. Cheryl rejoined them, running her hands down between their bodies, touching them both.

In apparent desperation, Rick looked up at Fran and Traci, holding the knife up as if offering it to them; this netted him twin looks of horror and revulsion, nothing more.

He looked back at the three bodies intertwined on the floor. "No," he murmured. "No, Jennifer isn't going to be the only one!" Only Sam realized what he was about to do, and he didn't react anywhere near quickly enough; Rick touched the knife to Art's side, between his ribs, and quickly ran the full length of the blade right into him.

Fran and Traci both screamed. Sam was stunned; Art, apparently, was equally shocked. His eyes flew wide open and he grunted loudly; blood spurted from his side, and it almost immediately appeared on his lips as well. Still, he didn't try to get up, didn't stop making love to Stephanie. "You did it," he whispered. "You really did it . . . !"

For just an instant her reaction to realizing that her husband had just been stabbed was almost normal: she looked horrified. But then she ran her hand down over his side, and, when it came up bloody, the sight of the redness seemed to wipe such questions from her mind. Her eyes half-lidded, an expression of wild passion on her face, she threw her arms hard around his neck, squeezing his hips with her legs at the same time. She muttered something about not having done it, told him that Cheryl must've; Cheryl didn't hear and she had not seen Rick stab him. But she saw the blood, and she touched her lips to the wound, licking at it avidly.

Like a man caught in a nightmare, Sam once again tried to say something, tried to do something, but he could not make his mind work clearly. While he struggled with himself, feeling his passions rise again in spite of everything, Rick stabbed Art again, in his lower side this time, just above the joint of his hip.

Again, blood almost shot out of him. His knees slid backward a little, and he moaned softly. "I'm cold," he complained. "Cold and weak, I can't go on and on like Jenny did, I'm slipping away . . . Finish it, Stephanie. Just finish it, finish it now, I'm ready, I don't want to pass out . . . !"

"But I'm not doing it!" she wailed, the war among her conflicting emotions more than apparent in her tormented face. "I'm not, I can't—!"

Rick had heard too, and he responded to Art's request immediately. Slipping the blade under Art's chin, he pressed upward and started drawing it toward himself. Art, accepting it fully now, pushed his head downward against it, and it slipped deeply into his throat. Rick drew it all the way across and upwards toward his ear, creating a long and deep incision.

Somehow, Art managed to hold his position, raised on his arms, looking down at Stephanie's face. A huge amount of blood was pouring from his open throat, soaking her upper body; she looked stunned. Fran and Traci were screeching at an impossible volume. Sam felt like he was enveloped in hardening cement, he couldn't move, couldn't do anything.

Then, as if Art were some sort of giant puppet and the strings holding him up had suddenly been cut, he collapsed on Stephanie, his muscles jerking without coordination. Suddenly the flow of blood from his throat slowed. That was reasonable, Sam told himself dazedly. It wasn't being driven by a beating heart, not anymore.

Stephanie rolled him off herself; to Sam, it looked like her mind —and Cheryl's, as well—was completely gone. Her eyes were blank, staring. Once she'd gotten him on his back on the floor, she and Cheryl both began rubbing their bodies against his, like two cats with a large bag of catnip, smearing his blood everywhere, mixing it with their own. Fran and Traci had fallen into a wide-eyed, almost catatonic, silence. Sam, too, felt as if he were falling; now that there was clearly nothing he could do to save Art, he couldn't seem to find anything to hold on to, and he started sliding back into the place he'd been before, the place where he was, like Rick and the two women, totally ruled by these insane passions.

So driven, he went to the women and folded Stephanie's blood-soaked body into his arms. She and Cheryl literally attacked him; for a few seconds he truly believed that Cheryl was going to rip his penis off his body with her teeth.

"Get the knife, Sam," Stephanie begged, holding handfuls of his hair, her lips pulled back to expose her teeth. "Get the knife, do me now! Stick it in me, oh, God! I want it, kill me, kill me, I want you to kill me . . . !"

By force, he drove her to the floor; she swung her legs forward and stuffed his erection inside herself. "Not yet," he told her, his own voice so harsh it was startling to his ears. Reaching out, he grabbed Cheryl's shoulder and pulled her to himself. "Not quite yet, not for either one of you, but . . ."

He stopped speaking; something was distracting him, and he thought it was new shrieks from Traci and Fran. He looked around, ready to yell at them to shut up, and was startled to see that only Traci was still there, and that she had tipped herself over, burying her face in the cushions. It was just then that he also realized that he didn't know where Rick was, that he'd gotten up shortly after he'd cut Art's throat. He turned his head the other way, looking around for his friend.

What he saw shocked him so that it snapped him back to something close to normal. Fran, her wrists and ankles still tied, was dangling from the ceiling hook. She was nude, and, though she was screaming incoherently, she was not struggling, she was not moving at all. Rick, his eyes so wild they made Stephanie's and Cheryl's look calm, stood in front of her, his left hand on her thigh. In his right was the knife, and he was running the tip of it around her body, up over her smallish breasts, down across her flat tanned stomach.

"You just don't understand," he almost crooned. "You just don't. You can't, unless you experience it. I have to show you. I have to."

"No!" she screamed. "No, please, Dr. Mason, don't!"

"Rick, stop it!" Sam yelled. He started struggling to get free, but

Stephanie and Cheryl were piled on top of him, their combined weight preventing him from rising. "No, leave her alone!"

Rick glanced at him and frowned. He stopped moving the knife, but left the tip of it resting against her abdomen, a little below her navel. "Come on, Sam," he said irritably. "You know how good it feels, you know how good she'll feel once she gets into it!"

Sam struggled some more. "No, no, you can't, Rick, think about what you're doing, the rest of us did this because we wanted to, if you do it to her it's just murder!"

He looked back up at Fran, ran his hand down from her breast to her hip, then moved it around to the small of her back. He pulled her body toward his a little. "Shit," he muttered. "No, it isn't."

Then, leaving the knife point where it was resting, he started pushing it in.

"Ah, oh, God, no, please!" Fran howled. She went stiff, as if struggling to remain still, as if hoping he'd stop. He did not; the razor-sharp blade kept sinking slowly and softly on in, deeper and deeper. Her blood began flowing profusely; she started trembling uncontrollably. Cursing, Sam grabbed Cheryl's shoulders, tried to force her off his lap. She merely smiled and continued to cling to his neck. If she was aware of what Rick was doing she showed no sign of it at all, and neither, for that matter, did Stephanie, who was lying across Sam's hips and legs, his fading erection in her mouth.

"God damn it, Cheryl!" Sam screamed, right in her face. He glanced at Rick and Fran, saw that the blade had been fully buried in spite of her screams and protests. "Let me up, please!"

She opened her eyes, blinked. "What—what's going on?" she asked, her face blank.

"He's killing Fran, God damn it! Let me go!"

To his absolute frustration, she did not. Instead, she looked up, to see what was happening for herself.

Rick had withdrawn the knife from Fran's abdomen by then, and again the tip was gliding over her skin as if it were itself searching for the correct spot. Blood pulsed steadily from the puncture he'd already inflicted. "Oh, please please please, don't hurt me again!" the girl wept. "Please, please, I'll do whatever you want, just please don't, please don't—!"

He was looking at her face as the knife searched around on her chest. "You have such lovely eyes . . ." he mused softly, his voice gentle. "I have to make you understand. I did this to Jennifer, you see. I did it and she loved it, she really loved it . . ."

"But I don't!" Fran shrieked. "I—ahhhhh! Ahhh! No! No!"

Sam screamed too; the knife was on its way into her body once more, passing slowly through her right breast and slipping between her ribs, freeing more of her blood. Now she seemed to understand that Rick was not going to stop, and she began kicking out at him wildly. Grabbing Cheryl's arms, Sam tore them away and pushed her backward. As she sprawled awkwardly on the floor Stephanie tried to take her place. But Sam shoved her away too, and managed to get to his feet.

Lunging across the room, he crashed into Rick, knocking him away from the dangling girl. Rick careened backward, trying to catch his balance, but he stumbled over one of the cushions and went down. Sam ignored him and looked up at Fran.

When he did he almost lost it again, almost slipped back down into whatever well he'd just climbed out of. Fran was calm now; her eyes were sleepy-looking, she was sighing and shuddering slightly, she looked precisely like a woman who'd just had a potent orgasm. The knife remained in her breast; almost the entire blade was hidden. Blood ran from around it and from her lips as well. Sam understood what was happening to her, all too well. She was sinking into shock, she was dying. No more, no less.

Cursing himself for fumbling, Sam carefully removed the knife and used it to cut her down. The puncture in her chest whistled when she tried to breathe. "Please," she moaned softly as he helped her lie down on the floor, "please, please, help me, I feel so funny, I don't want to die . . ."

"You'll be fine," Sam told her, recovering a persona he hadn't used since he'd taken his residency. "You'll be fine, just relax." As he spoke he was examining the wounds, and he knew he was lying to her. If she'd arrived at a hospital emergency room in this condition it'd be touch and go, the odds wouldn't be good.

Rick came up on the other side of her. Reaching down, he pushed her legs apart. "Let me get on top of her," he told Sam, his breath coming in quick ragged gulps. "Then she'll start to—"

"No!" Sam shouted. "No, it's gone too goddamn far! It's over, you hear me, Rick? Over!"

Rick bounced back as if Sam had punched him. "Over?" he echoed. "Over?"

"Yes, over! God damn it, God damn it! Help me with her, will you? Maybe we can do something—"

"It can't be over!" Rick howled, incredibly loud. "It can't be over, Jennifer is dead!" He sprang at Sam, falling over Fran's body, grabbing at the knife in a frenzy. For a few seconds they pawed at each other like two small boys, but Sam managed to keep the knife away from him. Rick gave it up far more quickly than Sam had anticipated, jumping up and running off across the room.

Again, Sam ignored him and turned his attention back to Fran, who was staring up at him with bright and terrified eyes. He cursed, wondering what he could do, with no instruments, to help her.

"It's . . . over?" Stephanie asked, her voice plaintive, little-girl.

He glanced up, only then aware that she and Cheryl, blood-soaked and hardly appearing human, were beside him. "Yeah," he said, almost coldly. "It's over."

Tears welled up in Stephanie's eyes, impossibly fast. "But Art is deeeeaaaaad . . . !" Her voice built to a scream; she began tearing at her hair like some heroine from a Greek tragedy.

Cheryl, too, seemed like something out of a Greek play—but something quite different. She danced away, smiling and sighing. "Not over," she sang. "Not over." She shook her head wildly, now fully the dancing Maenad from Sam's vision, her body swaying in time to some unheard beat, singing words that Sam knew he'd heard before, about Romeo and Juliet, about being able to fly, about having no fear—and, repeatedly, the title line from the Blue Oyster Cult's song "Don't Fear the Reaper." Sam shook his head. That song, always Cheryl's favorite, could long ago have told him a great deal about her deepest thoughts—if only he'd paid attention.

But she wasn't trying to interfere with him, and he understood that he'd have to try to deal with her later. He turned back to Fran again; she was still alive and still conscious, still had a glimmer of hope in her eyes. But she'd lost a lot of blood already, and she was losing more every second.

"It doesn't hurt anymore," she said in a weak whisper.

Not a good sign, Sam told himself grimly. Not a good sign at all. He forced himself to smile at her as he reached for a piece of her torn clothing to try to staunch her wounds.

He didn't get the chance. From behind him, Rick pushed his way violently past Stephanie, knocking her to the side. Again, Sam had no chance to react. Rick's arm came down violently. In his hand was another knife, an ordinary one used for cleaning fish, one he'd gotten from his tackle. Large, single-edged, serrated. It bore no resemblance to the other.

But its effect, as it sank to the handle into the vicinity of Fran's solar plexus, was even more devastating.

The girl stiffened, her legs quivering, her toes curling hard back; blood spouted from her mouth. Then she suddenly relaxed, her eyes began to glaze, her pupils enlarging.

Rick jumped up again, snatching the knife out of the girl's body. "There's no turning back!" he hissed at Sam. "We're all going to die, that's the only way!"

Jesus Christ, Sam told himself. He is totally gone, totally lost to us. "Okay, okay," he said soothingly, getting to his feet. "But we want to do it right, like Jennifer and Art did, not wildly, not like this!"

Rick looked dubious for an instant, but then he smiled like a happy child. "I knew you'd stick with me in the end, Sam," he said. "You're my best friend, we've always stuck together, through everything, always . . ."

"Right," Sam told him. He reached out, took the fishing knife from Rick's unresisting hand, breathed a sigh of relief.

Rick kept smiling beatifically for a few seconds before he realized what had happened. Then his eyes, like Stephanie's a few minutes earlier, filled with tears. "No!" he cried. "No! You're going to kill me and then none of you will go through with it! You just want to have all the women for yourself, Sam, that's the way you've always been!" Before Sam could say a word in protest Rick bolted from the room, racing up the stairs. "You'll see!" he screeched. "You'll see! You're all going to die, too, Sam! I'm going to make sure of that!" Then he was gone.

Sam sighed deeply, not knowing what to do first. Fran no longer commanded much of his attention; he did check to make sure, but she was, as he'd known anyway, dead. Stephanie seemed to be in shock, sitting and staring blindly into space, her tears now dry; Cheryl continued to dance around like a madwoman, still singing the Blue Oyster Cult song. He got to his feet, headed toward her. He had some notion about trying to bring her back down to earth before trying to reach Stephanie or going after Rick.

He didn't get a chance. He'd only begun to try to talk to her when a thunderous roaring shook the house, a sound much louder than the storm. They all saw it happen, they all saw the roof in the kitchen suddenly come crashing down to the floor, throwing up a huge cloud of dust that was washed away almost instantly as the rain came pouring in. Water swirled in, sweeping around them and tugging them toward the ruins of the back of the house.

Sam didn't have to ask what was happening, he knew. The new inlet had now advanced this far; the house, like all structures here, was built on sand. The same processes that had formed the inlet were now stripping that sand out from under the foundation, and it was collapsing, falling into the Sound.

Fifty-Eight

IN THE SPACE of less than a half hour, Stephanie's world had fallen apart. Still kneeling on the floor, she watched the water swirl around her legs; it had already reached a depth of six inches. Ribbons of blood ran in it, and it had lifted the three bodies off the floor. The corpses bobbed slightly as they moved, rather slowly, toward what had been the kitchen, where the cracking of beams told of the destruction of the house. From the couch, Traci was screaming at the top of her lungs; from somewhere upstairs she could hear Rick running about, shrieking just as loudly, insisting that he was going to make sure they all died. Across the room a table bearing a hurricane lamp tried to float, became unbalanced, tipped over. The lamp, in falling, struck another piece of furniture and shattered; the oil ignited, spreading out quickly on the surface of the water, breaking up here and there into little round lilypads of flame. One of them touched some curtains and they went up too, amazingly fast, whipped by the wind that was blowing inside the house.

Sam stood with his hands on his hips for a moment, surveying the disasters. "God damn," he muttered, almost mildly. "Does everything have to happen all at once?"

"Let me loose!" Traci screamed. "Let me loose, this whole place is coming down!"

Still holding the little knife, he splashed over to her; she cringed, wide-eyed, obviously unsure of his intentions, not knowing if she, too, would be stabbed. But Sam merely used the blade to sever the pieces of swimsuits at her wrists and ankles. She stood up, gazing uncertainly, from his face to the knife that was still in his hand.

"It seems stupid," Sam said, "to go out there into the storm. But I guess we don't have a choice." Nonchalantly, he watched the burning oil move closer. "Unless we want to stay here and go down with the ship, as it were . . ."

Traci waited only until he'd looked away. Then, like a captive wild bird whose cage had been left open, she made a break for the still-usable front door, high-stepping her way through the water. Sam watched her go; as she opened the door more wind and rain swirled through the house, but she darted through anyhow, disappeared into the storm.

Sam nodded sagely. "We should do the same," he observed. He looked over at Cheryl, who had stopped her wild dancing and was looking down at the water with an expression of confused concern, and then at Stephanie.

She smiled back up at him happily. In her mind, she had, by now, straightened it all out—more or less. Some confusion remained, though; Daddy, she told herself, was dead. There was his body, floating away. But there was Daddy too, telling her they had to leave. And Daddy was upstairs, telling her to stay and die. She looked around the room; it was so big. She remembered smaller rooms; it couldn't've grown, so that must mean she was very small.

That wasn't a problem. Figuring how to do what Daddy wanted when he'd told her two different things, that was her problem.

But it was easily resolved. She'd just do whatever Daddy told her, whenever he said it. She stood up and stepped around Fran's drifting corpse, wondering idly who she was, and went to Sam. "Whatever you say," she told him docilely, putting her head on his shoulder. If it had been the other Daddy—the one who wanted to stick a knife in her—she would've accepted that just as freely. That Daddy, she told herself, was really more right. She remembered him telling her—once when she was about eight or nine, when he'd gotten drunk and she was putting him to bed—telling her that someday he'd probably kill her, and that he was sorry about that because he really loved her, but that he probably would because he was such a piss-poor excuse for a man.

She didn't agree. For her, Daddy epitomized everything that for her defined "man." She felt sure of his love, no matter what he did; for the most part, her object was simply to please him. Long ago, before things had gotten bad, she'd developed a habit of baring her rear whenever a spanking was due, and of repressing her tears—Daddy hated tears. Later she similarly presented her face and body to be hit, and she almost never cried or screamed. Daddy didn't like that, he liked courage. She was strong now; if Daddy wanted to kill her with his knife she would let him do it, she would not scream; in this way she'd show him how much she loved him.

Sam-Daddy was frowning at her; she, too, frowned, not knowing exactly what was wrong. But then, leading her by the hand, he went to get Cheryl—whom Stephanie had more or less identified with her childhood friend Lacey from down the block.

As he came, Cheryl looked down at his hand, at the slender little knife he was still holding. She threw her arms around his neck. "Come on, Sam," she cooed. "We don't have much time, the house is falling down! Come on, let's make love, let's make love and we can use that on each—"

"No," he snapped. "No, it's over. God damn it, Cheryl, we have to get out of here!"

She drew her face back a little, blinked. "You don't want to?" she asked, her voice small.

"No, I don't! I never agreed to this, I want us to get out of this!"

She blinked again, several more times. "But I want—"

"Later! We'll talk about that later! If we don't get out of here now there isn't going to be a later!"

Tears appeared in her eyes; she dropped her arms, let them hang limply by her sides. "All right, Sam," she said quietly. "If you want to . . . I'll help you . . . I guess . . ."

He seemed to feel that this halfhearted acceptance was the best he was going to get. "Good," he said, a little lamely. Leaving them standing together, he returned to the stair. "Rick!" he yelled. "Come on, man! The house is going down!" There was no answer. After shouting again, with the same result, Sam put his foot on the stair as if he were going up. Behind them, another part of the kitchen roof went down, as if warning them that they had little time. Stephanie looked at that end of the room, saw that all the angles were now distorted, as if the whole house were leaning in that direction.

Still, Sam went up a few more steps. "Rick!!" he bellowed. "God damn it, man! Get your ass down here, now!" There was again no response, and he started on up.

He didn't get far; up near the top, the stairway started to give way, started to splinter and crack. "Sam!" Cheryl cried. "Don't go, Sam! If you go now you won't be able to get back down!"

He looked back at her, then back up the stairs; it sagged some more, a few of the banister supports snapped and popped out at angles. For what seemed to Stephanie a terribly long time he just stood there on the crumbling stair, looking up, then back at them.

Then, abruptly, his whole face contorted. "All right!" he screamed, stepping off the stair and splashing back toward them. "All right, one more, what difference does it make, God damn, God damn you, Rick, God damn!" He waved his hands at them impatiently. "Let's go, let's go! I don't know what difference it makes, I don't. Die here, die out there, who gives a shit? Death is all there is! I can feel it sitting on my left shoulder now, I sure as fuck can, and by God, the motherfucker is laughing at us!"

With that, he yanked open the door. The wind and rain shrieked in, right in their faces, soaking them all instantly, causing them to stagger backward. Leaning into it and holding hands, they forced their way out.

Stephanie was hardly focused on the storm—she was, by then, only vaguely aware of it—but that didn't mean she wasn't shocked when they actually went out into it. The rain was falling in such torrents that it wasn't easy to breathe; it stung as it pelted her bare skin, it made her injured breasts hurt worse than ever. Keeping close to the side of the house, they began trying to make their way back around to where the vehicles were parked. The sand beneath their feet was covered by two or three inches of water, it gave way repeatedly, and they couldn't manage more than five or six steps without someone falling.

Nor could they see much; the only illumination was from the flashes of lightning. Those were fairly frequent, but the walls of falling and blowing water still limited visibility to a few feet.

They could, however, see what had happened to the cars once they'd gotten around the corner of the house. The sandy area that had been used as a parking lot had been undermined; all the vehicles sat at crazy angles, the Isuzu Trooper lying on its side, the Dixons' Comanche nearly buried in sand and water, Sam's rented Jeep tilted far over. The last one, Traci's company truck, sat with its nose in the air and its front wheels off the ground, the rear end far down in some deeply-excavated hole in the sand.

For a long moment they stood in the driving rain, staring. "It doesn't really matter much," Sam said. Weirdly, he laughed. "We don't have any keys to any of these anyway!"

"You didn't bring the keys?" Cheryl asked. Her tone was quite mild. "Where are they?"

"In my pants pocket," he told her. "And as you can plainly see I'm not wearing any pants or anything else! All our clothes, God damn it, are inside the house!" He waved his hands at the cars. "But we can't drive them anyway, look at them!"

"What're we going to do, then?" she asked. She looked back toward the house, a longing in her gaze.

"Shit, I don't know. I wish Traci hadn't run off, she probably knows this area a whole lot better than—"

He was interrupted by a loud noise from the house; looking up, Stephanie saw that it was moving. She was amazed; the whole thing was slowly sliding toward the inlet and sinking slightly, as if it were mounted on a rail car. Part of the upstairs was already leaning precariously over the collapsed kitchen. A chimney burst asunder; bricks showered down, thudding into the sand not too far from where they were standing. The house groaned like some dying behemoth, and the groan was followed by a loud cracking, splintering sound. Fully half of the upstairs area sheared away, rocking forward and then crashing down into the water where the backyard used to be, sending a huge spray into the air. A remaining piece of the corner toppled sideways, toward them, moving in apparent slow motion. As one, all three stepped back.

It didn't come that close. Instead, it hit the nose of Traci's truck, splintering over the vehicle in a welter of plaster, pieces of broken stud, a few shingles, crushed lathing. As this noise subsided, they all heard, quite clearly, an anguished cry from the truck.

"Oh, shit," Sam cried, starting forward. "Traci." With the two women close behind, he hurried on to the vehicle.

At first, Stephanie could see nothing except the front end of the truck and the mass of broken wood that half covered it. Then, through a section of exposed and cracked windshield, she saw the girl—inside the cab.

"Well, God damn," Sam groaned when Stephanie pointed her out. "She's pinned in. We'll have to dig her out!" Matching action to words, he started grabbing the larger pieces of wood piled by the door, jerking them away. The women pitched in, and in a very few minutes they had enough of the debris cleared to get the door open.

Traci did not come out immediately. Huddled against the far door, she stared at them fearfully.

Sam offered her his hand. "Come on out," he said in a tired voice. "We aren't going to hurt you, Traci."

"I don't know that!" she shouted back. "How can I know that? You're all crazy, crazy!"

He laughed. "We do know that!" Shaking his head, he moved away from the truck and stood staring up at the house—which, for the moment, had stopped moving. "Rick's still up there some-where," he mused. "Damn it, I hate to leave him, I just hate to . . ."

Traci, looking almost as wild and haggard now as they did—her appearance mitigated somewhat by the fact that she, unlike them, was still wearing clothes—heaved herself up and out of the truck. She circled around them warily. "Why?" she demanded, weaving in the wind, trying to stand upright. "Why'd you bother to get me out? I'd've drowned in there, sooner or later—you wouldn't've had to worry about me, about what I might say—"

Sam shook his head. "We don't want to see you hurt," he told her. "We never did, you or Fran. You never were a part of this, I said that before. I don't care what you say. I don't."

. She didn't say anything for a few seconds. "I'm going on, then," she said finally, hesitantly.

"Where? You think you can make it back to Corolla on foot, in this storm?"

Again she hesitated, but she nodded. "Trees come down in these storms," she told them. "And sometimes houses and stuff fall into the ocean or the Sound. But the dunes stay, they're always the same." She pointed to the trees. "I'm going through there, to the dunes, then south to Corolla." As she spoke she started edging away, toward the treeline. Then she was running, her legs flashing white in the darkness vanishing among the trees.

"We'd better do the same," Sam observed. Neither Cheryl nor Stephanie made any response, but they allowed themselves to be herded toward the trees.

As they went, a voice, loud enough to be heard above the wind, yelled at them from the house. Stephanie turned her head; a flare of lightning showed her Rick, standing out on the remains of the balcony, a surreal figure, naked, leaping up and down insanely, waving some large knife he'd gotten somewhere, maybe a kitchen knife. "I won't let you go!" he shrieked. "I'm coming after you! I am the storm king, I am the rider on the storm, you cannot escape me!" He vaulted over the now-broken railing, tried to run down the front slope of the roof. But he lost his footing and fell head-long into the yaupon below, disappearing from their sight.

"I'm glad to see," Sam observed with a slight smile, "that he's alive. I can't imagine he'd've been seriously hurt in that fall."

"I'm sure he isn't," Cheryl agreed, smiling too. "And he'll be coming after us . . ."

Sam's smile faded. "Uh-huh," he said noncommittally. "And so, we'd better get moving! I don't want him hurting us and I sure as hell don't want to hurt him, and the best way to do that, right now, is to avoid him!" He sighed. "And hope he manages to get back, and hope he comes to his senses. Somehow."

They did start moving then; Stephanie heard Sam saying he hoped they were headed eastward, toward Currituck Beach, but she didn't really know where that was anymore, she had no idea where they were going; she could see almost nothing, despite the near-continuous flashing of the lightning. Wet sand whirled up off the ground around them, hammering at their legs; pine branches and yaupon leaves, along with whatever other debris the storm winds could carry, flew about their heads. The noise of wind and rain was continuous, distracting, almost hypnotic. Still holding hands, forming a chain with Sam, who was still clutching the knife, in the lead, they moved on through the pine forest, searching for the dunes. Behind them, another section of the house fell into the Sound, and more of the pines and yaupons followed; it seemed to Stephanie, who was at the end of the human chain, as if the inlet itself were in pursuit of them, eager to overtake them and sweep them away.

Right over them, a large bough broke loose from one of the pines and came crashing down through the branches; the two women, seeing it coming, jumped to avoid it, but they jumped in opposite directions, their hands were torn apart. Instantly Stephanie found herself alone, unable to see the others, not knowing which way to go. She screamed in the darkness, heard Cheryl's voice answer from her right, and slowly began moving that way. Lightning burst over the sky again, and she felt a hand take her wrist—from the left.

She turned to look. Rick, looking as if he'd been transformed into something not even close to human, held a finger up to his lips for quiet; in that same hand he held a huge kitchen knife, the blade more than a foot long. He jerked at her arm, pulling her close to himself. He's been following us, she realized. Stalking us, waiting for an opportunity.

"Be quiet, Stephanie," he said, reinforcing his gesture. Then he giggled. "Or no, no, don't be quiet. Call Cheryl. Get them over here, just don't say anything about me!"

Still completely confused, she smiled at him and prepared to do what he was asked. Then, as if from nowhere, a little voice of reason, provoked by the crisis, rose up inside her. This was not Daddy, it cried. This was Rick, this was Rick, and he meant to kill Sam—who'd said, very clearly and plainly, that he didn't want to be killed.

Holding on, her rationality balanced on an edge narrower than the blade of Rick's knife, she managed to shake her head. "No, Rick," she told him. "I will call him, but—no, you call him. And put the knife down, Sam doesn't want to, you can't—"

"No! Nononono. It doesn't matter what Sam wants. We have to die, all, we have to die. Call them. Call Sam, call Cheryl."

She faced him, pulled her wrist free from his grip, put both her hands on his shoulders. "No," she said softly. "I won't do it. Kill me if you want to, Rick. I don't really care." He lowered the knife as if he were going to do just that; she watched him aim it at the vicinity of her navel, the same place he'd first stabbed both Jennifer and Fran. "Go ahead," she repeated, not moving her hands. "It's all right, I won't fight you, I won't scream."

He shook his head violently. "No, I want Sam too, I want Cheryl too, all of us, all of us. It's Sam I've got to take out, Sam's the one that's stopping me. Call them, Stephanie. Please. Please."

"No."

She'd no sooner gotten that word out than she heard Cheryl's voice, calling her name, close behind her. They'd found her, and she knew that Rick would take full advantage, that he might very possibly kill Sam before his old friend even knew he was there.

She made her decision. Pushing forward, she wrapped her arms tightly around Rick's neck and pushed her body against him; the point of the kitchen knife pressed hard against her belly, pricking it, but it was not nearly so sharp as that dark little blade of Sam's, it did not even nick her skin. Stephanie wasn't concerned. All Rick had to do was shove it in, and she would be dead or dying; she knew that well enough.

Still, she held Rick tightly and screamed out at the top of her lungs, warning Sam and Cheryl that he was there. She heard Cheryl's voice stop calling, and she, too, fell silent and waited, waited for Rick to kill her, waited to die.

Reaching up, he grabbed one of her wrists and pried it away

from his neck. The muscles in his arm rippling, he forced her back, jerking his head free when her other arm was extended. "I don't know why you did that," he said, his voice quite calm. "But it won't matter. I'll see you again, Stephanie, soon."

"Why didn't you kill me?" she asked. "You had the chance . . ."

"I don't want to do it like that." He stepped forward, touched her face gently. "I love you, Stephanie. I want to kill you gently, lovingly." Then he turned away, vanishing almost immediately among the trees, in the darkness.

She looked for him for an instant, then turned around and moved off to her right. "Cheryl?" she called. "Art? Sam? He isn't with me now I don't know where he is he's got a big big knife oh God where are you where are you?"

She fumbled around in the trees for a moment, then saw a flash of white; she rushed to it, fell weeping into Cheryl's arms. Sam stood nearby, the slender little knife still in his hand, his back against a thick trunk, his eyes searching the darkness.

"God damn it," he muttered as the women gathered around him. "God damn it, there's nothing worse than this. Your best friend, a person you love, trying to kill you. It doesn't get any worse!"

"Where's Art?" Stephanie asked innocently. "I don't see him. Where is he, Sam?"

He looked hard at her, frowned. "Let's talk about Art later," he said. "All right, Stephanie?" She pouted like a small child, but, now that the immediate crisis was past, the images of the three men were again merging with her father's; she nodded sullenly.

"We have to keep going," Cheryl said, though her voice sounded listless. "Have to keep moving. Unless you want to finish it up right now . . ."

"No. Let's go," Sam said firmly. He took her hand; she held Stephanie's and again they were off, glancing around as they went, each expecting Rick to jump out at them at any moment, each expecting the silvery flash of the big kitchen knife coming out of the rain, appearing among the dark trees.

But then, abruptly, the trees were gone. For the first time in quite a while, they stepped on sand that was not covered by rain-water, and they found themselves struggling upward, up the side of a rather modest dune.

At the top of it they paused. Back toward the house—or where the house had been—an orange glow lit the night; it was burning, or rather, the remains of it were burning.

Eastward, on the other side, all they could see, at first, was the next, somewhat higher, dune. The beach strand itself wasn't too far, Bodie Island wasn't that wide here. As they watched, a bolt of lightning lit the sky at the same time that a heavy, low-pitched roar shook the ground. They could see parts of that ocean wave flying high into the air after smashing on the beach, diamonds of seawater flickering in electrical light.

"Jesus Christ," Sam mumbled. "Jesus."

"We'd better not get any closer to the beach," Cheryl said, standing beside him.

"You are sure as hell right about that!" He looked to his right, then led them down the seaward side of the dune, entering a sort of a trough between two sandy ridges. Soon they were sloshing through calf-deep water again. The rain continued unabated, but the wind did not seem nearly so severe down here.

Still, as far as Stephanie was concerned, this environment was not much more comforting than the pine forest had been. In full sunlight, she was sure, the roll of these dunes would seem gentle, the valleys between them would seem open. But now, in the stark light from the storm's bolts and through the haze of the rain, they were severe, steep, ominous. Almost like desert canyons and arroyos. She wouldn't've been surprised to see rattlesnakes, coyotes.

Moving slowly—Sam was trying to keep an eye on the rim of the dune above them and to the west, trying to make sure Rick didn't surprise them—they struggled on southward toward Corolla. Twice Stephanie thought she saw movement near the top of the dune on the seaward side, but each time she could pick out nothing, and she convinced herself that it was just debris flying in the wind.

Ahead of her, Sam paused. The dune on the west had broken away somewhat, leaving a fairly steep wall where sand ran down with the water; it made walking difficult, and it also created a place admirably suited to an ambush. Dropping down on his hands and knees, Sam went on ahead, holding his knife at the ready, looking upward as he passed the wall.

Nothing happened. He stood up, motioned for the women to come on.

And at that moment, Rick, who'd obviously been waiting for him to turn, appeared at the top of the opposite dune, on the seaside. The knife was in his hand, brilliant silver; his knees were bent, ready to spring. Stephanie could have sworn his eyes were glowing with a hellish red light.

"Sam, look out!" someone screamed—herself or Cheryl, she wasn't sure which.

He turned, but he turned the wrong way, toward the Sound. Rick came hurtling down behind him, half leaping and half running, the knife ready, ready to plunge into Sam's body. Again, in the bright light of an immediate crisis, Stephanie's confusion departed and she could see things very clearly. And what she could see was that Sam was about to die; there was little he could do to prevent it, and nothing the women could do—even if they hadn't been paralyzed by confusion.

Fifty-Nine

WHEN ONE OF the women screamed and Sam turned to see nothing at all, he knew, immediately, the nature of his mistake. If he turned again, it would only mean that he would get Rick's knife in his chest, not in his back. He could think of only one possible plan of action; he hadn't time to think further, he just threw himself face down on the sand.

Rick wasn't expecting it; he stumbled over Sam's feet and fell on top of him, the knife sinking harmlessly into the sand. Rolling over quickly, Sam started to lash out at him with his own knife, but a voice inside him held him back. *This is Rick, Rick Mason, more of a brother to you than any blood brother, closer to you than any relative. You cannot harm him, you have to find some way to bring him back to his senses.*

As he hesitated, indecisive, Rick's hand whipped out and closed over his wrist. "You don't want to do this, Sam," he panted. "Not really. Come on now, Sam, we can finish it all right here, out here in the storm—"

"No!" Sam insisted. "No! It's over, Rick, try to get hold of yourself! Come on, man, I don't want to have to—"

Rick giggled. "Hurt me? You know better than that, Sam. You can't, even if you wanted to, you can't. You never were a match for me physically, Sam, you never even tried to be. You always were the smarter one, you always threw that in my face—"

Sam was so surprised he stopped struggling for a moment. "I did not! I never felt that way!"

"Yes, you did!" Rick screeched. He swung a fist wildly; it caught the side of Sam's head, half stunned him for a moment. Taking full advantage of the opportunity, Rick twisted his wrist; Sam dropped the little knife, and worse, did not see where it had gone.

Rick let him go, jumped to his feet, pulled the big kitchen knife up out of the sand. "Now," he said, while Sam scrabbled around desperately looking for the other one, "now are you willing to listen to reason, old buddy?"

"No!" he shouted, still looking. "No, I'm not going to let you do this! God damn it, Rick! Can't you just—"

"If you don't," Rick went on, his voice just audible over the continuing howl of the storm, "I'll hamstring you. I'll take this knife and I'll cut the tendons in your arms and legs so you can't do much of anything. I don't want to do that, but I will if I have to. It's got to go down my way, Sam. My way."

It was hopeless, Sam told himself. There was no way to deflect him now. There hadn't even been a chance, not since Jennifer had died.

"He's right, Sam," Cheryl said unexpectedly. "He's right. We should stop fighting it."

He looked up at her. She and Stephanie had drawn close while they'd been fighting, and now Cheryl's eyes were fixed on Rick, her hands clasped behind her back. "No," he said, resuming his search for his weapon, cursing when he could not find it. "No, we can—"

"We can't do anything. We shouldn't do anything." She took a few more steps toward Rick, passing Sam, shuffling her feet in the sand and water. She smiled, sexy-sleepy. "Come on, Rick," she asked. "Come on, do me now. I want it, Rick."

Sam stared in disbelief; she seemed to have reversed field completely. Stephanie, too, was just standing by watching, saying nothing, doing nothing. Weaponless, he struggled to his feet; Cheryl had almost reached Rick, and he was holding his knife with the point slightly up, very suggestively. "No, Cheryl!" Sam screamed. "God damn it, no!" He could see the whole scene very clearly—if intermittently—in the strobe-light illumination of the frequent lightning.

But she ignored him, she went on to Rick; he put his left arm around her. Looking up, he waved the knife threateningly at Sam. "Don't try it," he warned. "Don't try it. You need to listen to your wife, Sam. She knows what's right. Just get into it with us, will you? Help me make it good . . ."

"Yes," Stephanie said, laying a hand on Sam's shoulder. Her hand slid down, her fingers wrapped around his upper arm, dug in. "Yes, let it go. Just watch, just watch, Sam, okay?"

"No, it isn't okay!" He shook her off; by that time Rick was kissing Cheryl passionately, his arm around her shoulders, the knife resting against her belly. He was erect already; Cheryl was holding his penis with her left hand. Sam moaned, knowing what was about to happen and knowing he could not stop it.

But instead, Cheryl's other hand came around from behind her, and in it she was holding Sam's knife. Without warning, she stabbed it into Rick's chest, a little to the left of the center line.

Rick's head jerked back. "Ahh! Oh, Cheryl!" he groaned. Sam held his breath, afraid he'd drive the kitchen knife into her, she was doing nothing to prevent that, she was concentrating on the other, concentrating on forcing it deeper and deeper into his chest. Stephanie was floundering toward them, she was reaching for the knife in Rick's hand, obviously they'd planned this whole thing when they'd found Sam's knife. If only Rick didn't stab her before Stephanie got there . . .

He didn't. He dropped his knife, it bounced on the sand, splashing the water. Blood was literally squirting from his chest, he was obviously fading fast. "Please," he begged. "Let me get inside you, I want to, please, Cheryl, please, I love you . . . !"

She kept grinding the knife in, but she kissed him, too. "Yes, come on," she urged, spreading her legs. "Come on, come on . . . I love you too, Rick, I really do . . . I wanted to go with you but Sam wants to live and I love him Rick I love him . . ."

He couldn't manage it, the best he could do was to get his now only half-erect penis up against her vagina. He started to sag downward, his knees buckling, and she wasn't able to hold him. Stephanie tried to help, failed; they all went down in a heap on the sand.

"Damn," Rick sighed. "Damn, I just can't." He stared at her face. "Just hold me," he pleaded. "Just hold me, let me look at you. Beautiful . . . green . . . eyes . . . !"

Then he coughed up an enormous amount of blood, his body shuddered once, and he sank backward, his hands clutching at Cheryl's thighs. Sam, feeling like a sleepwalker, went to him, checked for any sign of life. It was a formality. He knew full well that Rick was dead. He started to cry, great wracking sobs bursting forth from his chest, sobs that threatened to tear him apart.

Kneeling beside them, Cheryl pulled the knife out of Rick's chest and handed it to Sam. "Kill me," she begged. "I mean it, Sam. Kill me. That's what I wanted anyway and I can't live with this, I can't. Kill me, then go on, take Stephanie back . . ."

"God damn!" he screamed. He stood up, hurled the knife as far as he could, over the dunes, out toward the ocean. Stephanie was holding the other one; he took it from her, threw it the other way. "No more!" he yelled. "No more! Nobody's killing anybody, no more, no more, no more!"

Cheryl broke down too, sobbing bitterly, but she allowed Sam to hold her. Stephanie came to them and they pulled her into their embrace as well. Huddled together, the three of them sank to their knees and clung to each other, ignoring the wind and the rain, for quite a long time.

Eventually, though, Sam got them moving again, headed on toward the south, toward Corolla. For what seemed like hours they struggled through the rain, staying down in the valleys between the dunes, listening to the waves smash at Currituck Beach on their left and only in that way, really, knowing that they were still headed in the right direction. Each time they topped a rise Sam hoped they might see the town on the other side; each time he saw only darkness and more rain, more dunes.

And when, finally, they did see lights up ahead, he could not, for a few seconds, imagine what they could be. Still, they pushed on toward them; in a few moments it became clear that they were the headlights of a military-style truck. Two poncho-clad men, bearing more ponchos in their hands, jumped out and approached them; another remained near the truck, keeping what appeared to be a shotgun trained on them.

One of the men came up to Sam, pushed a poncho at him, tossed two others to the women. "You got a beard. You're Dr. Sam Leo, right?" he demanded, his manner identifying him as a policeman of some sort. "Where's Richard Mason?"

"He's dead," Sam answered as he put the poncho on. "We killed him, his body is up there in the dunes some—"

"No, I killed him," Cheryl announced, pulling her poncho down over her head and peeking out. "I did it, just me, I stabbed—"

"Yeah, okay," the cop said, waving off her confession. "We can get all the details later. Traci Melrose has already told us about most of it."

Well, Sam thought as the man guided them back to the truck and helped them up in the back, when are you going to tell us we're all under arrest? The policeman said nothing; after they were in he jumped in, too, pulling back his poncho as he sat down and revealing that he, too, was carrying a gun, a revolver, and that he'd had it out and ready.

But he holstered it, and the handcuffs Sam expected remained on his belt. "You folks musta been through hell," he noted, shaking his head as the truck started to move. "Runnin' around out here in this storm stark naked. 'S one for the books, it is."

Sam was frowning. "What," he asked hesitantly, "did Traci tell you?"

A flicker of suspicion passed across the policeman's face, but it didn't last. "Well, I 'spect she didn't go inta all the details," he replied. "Said your friend Rick Mason went nuts. Killed little Frannie Retton, killed one—lessee, Arthur Dixon, I b'lieve 'twas —killed his own wife, too. She told us you three cut her aloose, and that you dug her outta her truck when parta the house fell on it. She says you all saved her life twice over. Wanted us to go up and find you, but we couldn't 'spect to do that with the storm still blowin.' So we waited, we figured you'd turn up around here." He looked at the three of them in turn. "Is it true?" he asked. "He killed all three of them?"

Sam hesitated again. He could hardly believe it, but Traci had evidently told a story that cleared all of them—maybe she felt she owed them for digging her out of the truck.

It wasn't satisfactory for him, though, to let all the blame fall on Rick, to let his friend's reputation be destroyed. It was true enough, he told himself, that Rick had indeed done all the actual killings, but he was also aware that that was very likely a mere matter of chance—it had been his wife who'd been the first of them to die, and Sam understood, perfectly well, that not one of them was guilt-free.

"Yes," Stephanie said suddenly, taking the decision away from him. "Yes, that's true. And it's true that Cheryl here did kill him, but it was in self-defense, he was holding a knife against her at the time, and she—"

"Yeah," the cop said, sympathetically. "The girl told us Mason was chasin' after you, sayin' he was gonna kill you. Now I can't say 'cause t'ain't up t'me; we'll hafta wait, see what the county D.A. has to say. But I don't think there's gonna be much of a question about it bein' self-defense, I really don't." He smiled at them as the truck rolled slowly onward, rocking in the wind. "I think the nightmare's over for you all."

Suddenly exhausted, Sam leaned his head back against the side of the truck and closed his eyes. You don't know, he told the officer silently, how wrong you are. You just don't know.

Sixty

SAM CAME BACK across the Blue Heron's parking lot to the rented Chevrolet, opened the door, sat down behind the wheel. He glanced at Cheryl, then at Stephanie in the back seat. Outside, the morning sun was shining brightly; it promised to be another hot day. The towns along the Outer Banks had weathered the storm well; other than a few downed trees and power lines, a mangled roof here and there, there was little damage to be seen.

"Gone?" Cheryl asked after the silence had grown a little long.

"Uh-huh. Left before the storm hit. Naturally, she didn't say where she was going or anything."

"I can get in touch with Dave Brennan when we get back," Stephanie told them. Her voice was flat, emotionless. "If anybody can find her, he can."

Sam shook his head. "No, somehow I doubt that Selinde will be found if she doesn't want to be. Maybe that's irrational. I don't know. I don't know what's rational and what's not anymore." He closed the car door, pulled the seat belt over his shoulder, started the engine. "Gonna be one damn long drive back to Raleigh," he observed. "We might as well get at it." He slipped the car into gear and pulled out onto the road. For a while, as they left Bodie Island

and passed through Manteo, they rode in silence, three serious faces.

"It's hard for me to believe," Cheryl said eventually, "that you were having an affair with this woman and I didn't even suspect it. I always thought I'd know, right off."

"Frankly, I always thought you would too," he admitted. "I'm just glad you aren't angry—"

"Don't make that assumption," she said quickly. "It's just that I can't really think about it clearly right now, not in that way. It'll be a while. But then we'll talk about it, Sam. We'll talk about it."

He nodded as he drove on; pine forests rushed by, the long bridge over the Sound appeared, they drove onto it. Closure, he told himself. Get across these two bridges and you leave all of it behind, leave it out there on the island. This is the gateway. Days had passed since they'd struggled back to Corolla during the storm; long hours of discussions with the police, discussions with the lawyer friend of Art's they'd called. As the officer had indicated that night, Traci's statements had placed virtually all the blame squarely on Rick, and the police seemed inclined to accept Cheryl's actions as self-defense. No charges had been filed against any of them, and as far as they could see, none was being seriously planned—though the police had not really closed the books on this matter, not yet.

They of course had been taken to a hospital, their wounds had been cleaned and treated—and had provoked a few questions from the doctors that none of them had been able to answer satisfactorily—but still, the physical scars from those injuries were already beginning to disappear. None of them was unaware that the psychological scars ran far deeper, that they would take a lot longer to heal—that they would never really be gone. Bridge or no, none of the three were the same people who'd happily driven onto these islands for what should've been—what had started out to be—a pleasant vacation.

He glanced over his shoulder at Stephanie. He was concerned about her; there were problems there, problems not easily solved. Initially, after their rescue, she'd persisted in calling Sam "Daddy"; after that phase passed she began asking about Art, with increasing urgency, and had gone into hysterics when Sam finally told her that Art was dead. Even now, she claimed to have a gap in her memory that extended from the time they'd been having the drinks until the moment she'd first encountered Rick, out in the storm. Any attempt to discuss those events with her led quickly to hysteria; Sam and Cheryl had already learned to avoid it. Not that such avoidance was, in the long run, going to solve anything.

Other than that, though, she was well able to discuss their experiences—though her tears came often and freely. "I just couldn't believe it," he said to her as they passed the drawbridge section, "when you told me that there was a connection between Selinde and the Alice Near murder. Just couldn't believe it. I swear, it does make the virus idea tenable. When I get back I'm going to go over that data again, I want to see if her name pops up anywhere else. If it does, I think we have to assume she's the carrier."

"There's no virus," Stephanie said flatly, looking out over the water. "No virus. Just us. Somehow what was buried inside us got released. I think it would've, sooner or later, anyway. Selinde and her jalapeño games were just triggers, that's all."

"Then why'd she give me that knife?"

"Maybe nothing more than what she said, a gift to remember her by. You told us you got the idea she was going to kill herself with it. Maybe you communicated that somehow."

He nodded again. "Maybe. All I know is it roused up in me things I didn't really want to face. The things we've all faced this summer." He shook his head as if to clear it. "I had no idea things like that were hiding inside me; inside any of us, for that matter."

"None of us did," Cheryl mused. "I do have to say this, though; the idea that six people chosen at random would all have these quirks—well, it just seems like an enormous coincidence to me!"

Sam shook his head. "It would be," he agreed. "But your first premise is wrong—that the six were chosen at random. We were all the closest of friends—we couldn't've been that close if there weren't similarities among us. Maybe that was one of them; maybe we just didn't recognize it."

"But how did we all just happen to get set off at the same time?"

He shrugged. "A couple of maybe-coincidences there," he replied, "and maybe not. Rick, well, he was into this stuff for years, it was always there—so was Jennifer, she just needed permission to express it. For me, Selinde—and Ken's data—got me thinking about it. For Art and Stephanie, Alice Near—part of Ken's data. And Selinde may be tied up with that somehow. You're the only exception, Cheryl."

She nodded slowly. "It was there for me too," she said. "Just like Jenny, all I needed was permission to express it, to let go . . ." She sighed. "God, we are so sick!"

"That's what I've been saying too," Stephanie put in. "But I don't know; I think these things are hiding inside a lot of people. A lot more people than anybody thinks."

"Yeah, I'm sure you're right," Sam agreed. "All you have to do is look around you—MTV, the movies, advertisements—the violent and the sexual are blended in some way in half the things you see. It's subtle, but it's there. The old general adaptation syndrome—flee, fuck, or fight. All locked together inside us; we probably have some kind of fragile lock, some inhibitor like the one dogs have, that prevents a male dog from biting a female. Some little repressor that keeps us from killing each other when we're trying to propagate the species."

"Something easily broken down," Stephanie agreed.

"It makes the notion of a virus possible."

"It's simpler than that, Sam. Triggers. The right environment, peer pressure or just peer acceptance. Like you said, we were all getting into this in little ways at the same time, and when we got together it just spiraled out of control."

"What about the kaleidoscope?" Cheryl asked. "Do you think it played any part?"

Both Sam and Stephanie shook their heads. "Just another trigger," Stephanie insisted. "We saw what we wanted to see in those patterns. You two didn't need them, I guess that's all. We did. To bring these things up from the darkness, to let us see them."

"I think there has to be a little more to it than that," Sam mused. "There's one matter there that just can't be ascribed to coincidence—the fact that the carvings on the kaleidoscope and on that knife that Selinde gave me were identical. There isn't any way that could happen by chance."

"No," Stephanie agreed, "there isn't. But look, the girl at the Dancing Moon told me that someone—I think she said a woman —came in and sold them that kaleidoscope. The bookstore really isn't that far from where you said Selinde lived, maybe she was the seller. Maybe those two things were, at one time, a matched pair, maybe part of a set. That I was the one to come in and buy it— well, that just has to be a coincidence, there isn't any other way to explain it."

Cheryl turned her head, looked back through the windshield. "Maybe," she said after a long pause. "Maybe. The simple truth is, we probably won't ever know for sure." She glanced quickly at Sam, turned her head back. "You think it'll come up again?" she asked. "You think we'll ever see old age?"

"I don't know," he said grimly. "Right now it's buried again, and we shouldn't go digging it up. We should be making plans for the future."

"I'm not so sure," Stephanie said wistfully, "that I even have one. I'm so alone; I'm not sure it wouldn't've been better if you hadn't just let Rick go ahead and—"

"You aren't alone," Sam said strongly. "Not as long as one of us is alive. You hear me, Stephanie?"

She smiled a little. "I hear you, Sam."

"We have to think," he went on, "about Paul." He glanced at Cheryl. "We have legal documents that say we're to adopt him now," he reminded her. "We have to follow that up, we have to—"

"We can't!" Cheryl cried, sudden tears already streaming down her cheeks, "I want to but we can't, we can't even go see him! What're we going to tell him, Sam? Are we going to tell him that we all killed his mommie and that his Auntie Cheryl—his new mommie—killed his daddy?"

"No, of course we aren't going to tell him that. Not for a long time, anyway, if ever. I don't know what Jennifer's parents have told him already; we'll ask them, and we'll go from there."

She wiped her eyes, stared through the windshield. "You think they'll let us see him? We're probably not their favorite people right now!"

"Well, you know I talked to them on the phone. They're broken up, naturally, but they don't seem to be holding it against us—the police reports they have say Rick went insane. I don't think they'll challenge the custody." He hesitated, shuddered. "Rick's mother —I don't know. I have to call her again. She wants answers, and I don't have a way of giving her any that she could understand or accept."

"We'll just have to take those problems one at a time, I guess," she agreed. "You're right, Sam. We have to do everything we can for him. Give him the best life we can." Her voice started cracking. "Make it up to him somehow . . ."

"You can't make it up to him," Stephanie pointed out reasonably. "And if you try, you'll create new problems—for him and for you. All you can do—all we can do, I don't want to be left out of this—is our best; love him and treat him like he was our own. That's all."

Cheryl nodded agreement; a period of silence followed.

"What are you going to do about Ken, Sam?" Stephanie asked then. "I know it may not be the main thing on your mind right now, but he is going to be a problem. From what you've said about him, I don't think he's going to have any sympathy for you; he's going to go right on blackmailing you."

Sam grinned; the expression felt almost peculiar after the last several days, and he was not unaware that he was smiling with his mouth only, not with his eyes. "That," he told them, "is one part of this that has a happy ending. We've had too much to talk about, I haven't told you yet—Ken isn't a problem, not anymore. He is, as a matter of fact, in jail in Raleigh."

"In jail! How'd that happen? What's he charged with?"

"About a million things—the big one is rape. I don't know if it'll stick, the circumstances are peculiar, but he has been charged." He went on, explaining about Cindy Ellison and what Ken had done to her—and how she, once freed of his blackmail, had proceeded to bring charges.

"I still don't understand how this happened!" Stephanie said.

"Well," Sam told her, his dark grin returning, "I'll readily admit that I'm not Ken's equal when it comes to computers, but I'm not ignorant, either. When he set up the laptop to access his data, he neglected to lock me out of the rest of his files if I aborted a program rather than exiting it. The laptop had already given the password; I was inside, I could do whatever I wanted."

"So what'd you do?"

"I found his password controller file, and I changed the password; I locked him out of his own files. Then I called the Institute and gave them the password, told them the whole story about my data and about Cindy's, and let them take it from there. Now, Cindy's brought charges, the IRS has brought charges, several banks—he's been fired, of course—" Sam shrugged. "He's had it. Even if he doesn't do jail time, he'll have a hell of a time finding another job, I'm sure." He looked over at Cheryl. "You, however, will be getting a letter from him. That I'm sure of."

"A letter? Why me?"

"A letter telling you about me and Selinde." He shook his head, then went on to explain that his affair had been a part of Ken's blackmail too, telling her how Ken had learned of it by effectively tapping his phone.

"Well," Cheryl said, nodding, "if I do, then I'll just have to write him back. At Central Prison or wherever, and tell him my opinion of him."

There was brief and far from hearty laughter among the three of them, after which they all fell silent again. They were just then reaching the western end of the Alligator River bridge, the second and final one, crossing—as Sam saw it—back into whatever remained of their old lives. He reached over and toyed with Cheryl's hair affectionately. She smiled at him, and Stephanie, leaning forward in the back seat, laid her hand on his arm. There's a lot of love in this car, he told himself, a lot of love.

But he also understood that any rose, no matter how splendid, eventually dried up in the very sunshine that once nourished it, that it fell to dust and was blown away on the winds of time.

If you let it, of course. One always has choices.

Epilogue

THERE WAS A great deal of noise from next door, a slamming of car doors, a few shouts, a lot of laughter. Bobby Gilman stood up, went to the window, pulled a slat of the blind down, and looked out. Mexican migrant workers; a whole carload of them, up from Florida for the harvest season here in southern Virginia. This inexpensive motel just outside of Petersburg would be the sort of place they might stay in transit. He watched idly for a few moments while they unloaded some of their things and piled into their room. On the door of the battered '71 Dodge they were driving was painted the familiar image of the Virgin of Guadalupe, the dark patroness of the Indian peoples of America, surrounded by her characteristic penumbra of white brightness.

He'd seen that icon many times before, but he hadn't known much of anything about it; then, just this morning, he'd read an article in the newspaper about an apparition of the Dark Virgin appearing on an oak tree in California. The article had given the background—how an Aztec named Juan Diego had, in the year 1531, seen the Virgin in person on Tepeyac Hill outside of Mexico City, about how she'd made the hillside bloom with roses even though it was December, about how this Indian had taken word of his vision back to Bishop Zumarraga, about how the image of the Virgin and the roses had been imprinted on his *tilma,* his cotton shirt. The bishop, impressed, had then ordered a shrine built on Tepeyac. That shrine stands today, and pilgrims still flock to see Juan Diego's miraculous *tilma,* enclosed in glass high above the altar.

Neither had the article neglected to mention that Tepeyac had been an important religious site for centuries before Zumarraga had the shrine built there, that on the crest of the hill of Tepeyac there'd been, before the coming of the Spaniards, an important Aztec temple. Just as the shrine of Guadalupe had been dedicated to the Christian mother image, the temple that preceded it had been devoted to the Aztec mother goddess, the one they often referred to as Tonantzin—a name that meant, simply, "our mother."

Such matters did not interest Bobby much now, though. Turning away from the window, he sat back down in a nearby chair. He looked sad.

"Is something wrong?" the beautiful black-haired woman sitting on the edge of the bed asked him. Her white shorts and shirt seemed incredibly bright in the subdued light of the room.

"Ah, no, not really," he told her. "I was just thinkin' about stuff, that's all." He looked down at his hands, at the black dirt ingrained around his fingernails. "When I was a kid I wanted to go to th' University, up at Charlottesville. But then Ellie got pregnant, and I hadda drop outta school, hadda take that job over at the machine shop, and . . ." He stopped, shook his head. "Don't wanna talk about Ellie," he said morosely. "Makes me feel bad. I never cheated on her before. Ain't that kinda guy."

The woman smiled richly. "You aren't really cheating on her now," she said. "She's busy, isn't she? Didn't you tell me that?"

He scowled. "Yeah. That damn dumb kaleidoscope. Seems like that's all she wants to do, sit around lookin' in it, ever since she found it in that little store downtown. Don't even wanta get up and fix the kids no breakfast. I don't know, I just don't." His sigh was long, drawn-out. "But she ain't busy at nights . . ."

"It isn't night," the woman pointed out. "It's Saturday afternoon." She looked off into the distance herself. "A Saturday that shouldn't be wasted in vain regrets," she went on. "I'm moving on, tomorrow."

He looked up at her. "Where you goin,' Selinde?"

She shrugged. "It doesn't matter. On north, I think. Toward Washington."

"You don't like Petersburg?"

"I never stay in one place very long, Bobby."

He looked at the floor, shook his head. "Shit," he muttered. "I'm really gonna miss you."

She stood up. "Let me give you something," she said, walking to the cubby where her clothes were hanging. She pulled out a small bag, dug around in it for a moment, came back, handed it to him.

He stared for a moment, then drew it carefully out of its finely tooled leather sheath. The blade seemed dark, reddish. A few grains of white beach sand came with it, falling lightly to the carpet.

"It's real pretty," he said. "But why're you givin' it to me?"

"It's—an heirloom. It's been with me a long time. I wanted you to have it. As a memento, let's say."

He shrugged. "Funny," he said, tipping it toward the light. "The carvins' or whatever look just like those on that kaleidoscope. That's funny." He held it up, point skyward. Like a fast-forward movie a fantasy flashed through his mind; himself and Ellie, on their bed, making love, he pushing this knife into her body, blood spilling, she sighing, sighing, clutching at him . . .

He flushed guiltily. Not the first time you've had a sick idea like that, he told himself. Gotta keep those down. Gotta keep that under control. He'd never had an urge to actually bring those fantasies to reality, but they sure seemed to be more common in the last few days.

"Well, I thank you," he said, stuffing the knife in his pocket. He grinned. "What you think we oughta do now?"

She smiled. "The choices are all yours, Bobby."